ABSOLUTELY LOVE

Mary Bond has been writing since childhood and began her writing career with short stories and freelance articles. She is a skills trainer in the civil service and lives in Dublin with her husband. She has two daughters and a son. *Absolutely Love* is her first novel.

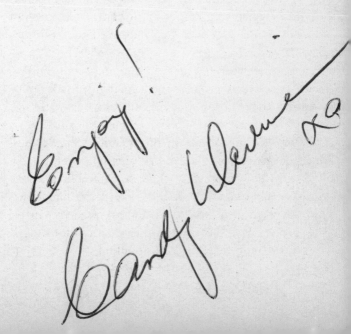

MARY BOND

ABSOLUTELY LOVE

TiVOLi

Tivoli
an imprint of Gill & Macmillan Ltd
Hume Avenue
Park West
Dublin 12
with associated companies throughout the world

www.gillmacmillan.ie

© Mary Bond 2005
0 7171 3901 8
Print origination by Carole Lynch
Printed and bound by Nørhaven Paperback A/S, Denmark

*The paper used in this book is made from the wood pulp
of managed forests. For every tree felled, at least one tree is
planted, thereby renewing natural resources.*

A catalogue record is available for this book
from the British Library.

1 3 5 4 2

To the memory of my lovely dad,
Loughlin Morris, who bought my first
typewriter and made me a desk.

Acknowledgments

Thanks a million to Alison Walsh, my lovely editor, for her kind encouragement, inspiration and expert guidance. To all the team at Gill & Macmillan, I really appreciate your hard work and enthusiasm on my behalf.

A very special thanks is due to my wonderful agent Sheila Crowley for invaluable support and dedication and to all at AP Watt.

For encouragement along the way, I would like to thank David and Kathleen at the Killaloe Hedge School, and authors Rose Doyle and Richard Lysaght.

Thanks to my family for lots and lots of love; Derek, my best friend, for always putting me first; Michelle and Barbara, for enthusiasm, tons of support and gems of advice; Declan, for contagious confidence and for rescuing my precious novel from accidental deletion in addition to rescuing me! Thanks to Mam, for instilling a love of books and writing, and our Friday night book club; to Margaret, best sis; Peter, David and Kevin – photographer supreme!

Special acknowledgement to Brid, for pointing me in the right direction. Thanks to Dara and Tony, for all the hard work; to Colm and all my extended family and many friends, too numerous to mention. One of the best things about having my novel published is the delighted response and encouragement I have received from all of you. Thank you, reader, for choosing this book, hope you enjoy it.

And thank you, God.

Mary Bond
March 2005
www.mary-bond.com

Prologue

London, the early eighties. A sunny afternoon in August. A perfect day for a picnic.

They laughingly load the red Ford Cortina with rugs, sandwiches, snacks and drinks and the double buggy. They strap the twins into their car seats and carefully secure the sleeping infant. They set off for the park.

Summer sunshine blazes in a cerulean blue sky. They relax under the shade of a great sweeping oak where dappled leaves interlace above their heads and gently filter the dazzling sun. A heat haze shimmers in the air and drifts like a gossamer veil over the green swathes of the park, so tangible you can almost reach out and touch it.

They laugh and chat and make daisy chains for the twins. The baby, swathed in soft pink cotton, sleeps the dreamless slumber of the new and innocent. The twins play with a brightly coloured ball and roll about on warm-scented grass, then are carefully tucked in for a nap in their buggy. The sound of David Bowie's 'Space Oddity' flows across the heat haze.

Soon after, they drive home through drowsy London streets. They look forward to the evening ahead, when they will sit in the quiet back garden as the sun slides westwards in the sky and scents of flowering shrubs waft in the calm evening air and birds sing into the hush of a gathering twilight.

Then a car comes out of nowhere. It crashes into the red Ford Cortina, and now the sun glitters on shattered glass, twisted metal and a brightly coloured ball that bounces freely down the road....

Part I

Chapter One

Daisy paused to examine her reflection before she faced the world. Her brown eyes gleamed with wry amusement.

To look at her now, the perfect image of the assured and professional Ms O'Neill, no one would have guessed that only last night she had been in a blind panic as she scrabbled her clothes together and rushed out of a boyfriend's apartment. No one would have realised, either, that she was feeling on edge because Sam Heffernan, due back today from a marketing seminar and newly invigorated, was bound to be prowling around her office. On top of all that, she had a demanding schedule lined up for the day so she needed to look calm and in control.

And there was no arguing with the sharply cut pinstriped trouser suit that camouflaged the slim contours of her body, the steel-rimmed glasses that shielded her soft brown eyes or the cropped blond hair that was lightly spiked around a fine-boned face with a neat, slender nose and a small, determined-looking chin.

Daisy lifted that chin, smiled a mocking smile at the uncompromising image of Ms O'Neill, human resources manager, and picked up her black leather briefcase. Even though she never managed to feel half as cool and confident on the inside as she appeared on the outside, looking the part was half the battle, wasn't it? With her bullet-proof suit and armour-plated glasses, as well as the advantage of being five feet ten in her stocking feet, she looked as though she was ready to conquer the world.

She scooped her car keys off the hall table and reminded herself that in spite of her busy schedule she would have to find time to phone her Aunt Liz about her mother's birthday. After all, fifty years of age was a milestone and Daisy wanted to make sure Marina enjoyed the occasion.

She threw a sharp glance up the staircase, almost as though she expected to see Marina drifting about in her blue velvet dressing gown. But save for the rain tapping on the front window and the swish of early morning traffic on the road outside, the house was cloaked in thick silence and there was no sign of life from Marina's bedroom.

Daisy opened the door and tasted the fresh, damp-scented air that rushed into the hall. She threw a final glance up the stairs, then firmly closed the door. Despite the soft drift of April rain beading her hair, she paused to take a deep, calming breath, then strode over to her silver Toyota Yaris, switched on the ignition, reversed out of the driveway and with a twirl of the wheel, turned to face the wet Friday morning.

The car park of Cardinol Electronics was deserted except for the red Volvo parked outside the reception area.

Sam Heffernan was back.

Daisy stepped into the foyer and hurried across to the lift. She wondered if by some miracle she could avoid bumping into him, considering that her kitten heels sounded like the rattle of a machine gun on the tiled floor. Despite her best intentions, she was already feeling tense even though the day had scarcely begun. Thankfully, though, she reached her office undetected and with a sigh of relief, she closed the door. She sat down at her desk, flicked open her diary and switched on her computer. As she began to scroll through her e-mails, her mobile buzzed.

'Good morning, Daisy.'

Keith Kinsella. Her heart skipped a beat. God, she wasn't ready for this. Not yet. After all, it was barely half past eight.

'I prefer not to take personal calls in the office, Keith,' she began crisply.

'Look, Daisy, we need to talk.'

'What about?'

'You know exactly what about.'

Yes, of course she did. She had met Keith a month ago at a mutual friend's wedding and had gone out with him on a few casual dates. Then last night he had brought her back to his apartment and it had ended in total disaster.

'What's the point in talking, Keith?' she stalled, fidgeting with a pencil and tapping it off the desk. She wondered if Keith could possibly come up with anything she hadn't already heard.

'The point?' he spluttered. 'Would you mind telling me what the hell I did wrong last night?'

God, he was taking it personally. 'What do you mean?'

'C'mon, Daisy, what happened? You weren't exactly....' he hesitated.

'I wasn't exactly what?' she drawled.

'It was a bit of a shambles, wasn't it? I tried hard, but despite my best efforts, you weren't very, well, up for it.'

'"Up for it"? Is this your way of saying I wouldn't sleep with you?' Daisy sat up straight in her chair and swung into attack mode.

'I must have done something wrong—'

She cut him short. 'Is that what this phone call is about? Worried about your performance? You have some cheek. While we're on the subject, do you really mean to say I was treated to your best

8

efforts? I find that hard to believe,' she finished, her heart thumping as she injected as much icy scorn as possible into her voice.

'That's totally out of order,' Keith blazed. 'You should do yourself a favour and chill out.'

'Get lost.'

'You might have enjoyed it, you know. Most women do.'

'Go to hell.'

Men. You could keep them. She tried not to think about last night with Keith. There was no point in remembering the look of astonishment on his face as she had suddenly called a halt to his advances, pulled her clothes together and scurried out of his apartment. No point whatsoever. She had more than enough on her plate for today, and she was supposed to be thinking positively, wasn't she? She didn't need to be reminded that she had notched up yet another humiliating experience.

The story of her life.

She had even left her previous job in rather a hurry on account of a run-in with an over-amorous accounts executive. Now, after the latest disaster with Keith, she was beginning to think that her romantic life was destined to be a series of ill-fated encounters.

She opened her briefcase and searched in it for her lavender-scented pulse point. It said it was supposed to aid a relaxed state of mind. She rolled it across the inside of her wrists and raising one wrist to her nose, she closed her eyes and inhaled deeply.

When her office door opened, she hastily pulled a file across the desk, pretending to be absorbed in it, barely registering the fact that it was upside down. So much for inducing a state of relaxed calm, Daisy fretted, but she summoned a smile when a friendly face popped around the door. It was Paula McCullagh from the office next door.

'I see Sam Heffernan's back.' Paula's blue eyes danced with amusement.

'Oh, I'm far too busy to talk to him today,' Daisy smiled as she sat back in her chair. 'I have to read the riot act this morning to two of the process operatives about their atrocious timekeeping. And this afternoon, I have the delightful job of delivering the summer leave presentation to the factory floor.'

'Sounds fun. Rather you than me,' Paula grinned. 'I would hate to work in human resources. Give me accounts any day of the week. At least figures don't answer you back. And what delights have you lined up for the weekend?' Paula asked as she perched on a corner of the desk.

'I haven't decided yet,' Daisy said.

'Finding it hard to choose between the men in your life?'

'Exactly. What about you?'

'I'm hoping that Tom's sister will come over to babysit the kids and let us off the leash tomorrow night.'

10

'I've told you before, I'll babysit for you anytime you're stuck,' Daisy offered.

'I wouldn't dream of asking you. I'm sure you've far more exciting things to be doing on a Saturday night than looking after Sean and Lorna.'

'Of course,' Daisy was nonchalant. 'But I don't mind curtailing my wild nightclubbing adventures occasionally.'

'If Sam Heffernan has his way, you won't be free to babysit on a Saturday night,' Paula grinned. Daisy firmly shook her head.

Along with all the female staff, she had noticed Sam the first day he started in Cardinol Electronics, almost a month ago. As head of marketing, he was someone you couldn't fail to notice. He didn't need to stand tall or dress the part in order to look confident. Sam had been blessed with sexy good looks and he knew it, all six feet of him.

The kind of man to be avoided at all costs, Daisy had instantly decided.

'Might be worth going out with him even once,' Paula said. 'I think you'd really suit each other.'

'Don't be daft.'

'You're both tall, you'd fit together well, you're both attractive….'

'Yeah, sure.'

'Behind your cool exterior,' Paula's voice dropped, 'I'd say there are hidden, volcanic depths.'

'How on earth did you guess!'

11

'There are times, you know, when I wish I was young, free and single like you,' Paula sighed. 'Don't get me wrong, I love Tom and the kids, but with all the fun you young ones are having nowadays….'

'I'm not all that young.'

'What are you, twenty-three, twenty-four?'

'I'll be twenty-six this year. And before you go any further, I have no intentions of having fun with Sam.'

'Don't sound so cross. There's nothing better than a bit of office romance to brighten up the daily grind. Think of it,' Paula said as she headed towards the door. 'You'd be the envy of every woman in Cardinol.'

'I can't think of anything more exciting. Sorry to disappoint you, Paula, but I don't mix business with pleasure.'

'Not even for the sexy Mr Heffernan?'

'Especially not him.'

'You must lead one hell of a charmed existence if you can afford to turn him down. I'm going up to the canteen at lunchtime. Care to join me?'

'Yes, please. You never know, by the time I'm finished dishing out a lecture on good timekeeping to my two charmers, I might be in need of some moral support.'

'As if,' Paula scoffed. 'You're well able for it, Daisy. You always manage to stay cool and calm.'

'Nothing to it,' Daisy casually shrugged.

12

A charmed existence, Paula had said. How easy it was to pretend, to look the part on the outside, to face the world with an up-tilted chin and shield her eyes with steel-rimmed glasses. So long as no one got anywhere close to the real Daisy O'Neill, of course, she was fine. As far as the world at large was concerned, she was a capable, confident person.

Men. They weren't worth getting into a heap over. Keith was history now, and she would tell Sam where to go if he came looking for her.

Chapter Two

At quarter to ten in a third-floor office on St Stephen's Green, Eve Andrews threw a mocking glance at the wall clock as she strolled through the door.

Late again. So what? They were lucky she was putting in an appearance. And that's all it would be – an appearance. It was such a wet morning that she'd been tempted to stay at home and pull a sickie, but two Fridays in a row was pushing her luck, even for her. At least she could spend most of the day crashed out at her desk. After all, nothing remotely exciting ever happened in Foley Financial Services, and today, surely, would be no different.

As she glided past Daniel Richards, he fumbled with his mouse and sent a dish of paper clips flying through the air. As he bent down to pick them up, he banged his head off the edge of the desk.

Eve laughed at his beet-red face. 'Daniel,' she mocked, 'you must learn to control your mouse.'

'Give over, Eve,' Rachel Williams frowned across the desk.

'What's this, a mutiny?' Eve's blue eyes gleamed.

'You should leave Daniel alone.'

'I can't help it if he has a panic attack whenever I'm within a certain radius.' Eve winked at Daniel, chucked her soggy umbrella in the waste bin, draped all five feet two of herself at her desk and calmly surveyed the office.

'You should give Daniel a chance, he's only here a wet week.' Rachel gave her a disapproving look. 'Isn't he a little young for you?'

Eve flashed a mischievous grin. 'Don't you know that most boys – sorry, *men* – reach their sexual peak at nineteen?' she said in a whisper loud enough to reach Daniel's crimson ears. 'It's a shame to let that go to waste.'

'I give up,' Rachel huffed. 'There's no point in talking to you when you're in your contrary mood.'

'Lighten up. Daniel knows I'm only having fun, don't you, Daniel?' Eve directed her last remark at the shy, sandy-haired office junior and was rewarded with the barest hint of a smile.

'Whatever you say, Eve,' he shrugged.

'I suppose you're heading home to Cork for the weekend?' Eve asked him.

'No, not this weekend,' Daniel mumbled.

'Must have a love interest in Dublin already. How exciting,' Eve grinned. 'God knows, you'd need a bit of distraction around here.' She took out a mirror from her desk drawer and examined her reflection. Thankfully her eyelashes were still in a state of perfect definition in spite of the rain that morning. Her mascara was supposed to be water-proof, but you couldn't always trust the advertising blurb. Her bob of glossy dark hair was sleek and smooth, with no sign of the dreaded frizz. Maybe that new humidity-resistant serum was resistant after all. She made a mental note to stick with it for another couple of weeks rather than testing out another revolutionary innovation. She replaced her mirror with a sigh of relief and caught Rachel look-ing at her with a mixture of exasperation and envy.

'What's up now?' Eve asked.

'I knew you'd forget,' Rachel shook her head.

'Forget what?'

'It's D-Day for the go live.'

'The go live? You're joking!' Eve frowned as she scanned the length of the office. Everyone was busy. Even Katie and Susan, her socialising pals, displayed an almost traitorous exertion as they pounded their keyboards. Usually by now they were barely finished circulating their jokey e-mails. For the first time since she entered the office that morning, Eve was aware of a muted frenzy in the air. 'Is that why everyone is glued to their computer?'

'Yeah, everyone except you,' Rachel pointed out. 'Full marks for being the only member of staff who has completely forgotten about it.'

'I can't help it if it slipped my mind. And I have no intention of killing myself,' she said as she glanced at her overflowing in tray. 'I don't give a toss about the go live.' She fiddled with her miniature Forever Friends teddy, tweaked his ears, straightened his jumper and repositioned him on top of her computer. She took her mobile phone out of her bag and checked it in case she had missed any calls and put it on her silver star-shaped mouse mat.

'We have to clear our monthly statements by lunchtime,' Rachel informed her.

'What's got into you today?' Eve asked with a hint of impatience. 'First you come to Daniel's rescue, now you're telling me about this ridiculous deadline. Have you been promoted or something? Or has old Fogy offered you a bonus?'

'It's all right for you, Eve,' Rachel sighed. 'You're not like the rest of us ordinary mortals. You might have Mr Foley wrapped around your little finger, but some of us have to work at making a living.'

'Wow, we *are* tetchy today. But I'll make an effort this morning,' Eve promised. 'If it makes you happy, I'll leave Daniel alone, seeing that he's under pressure. No attempts at wild sex under the desk. And,' she smiled impishly at Rachel, 'I might even make a dent in my in tray. Don't want you

17

thinking that I'm getting away with murder just because old Fogy has the hots for me.'

She glanced around the floor, but there was no sign of the bear-like man who had taken over the running of his father's business on his retirement and who worshipped the ground Eve walked on. She reluctantly edged her in tray forward and switched on her computer, and as she waited for her program to download, she suddenly remembered.

'By the way, Rachel,' she said, feeling instantly cheered, 'my credit card has been restored, at last!'

'That's great.'

'Isn't it? I can't believe I'm in the clear again – well, almost. The last few months have been the worst of my life.'

'Lucky for some,' Rachel said.

'Yes, I know I'm lucky,' Eve said. 'I do appreciate my life. Really. I'll never moan about the fact that I'm still living at home, because it certainly has its compensations. Thank God I haven't got a mortgage, or I would've been in serious trouble. The last few months have taught me a lesson.'

'I'm impressed.'

Eve grinned. 'Seriously, Rachel, it was awful to be short of funds.'

'It must have been terrible to miss your annual skiing trip. I can just imagine the sense of deprivation,' Rachel said dryly.

'Not only that, I missed the sales as well.'

'So that's why you're still wearing last year's designer coat.'

'Yes, well....'

'I'm only teasing. I wish I had a designer coat to wear, no matter what vintage it was. You really have it good, Eve Andrews. Anyway, I'd better get on with my work,' Rachel sighed.

She certainly had it good, Eve admitted to herself. Her parents had scarcely batted an eyelid when she casually informed them of her dire financial circumstances. Better yet, they had bailed her out by immediately waiving her modest monthly contribution to the phone bill until such time as she was back in funds. Her mother had included her not inexpensive toiletries as part of the weekly shop, and quite often her father had slipped her a fifty-euro note whenever he ferried her into town to meet her pals on a Saturday night.

But then Liz and Harry Andrews had always been good to her. Almost too good. Sometimes, growing up, comparing herself with her peers, Eve wondered what exactly she had done to deserve being cherished like a precious gift, when she knew that she was far from perfect. And although she rarely admitted it, even to herself, deep down she sometimes felt a little uneasy at the level of unending adoration that surrounded her. But she usually tossed aside any misgivings as rapidly as they had surfaced. Far better to enjoy it and bask in the glow of unconditional love. It was nice being the one who had it all, the girl everyone envied. She had quite a lot to be thankful for, Eve realised. Everything she had ever wanted had fallen into her lap without much effort, apart from the recent hiccup she had had with her credit balance. And now, thankfully, she was back in funds again.

An assault on her favourite boutiques was definitely on the weekend agenda, she decided, and in spite of the wet Friday morning she felt a glow of anticipation. Maybe she would book a deep conditioning treatment in the hairdressers. She might even have time to fit in a pedicure.

'Doing anything exciting this weekend?' Rachel asked as she paused again in her data entry. 'Going out with… what's his name again?'

'He's dumped,' Eve said firmly. 'I sent him a text he can't fail to understand.'

'A text?' Rachel's eyes widened.

'It was all he deserved. He turned out to be a right pain in the ass.'

'You must have been going out with him for, what, two weeks now?'

'Two weeks too many,' Eve said with conviction.

'Don't you ever get fed up?'

'Fed up with what?'

'Flitting from man to man.'

Eve laughed. 'Are you for real? Isn't variety the spice of life? I'm on the tear again, and I'm going to have a blast. I've told Katie and Susan to include me in their weekend plans. How about you?'

Rachel gave Eve a half smile, but all of a sudden her face dropped. 'Don't tell me. Love life on the blink?'

'What's new?' Rachel sighed.

'God, I'm really sorry.' Eve was instantly sympathetic.

'I'm beginning to think I should never have moved in with John.'

'Look, we'll go for a drink straight after work and I'll give you whatever advice you need to have him eating out of your hand,' Eve offered.

Rachel hesitated. 'I don't want to mess up your Friday night plans.'

'Nonsense. What are friends for?'

'I'd need a miracle.'

'No problem. We'll get you a miracle.'

'Anyway, right now I'm off to the photocopier.' Rachel got up from her desk and smiled shakily.

'Chin up,' Eve said encouragingly.

Eve's attention drifted to her overflowing in tray. Where the hell had all that work come from? Did they think she was some kind of robot? She scowled as she opened a spreadsheet and lifted a piece of correspondence from the top of the brimming pile, fingering it as though it carried a health warning.

She sensed someone beside her desk and was still scowling as her eyes collided with a pair of grey ones. Grey eyes that were dark and sexy. Seductive grey eyes that held hers in an unwavering gaze. For

21

the beat of a millisecond her life went into freeze frame mode. She wasn't even conscious of breathing. She wasn't conscious of anything except the stunningly attractive man standing beside her. After a long, dizzying moment she managed to wrench her gaze away from his eyes, only to find herself staring at the most sensual mouth she had ever seen. Something inside her melted and dissolved and she felt unusually defenceless as she sat at her desk.

After that, nothing was ever the same.

'Excuse me,' he said, 'I need to check your access.'

This couldn't possibly be happening. Not to her. And not in Foley Financial Services at half past ten on a Friday morning.

'Excuse me?' he lifted an eyebrow and looked at her with those amazing grey eyes.

Oh yes, Eve silently gulped, it was happening all right.

'I need to check your access for the go live. If I could just interrupt you for a minute?'

'Sure, no prob.' She edged her chair away from her desk and watched, mesmerised, as he turned his attention to her computer.

He could interrupt her for the rest of her life. That tantalising thought seemed to quiver so strongly in the air around her that for a moment she thought she had said it out loud. He checked some details on his clipboard sheets, inserted a disc into her computer and ran his fingers across her keyboard and newly ruffled mind.

Just as well Rachel was still down at the photocopier. One look at Eve's glazed eyes and she would have instantly reacted, making faces or funny gestures that would have frazzled Eve even more. This gorgeous man was obviously one of the consultants appointed for the go live. She had heard that a firm of consultants had been hired to implement an upgrade to the computer system, but she hadn't paid much attention. After all, most computer experts were dull, nerdy types, weren't they?

Oh no, they weren't.

He was about six feet tall and his dark hair was untidily slicked back from his face. The assured look in his grey eyes as he focused on her monitor, his air of calm authority as his fingers ran decisively across her keyboard and that upward tilt at the corners of his sensual mouth gave him a kind of magnetism that made Eve feel as though she was on fire.

'I suppose you'll be very busy today,' she croaked, anxious to remind him of her presence, willing him to look at her with the same level of attention he was giving her computer.

'Sorry, what?' he asked, and once more she was treated to a glance from him. Even his voice was sexy. It had a gritty edge to it that sent fingers of pleasure slithering down her spine.

'Oh, nothing important.' She smiled her renowned Eve Andrews smile, the smile that normally guaranteed results, but this drop-dead gorgeous man turned his attention back to his clipboard. He began to scribble some notes, his eyes narrowed in concentration. Then he pressed some buttons on her keyboard, brought up the spreadsheet she had been updating and ejected his CD.

'That seems to be fine,' he said. 'You'll be all set for action on Monday morning.' He gave her a brief, businesslike nod and picked up his pen.

Was that it? Was he about to move on and out of her life? Hang on a minute! She took a deep breath. 'I'm not so sure about that.' Her voice was husky and she smiled what she hoped was her most beguiling smile.

'Is there a problem?' he asked in that gritty voice. 'Everything appears to be in order with your PC. The new system will be up and running on Monday morning.'

'Oh, that's not quite what I meant.' Eve was appalled to feel the colour mount in her cheeks. Why the hell was she feeling so flustered? What had happened to her smooth chat-up technique? Easy – this man standing in front of her had demolished it with a flick of his grey eyes. He was waiting for some sort of explanation, so once more she plastered a dazzling smile on her face. 'I'm sure you'll do a great job. What I meant was me,' she said, realising to her horror that her nipples were hard and taut.

'Surely you've had familiarisation sessions?'

Her face flamed and she prayed his glance wouldn't stray to her boobs. No point in being too obvious. 'Oh yes, but what I mean is, I'll scarcely be ready for action on Monday morning, not with the hectic weekend I have planned. I probably won't even notice the difference in the computers,' she giggled light heartedly, trying to diffuse her tension. 'Oops! I probably shouldn't have said that.' She gave him a conspiratorial glance. 'Pretend you didn't hear.'

'I've forgotten already.' He finally smiled at her, an indulgent smile that demolished the last remnants of her defences. 'You know, you're supposed to notice an immediate improvement in response times.'

'Response times?'

'The time it takes to clear a transaction off your screen. In other words, your routine work will be done in half the time.'

'That's a good advantage,' she said, struggling to look knowledgeable – rather a tough call when she hadn't a clue about the new computer system. And whose fault was that, she quietly simmered. She tried to look intelligent as she continued, 'It sometimes takes me ages to get through my statements. I always seem to lag behind. Does that mean I'll have twice as long to do my keying in?'

'Not quite,' he frowned, but she thought she saw a grin tugging at the corner of that sensual mouth and she threw him one final smile, knowing in her sinking heart that she had no justification to detain him any further.

'I'm sorry, I never introduced myself. I'm Eve, and you're…?'

'Alex,' he answered, 'Alex Gallagher.' And with a nod of his head and a final glance that Eve felt all the way down to her toes, he crossed the floor and began to talk with one of his colleagues.

Work was impossible. After all, how could she deal with boring data entry when the most devastatingly sexy man she had ever laid eyes on was here, in her office, just several feet away? She spent the remainder of the morning with one eye on her spreadsheet and the other one feverishly following Alex's progress around the office. There appeared to be three consultants altogether, but luckily for her it was Alex who had happened to check her computer.

She dredged the corner of her mind for details of the go live procedures. She had attended staff meetings and training sessions, but most of the details had gone in one ear and straight out the other. Why the hell hadn't she paid more attention? She was desperate to know if Alex had anything more to do with the computers. Would he be around if there were problems on Monday, like if she forgot her password over the weekend, as frequently happened? Were there any further chances of getting a bit of undivided attention from him?

Chapter Three

It was after six o'clock by the time Daisy switched off her computer. The day had been just as busy as she had expected. In the canteen at lunchtime, the two operatives she had cautioned had spent the best part of their lunch hour throwing surly glances at her, which she had coolly ignored. The presentation that afternoon had gone on longer than scheduled and the resulting discussion had been quite contentious. Nonetheless, she had handled it all with a cool aplomb, reminding herself that just a year ago she had been only too relieved to accept her position in Cardinol.

She grabbed her briefcase and car keys and headed for the lift. The building was quiet, as most of the process staff had already gone home. But just as she was striding down the corridor, Sam Heffernan walked out of the boardroom and fell into step beside her. It was almost as though he had been lying in wait, she immediately suspected, after her efforts to avoid him all day had been successful.

'Daisy! This is a pleasant surprise,' he smiled. 'You and me, alone at last. It was worth staying late for this. It was even worth coming back from a most interesting seminar to see your face again. Did you miss me?'

'Sure, Sam.' She quickened her stride, the sooner to reach the lift.

'Good. Any plans for the weekend?'

'I might have,' she said cheerfully.

'I suppose you're tearing out on the town.'

'Could be.'

'And what about us? Why can't we tear out on the town together?' They arrived at the lift and he stood there looking as though he had all the time in the world.

Daisy took a deep breath and drew herself up to her full height. She had read that it was an effective way of radiating confidence and authority, so she hoped she oozed self-assurance as she faced Sam. 'No thanks, Sam, I don't think so.'

'Why not? What's wrong with a sociable drink?'

'Look, Sam, I'm not into a sociable drink with my colleagues,' she said with a half smile, resisting the urge to fidget with her glasses.

'C'mon, Daisy, that's what you said the last time. Surely by now you see me as more than just a colleague?' He gave her an entreating look with his blue eyes.

'I really prefer not to mix business with pleasure.' She deliberately leaned past him and stabbed the button for the lift.

'Pleasure? So you agree there would be an element of pleasure involved? I suppose that counts for something.'

'Look, Sam, if you don't mind, I'm late already.' She began to edge towards the lift door, watching its ascent to her floor on the illuminated strip.

'You sure I can't tempt you? I promise I won't even breathe a word about my innovative marketing strategies.'

'I'm sure the seminar was terrific, but sorry, no.'

'Don't worry, Daisy, I'm not giving up just yet. Next time, you won't escape so easily.' Sam's blue eyes twinkled at her.

Outside, the damp air was cool and fresh, and thankfully the rain had stopped. As she got into her car, she wondered why she couldn't just be like everyone else. As Paula had pointed out, half the girls in Cardinol would jump at the chance of going out with Sam, and jump into bed with him just as easily. But not Ms O'Neill. What was wrong with her that she couldn't relax? Chill out, Keith had said, she might enjoy it. She sighed as she switched on the radio, and despite the heavy Friday

29

evening traffic that clogged the roads of the business park, she made a conscious effort to unwind as she headed home. The tough, uncompromising Ms O'Neill could stay in her office for the weekend. All she needed to do in the next couple of days was to find out what Marina wanted for her birthday.

Should be straightforward enough.

Chapter Four

'So you see, Eve, this time the row was really all my fault.' Rachel's green eyes were huge with distress. She took a hurried gulp of her drink, plonked her bottle of Smirnoff Ice on the table and continued. 'I overreact to the slightest thing.'

'You're far too soft and sensitive, that's what's wrong. You just need to stand up for yourself a bit more. Hold on till I get us another drink,' Eve told her. She had to raise her voice against the voices shrieking all about them. Friday evening after work in a Dublin city centre pub heaving with bodies, noise and music wasn't really the best place for dishing out advice. Aside from that, on this particular Friday evening the last thing Eve felt like was an in-depth analysis of Rachel's troublesome love life.

Eve drained her own bottle of Smirnoff Ice, then shoved her way through the crush of people. She squeezed into a spot by the bar, gratified that the bloke standing next to her took one appreciative glance and gave her space to signal the barman.

She was glad to get away from Rachel, even for just a few minutes. Sorry and all as she was for her friend, Eve desperately needed some time to herself – time to clear her head and think about Alex and the likelihood of bumping into him again.

Alex Gallagher. Even his name brought goose-bumps to her skin. He had stalked off the office floor that morning at twenty to twelve. After that she hadn't laid eyes on him. She still hadn't managed to find out what further arrangements, if any, had been made with the consultants. Asking Rachel was out of the question. Rachel was so sunken in gloom over the latest row with John that, apart from raising her suspicions, any info she had would surely be questionable.

She hadn't wrangled anything out of Katie and Susan either. Tempted as she was, she realised that she could hardly make a point of strolling down to their desks to ask questions about the new computer system – they would think she'd had a brain transplant or something. Nor was there any point in asking Daniel Richards, since every time she looked at him he became incapable of basic communication. Why hadn't she paid more atten-tion in the first place?

But how could she possibly have known that the likes of Alex would turn up at her desk on a Friday morning?

'You know, Eve, I really admire you,' Rachel said after Eve had pushed her way back to the table with two more bottles.

'Admire me?' Eve grinned, running a hand through her hair and pushing it back from her face.

'Yeah. I wish I was more like you, relaxed and confident with men.'

'It's just a question of not letting them get under your skin,' Eve said.

'That's easy for you, you're always having to fend them off. I've never had that problem,' Rachel sighed.

Eve was thoughtful for a minute. She was so used to fending them off, as Rachel had put it, that she supposed it had become second nature to her.

'The main thing is not to take them seriously. You really should lighten up and not worry so much. I bet your row with John wasn't half as bad as you think. He's probably back at the apartment right now with a bunch of flowers or something, waiting to make up.'

'Do you think so?' Rachel half rose to her feet.

'Sit down,' Eve commanded. 'That's all the more reason for you to relax and enjoy a few drinks. Why shouldn't he wait? All the better if you're late home. You can float in looking as though you've had a brilliant evening. That'll make him sit up and take notice.'

'I suppose.' Rachel didn't look too convinced.

'You asked for my advice, Rachel,' Eve pointed out.

'You're right. What am I thinking of? You're the expert, after all,' Rachel smiled faintly. 'I'm the one who's always in a mess with my love life. You just have to click your fingers and men come running.'

'Yeah, well, I can't seem to help that.' Eve gave her an impish grin.

* * *

Daisy's bedroom was an oasis of calm. It was somewhere she immediately relaxed, a quiet space she loved returning to after a day at the office. Pale blue walls contrasted with generously draped cream cotton curtains. Her bed was arranged with blue and cream cushions and a thick matching duvet. Her favourite books, some of them revered since childhood, jammed her pine bookshelves in the corner. Her first-class business degree from the Institute of Technology was framed on the wall.

And tucked into a corner on the top shelf of her bookcase was a small photo of her mother and Liz.

Daisy picked it up on impulse. In the photo, they had their arms around each other and were laughing and squinting into the sunlight. Marina's hair was long and blowy and she was wearing a bright cheesecloth top, purple satin trousers and platform sandals. She looked about nineteen. Liz had on a multicoloured flower-patterned blouse and bell bottom trousers. Rising in the background, London Bridge formed a surround that held the sisters in a permanent embrace.

Marina didn't know she had the photo. She rarely ventured into Daisy's room. She didn't know that Liz had given it to Daisy ages ago so that she could see what her mum had been like as a young woman.

Daisy remembered that afternoon with painful clarity. She had been about thirteen, and had been staring at a portrait of Eve in Aunt Liz's lounge, a smiling, bandbox-pretty Eve on her Confirmation day, beaming down at all and sundry from the security of her gilded frame. It was the latest addition to join the swelling collection of portraits on the wall, beginning with Liz and Harry on their wedding day.

'Do you like it?' Liz had asked.

'Yes, it's lovely,' Daisy had said, ignoring her spasm of jealousy.

'It's good to have photographs of special occasions.' Liz smiled at Daisy with tender blue eyes in that special way of hers.

'Mum doesn't seem to think so,' Daisy quietly ventured, feeling suddenly emboldened by the smile.

Their eyes met and held, and in those few fraught seconds Daisy wondered if Liz recalled the time that a photo had once graced Marina's mantelpiece, the photo of a tall, smiling young man. One fateful afternoon Daisy had innocently asked if it was her father and Marina had flown into a rage. When Daisy arrived home from school the following day, the photo had disappeared and she couldn't wake her mother. It was the first time she remembered having to phone Liz.

'I suppose some people don't set too much store by photographs,' Liz said calmly. 'Don't mind me, I'm just camera mad. And they're only pictures, after all. It's nice to have special memories, but the past is in the past and what's really important is what's going on in the present moment. Do you understand?'

What Liz was telling her was that Daisy needn't worry because there were no photos on the wall in Marina's house. Not any more.

'Do you have any of Mum? Like when she was younger?' Daisy croaked, briefly wondering how the words had managed to come out of her mouth and form themselves into a coherent sentence.

Straight away Liz had given her one of herself and Marina, taken years ago when Liz had visited Marina in London. 'You hold onto that,' Liz had said, tucking it into her hand.

In other words, don't tell Marina.

Daisy had secretly hoped that Liz might have a photo of her mum and dad together, if there were any such photos in existence, but she couldn't possibly have asked her. She would have felt like she was being disloyal to her mum. And she was glad she held her tongue, for just at that moment Eve had pranced into the lounge. Eleven years old and glowing with pre-teenage assurance, she looked at them suspiciously. Tall and gawky by comparison, Daisy immediately coloured and felt as though she had been caught in some underhand act.

'What's going on?' Eve was slightly hostile. 'What are you two up to?'

'Nothing, darling,' Liz had swiftly said, smiling at her daughter. 'Daisy was just admiring your beautiful Confirmation portrait. Weren't you, Daisy?'

* * *

Daisy replaced the photo of Liz and Marina in her bookcase. She had learned long ago to stop asking questions about her father and London, though nowadays she didn't have to phone Liz on occasions when she couldn't wake Marina up.

She knew Marina had lived in London for several years and that she herself had been born over there. Marina had brought her back to Dublin when she was still quite young. But there were plenty of questions she didn't think she'd ever find the answers to, like why her father had done a runner at some stage. Had Marina been in love with him, or had it just been a casual relationship? Why did she never discuss what had happened in London all those years ago? Was it really too painful, still?

On and off during the years, when a hotly embarrassed Daisy had come home with a school invitation that included fathers burning in her fingers, Marina had merely scoffed that men were not to be trusted and that she was far better off without a dad. There were a handful of other girls in her class whose fathers weren't around much, but almost all of them had some idea of who and where they were. However, Marina remained tight lipped on the subject and by now Daisy had completely forgotten what the young man in the photo had looked like. If it had, indeed, been her father.

She had learned not to lose any sleep over it. Something Liz had said about the present moment being the most important had stayed with her throughout her childhood and she reminded herself of that now.

She felt more refreshed after a quick shower, changing her pinstriped suit for a comfortable tracksuit and putting aside her glasses in favour of contacts. In the hallway downstairs, she hesitated outside the front room and crossed her fingers. How many times had she done this, wondering what might be on the far side of the door? Daisy had lost count, but the childhood habit remained. There were lots of days when Marina was fine, but the problem was that you just never knew.

When Daisy opened the door, everything was okay. Marina O'Neill wasn't slumped over her sewing machine in vodka-induced withdrawal – she was busy at work. She looked up from her sewing machine in the corner and lowered the volume on the radio. Daisy didn't realise that she had been holding herself tensely until her shoulders suddenly relaxed.

'Hi, Mum, how are you today?' She adopted an exaggerated cheerful tone that suggested everything was fine.

'I'm okay.' Marina's stock answer, whether she was okay or not.

'Are you hungry?' Daisy spoke as though she was calming a querulous child.

'I might be. I don't think I've had much today,' Marina said vaguely.

'Would you like me to order a Chinese?'

'Hmm, I suppose so.'

They didn't look alike. Marina was petite in contrast to Daisy's tall stature, her eyes were blue like Liz's and her dark shoulder-length hair was sprinkled with grey. Sometimes her hair was tossed and unruly, but today she had it pinned back in a large clip at the nape of her neck. She was wearing a green velvet kaftan that floated around her slender figure, under which she wore a pair of black palazzo pants. With the heavy beaded cross hung by a leather cord around her neck and the often ethereal look in her eyes, Daisy sometimes thought that her mother resembled a new age hippy.

The front room of the house was her mother's

sewing room, complete with cutting table, sewing machines, samples and oddments of material, spools of thread, a higgledy-piggledy sheaf of patterns and whatever set of curtains or furnishings Marina was working on.

This evening, the curtains were closed, the linoleum floor was flecked with swirls of yellow threads and shards of material, the lights were blazing and a sheet of yellow cloth flared out from the sewing machine where Marina sat.

'What are you working on?' Daisy asked, venturing across to the sewing machine.

'Curtains, of course. Two sets with pinch pleats. They're to be collected on Monday,' Marina said anxiously. 'I don't know if I'll have them finished on time.'

'I'll give you a hand,' Daisy said automatically, pleased to see that some progress had been made on the work. 'This is lovely,' she approved, fingering the heavy material. 'And you've got quite a lot done. Why don't you leave it for now and I'll phone the Chinese?'

'Okay. I suppose I'll have the usual.'

Daisy phoned in the order for delivery and went out to the kitchen cum living room that ran across the back of the house. So much for tearing out on the town or enjoying wild nightclubbing adventures, she thought ruefully. Her normal Friday night usually consisted of Chinese takeaway and *The Late Late Show* or whatever Marina wanted to

40

watch. Perhaps tomorrow night she would meet some of her old college pals for a drink in Temple Bar – though on second thought, she decided to forget about it. She still felt raw after last night with Keith and a weekend hibernating at home might be better.

Thankfully Marina had had one of her good days – the perfect opportunity, Daisy realised, to ask her what she would like for her birthday.

'I want to ask you something,' she began when they were sitting down to their chicken curry, 'and I want your honest answer. It's about your birthday.'

'My birthday?'

'I think it's an important birthday, a kind of a milestone, and I want to get you something really special, whatever you'd like.'

'You do?' Marina threw her daughter an engaging grin that suddenly gave Daisy a glimpse of the once young and beautiful Marina O'Neill, and it made her wonder all over again what the hell had happened, and when and how.

'Yes, whatever you'd like,' Daisy repeated. What she really would prefer would be to take the two of them away to a whole new life where they could begin all over again, away from the shadows of the past. She longed for a new start herself. She wanted to get away from cool, calm pretences and Friday night takeaways, not to mention passionate disasters, but God only knew what Marina would resort to if she was left on her own.

'Do you mean it? Anything I want?'

'Of course,' Daisy smiled. 'Whatever would make you happy.'

'Let me see....' Marina said slowly.

In those few minutes as she waited for her mother's answer, Daisy thought that perhaps Marina would like some nice jewellery, or a slim gold watch like the one Liz wore. Or maybe she could persuade Marina to join her in a weekend away in a luxury hotel with a range of pampering facilities. That would be relaxing for them both.

'I do know what I'd like,' Marina said. 'I'd like a party!'

'A party? What kind of a party exactly?'

'A proper party, just like the one Liz had,' Marina announced with satisfaction.

Daisy felt a cold wave of dismay wash through her and settle like a lead weight in the pit of her stomach. Two years ago, Liz had celebrated her fiftieth birthday in style. Harry had whisked her off to a chateau in the Loire valley for a week, and on her return she had had a lavish, no-expense-spared bash with over a hundred guests. A party for Liz was one thing. A party for Marina would be a recipe for disaster.

'Liz had a great night, remember?'

'Yes, she did,' Daisy found her voice. She'd had to bring Marina home early and put her straight to bed. That was the bit she remembered the most.

'She was really the belle of the ball. Surely I deserve a party just as much as she did,' Marina suddenly challenged.

'Of course you deserve it,' Daisy hurriedly agreed.

'We could ask all the family and our friends,' Marina suggested.

What family? What friends? What the hell was the normally reclusive Marina thinking of?

'And it would be a chance for me to see all your friends, Daisy, seeing as you hardly ever bring them home.'

Good grief. How could she possibly bring friends home when she never knew what Marina was going to be like?

'That's what I want. A party.' Marina smiled happily as she warmed to her idea. 'Can you just imagine it?'

She could imagine it only too well. Marina was bound to make a show of herself in front of everyone – in front of Liz and Harry, but worse again, in front of their spoiled daughters, Eve and Victoria. Eve in particular, who always took some perverse pleasure in looking down at Daisy.

'Well? What do you think?' Marina persisted. 'I'm sure Liz will help. She'll be glad to, especially after the success of her party.'

Daisy felt as though she could barely talk. 'Tell me, Mum,' she asked, 'is this what you'd really like?'

'Of course,' Marina said forcefully. 'Most people have parties for their fiftieth, don't they? It's an important milestone, after all. You said it yourself, Daisy, it's a special birthday. And if Liz could have a party, then why shouldn't I?'

Yes, of course, Daisy simmered as she began to clear the table. Why shouldn't Marina have a big party like most people? Only her mother wasn't like most people, was she? That was the problem.

Wait till Liz heard about this. She could just picture her reaction, almost as easily as she could picture the ridicule in Eve's mocking blue eyes.

Chapter Five

Eve wasn't the kind of person who believed in fate. Life was what you made it, she reckoned, so she rarely pored over her horoscope like Rachel or the other girls in Foley's, firmly believing that your destiny was in your own hands and under your own control.

But when she and Rachel finally emerged from the stuffy warmth of the pub later that evening, Eve wondered if there was something to be said for fate after all. As they began to head down Grafton Street, thronged with the Friday night crowd, who did she spot striding along the other side of the street, threading swiftly through the crowds and silhouetted against brightly lit shop windows, but Alex.

There was no mistaking his tall, broad figure. Hadn't she spent most of the morning committing it to memory?

'What's up?' Rachel asked as Eve faltered in her stride.

'Oh, nothing.' Eve turned up the collar of her coat. 'Just feeling a bit nippy.' Nothing? Then why had her heartbeat suddenly accelerated? Why had the cold Friday night taken on such a distinctly magical air that she could almost sense it?

She felt as though her eyes were out on stalks as she followed Alex's swift progress down the street. They reached the corner just in time to see him disappearing into a pizza restaurant.

'Tell you what, Rachel,' Eve said with a determined look on her face, 'let's go for something to eat. It'll delay you even more.'

'I'm not sure,' Rachel hesitated. 'I think I'm late enough already.'

'C'mon, the night is only starting,' Eve scoffed. 'You want to make sure that John will be ready to fall all over you by the time you get home. And you'd be doing me a favour. I'm supposed to be meeting Susan and Katie later on, but I need to grab something to eat first to soak up the booze.'

'Me doing you a favour? As well as John falling all over me?' Rachel laughed. 'Okay then.'

The restaurant was almost full. Once she spotted Alex sitting alone at a table for four, it was the easiest thing in the world to allow a glance of recognition to flicker in her eyes, to pause and hesitate until he suddenly recalled who she was and insisted that they share his table.

'We can't possibly intrude,' Eve demurred.

'Not at all, I insist.'

Eve sent up a swift thanks to whatever destiny had given her a second chance and smiled at Alex as she shimmied out of her coat, sat down and invited Rachel to do the same. There were introductions all around, as Rachel didn't recall Alex from the office that morning.

'You were down at the photocopier when your computer was being checked,' Eve informed her.

'Otherwise I'm sure I would have remembered you,' Rachel smiled, naked admiration beaming from her green eyes as they ordered food. Eve felt as though she was in some sort of trance. She was scarcely able to believe she was sitting here beside the man who had distracted her all day long. She tried to rein in her thoughts, afraid that even in the busy ambience of the restaurant he would somehow sense her exhilaration. It seemed to have a life of its own as it washed over her in sparkling, glittering waves.

'I still can't understand why I didn't see you out on the floor,' Rachel was saying breathlessly. 'Of course, we were all so busy today, even you, Eve, that we had no time to notice anyone out of the ordinary.'

'Yes, very busy,' Eve agreed, almost falling off

her chair when Alex shot her a knowing, amused glance. Had he noticed? Had he spotted her following his progress around the office floor when she should have been concentrating on her spreadsheet?

'In that case,' he smiled, tiny lines fanning out from his dark eyes, 'I'm glad I could offer you a seat. Can't have hard-working girls like yourselves unable to find somewhere to sit down and relax at the end of a long day at the office.'

'Well, that's not the real reason we came in here,' Rachel began.

'Oh?' Alex asked. Eve immediately wished that Rachel hadn't had quite so much to drink.

'You see,' Rachel began in a sudden rush of confidence, totally oblivious to Eve's warning glance, 'I'm trying to delay going home.'

Alex's eyebrows shot up in surprise.

'What Rachel means is that we're out for the night,' Eve said smoothly.

'Yes, sort of. The later I'm out, the better,' Rachel said firmly. 'That's what Eve suggested, so I'm taking her advice. She always knows best.'

Eve smiled blandly across at Alex and resisted the urge to kick Rachel under the table. 'Have you just come from work yourself?' she asked.

'I have. Busy day today.' He ran a distracted hand through his hair, looking suddenly boyish and even more appealing. Eve silently absorbed every inch of his face, from the faint stubble on his angular jaw line, to his enticing mouth, to those stunning grey eyes. 'I had to run some back-up files for Foley's just in case there's a problem on Monday,' he explained

'Will you be in our office on Monday?' Eve asked.

'No, I'm involved in a different project,' Alex said, instantly dashing her hopes. 'I was just helping out today because one of my colleagues came down with flu. It means I'll be spending Monday catching up on stuff I neglected today.'

So he had been in her office purely by chance, filling in for a sick colleague. Eve shivered when she thought of how easily she had almost taken the day off and stayed in bed. It was definitely fate.

'Is this your usual Friday night thing, a few drinks and a meal?' Alex asked.

'Oh no. Well, maybe for Eve, but I should really be going home to John,' Rachel said, glancing at her watch and suddenly looking apprehensive. 'Look, Eve, are you sure I'm doing the right thing?' she asked, and she looked so genuinely worried that all Eve could do was smile.

'Of course you are, trust me,' Eve said, wondering if she needed to get her head examined. She had had the perfect excuse to get rid of Rachel and leave the field clear for her to concentrate on Alex.

'What do you think, Alex?' Rachel turned to him suddenly. 'If you had a row with your girlfriend, would you think more of her for deliberately

49

keeping out of your way? Or would you prefer her to be at home, waiting to fall into your arms?'

'That all depends,' Alex said.

'Although I can't imagine you having girlfriend problems,' Rachel continued innocuously as she lifted a slice of her pizza. 'You're probably like Eve. I bet you spend all your time holding them at bay.'

'And does Eve spend all her time fighting off admirers?' Alex smiled, throwing Eve an amused glance.

She almost melted, but she tried to look detached. There was no harm, she supposed, in letting him know that there was plenty of competition, although he didn't look like the type who would be happy to join a queue. But neither did she want him to think she was an empty-headed flirt. For someone as obviously intelligent as him, that would never do.

'Eve could have a different man on her arm every night of the week if she wanted,' Rachel boasted before Eve had a chance to speak. 'And she usually does.'

Thanks Rachel, Eve fumed. She was sitting beside this gorgeous man who had come into her life for the second time that day, and Rachel was making a mess of everything. But it wasn't only Rachel making a mess, Eve silently admitted. She was as much to blame herself. She felt as though her brain had seized up, for she seemed suddenly incapable of her usual flirty conversation.

'Where do you work, Alex?' Eve asked, swiftly changing the subject and taking the attention away from herself.

'Citimex Systems,' he said, looking surprised.

'Of course, silly me.' She could have kicked herself. Anyone with a bit of cop on would have remembered the name from the training handouts they'd been given.

'I'm mostly based in the head office,' Alex said.

'So you kind of direct operations?' she asked.

'You could put it like that.'

'Sounds interesting,' she continued. 'A lot more interesting than boring old data entry. We've worked in Foley Financials for almost two years now, haven't we, Rachel?' she said.

'Is it that long?' Rachel frowned.

'Yeah, we started within a week of each other,' Eve continued, explaining that she had done a basic ECDL course on leaving school and never stayed in a job longer than a year or two. 'Foley's is my third, or is it my fourth, job?' She held up her hand and silently counted across her fingers. 'Whatever. I like to broaden my experience,' she hastily added. It sounded a lot better, after all, than admitting she got bored easily.

'So you'll be saying goodbye to Foley's soon?' Alex asked with a glint in his eye.

'No, not quite yet,' she backtracked, feeling suddenly foolish. No way could she leave Foley's until her finances were in some sort of reasonable order. 'This time I'm not moving until I get the kind of job I really like.'

'Makes sense.' Alex looked at her approvingly and she felt a wave of excitement going down to her toes.

They talked about the job market and Eve tried to look enlightened, even though the only criteria from her point of view was the size of the pay cheque at the end of each month. But it didn't really matter what they talked about. She was sitting beside the most attractive man on the planet and she felt on a high, so she smiled in all the right places and flirted with her blue eyes and didn't want the night to end. Time flowed by in a blur of heady expectation, and before Eve knew it their plates were being whisked away.

'Will you join me for a coffee?' he asked. 'I'm sure it won't delay you for too much longer, Rachel.'

'It's okay,' Rachel smiled. 'Another few minutes won't make much difference. It's Eve you should be asking. She's all set to go out on the tear.'

'I'm sorry, Eve,' Alex apologised. 'Am I delaying you?'

'Not at all.' Eve forced a nonchalant expression into her eyes. 'I'm not rushing anywhere.'

'Aren't you supposed to be meeting up with Katie and Susan?'

'No, not tonight.' She met Rachel's puzzled glance head on. No way was she going to dash off if it meant leaving Alex's company any sooner than she had to. She knew by the alertness in Rachel's green eyes that her friend had finally copped on. It wouldn't make much difference now, Eve fretted. Fifteen minutes max to linger over coffee, then that was it, over and out. She felt a mounting panic as their small talk gradually came to an end. They argued pleasantly over the bill before dividing it three ways, stood up, pulled on coats, threaded through the packed restaurant and went out into the chilly air. The night breeze was sharp after the insulation of the restaurant as the three of them headed down the street.

Alex stopped at the corner of Dame Street. 'Nice meeting you both,' he said, looking down at them. Eve realised that he was even taller than she had first thought. The top of her head barely came up to his broad shoulders and she imagined for a wild, wonderful moment what heavenly bliss it would be to be swept into his arms.

'Off anywhere exciting?' Rachel asked him, throwing a loaded glance at Eve.

''Fraid not,' he said, 'I'm off home. I didn't take the car this morning so I'm heading across to College Green to get a taxi. Unless either of you are interested in sharing a taxi?'

'That depends,' Rachel said. 'I'm going north-side and Eve is headed for the leafy suburbs of Templeogue.'

'Templeogue? You could come with me if you want, Eve, I'm off to Rathfarnham.'

Eve ignored Rachel's frantic nudge as she said, barely able to articulate her words, 'Sure, thanks, that would be handy.'

Handy? She felt almost dream-like as she watched while Rachel jumped into the first available taxi and was borne away in the swirl of traffic, then she was climbing into the warm interior of another taxi, with a thumping heart and jelly legs. Traffic was light at this hour of the evening – it was early yet and most people were just getting comfortable in pubs and bars. As the taxi bore them swiftly through the Dublin streets, Eve looked across at Alex's profile against the streaming lines of streetlights and wondered why her normally chatty voice had deserted her.

'This is probably an early night for you,' he said. 'I'd guess you're usually out till the crack of dawn.'

Oh, God, surely he didn't realise that she had abandoned her plans for the night in order to share a taxi and some more precious minutes with him? 'Yes, sometimes,' she said lightly. 'But I'm pacing myself tonight. I have a hectic schedule lined up for the rest of the weekend.'

'I'd say you have. All those admirers.' He grinned at her in the close confines of the taxi.

'Well, life's to be enjoyed, isn't it?'

'I suppose it is,' Alex said.

'You suppose?' She suddenly found her voice and continued in a burst of confidence, wondering at the back of her mind why she was blabbering on like this. 'I consider myself one of the lucky ones. Even though I don't particularly rate my job, I've always enjoyed a busy social life. And so far, it's been fun. That's what it's all about, isn't it?'

He fell silent again, staring out the window as they headed along Templeogue Road, and she wondered if she had said something wrong. When he spoke again, his next words threw her into a tailspin.

'I'm going to a party in the Burlington next weekend. A friend of mine is getting engaged. Would you be interested in coming with me?' he asked. 'If, of course, you can find a window in your hectic social schedule?'

Chapter Six

Liz picked up a sliver of beef Wellington and realised she wasn't tasting it at all. She hadn't tasted anything since the phone call from Daisy last night telling her what Marina wanted for her birthday.

'What's up?' Harry asked.

'Nothing. Why?'

'C'mon, Liz, you haven't been yourself all day. What is it?' They were out for a Saturday evening meal in their favourite restaurant in Templeogue. All around them diners were relaxing, sharing bottles of wine, soft laughter and intimate conversation, while music wafted in the background – the recipe for a perfect Saturday night. But Liz was tense and edgy and had been deliberately waiting until Harry had finished his sea bass before she broke the news.

'I wasn't going to tell you just yet….' she hesitated.

'I knew there was something bothering you. You might as well tell me.'

'I had a phone call from Daisy last night,' Liz began.

Much as she had expected, Harry put down his knife and fork, pushed away his plate and faced her squarely across the polished wooden table as she told him what Daisy had said.

'You're scarcely going along with this!' Harry was incredulous.

'What can I do?' Liz asked. 'Daisy was keen to do something special for her mother.

'God.'

'The way it is, Marina seems to think that because I had a party, surely she should have one. And my fiftieth was so successful that she suggested I help.'

'For heaven's sake, Liz, you're opening a can of worms here.'

'In fairness, Marina's right in a way. Why shouldn't she have a party?'

Harry spluttered. 'Are we talking about the same person here? I can think of plenty of reasons.'

'Maybe if I look after things….' She began to fidget with the flower arrangement in the middle of the table.

'Liz to the rescue once more? Is that it? You do realise, I hope, that you're far too soft.'

Soft? She wasn't too soft, was she? She'd hate to think she was being taken advantage of, Liz realised as she faced her husband across the table. But this was Marina, of all people, and Liz would go to the ends of the earth for her. 'Look, Harry,' she said, 'I told Marina she would always have me – have *us* – to turn to for help. And there were lots of occasions when she refused any offer of help, weren't there? Financial or otherwise.'

'It's scarcely your fault if your sister decides to be stubborn.'

'Harry, it was important for Marina to hold on to some basic dignity and pride. But now she's actually asked for my help, and I'm not going to let her down. And you never know.' Liz marshalled her arguments, took a bracing sip of wine and tried to sound convincing. 'It might do Marina all the good in the world to have a little fuss and attention. Maybe it's just what she needs. And I'm doing this for Daisy as well. I don't know how Daisy has stuck it out for so long, but she's bound to be leaving home soon. If Marina could be encouraged into getting some sort of a life, even at this stage, it would certainly help all around.'

'I think you should have knocked the whole idea on the head straight away. I don't see why it has to fall on your shoulders.'

'I'm trying to do a bit of damage limitation. Daisy said she'd organise things, but the more input I have, the better. Hopefully I'll nip any possible problems in the bud.'

'Personally I think you should leave well enough alone.' Harry shook his head. 'You tried to help Marina before and it didn't work. Don't you think there's far too much water under the bridge?'

Liz was silent for a few moments. 'Maybe the lapse of time is all for the better. Who knows?'

'Well, Daisy certainly doesn't,' he commented darkly, deliberately misinterpreting her remark.

'That's Marina's business, not ours,' she gently reminded him.

'Point taken. But as far as I'm concerned, she has a right to know what happened.'

'Perhaps,' Liz conceded. 'Anyway, back to the party. I intend to keep a very close eye on Marina. I'll do my big sister talk and tell her she has to behave for Daisy's sake. Maybe having a reason to dress up and get her hair done might just do the trick for Marina.'

'Do you really believe that, Liz?'

'Daisy had almost come around to that way of thinking by the time I was finished talking to her.'

'You mean you used some subtle persuasion?'

Liz smiled. 'She was so upset about the whole thing that I tried to make her see it from another angle. Another reason I'm helping out is that if things go pear shaped, I don't want Daisy blaming herself. God knows she's had enough to put up with over the years.'

'Yes, she has.'

'I know it might be a bit late in the day to rescue Marina,' Liz admitted. 'And I know I tried before and failed. But let's face it, Harry, we're the lucky ones, aren't we? We really have it all. Doesn't Marina deserve at least one more shot?'

'I suppose, if you put it like that,' Harry sighed. 'And if there's anything I can do… as usual.' He raised an eyebrow and gave her a quick grin of capitulation before signalling for the bill.

It was a grin she was only too familiar with, after almost thirty years of marriage. They had everything to be thankful for, she reminded herself as they purred home to their luxurious house in Templeogue in the comfort of Harry's Mercedes. She had every reason to be grateful to whatever destiny had given her this particular path.

She also knew that in spite of Daisy's best intentions, it would be almost impossible to make her sister happy.

Growing up many years ago in Crumlin, Marina had been her adored younger sister who had danced her way though life, pretty, petite and happy go lucky. Liz had been the quiet one, far more reserved and studious. Two years younger than Liz, Marina had been a constant source of wonder and delight to Liz and their parents, with her vivacious gaiety, her infectious happiness and her stylish personality, so loved and loveable that Liz couldn't possibly feel the least bit jealous of the way she sailed through school and the ease with which she collected a string of boyfriends. Nor the least bit jealous of Marina's exciting talent.

Then, when she was twenty, Liz had met Harry Andrews, a steady young trainee banker, and quietly fallen in love. Marina had teased her loyal devotion to him and followed a glittering dream of her own – fashion design and London.

Yes, Harry's hair was a lot sparser now and salt and pepper grey, and maybe he didn't visit the gym quite as often as he should. And sometimes, too, steady and reliable could be interpreted as boring and predictable, depending on the humour she was in, but she usually squashed that thought straight away. In a world where life could be unfair and the rug could suddenly be pulled from under you, there was a lot to be said for sound and solid predictability. Although they had had their ups and downs, they were one of the lucky couples, more in love now than on the day they had walked up the aisle of St Mary's and out into the rest of their lives.

At fifty-five her husband had settled into middle age quite comfortably. Harry might have a high-profile investment banker job, but his wife and daughters were his pride and joy and he was like putty in their hands. He poured his energy into his job and was quite happy to sit back and give his wife free rein when it came to domestic matters. Her part-time job in a local solicitor's office gave her a pleasant social outlet as well as free time during the week. Together they had provided a lovely home and the stability of unconditional love for Eve and Victoria, their two daughters. They were spoiled, but so what? Liz was so grateful to have them, especially Eve.

Liz and Marina's parents were long dead now, both succumbing to cancer within a year of each other. As for Marina… how things had changed. Liz sighed and wondered how a carefully chosen birthday present could possibly make any difference.

'You're very quiet. Are you okay?' Harry asked as the car whispered up the avenue, turned in between imposing black wrought iron gates and crunched up the driveway.

'Just thinking,' Liz shrugged.

'Happy thoughts, I trust,' he said, turning towards her with a note of caution in his voice.

'Oh, very happy.' She deliberately brought her focus to the here and now. 'How about a relaxing brandy, and then….' she hesitated for extra emphasis and continued with a smile in her voice, 'maybe an early night?'

Harry cut the engine, turned to her and, much as she had anticipated, gave her an affectionate hug. 'Sounds perfect, my wonderful, sexy wife.'

Lovemaking was better now, Liz thought as they lay close together in bed. No doubt Eve and Victoria thought their parents were way over the hill and gone beyond sexual enjoyment. Although the heart-thudding excitement of their youthful days may have slightly diminished, by now they knew each other intimately. They knew what pleased and what impassioned, and, she thought as she smiled into Harry's eyes, knew how to keep the magic going. Lovemaking was also somehow more meaningful, and it was all the more special with someone you had entrusted most of your life to. Feeling grateful for her blessings, Liz drifted off to sleep.

* * *

Rachel was ready and waiting when Eve stalked up the office floor on Monday morning. 'Well?'

'Well what?'

'How did you get on with that fab hunk on Friday? What a coincidence, bumping into him like that. I can't understand how you never once let on that he was prowling around the office,' Rachel huffed.

Eve shrugged. 'Last Friday you were in the rats,' she pointed out. 'Not even Jude Law in the nude would have cheered you up.' She plonked her make-up bag on her desk and pulled out her mirror.

'I dunno. Alex Gallagher stalking around my desk would have been a major boost. Even fully clothed. Did you manage to make a weekend of it?' Rachel grinned.

'I had a great weekend,' Eve said airily. 'I went shopping on Saturday and picked up three new tops

63

and got my hair done. On Saturday night I met the gang in Samsara and afterwards we hit D2.'

Rachel frowned. 'I thought you were trying to make out with that Alex bloke.'

'Oh, did I not say?' Eve feigned innocence. 'He's invited me to a party next Saturday night.'

'See? I told you. Eve Andrews just has to click her fingers.'

'Course, I have to decide if I'm going or not.' Eve was triumphantly nonchalant.

'I'd say that's a very difficult decision,' Rachel grinned.

The only decision she had to make, Eve thought as she checked her lip gloss, was when exactly to phone. Not too soon, of course. But how long could she hold out? The delicious prospect of even hearing his gritty voice on the phone was already sending flutters of anticipation through her. No wonder she was feeling so absurdly cheerful about life this morning.

'How about you, Rachel? You look a lot happier than you did on Friday,' Eve said brightly as she took out a comb and smoothed her already smooth, frizz-free hair.

'Oh, I am,' Rachel beamed. 'John and I had a great weekend. Thanks a mill for listening to me and giving me advice.'

'Anytime,' Eve smiled.

On Wednesday afternoon she took Alex's business card out of her purse and fingered it for several moments, then resolutely put it back. One more day to keep him on ice and then she'd phone. On Thursday morning Eve picked up the phone, took a deep breath and dialled Alex's number.

'Alex Gallagher.' He answered immediately, his voice sending shivers down her spine.

'Hi, Alex, it's Eve.'

'Eve? Oh – yes.'

'I'm phoning you about Saturday night? The engagement party?'

'Sure. Sorry, I'm just in the middle of something. Um, give me your number and I'll call you back in a few minutes.'

The minutes dragged by. Eve didn't realise that she had been staring blankly at the same statement over and over until she tried to key in data that she had already entered onto her spreadsheet. After ten minutes, she told herself that he had forgotten all about her. He had changed his mind. After fifteen minutes, she felt a cold dismay running through her as she convinced herself that she had waited too long to phone and that things were finished before they had even begun.

Chapter Seven

As Eve sat panic stricken at her desk, Alex was staring out through the fifth-floor window of his Citimex office. Down below in the city centre street, Thursday morning traffic was still gridlocked. In the distance, the familiar sweeping curves of the Dublin Mountains were shades of misty blue.

Eve. He had totally forgotten about her. He had also totally forgotten about the engagement party that he had promised to attend Saturday night. He had even forgotten that his friends had vowed to drag him along by the scruff of his neck if he didn't go voluntarily.

'We're going to wash our hands of you if you don't put in an appearance,' they had warned. 'You have to get your life back. You can't hide away forever.'

And then Eve Andrews had sashayed into his life, bumping into him in a pizza restaurant, practically hijacking his table just hours after she had batted her endless eyelashes at him in the offices of Foley Financials. Flirty, empty-headed Eve, with her frivolous, carefree attitude, who probably had as many boyfriends as he had had hot dinners. It had seemed a good idea last Friday night to suggest she accompany him to Maurice and Karen's engagement party. It seemed like a perfect solution. It would at least keep his friends happy and it would probably do him good to get out on the social scene again. But then when Eve had phoned him in the cold light of Thursday morning, he had hesitated.

Right now, he had other things on his mind. A detailed report was sitting on his desk awaiting his recommendations. He had picked it up several times and tried to absorb the salient points, but he couldn't concentrate. As he stood by the window looking at the mountains, that morning's meeting he had had with his boss kept running through his head.

Alex sighed as he turned back to his desk. Mark Dowling had just offered him a huge job in London and here he was dithering about going out on a Saturday night. How ridiculous could you get? It was only a casual date, after all. One of thousands for Eve. It wouldn't mean anything much to either of them. He reached for the phone.

* * *

Alex spent his lunch hour eating with his mother.

Jane Gallagher was seated in the foyer of the Madison Hotel in Harcourt Street when Alex arrived. In her mid-fifties, she was trim and youthful looking. Jane came into Dublin city centre two days a week and served behind the counter in a charity shop for a few hours. It gave her something meaningful to do, she said, in between her choir practice and her book club. It also kept her out of mischief and saved her from becoming a total leech on the economy, she often joked. She rose gracefully to her feet and smiled at Alex with similar dark grey eyes as soon as she spotted him arriving.

Jane lightly bemoaned the latest traffic hold-ups as they got comfortable, then turned to Alex and asked him what was wrong.

'There's nothing really wrong....' he hesitated.

'You have something to tell me but you don't know how to begin.'

Alex smiled. 'I just want to run something past you. Mark Dowling has offered me a job in the London branch of Citimex. Just temporary, several months, maybe a year. But he wants me in place before the end of the month.'

'I see,' Jane said slowly. 'Tell me about it.'

Alex filled his mother in on the meeting with Mark and the generous offer he'd made, explaining that the head of Citimex operations in London was seriously ill and would be out of action for several months. 'Mark needs him replaced as soon as possible. There's no one at the helm in London right now, so I have to keep this to myself until I come to a decision, as Mark doesn't want word leaking out.' He left out the bit about Mark assuring him that he had the requisite talent and full capabilities for the challenge. There were tough decisions to be made, Mark had said, decisions that he could entrust quite happily to Alex.

'What do you think?'

'It's not a question of what *I* think. You have to make up your own mind,' Jane said.

'I know that,' he said with a hint of impatience. 'I'm just asking you for your opinion.'

'Well then, for what it's worth, I think it's a great opportunity. And I also think it's come at a very appropriate time. It'll do you good to get away, even for a few months,' she continued firmly as Alex tensed.

'I'm not sure I'm so keen on going away.'

'Nonsense. You never regretted going to America, did you?'

'No, but things are a little different now, aren't they?' Alex said pointedly. He looked out the picture window to the beer garden. The patch of sky above was a clear, crystal blue and the landscaped greenery was covered with fresh green fuzz – unmistakable signs of spring and new growth. He turned back to his mother and smiled apologetically.

'At the end of the day, it's up to you, Alex. London's not that far away. It's exactly what your father would have wanted.'

'Do you think so?'

'Of course. And think of the girls. They could have great fun going over to visit you and updating their wardrobes,' she added with a gleam in her eye.

'Why do I suspect it would be more of a shopping expedition than a chance to visit me?' Alex grinned.

'And maybe I'll get a chance to drive the BMW,' Jane continued. 'No sense in leaving it languishing in the garage while you're away.'

'All right, that's enough.' Alex put up his hands in mock surrender. 'I'll consider it.'

'Seriously, Alex, I think this has come at a fitting time. A change of scene will do you good.'

'Yeah, well, I'll think about it,' he said, signalling the waitress for two coffees.

London. A new job, something to get his teeth into, something to keep him on his toes, he thought as he strolled back to the office afterwards in pale spring sunshine. A challenge that would give him little time to think, and certainly no time for raking over the past.

Chapter Eight

Daisy awakes suddenly, her heart thumping erratically and her face slicked with sweat. Her bedroom is full of dark shadows and brooding silence. She realises instantly what has happened. After years, she has had the nightmare again.

She waits and tries to hold onto the tail end of it, but it vanishes with its usual elusiveness, slipping out into the dark well of the night, leaving her with a thudding heartbeat and a feeling she can barely describe. Where are these shadowy images and frightening emotions coming from?

All she can remember is the little girl dressed in white, a little girl who laughs and giggles and holds out her hand towards her as though she wants to play. Then she hears a loud bang and the little girl disappears. Daisy searches and searches, but she can't find her anywhere.

She closes her eyes once more and tries to pull together the threads of her nightmare, to make sense of it, but it's impossible. She focuses for a moment and tries to make sense of the feeling. It's like the feeling you'd get if someone you love is snatched away, leaving you alone in terrifying emptiness.

Chapter Nine

Eve swanned into the bathroom, where fragrant steam clouds were rising from the whirlpool tub.

'You'd better not be all night in there,' Victoria glared as she flounced out of her bedroom.

Eve draped a bath sheet over the heated rail. 'I'll take as long as I want,' she taunted.

'I want to have a bath,' Victoria huffed.

Eve ignored her as she checked the temperature of the water. Trust Victoria to be awkward. She had spent most of her childhood looking up adoringly at her elder sister. Now, at the age of fifteen, not only was she four inches taller than Eve, but everything Eve said or did was cause for revolt. It was a bit hard for Eve to get used to after all the years of unswerving adoration.

'Look, Victoria, you only want a bath because I'm having one.'

'Hello? How many times do I have to tell you that it's Vikki now, not Victoria? And no, smarty, as it happens I've bought this new bath oil I want to try out.'

'Tough. You'll just have to wait until I'm finished.'

Eve locked the door, slid out of her robe and relaxed into the water. Saturday night at last. She had thought it would never come. She didn't spend too long in the bath – she needed plenty of time to get ready for her date with Alex. Not that she expected anything much to happen tonight. Her plunge bra and matching lace thong would scarcely get an airing, as she sensed that Alex was far too much of a gentleman to initiate anything on the first date. She shivered as she imagined those grey eyes raking over every curve of her body.

* * *

Daisy blindly moved along with the crush of people exiting the darkened auditorium, blinking as she came out into the brightly lit foyer of the cinema in Liffey Valley.

'There you are.' Sam Heffernan laid a possessive hand on her arm. 'Thought I'd lost you in that crowd. Good film, wasn't it?'

'Yeah, quite good,' she answered as he fell into

step beside her, joining the straggle of cinema goers making their way out of the complex.

He couldn't have chosen a better time to ask her to the cinema.

All week she had felt out of sorts, and no amount of power dressing or deep breathing or positive visualisation could shake off the black clouds gathering ominously above her head. All week she had fretted over the party for her mother, and phone calls to Liz hadn't reassured her. Really, what kind of a celebration could you have with Marina? Liz had said optimistically that she would take care of everything. Daisy just had to turn up with her friends. Her friends? Like who, precisely? The old college gang that she often met up with on a Saturday night when she wasn't picking up the pieces with Marina's sewing and pretending to Paula that she was painting the town red? The college gang that was getting smaller and smaller as friends spread wings or moved abroad? The gang she had always kept at arm's length from both herself and Marina?

No thanks.

As for Eve, how was she going to suffer her at Marina's party, flaunting herself in some sexy creation? She would certainly have something sarcastic to say if Marina let herself down. Although Daisy had spent a lot of her childhood in Liz's house, she and Eve had never really hit it off. Somehow Eve seemed to regard her as a rival for her parents' affection, which was ridiculous because it had always been blatantly obvious that Liz and Harry were completely besotted with their pretty, effervescent elder daughter.

When she had come down the back stairs of Cardinol Electronics last Thursday evening, she had been so distracted with thoughts of Marina's party that when she ran into Sam Heffernan, Mr Confidence himself, leaning lazily against her Yaris in the car park, quite clearly waiting for her, she had unthinkingly agreed to go to the cinema with him.

Only the one date, she'd assured herself. No more getting into compromising situations. Not with work colleagues.

Plus a date with Sam would give her a chance to practise being cool and confident with him outside the four walls of Cardinol, without the shield of her authority suits and the safety screen of her status as human resources manager. Good practice, in other words, for Marina's party.

'So long as the film isn't too gory,' she had qualified as she faced him in the car park. 'And nothing creepy either.'

'Don't tell me you're afraid of creepy things,' he had teased.

'I like to enjoy the cinema,' she said, 'not be scared half to death.'

'Being scared half to death is part of the fun,' he challenged, his eyes on a level with hers.

I've been scared half to death for most of my life, she felt like admitting, and believe me, it's not fun. Instead she said she would leave the choice of film up to him, but he needn't expect her to hang about if it fell into the wrong category.

'Okay, point taken. I'll pick you up around eight.'

She almost changed her mind when she had to give him her address and mobile number. The less he knew about her private life, the better.

'I can hardly collect you if I don't know where you live,' he had said, sensing her reluctance. 'Don't worry, I'm not expecting to be invited for Sunday lunch. I won't even knock at the door in case your dad comes out with a frying pan.'

She smiled ruefully. No chance of that happening, Mr Heffernan.

Sam brought her to an action-packed comedy and at times she almost forgot she was sitting beside him in the cinema. She was brought back to reality when they left and headed to the exit doors, walking under a blast of warm air before they went out into the cool April night. She was only too aware of him now as he guided her across the floodlit car park with his hand on her arm.

'Did you like my choice?' he asked. 'No blood or guts or spooky things.'

'I watched it to the end, didn't I?' she said lightly, gently disengaging her arm as they reached his car. As he swung his red Volvo out of the car park and took the lane for the southbound M50, she told herself so far, so good.

When he pulled up outside her house, she decided that he must have studied first aid some-time, because he gave her what could only be described as a practical demonstration of mouth-to-mouth resuscitation. Although there was nothing to resuscitate, she thought wildly, nothing whatsoever. What the hell was wrong with her, that his mouth just felt wet and rubbery against hers? That she almost choked on his delving tongue? Why didn't she feel even the least bit pleasured or excited?

She eventually disengaged herself from his arms and said goodnight, utterly relieved to reach the hall door.

* * *

On Wednesday evening when she heard Eve arriving home from work, Liz decided that, loathe as she was to do it, she couldn't put off telling her daughter any longer, so she followed her up the stairs and into her bedroom.

'Eve, before you do anything else....'

'What, Mum?'

'There's something I need to tell you,' Liz hesitated, sitting down on a corner of the flouncy bed and marshalling all her defences, knowing only too well what her daughter's reaction was going to be.

'Well? What's up? I'm going out soon and I need to get ready.'

'This won't take long. I just wanted to let you know that I'm holding a party for Marina, for her fiftieth birthday.'

'Is that all she is?' was Eve's first reaction, delivered in a tone of mild disbelief. 'I thought she was about sixty.' After a beat she added, 'Did you say you were holding a party?' Now Eve's tone of voice was incredulous. 'You've gotta be kidding, Mum.'

'No, I'm not.'

'But this is a mad idea.' Eve ran a hand through her hair and made a face at her reflection in the mirrored wardrobes. 'What does Dad think?'

'Your father is quite happy to go along with it.'

'I bet this is Daisy's idea. Trust my ditzy cousin to come up with such a crazy idea. Is that why she was on the phone the other night?' She whirled around and confronted her mother.

'No, well, yes….'

'Naturally, you couldn't say no to Daisy.'

'It wasn't Daisy. It was Marina's idea. This is what she wants for her birthday.'

'God, Mum. This gets better and better. Mad Marina snaps her finger and everyone jumps. You, of course, jump the highest.'

'It's not like that, Eve, and I won't have you being disrespectful about my sister.'

'Okay, but I can't understand why you didn't talk her out of it. Marina's such an oddball that it's bound to be a disaster. Why put yourself through this? Why bother? I hope to God you're not expecting me to go.'

'As a matter of fact, I am.' Liz pretended a calmness she didn't feel. 'It would be insulting to Marina, never mind me, if you didn't bother to show up.'

'C'mon, Mum, get real. The whole idea is farcical.'

'I suppose it is, but it's the one thing Marina wants for her birthday,' Liz tried to explain. 'And if it's what Marina wants, I'm happy to go along with it. She's had such a raw deal in life that I can't very well refuse her.'

'Here we go again with the sob story. Poor Aunt Marina.'

Eve was looking at her, Liz realised, as though she was soft in the head. But then, she had scarcely expected anything else from her fun-loving daughter. Eve didn't think much of her aunt, having more or less witnessed at second hand the problems caused down through the years by Marina's drinking. And now, to judge by the expression on her face, Eve didn't think much of her mother either.

Liz unexpectedly caught sight of her reflection in the mirror, her whole demeanour a blend of solicitous appeal, and she was suddenly tired of it all, tired of battling on Marina's behalf and trying to keep the slender peace that existed between Marina and her family. She was tired of making excuses for her to Harry, of trying to get her daughters to make allowances for her, her happy-go-lucky daughters who were completely oblivious to their aunt's sad history. This party was really the last straw. She was anxious enough about it already without Eve unintentionally adding more fuel. She could do with Eve's support. At twenty-four years of age, surely it was about time she could be trusted to have a more adult outlook? Maybe Marina had lost all credibility with Eve, but that didn't mean that Liz had to go down that route.

She tried to salvage some of her self-respect with her daughter, saying, 'You don't know the half of it, Eve.'

'No, I don't know the half of it, do I?' Eve said firmly. 'And I don't understand why everything is such a big dark secret.'

'Like what?' Liz faltered.

'Like Daisy's father, for instance. Why doesn't anybody talk about him? Ever? Daisy must have had a father, yet he doesn't seem to exist. I mean, so what if Marina had a one night stand when she was over in London and got pregnant?'

'That's enough, Eve. Your aunt wasn't like that,' Liz said sharply, springing automatically to her sister's defence. 'Marina was very much in love.'

'Marina in love?' Eve chortled. 'The mind boggles. What went wrong?'

'He left her,' Liz said.

'So? What's the big deal? It happens. It happens

81

all the time. It doesn't mean that Marina has to spend her life lamenting a lost love. And it doesn't mean you have to jump through hoops to try and make up for it.'

'There's a bit more to it than that.' Liz picked a fluffy pink cushion off Eve's bed and hugged it to herself. 'For starters, his timing was way off line. He left her when Marina was at her most vulnerable.'

'Oh yeah?' Eve's blue eyes were full of bored contempt. 'Marina, vulnerable?'

'Yes, Eve, and you needn't look so mocking. You see….' Liz paused.

'What?' Eve sounded impatient.

Liz took a deep breath and said, 'Thing is, Marina had just given birth to twins when he walked out on her.'

'Twins? What twins?'

Liz looked at Eve's confused face and realised that in a matter of minutes she had broken a silence that had lasted for over twenty years. 'Never mind.' She shook her head, feeling suddenly weak. 'Forget what I said. You're not supposed to know anyway.'

'Obviously.' Eve's eyes were alight with curiosity. 'So. The family skeletons are finally beginning to come out. I always knew our family had a colourful past. C'mon, Mum, you might as well spill the beans. Where are the twins now?'

Chapter Ten

London, years earlier. Liz comes over to visit. She has to meet him, she tells Marina. To see if she approves. You'll definitely approve, Marina laughs. She looks happier than Liz has ever seen her. When she finally meets him, she sees why.

He's blond and his brown eyes are smiling. He's carefree and untroubled. Much taller than Marina, he swings her right off her feet as he whirls her around.

They spend the weekend having fun. Liz has never heard her vivacious sister laugh so much. They sit and gossip, chatting to the backdrop of his strumming guitar. He can't pass Marina by without dropping her a kiss or smothering her in a hug.

They go sightseeing and take loads of photos. Liz captures them wrapped around each other in front of

London Bridge. He takes one of the two sisters, and when he hands the camera back to Liz she's struck by the dreamy expression in his eyes.

Marina says she loves him. He plays music for her while she sketches and works on her designs. On summer afternoons he sits in the garden and plays his guitar and dedicates his songs to her. On winter nights, they curl up together in front of the fire.

Just before Liz leaves, Marina says she has the best news of all. Her eyes sparkle with secret knowledge and Liz has guessed before she even tells her.

A baby. Marina says she doesn't know what she's done to deserve such happiness.

Chapter Eleven

In one sense, it was a relief to have it out in the open with Eve, Liz argued with herself. It had all happened so long ago that time and distance had altered perception. The veils of secrecy that had been woven over the years had magnified and distorted details of the event. Now the whole sorry episode lay lurking beneath so many layers of sorrow and poignancy that it resembled a deep, shadowy cavern, a place that everyone concerned was afraid to venture near – herself, Harry and, of course, Marina.

Telling Eve went some way towards vindicating Marina's behaviour, and indeed her own, Liz assured herself. She looked at her daughter's inquisitive face and took a deep breath. 'Promise you won't repeat this,' Liz asked solemnly.

'I promise. Who'd be interested anyway?'

'And under no circumstances are you to discuss this with Daisy. Under *no* circumstances, Eve.' Liz was suddenly sharp. 'Have I made myself clear?'

'Yeah, very clear. Don't worry, I won't say a word.'

'You see, Daisy was one of the twins.'

'You're joking.' Eve's eyes widened in startled incredulity, and for a brief moment Liz entertained the trivial thought that she couldn't remember the last time she had so totally engaged her daughter's attention.

'And the other twin, little Jessica....' she sighed, 'well, she was killed in a car crash.'

'Oh my God, Mum, that's awful.' Eve's eyes were saucers of astonishment. Liz fervently hoped she was doing the right thing. 'When did this happen?' Eve asked.

It happened so long ago that we should all be reconciled to it by now, Liz felt like saying. Instead she cleared her suddenly constricted throat and continued, 'Years ago, when we were over in London, just before Jessica was two. And please don't expect me to go into the gory details. It was far too upsetting.'

'God, I'd say it was. No wonder Marina hit the bottle.'

'Yes, well, she never really got over it.'

'I'm not surprised. But is that it? The dark family secret?'

86

'More or less.' Liz shrugged and gave her a half smile. Eve didn't understand, not really. But then, words couldn't explain, couldn't possibly do justice to the awful nightmare.

'It's sad all right, but I still can't understand why this all has to be kept under wraps. I mean, couples are splitting up every day of the week, that's nothing new, and I know the car crash must have been truly dreadful, but unfortunately they're happening every day too. Why the secrecy? It was a whole lifetime ago.'

'Eve, it was Marina's choice. She was totally destroyed, as you can imagine, and she didn't want any mention of it whatsoever. That was her decision and you have to respect that. Your father and I had to promise her.' Liz sighed at the haunting memory of a grief-stricken Marina, fresh in her mind now in spite of the passage of time. 'And don't forget, this conversation has to stay between the two of us. I'm not going to refer to it again, Eve. And I want no gossiping to Victoria or any of your friends. And certainly not to Daisy. It would be far too upsetting for her.'

'I hardly see Daisy any more, and I'm scarcely going to waste my time upsetting her about something that happened light years ago.'

'Promise?'

'I promise.'

'So now you've got some idea of what's going on, including why I'm organising this party, don't you?'

'Yeah. You're trying to keep Marina happy. But if you ask me, so long as it's all festering under the carpet and Marina's letting on it never happened, she'll never be happy.'

'You're probably right.'

'It stands to reason,' Eve shrugged. 'I feel sorry for Marina, I really do, and it must have been terrible, but life goes on, doesn't it?'

'Of course it does. You can only live in the present.' Although try telling that to Marina, Liz thought, feeling a helpless mixture of sadness and anger at the way her sister's life had been ruined.

'And right now, tonight is very important to me.' Eve reached out a hand and pulled Liz up off the bed. 'You'll have to leave me in peace, as I need to get ready for a date.'

'Anyone special?' Liz asked, relieved to change the subject.

'Very special!' Eve grinned.

Liz suddenly found herself on the far side of the bedroom door. Her head was swimming, her legs were weak and she was scarcely able to believe that a casual chat in Eve's bedroom had led her to finally break the years of silence. It was about time that she had confided in Eve, and in a way she was glad that her daughter had simply accepted everything without digging too deeply. Liz had said all she wanted to say on that sad matter. As well as that, Eve could be trusted to keep her word. Flighty and all as she was, she could be relied on to stay quiet.

From now on, Liz realised gratefully, Eve would surely understand whenever she went out of her way for Marina instead of looking at her as though she was daft.

She thought of Eve's words as she began to prepare dinner. Truly dreadful, she had said, but a lifetime ago, and Marina would never break free as long as everyone pretended it had never happened. Certainly a present-day, clear-cut perspective. And all too easy to say when you were coming at it, years later, from the outside.

* * *

Her mother was a true martyr to the cause, Eve decided as she rushed around the bedroom, pulling out wispy underwear, tight tops and trousers and her new spiky heels. She'd be better off saving her energy. But that was Mum for you. Every so often she tried to rescue her sister, and her efforts usually met with failure.

No wonder. Sorry as she was for her aunt, Marina was definitely a lost cause from the sound of things. She had obviously never got over her broken relationship. These things were common-place nowadays. You just had to move on.

Still, the car crash was something else. Eve didn't want to think about it as she ran into the shower; it was far too horrible to contemplate. No wonder Marina had turned into a basket case.

Maybe she was right to bury it in the past and pretend it had never happened. It was probably the only way she could live with it, if living was the appropriate word in her case.

Thank God she had Liz for a mother instead of Marina. A mother who was clued in – most of the time – who had always spoiled her rotten and who told her she was special and impressed upon her that she could have whatever she wanted out of life.

Anyway, Eve reminded herself that she had other things on her mind as she tried on one slinky top after another and admired her reflection in the mirror. Exciting things. Alex things.

He was collecting her at seven o'clock and they were going to a gig in Vicar Street. The chat with her mother had delayed her and she was just putting the finishing touches to her new lip gloss when the doorbell rang. Eve flew into a blind panic when she heard Victoria's voice in the hall and pictured her sister and her turbulent teenage hormones coming face to face with Alex. She flew down the stairs, almost tripping herself in her heels, and glared at Victoria behind Alex's back while she urged him out the door.

'Your sister seems very nice,' Alex said as they headed down the path.

'I hope so,' Eve grinned. 'I'm her role model, after all.'

'I might have guessed,' he laughed as he opened the door of the taxi for her.

Chapter Twelve

Their first date at the party in the Burlington had gone by in a haze. All night, as she was introduced to his friends, chatted to Alex and slow danced on the dance floor, Eve had felt as though she was wrapped in a magical glow. The only niggle at the back at her mind was the fact that not once did Alex look at her as though he couldn't wait to drag her off to his bed. But she had sensed from the beginning that he was a gentleman, hadn't she?

On the way home in the taxi, she had casually mentioned that she had tickets for Vicar Street and she had asked him if he would be interested. Her careless tone had belied her frantic run around to get her hand on some tickets, any tickets, anything at all to have a ready-made excuse to see him again.

'Next Wednesday?' he had asked.

'Yes, it should be a good night.' He had hesitated for a moment and her heart had given a dangerous lurch, then with a smile and slight nod of his head he had put her out of her misery.

And now, as the night in Vicar Street slid past all too swiftly for Eve, once again Alex was the perfect gentleman. Eve wasn't interested in the musician that night – it was magical enough to be sitting beside Alex, catching the scent of his aftershave as she leaned closer to exchange smiles and small talk with him during breaks in the performance, and hoping with an almost adolescent anticipation that he might suggest going for a drink afterwards. Might even suggest bringing her back to Rathfarnham....

He didn't.

At the end of the concert, they joined the crowd surging through the exit. Eve was acutely conscious of Alex's height as he towered protectively over her, her hand firmly tucked into his arm in case they became separated.

He immediately hailed a taxi, apologising for cutting her evening short.

'I'm in Galway tomorrow on business,' he explained. 'On the road at the crack of dawn. Otherwise I've have brought you for a drink or some food, seeing as you won't let me pay for my ticket.'

'No problem,' she said airily. Galway at the crack of dawn. Just her luck. 'Tell you what,' she suggested, 'we'll postpone the meal and drink till Saturday.'

'Saturday?' he frowned.

'Yes.' She smiled engagingly and allowed her hand to remain on his arm as she looked guilelessly into his eyes. 'We could go out for the meal and a drink on Saturday night. Would that suit you better?'

* * *

'Two Saturday nights in a row,' Rachel said the following day. '*And* out during the week. You'd want to watch your reputation, Eve.'

'What reputation?' Eve asked.

'Social butterfly? Never last longer than two dates with anyone? You'd get bored?'

'The words bored and Alex are completely incompatible,' Eve said.

Saturday night was shaping up to be far better than she could have imagined. Eve's heart raced as she sat at her desk. Only that morning her mother had reminded her that she and her father were going to a wedding in Wicklow and would be staying in the hotel overnight. That only left Victoria, who could be cleared out of the way, bribed if necessary, and the house would be free.

Just in case.

Maybe Alex was too much of a gentleman to bring her back to his place, but surely it would be no harm to have the right ambience ready and waiting in case he wanted to take things a little further.

* * *

'Twenty euro,' Victoria demanded. 'Boots has a great new glitter eye shadow I want. And a loan of your new pink top, the one with the slash down the front.'

'Aren't you a bit young to be wearing that kind of thing?'

'That's the deal, the money and the top.'

'Make sure you're not home until at least Sunday afternoon,' Eve warned.

* * *

On Saturday night, Alex called for her in a shiny black BMW and brought her to an Italian restaurant. It was crowded and lively; she would have preferred something a little more intimate.

'Cheers,' Eve said. She beamed at Alex across the table and raised her glass of white wine.

'Here's to a pleasant evening,' he said in reply.

'You can say that again,' she smiled. Alex was perfectly composed, his eyes as enigmatic as ever. He was wearing a black shirt and dark jeans and his hair was attractively tousled, as though he had towel dried it in a hurry. She tried to look as though she was enjoying her chicken and tomato compote, but she wasn't the least bit hungry. The sight of him sitting opposite her, chatting to her, smiling with her and giving her his undivided attention was sending her insides into somersaults.

'An Italian restaurant and you go and order steak,' she teased, feeling on a delicious high with his proximity. She could sit here forever and do nothing but look at him for the rest of her life.

'So?' He grinned boyishly. 'Steak is my favourite. Fillet, medium rare, chargrilled. And I like this restaurant. It's nice and busy.'

'So you prefer lively as opposed to a more intimate kind of atmosphere?'

'Why, don't you?' he asked.

'Depends on the occasion.' Eve gave him a meaningful look.

'I thought you'd prefer bright and cheerful surroundings instead of somewhere solemn and hushed.' He looked surprised. 'I hate those pretentious places where you can hear a pin drop.'

'I'm up for cheerful as well, but there are times when maybe a secluded booth is called for,' she said.

'Like you said, Eve, it all depends.' He smiled at her, but she didn't quite know what to make of it. Did he think they hadn't yet reached the secluded booth stage? Or had he brought her here because he sincerely believed it might be her favourite kind of restaurant?

'So how long have you been living in

Rathfarnham?' she asked, changing the subject.

'About six months,' he told her. 'When I came home from America I moved back to the family home for a few weeks and then I bought the apartment. My sisters were glad to get rid of me. I was always in trouble for leaving the top off the toothpaste.' Her blood pressure sky rocketed at the image of him in the bathroom with a towel slung around his hips and she felt like telling him that he could leave the top off her toothpaste anytime. She immediately latched onto the critical fact that he had returned home alone from America and had bought his apartment as a sole occupant.

Better and better.

'So you were in America? Did you like it over there?'

'I suppose so. It was hectic. I was there for nearly three years, working in Boston and New York. Not somewhere I'd like to live permanently, though.'

'I really loved America, but I only got as far as Florida a couple of times. My parents brought me to Disneyworld after Victoria was born as a special big sister treat for me, and I thought it was brilliant. Then we all went back together a few years ago. Working over there must have been a great experience for you.'

'It certainly broadened the horizons.'

'And where do you think you'd eventually settle down?'

'Dublin, of course,' he said. 'It's where family is.'

He had no doubt sown his wild oats in the States and was now back home in Dublin, where he intended to settle. Sounded very promising. She had figured he was about thirty years old, time to start planning for the future. 'Some people would prefer to put a lot of space between themselves and their families,' she remarked.

'Perhaps,' he nodded in agreement, 'but I've always got on well with my family and the extended relations.'

She wouldn't have expected otherwise. She could well imagine how nice Alex's family was bound to be and how easily he would get on with them all. 'That sounds good,' she said wistfully. 'I wish I could say the same.'

'Why, what's the problem?'

Eve shrugged. 'Nothing that would interest you. I can't fault my parents, they've always been great to me, but as for the rest…. The family's only small, but talk about the relations from hell.' She shook her head and laughed. 'I'm not even going to go there. So, do you think you'll stay in Citimex?'

'For the moment, yes.' Alex moved his plate to one side and poured more wine for Eve. 'I've been offered another position within the firm, but I haven't made up my mind. I can't talk about it yet as I have to keep it to myself until I make a decision.'

'Is it a promotion?'

'It is, in a way.'

'More money?'

'Yes….'

'Then you should accept,' Eve said brightly. 'Straight away, no questions asked.'

'I'll see,' he said good humouredly. 'Anyway, I'll let you know what I decide.'

That sounded even more promising – he intended to see her again, and he intended to keep her informed of his future career plans.

'I'd like to get a better job, but I wouldn't have that much scope for promotion,' she admitted. 'You see, I never went to college.'

'It's never too late,' he said.

'It would always be too late for me, Alex. I have to admit that I'm scarcely college material.'

'Not everybody is, but there's a lot to be said for the university of life.'

'That's what my parents told me when I barely scraped a pass in my Leaving Certificate. They insisted that I hadn't let them down and I wasn't to feel in any way disappointed. But let's face it, nowadays most people go on to third level. Even my tiresome cousin managed to do a business course with, believe it or not, my mother's encouragement. Of course, she's a bit of a brain box. But I suppose my talents lie in a different direction.'

He laughed outright and flashed perfect white teeth. 'We're not all clever clogs, thank God. You've a great sense of fun, Eve. I like that about you.'

She had a sense of fun. He liked her. She clasped the words to herself and embedded them in her heart. She resented the intrusion when the waitress arrived to clear away their plates.

'Care for dessert?' Alex asked.

Dessert? If he liked, she'd be giving him all the dessert he needed later on, Eve felt like saying. Instead she demurely asked for a bowl of ice cream.

'Ice cream?' His eyebrows rose.

'Yes, please, vanilla with butterscotch sauce,' she ordered. There was great potential for seductive body language with a spoon and a bowl of ice cream, all that flirtatious licking, and in case he needed a bit of encouragement from her, Alex was going to get the full blast.

However, she had just dipped her spoon into the mound of ice cream and was preparing to slide it seductively into her mouth when there was a commotion at a nearby table. A family party was having some kind of celebration. A birthday cake glowing with dozens of flickering candles was borne aloft to their table and everyone began to sing 'Happy Birthday'. An elderly man leaned forward and made an attempt at blowing out the candles as his family clapped and cheered.

Eve felt irritated with the disturbance and exchanged complicit looks with Alex, fully expecting him to be in tune with her annoyance, but to her surprise he was gazing into space and looking as though he was a million miles away.

'Alex,' she said, bringing him back to the crowded restaurant, 'aren't you having your dessert?'

He had taken two spoonfuls of his lemon sorbet. Now he pushed the dish away, looking at it with displeasure. 'No, I've had enough. Would you like tea or coffee before we head off?' he asked.

'No thanks,' Eve said, spooning vanilla ice cream into her mouth and fixing her gaze suggestively on his mouth as she ran the tip of her tongue across her lips. But the moment was lost as Alex excused himself and went off to the gents. She watched his tall figure weave authoritatively through the tables and decided that it was best to get going, away from the bustle of the noisy restaurant, into the relative intimacy of his car and on to the empty house.

When they drew up outside, she almost abandoned the idea of asking him in. Alex seemed to be quieter than usual. But when she suggested a glass of wine, he hesitated just briefly before agreeing to just the one. She felt on tenterhooks as she showed him into the sitting room, inviting him to take off his jacket and turning on soft shaded lamps. She put on her favourite Robbie Williams CD, adjusting the volume so that it flowed softly in the background.

She went into the kitchen to get the wine. It took her three tries to open the bottle, her fingers were so jittery. What the hell was wrong with her? Why was she so nervous? She opened a bag of ice, tearing it lengthways in her fumbling. She filled the wine cooler, jammed in the bottle of Chablis, fetched two glasses and sashayed back into the front room.

And almost dropped the bottle of wine.

Alex looked positively devastating. His head-to-toe black outfit was a stark contrast to the pale beige sofa. It was no wonder she felt jittery, but she walked across the room, her heart quivering as she set down the wine and the glasses on the coffee table, her legs trembling as she toed off her spiky heels and sat beside him on the sofa. She curled her legs up under her, letting her skirt ride up to her thighs.

'I'll let you pour,' she said.

They sipped their wine for a few minutes, the silence broken only by Robbie Williams crooning in the background, and Eve tried to think of something to say. Although her body was crawling with expectation, her mind was frustratingly blank.

'Do you like Robbie Williams?' she eventually asked, gazing at him with an interest that went far beyond his musical tastes.

'He's okay,' Alex shrugged.

'I went to see him in the Park,' Eve said. 'It was a brilliant concert.' She sipped her wine and looked at him over the top of her glass. 'Isn't this more relaxing than the noisy restaurant?' She raised her glass to his and smiled.

'Yes, it was busy all right.'

'Let's talk about us,' she whispered, edging closer to him.

'Us?'

She took a sip of wine and set down her glass. 'Yes, Alex. Us.'

Feeling as though she was in a dream, she moved across and began to kiss those sensuous lips. Her hand curved around the firmness of his jaw line and she felt the warmth of his skin and fine prickle of stubble under the pads of her fingers. He was unresponsive at first and she drew back for a moment and looked questioningly into his dark eyes.

Then he began to return her kiss, softly at first, then more firmly, his lips parting hers, his tongue dipping into her mouth. He stopped for a moment and she felt slightly dazed, but not too dazed to unbutton her blouse so that it opened to reveal her lace-covered breasts. She released the front catch of her bra and the cups fell apart. Her nipples were already rigid and straining for his touch.

'Yes, please,' she murmured. She thought she was going to melt when his dark eyes flicked to her creamy curves. She took his hands and placed them on her breasts, her skin tingling as she felt his touch. She slithered her fingers up under his shirt and grazed her nails along the indent of his backbone, drawing him closer.

'Alex,' she whimpered, loving the sound of his name on her lips in the intimacy of the moment.

102

She felt a craving deep inside her, sharper than anything she had ever felt before. He began to kiss her mouth again and she moved slightly on the sofa, still kissing him, while with a practised movement she got rid of her tights, working them down her legs until they dropped soundlessly to the floor. The ache in her body swelled as she moved forward onto his lap. She flicked her tongue into his mouth, arching her body into his, suddenly triumphant as she felt the hardness in his groin.

'You want me, don't you?' she murmured. 'Just as much as I want you?'

She couldn't wait to go upstairs. There was no need to go upstairs. She sat up on the sofa and never took her eyes off the inky depths of his. 'Let's not wait a minute longer,' she breathed, taking his hand and lifting it up under her skirt.

She thought she was going to erupt with need as she reached for his belt buckle. She was smiling in heady anticipation when his hand took hold of hers and stayed it; when he drew across the sides of her blouse to partially cover her breasts; when he shifted underneath her so that she was forced to suddenly put out a hand to balance herself on the sofa. It was only as he continued to regard her with that enigmatic look in his eyes that she sensed something was not quite right.

'Alex?' She was suddenly conscious of her heart pounding erratically.

He made no reply and just continued to look at

her. She couldn't read the expression in those steel grey eyes.

'Is anything the matter?' she asked, her voice high and tinny. She sat beside him, trying to ignore the surge of apprehension that gripped her like a physical pain and the sharp craving that pulsed deep inside. 'Did I do something wrong?'

'God, no. It's not you, Eve.'

'Don't you want me? You do, I know you do.'

'Look,' he sighed heavily, 'maybe this isn't the time or the place.'

'Yes it is, we have the house to ourselves for the whole night. We can go upstairs if you'd feel more comfortable.'

'No, Eve,' he said so gently that Eve felt like crying.

'So I *did* do something wrong,' she faltered, cold with disappointment.

'Believe me, you didn't,' he insisted as he finally gave her a lopsided smile. 'Look, it's not you, honestly. I just have something on my mind.'

'Something on your mind?' What the hell did he mean? 'Can I help?' she asked, trying to rescue whatever she could out of the situation.

'Not tonight, Eve,' he said. He drew his finger down the valley between her breasts, scorching her skin. 'You're really lovely, but I'm just not with it tonight. Sorry.'

She turned and looked away, focusing on the soft lamplight, the half-full glasses of Chablis on the coffee table, the gas fire throwing out warmth she was suddenly glad of, the sound of Robbie Williams singing a love song in the background – on anything and everything except the sight of Alex getting up off the sofa, pulling on his jacket, leaning over to kiss her softly on the top of her head and gently telling her he'd call her as he left the room and quietly closed the door. Afterwards, she couldn't remember how long she sat there. She only remembered hearing the click of the hall door closing, the slam of his car door in the quiet of the night and the thrum of his engine as it faded away down the avenue.

And then there was silence, for even Robbie Williams had come to a stop.

Chapter Thirteen

When Daisy came home from work and went into the front room on Tuesday night, she was momentarily startled. Marina wasn't working at her sewing machine, nor was she slumped over her cutting table with a bottle of vodka. Dressed in a long midnight blue sheath, lost in a world of her own, Marina was whirling around in her bare feet to the radio. Daisy stood there for several open-mouthed seconds before Marina eventually spotted her, stopping mid-whirl.

'Well, what do you think?' She flung her arms wide and invited Daisy to inspect her dress.

'It's lovely.' Daisy tried to recover herself as she frantically wondered what on earth had brought this on.

'Liz brought me to her local boutique today and insisted on buying this. It's silk crepe.' Marina glided her five-foot-one-inch figure across the room, weaving around the sewing machine, swivelling her hips with the sudden poise and conviction of a six-foot-tall svelte fashion model. 'It's so long since I danced, Daisy,' Marina said dreamily.

'Yes, I suppose it is.' Daisy decided it was best to humour her. 'We're going to have a great night,' she continued. Maybe if she said it often enough, she might begin to believe it.

'I don't know,' Marina fretted. 'I changed my mind, you know. I told Liz to cancel everything, but she said it was a bit late in the day to have second thoughts.'

'Look, Mum, we can do whatever you want,' Daisy began, wondering whether it was possible to call a halt to everything at this stage. 'You don't have to go ahead with the party if you don't feel like it.'

'Sometimes I don't know what I want.' Marina looked confused.

'You can change your mind at any time,' Daisy said with firm reassurance.

'Why, do you think I shouldn't have a party?' Marina quickly challenged.

'I think you should do whatever suits you.'

Marina put her head to one side and considered for a moment. 'Do you like my dress anyway?'

'Yes, it's really beautiful.'

'It is, isn't it?' She looked down at the flowing silk crepe and grasped the two sides of the dress, pulling it wide at hip level. 'I might just alter it slightly.'

At first Marina didn't know what had made her say that. Standing in her sewing room, she felt the delicate cloth beneath her fingers, so different to the usual thick texture of curtain material. She felt the shock of recognition and realised that she still instinctively knew where to fashion and trim, where to shape and sew.

For long years now she hadn't had any interest in style or design, but it hadn't gone away. It was still there inside her, like everything else. The important thing was that everything else stayed buried.

'Alter it, Mum? But it's lovely the way it is.' Daisy looked at her in alarm.

Sometimes she hated the nervous way Daisy looked at her; other times she felt gratified. It confirmed exactly how she felt about herself. Tonight, for some reason, she was edgy and confused.

'I'll think about it,' she said, taking a certain satisfaction in Daisy's reaction.

'You'll look great no matter what,' her daughter smiled tentatively.

That was why she had wanted a party for her birthday, Marina remembered. When Daisy had asked her, she'd had a sudden vision of Liz on the night of her party, twirling around in a yellow dress, happy, light-hearted and in love with life. Liz had looked great. She wanted to look like that. Then today she had realised how foolish she was, but Liz wouldn't hear of cancelling anything. Liz had given her a big bright smile and said it would be a great night.

'Liz said the DJ will play the best of the seventies and the eighties at the party,' she told Daisy.

'Sounds good. Any particular favourites?'

'David Bowie.' Again the words sprang from her lips of their own accord. Marina tensed as alarm flickered inside her. But there was need to worry. Daisy was already backing out of the room, telling her she was going out that night.

* * *

Daisy went upstairs to the calm of her bedroom, kicked off her mules and took off her sharply tailored charcoal grey suit. She wondered if there was a grain of truth in what Liz had said – the party would act as a starting point to encourage Marina to socialise a little more, she had told Daisy. Surrounded by a warm circle of well wishers, with food, music and laughter, Marina would relax and enjoy herself.

Wishful thinking on Liz's part, Daisy had cynically thought. But now, already, Marina had something really glamorous to wear and was chatting about her favourite music, never mind dancing in the front room. And if Liz was right, it would be a major stepping stone for her. It was about time that she had her own place. Up to now, some innate sense of loyalty, as well as a reluctance to move on and leave Marina behind, was keeping her at home. But that, of course, couldn't last forever.

And surely, Daisy reminded herself, the very worst that might happen on the night would be the necessity to bring Marina home early and get her to bed.

But she didn't have time to worry about it now. She opened the door of her wardrobe and selected black trousers and a pink chenille jumper. Contrary to her best intentions, she was going out with Sam that evening. Again.

Much to her consternation, he had dropped into her office that afternoon and calmly announced that he was taking her out to dinner in his favourite seafood restaurant. She didn't want to get involved with him. The last thing she needed in her life right now was the prospect of another romantic disaster, especially with a colleague.

But Sam had caught her on the hop. 'I'm collecting you at half past seven,' he had insisted, his blue eyes confident. 'And I refuse to take no for an answer.' She had no choice but to be ready and waiting for him when he called to avoid the possibility of a scene at the door within Marina's earshot.

By the end of the evening, though, she had to admit to herself that he was a pleasant dining companion. During their meal, Sam entertained her with funny stories of his soccer-playing days and talked about his favourite World Cup legends. And naturally, when he left her home at the end of the evening, he pulled her into his arms. Yet again, Daisy felt nothing, nothing whatsoever, as his mouth moved with increasing pressure against hers. She pulled out of the embrace before Sam could get too carried away.

Surely now, she hoped as she got out of his Volvo and said goodbye, he would finally realise that she wasn't interested and leave her alone.

Chapter Fourteen

'Eve?'

Eve's heartbeat immediately accelerated at the sound of his voice on the phone. 'Alex!' She swung away from her desk and turned towards the office window to give herself a little more privacy.

'I thought we might go out for a meal? Tonight?'

'That would be great.' She willed herself to sound normal.

'I'll collect you at seven o'clock. And it'll be somewhere quieter than the last time!'

Her heart sang as she gazed out the window. Life had never seemed so good as it did on this Wednesday morning, with the sunlight flickering over a vista of green-fuzzed branches in St Stephen's Green and the knowledge that she was seeing Alex again that night.

She had been going around in a daze since the previous Saturday night, counting the hours since she had felt Alex's arms around her and his mouth on hers. Yes, she had been taken aback by his rather abrupt departure, but during the intervening days she had consoled herself by remembering how he had told her she was lovely. Although she had ached for him, she knew he had desired her, even as he had gently told her that it wasn't the right time or place. And just now he had phoned. He was bringing her out for a meal, somewhere quieter....

'Good news?' Rachel asked curiously.

'Oh, that was just Alex,' Eve said offhandedly, suppressing a quiver of excitement. 'We're going out tonight.'

'This is getting serious, Eve. Your reputation will really be shot to bits.'

'Who cares?'

'Wow.' Rachel looked seriously impressed. 'He must be different.'

Yes, Alex Gallagher was different from anyone she had ever dated before. Eve didn't care if her social butterfly reputation was torn to shreds. For the first time in her life she had met someone who meant a lot more to her than just a casual date, who made her feel ridiculously happy, as though life was a very exciting place to be. How was she was going to get through the next few hours, let alone try to work?

She didn't even care if he wanted to wait until he knew her better before they went to bed. Alex was well and truly worth waiting for. And what she was beginning to feel for him was a lot bigger and a lot better than just a desire to get into bed with him.

'It's well for you,' Rachel sighed, dragging her back to a Wednesday morning in Foley Financials, with hours to go through before she saw Alex again. 'I wish I had someone to take me out for nice meals in his swanky BMW.' Rachel began to fidget with a pile of statements, and her mouth suddenly turned down at the corner and two fat tears ran down her cheeks and plopped on her desk.

'Rachel! What's wrong?' Eve asked, horrified to see her cry.

'Keep your voice down,' Rachel said fiercely. 'I don't want Mr Foley coming down on me like a ton of bricks.'

'Don't worry about him,' Eve said impatiently. 'What's up? I thought things were sorted between you and John.'

'So did I,' Rachel sniffed, trying to stem the flow of tears with her hanky. Eve silently passed her the box of tissues at the side of her desk and Rachel absently began to pull them out one by one. 'It's just that we've hardly talked since that weekend. He's either out at work or too tired when he gets home. We're going nowhere fast and I'm beginning to think I'm wasting my time with him. And I'm older than you, Eve, I'm almost thirty. I want marriage and kids and the whole lot.'

'You just need to inject a little fun and romance into things,' Eve advised. 'Make sure he's not too tired for you when he comes home from work.'

'That's easier said than done.'

'Tell you what. Have a relaxing bath ready for him when he comes home tonight and be wearing your sexiest underwear. By the time you're getting to work on him with the soap, I guarantee that he'll have forgotten all about his job.'

She was late returning to the office after lunch. Mr Foley was out on the floor and Eve smiled confidently at him and stalked down to her desk. She placed her carrier bag on her desk and winked at Rachel.

'Maybe I should tell him why I'm so late? Maybe show him what took me so long?' She dipped her hand into her bag, where a diaphanous La Perla concoction in filmy black lace nestled, wrapped in folds of tissue paper.

'Don't you dare,' Rachel warned.

'Or maybe I should ask Daniel for his opinion. I'm sure he's an expert on sexy underwear. I believe there are some hot shops down in Cork,' Eve said, just loud enough for him to overhear. She glanced sideways at him, causing a red tide of embarrassment to wash over his face. 'Although there's no point in giving him a massive heart attack,' Eve smirked as she sat down and put her bag under the desk.

When Eve arrived home from work in a state of bubbling excitement, she met Liz in the hall. 'I won't be needing dinner tonight,' she said. 'I'm going out for a meal.'

'Is it safe to ask if it's the same bloke you were out with last week?'

'Ask away,' Eve smiled.

'If you feel like bringing him or any of your friends along on Saturday night…?'

'Jeez, Mum, I couldn't possibly inflict that on him! Aren't you happy that *I'm* putting in an appearance?'

'I suppose I should be grateful for small mercies,' Liz smiled wryly. 'Daisy's out in the conservatory. She called in after work so that we could go over some of the arrangements. Why don't you go out and say hello? I'm just running upstairs to get my diary.'

'Oh, okay,' she said airily. She was so buoyed up with the prospect of seeing Alex that she felt particularly benevolent. A quick chat with Daisy was surely no hardship. 'Not that I have much time,' Eve added as Liz disappeared up the stairs.

Her tall, buttoned-up cousin would never change, Eve thought as she sauntered into the conservatory and looked at Daisy's crisp business suit, don't-mess-with-me glasses and short, sharp hair. What she needed was a man in her life, someone who would rumple up her strait-laced clothes, ruffle her hair and pull off those school marm glasses. Although Daisy would probably run a mile if any such man appeared on her horizon.

'All set for the great occasion?'

'Oh, hi, Eve,' Daisy said. 'Hopefully it will all go well.'

'It will, of course, seeing as how Mum is looking after everything.'

'I really appreciate what she's done.'

'She's a real pro. Naturally she'd want to help Marina, in the circumstances.'

'What circumstances?' Daisy gave her a sharp look.

'Well, you know….'

'No, actually, I don't.'

Of course, Eve thought with a flash of exasperation, as far as the world at large was concerned, there was nothing wrong with Marina. They all lived perfectly happy lives in their perfectly happy homes. 'That's a bit rich coming from you,' she taunted, unable to avoid the gibe. 'You've lived with her all your life. You should know.'

'I think that's slightly out of order, Eve.' Daisy's brown eyes hardened.

'Don't you think it's out of order that everything is kept in the dark?' Eve knew she wasn't supposed to breathe a word, but she just couldn't resist ruffling Daisy's cool demeanour.

'About what?' Daisy asked. Her voice was frosty

and her eyes held Eve's in an unwavering gaze.

'I suppose what I mean is that it's just tough that you've never had your father around.' Eve backtracked a little and decided to bring this conversation to an end. She had far better things to be thinking of. 'Anyway, I have to dash,' she said brightly. 'I have a very special date on tonight.'

'Make sure you enjoy yourself,' Daisy said with a tinge of sarcasm.

'Thanks, Daisy, but that's one thing I certainly don't need to be told!'

She turned on her heel and hurried upstairs to get ready. Enjoy herself? What an understatement. She forgot all about Daisy as she wondered what exactly Alex had planned for tonight. She put on the La Perla basque and admired her reflection in the mirror. Running her hands over the lingerie, she imagined Alex's hands feeling the heat of her skin under the thin, silky lace. She turned slowly in front of the mirror, looking at herself from every angle, feeling sexy and desirable. Then she imagined his hands slowly peeling it off her.

God. She had to stop thinking about taking off his clothes, of Alex naked in her arms. Of herself, naked in Alex's bed. It mightn't be on his agenda just yet. And at this rate, she thought as she grinned at her reflection in the mirror, she would never be ready.

She sprayed herself all over with Romance perfume, then put on a plain black dress with a hemline almost to her knees. Now she looked almost demure. She practised pulling down the zip and letting the dress slither to the floor, revealing her sexy underwear in one fluid movement.

Perfect.

* * *

Daisy left just after Eve. She had finished discussing the guest list with Liz and was ready to go when she heard the doorbell chiming and her cousin coming down the stairs. She stalled for a moment as Eve called out a quick goodbye in a voice that quivered with repressed excitement, waiting until the door had safely closed behind her before picking up her briefcase and going out into the hall.

It wasn't the first time that Eve had taunted her about the lack of a father in her life, Daisy mused as she drove home. It was something she had taken great pleasure in as a younger child, particularly on occasions when she had sensed that Liz had been extra kind to Daisy. But their days of childhood jealousies were long gone. Or were they? This time she had sensed something different in Eve's tone. It was almost as though her cousin knew something, something secret, something about which Daisy was unaware.

Impossible. She was only imagining things.

Chapter Fifteen

Eve didn't suspect anything until Alex ordered dessert.

It had felt so good to totter carefully down the driveway and sink into the luxury of his BMW, the sheer basque moving sensuously against her skin. It had felt even better to look at his hands as he put the car into gear and deftly turned the steering wheel. With a heady sense of anticipation, she thought of how those same hands had touched her the other night and how they would no doubt touch her again.

He brought her to a restaurant in Terenure. The rush hour traffic had dwindled and streetlights were beginning to glimmer in the purple-shadowed evening. Alex parked and they walked the short distance to the restaurant. Eve had to concentrate on keeping her balance in her killer heels, but it was a good excuse to hang onto his arm, her body tingling already with even this slight contact.

The restaurant was quiet. Easy-listening music echoed softly in the background. Couples were seated at white linen-covered tables, where cutlery and glasses shimmered in the candlelight, and conversations were low and muted. Now that she was the sole focus of Alex's attention, Eve felt on edge. When was he going to mention the other night? Or was he so much of a gentleman that he was going to pretend it hadn't happened? She would have to take the lead from him, Eve decided. She was relieved when they were handed their leather-bound menus and she had something else to concentrate on besides her fluttering heart and his dark eyes.

'Well, what would you like?' Alex asked, eventually looking up and smiling at her.

You, now, she thought, and for a moment she worried she had said it out loud. She felt like throwing aside her menu and saying c'mon, let's get down to the real business in hand. She thought of his apartment in Rathfarnham. She thought of her sexy underwear awaiting his discovery and she shivered.

'Cold?'

'No, just something I thought of made me shiver.'

'Nothing too bad, I hope,' he smiled at her.

121

'No, on the contrary.' She gave him a coquettish glance, half hoping he would ask her exactly what she had been thinking.

'Good. Are you ready to order?'

She was disappointed he didn't follow it up. She looked across the table at him, but his dark eyes were inscrutable.

'I'll have the avocado salad and then the baked sole,' she said.

He signalled the waiter and placed the order, requesting chargrilled steak and shallots for himself. Fillet, medium rare, Eve silently mouthed to herself. Her brain raced ahead and she pictured herself ordering it in the butchers and then cooking it to perfection for him on a cosy night in somewhere, sometime. Might be no harm to invest in a cookbook. After all, she wasn't quite sure what fillet steak looked like in the raw.

'And perhaps a bottle of Chardonnay? Is that okay, Eve?'

'Yes, lovely,' she smiled brightly as Alex nodded at the waiter. The night was young, she said to herself. It stretched ahead, full of glorious promise. She wasn't going to get unduly upset if Alex seemed a little formal. They had the whole night to relax and get to know each other even better.

'Would you prefer to order a red for yourself, Alex?' she asked.

'No wine for me, thanks. Not tonight. Tell me, how are things in Foley's?'

No wine, not tonight – what did he mean by that? And he was going to talk about work. A neutral topic for the moment.

'Don't talk. Half the office is down with the flu and it's murder in there at the moment.'

'Poor Eve,' he grinned, making her insides melt. 'It must be terrible to be under pressure.'

Eve sipped her wine. God, how she needed this drink. She took another sip, and another, and felt it hitting her empty stomach. Her salad arrived and she nibbled at it, all the time keeping up a flow of chit chat, mostly about the office and Mr Foley, who had suddenly turned into the boss from hell on account of the staff shortages.

'You sound like you had your nose to the grindstone this week,' Alex said as he poured her another glass of wine.

'And were you very busy this week?' she asked.

'I'm always busy,' he said in a matter-of-fact voice.

'I don't think I'd be able for a ten-hour day,' she said. 'Must be tough at times.'

'Sometimes it's twelve hours.'

'God.'

'You don't really notice if you're caught up in something,' he shrugged.

'They must have let you off the leash early tonight,' she said, trying to infuse her voice with a hint of intimacy.

'Obviously. More wine?'

She hadn't even noticed that her glass was drained. She held it out to be refilled, her hand shaking slightly. Alex's hand was steady as he held the bottle and when his eyes met hers they were cool and dispassionate. For a moment he seemed like a stranger and the other night seemed very far away. Eve picked at her sole, not tasting it, and watched him enjoying his steak.

He caught her staring at him and said, 'What's the matter? Aren't you hungry?'

Eve automatically fumbled for her glass of wine. This wasn't turning out to be the cosy tête-à-tête she had imagined. Could Alex be deliberately ignoring what had happened last Saturday night? There had been no acknowledgement of any kind of the time she had spent in his arms.

'There's nothing the matter,' she finally managed to say, despite the hard knot in her stomach. 'My fish is lovely.'

The thought coldly washed over her that perhaps Alex was so used to women making a play for him that it had meant absolutely nothing. Although she felt as though the earth had moved for her in those spine-tingling moments, maybe it hadn't tilted very much for him. On second thought, she had felt his immediate response, hadn't she? She had seen his face as he leaned over to kiss her.

'Would you like some dessert?' Alex asked as she finally pushed her plate away.

'Sure. I'll have my favourite.'

'Ice cream?'

'You remembered.'

'I should hope so,' he said. 'It was only the other night.'

She held her breath. He had mentioned it – the other night. He had remembered that she liked ice cream for dessert. Surely he had remembered everything else. She waited to see if he would make some kind of reference, but instead he called the waiter over and ordered ice cream for Eve, tiramisu for himself.

Her mouth was full of butterscotch and vanilla when he abandoned his dessert and told her he had some news.

'Oh?' She felt that the whole restaurant was suddenly hushed because the sounds of low conversation around her and the soft music suddenly fell away.

'Remember I told you that I had been offered a different position in Citimex?'

'Yes?'

'I've decided to take it and I'll be going over to London.'

There was a beat of silence. Eve swallowed. She stared at the candlelight flickering on the table for several long moments before forcing herself to meet his gaze.

'London?'

'Yes. One of our team over there has taken ill

and he has to be replaced as soon as possible.'

'And you've been offered his job.'

'They want me over before the end of the month.'

'So soon? But that's only days away.'

Alex smiled. 'I'll barely have time to pack.'

Eve toyed with her ice cream, making it into a mush. She couldn't possibly eat any more. It would surely stick in her throat.

London. Before the end of the month. He would barely have time to pack.

'It'll be a change for you,' she said, her voice light and brittle. Big change from Dublin and settling down.

'Certainly will,' Alex nodded.

'And will you be gone for long?'

'Could be almost a year,' he answered.

'A year? I'm sure you'll be home regularly. London's not that far away.' She flashed a bright, hopeful smile.

'Mmm. It's probably quicker than trying to get to Galway,' he said.

'So we can still continue to see each other, can't we?'

Alex looked startled. 'I'm not so sure about that.'

'What do you mean?'

'Well, Eve, we'll be on different sides of the Irish Sea for starters.'

'But you said it yourself, it's almost as easy as getting to Galway and you'll be home regularly.

And I could go over from time to time.' She hated the sound of her voice, a mixture of entreaty and desperation. She had the gut-wrenching feeling that she wasn't going to like what was coming next.

'Look, Eve, I don't think there's any point in expecting to see each other,' he said quietly.

'Why not?' she said encouragingly. She tried to dredge up a smile, but it seemed that her face had turned into some kind of frozen mask. 'It's only a short hop away. Plenty of people commute back and forth.'

'Eve, to be honest, as far as I'm concerned it's not really an option.'

She drained yet another glass of wine and Alex automatically reached across and poured her a refill. She wasn't totally stupid. She recognised a dismissal line all too well; hadn't she delivered plenty of them in the last few years? How ironic that she was now, finally, on the receiving end. And with Alex, of all men. She took a sip and raised her glass to him and gave him a mocking grin.

'Cheers, Alex. In other words, you're dumping me.'

* * *

Alex looked across the table at Eve. Her voice had risen slightly, but luckily enough her words hadn't carried in the general buzz of conversation and background music.

He should have waited until they were in the privacy of the car before he said his goodbyes. But he had totally misjudged her reaction. Bubbly and fun loving, with a string of blokes wrapped around her little finger, he had assumed that Eve had no intentions of getting involved with him. After the engagement party, it had been easier to go along with her, easier to accept the invitation to Vicar Street, easier to bring her out for a meal last Saturday night. Hell bent on having a good time and flitting her way through life, he had been sure that she would soon move on to her next conquest.

Going by the angry look on her face right now and her remarks, Eve seemed to think that they had been in the throes of a steady relationship. He had definitely got it wrong. How the hell had he been so thick?

'Dumping you, Eve? We've only gone out together a couple of times. Now I'm off to London, so we'll scarcely be seeing each other again. Look,' his tone softened, 'don't spoil things. We had a bit of a laugh, didn't we? I was going through a bad patch when I met you and you were just what I needed at the time.' He knew by the arctic look in her blue eyes that he had said the wrong thing and well and truly put his foot in it.

'Just what you needed?' she blazed. 'You make it sound like I was some kind of tonic, to be taken three times daily.'

'Eve,' he hesitated, searching for the right words.

'It would be easy to say yes, we'll keep in touch, I'm only a plane ride away. But the reality is that I don't know how busy I'm going to be. I may not be home all that often and I don't want to cramp your style. This way at least you'll know where you stand, and you'll be free to make social plans without wondering if I'm going to be home next weekend or whatever.'

'And naturally the same applies to you.'

'What do you mean?'

'You'll be free to gallivant all over London whenever you feel like it.'

Alex threw back his head and laughed.

'I'm glad you find it funny.'

'I'll scarcely have time to gallivant all over London. But I don't understand your attitude, Eve.'

'My attitude?'

'We've only gone out casually a couple of times. You scarcely considered ours to be an exclusive relationship? Don't tell me you haven't been out with other blokes over the last couple of weeks.'

'No, as a matter of fact, I haven't,' she said in a small voice. 'So that's it. I meant nothing to you beyond a casual date.'

'Look.' Alex put down his napkin and wondered how a couple of casual dates had suddenly become so complicated. 'We're far from infatuated teenagers. We went out a couple of times and had a laugh. Let's draw a line under it before either of us says something we'll regret.'

'And the other night, was that just for laughs as well?'

Eve's heart thumped as she faced Alex across the table. There. She had said it now. He would have to respond. Far from infatuated teenagers? Funny, that's exactly how she felt as she faced him across the table and he trampled all over her dreams.

'The other night was a mistake,' Alex said. 'I really didn't know what I was doing.'

There was a deafening silence. Eve felt cold all over. Eventually she found her voice. 'A mistake?' she said, her blue eyes twin chips of ice. 'No one calls making love to me a mistake.'

He looked flustered. 'God, I'm sorry, Eve, that's not what I meant.'

'That's exactly what you said, Alex,' she snapped.

A mistake. Where the hell had she gone wrong? Eve's face burned. She knew she had drunk far too much wine and she knew by the air of interest that her voice had carried across to the next table. What the hell, she couldn't care less. For the first time in her life she was being dumped. And by Alex, the first man she had tentatively considered the possibility of a future with, of a long-lasting relationship. And the first time she had ever had her lovemaking thrown back in her face.

'Look, Eve, from the bottom of my heart, I didn't mean it like that,' Alex said. 'I'm sorry if I hurt your feelings. I wasn't myself that night, I was a little upset over—'

'The hell you were. You let me make a right fool of myself, Alex Gallagher.'

Alex obviously decided it was time they left the restaurant, because before she realised it he had settled the bill, helped her into her jacket and had her out the door into the cold night air. She tripped on the pavement in her heels and had to grab hold of his arm to steady herself. It felt like a stranger's arm.

'Are you okay?' he asked as they walked towards his car, Eve staggering on her heels.

'What kind of a question is that?' She stopped so suddenly that he almost bumped into her. 'No, I'm not okay, you sad bastard. I want to know exactly what kind of mistake I was.' She was almost sobbing as she glared up at him.

'Please get into the car, Eve,' he said. 'I'd rather not talk about it out here.'

'Are you afraid someone will overhear what you have to say? Was I really all that bad? Well, I'm sorry if my technique wasn't up to your usual high standards.'

'Look, Eve,' Alex said, opening the passenger door, 'let's get you home. Somehow or other, I don't think anything I have to say is going to sound right to you.'

Where had she gone wrong, Eve agonised as she got into the car. *A mistake.* The words resounded in her ears as Alex accelerated into the stream of traffic and swept through Terenure. Her heart pounded. Everything had taken on an air of unreality. She felt as though she was in the middle of a hideous nightmare. She had a sudden memory of the previous Saturday night, a memory of how aroused she had felt as her mouth touched his, and she felt a physical pain in her stomach.

Outside the house in Templeogue, Alex doused the headlights and switched off the engine. 'Look, please let me explain.' He turned to her with an apologetic look on his face that further incensed her. 'I'm sorry if I hurt you, Eve, or gave you the wrong impression. Let's not part like this.'

'I'm not interested in your explanations,' she snapped. 'You've said more than enough.'

'Eve, it's not what you think,' Alex sighed, running a hand through his hair.

'It's exactly what I think. You just used me, Alex. You used me to put in time before you went swanning off to London. You knew you'd be going away, yet you kept your mouth shut, until now, when you're practically about to leave.'

'It isn't like that. I only came to a decision on Monday, and I brought you out tonight so that we could have a sort of farewell meal.'

To her horror, Eve began to cry. A farewell meal! It was the last thing she had expected. How had she been so stupid? How had she misinterpreted her relationship with Alex from day one? If relationship was even the right word to use in this case. She had obviously meant nothing to him. He had said it himself in so many words.

'Please don't cry.' To her renewed horror, he reached out and pulled her close so that her head rested on his shoulder. In spite of her anger and misgivings, she allowed herself a precious few moments to be close to him once more, to absorb his sharp masculine scent and the feel of his arms around her. Then she resolutely pulled away from him.

'You're a right bastard,' she sobbed shakily. 'I hope to God that you get exactly what you deserve over in London.'

Chapter Sixteen

This time the nightmare is different. Marina is crying as though her heart is broken. Daisy is looking up at her, but Marina doesn't seem to see her. Daisy is pulling at her skirt and eventually her mother looks down, but when she catches sight of Daisy it only makes her cry all the more. She stands there shaking until Aunt Liz's arms go around her and she lifts her away.

When Daisy abruptly awakes, it's impossible to go back to sleep. She lies tense and nervous in bed, her ears straining to hear, and she's so confused that at first she doesn't know whether Marina is actually crying in the next room, if it's another haunting nightmare or if she's recalling something that happened years ago.

She listens hard, but the house is silent around her. She closes her eyes and tries to recall what she has seen and heard in her disturbed sleep. She doesn't know where they were, or why Marina was crying, but it must have been years ago.

How else would Liz have been able to lift her?

Chapter Seventeen

When Eve walked into Foley Financials the following morning, she looked much the same as usual. Her dark hair was sleek and glossy, her make-up accentuated the blue of her eyes, her mulberry plum lip gloss a perfect cupid's bow. Not by the flicker of an eyelid did she betray the sleepless night she had just put in. She dumped her bag under her desk, pulled out her chair and calmly informed Rachel that she might as well know that Alex Gallagher was past history.

'Past history?' Rachel echoed.

'Yes. Finished,' she said firmly, wishing Rachel wouldn't look at her like that, with a mixture of shock and wariness, as though she was expecting Eve to burst out crying any minute. So far, she hadn't shed a tear. Alex Gallagher wasn't worth it.

'Don't tell me you dumped him with a text message,' Rachel said.

'Not quite,' Eve said as she reached into her desk drawer for her mirror. 'He's off to London for a year so I told him there was no point in continuing our relationship.'

'I see.'

'It's his loss,' Eve shrugged as she checked her hair. 'I have no intention of putting up with a long-distance romance and I'm not having my social life dictated to by his career.'

'God, Eve, I could have sworn that Alex was different. I really thought you were mad about him.'

'Mad about him?' Eve looked at her friend as though she had suddenly sprouted two heads.

'Well, maybe not quite that,' Rachel conceded. 'But I thought at least you were an item.'

'An item? Don't think so.'

'I wish I could be like you,' Rachel said. 'Cool as a cucumber. Anytime I break up with a guy, I usually spend the next day crying.'

'It was only a couple of dates, nothing to get excited about,' Eve said, wondering if by some miracle she would ever believe that. All the same, she congratulated herself when Rachel turned back to her computer with no suspicion that deep down, and for the first time in her life, Eve felt as though her heart was broken.

She felt like a zombie as the day dragged on and she went through her paperwork, wearily keying in figure after figure onto her computer screen. Then midway through the afternoon, just when she was beginning to think that half past five would never come, her attention was caught by a flurry of activity down at the door to the corridor. A porter carrying the largest bunch of long-stemmed red roses Eve had ever seen came in. He spoke to one of the girls just inside the door and she pointed down the floor in the direction of Eve's workstation.

Alex has come to his senses, she thought in a wild rush of elation. He was sorry for his hurtful remarks, and Saturday night hadn't been a mistake after all. What on earth had he been thinking of? Maybe she could just about forgive him his silliness on account of this grand romantic gesture. Maybe he deserved a second chance, she thought giddily as the porter stopped in front of her workstation.

Just as Eve was about to reach out her arms for the roses, the porter turned to Rachel.

'Rachel Williams?'

Rachel was about the only person in the office who hadn't noticed his approach. She wheeled around from her keyboard so quickly that she almost pulled the mouse from its socket.

'Yes?' she said, red faced with embarrassment. 'Are they for me?'

'Are you Rachel?' he asked her.

'Yes, but—'

'That's who they're for,' he said cheerfully, depositing the bouquet in her arms. 'Don't forget to check who sent them. He must be in love!'

Everyone on the floor began to tease Rachel. Katie and Susan scooted up from their desks and had a good look at the huge bouquet.

'Who are they from?' Susan gasped.

'You must have a secret admirer,' Katie teased.

'It's John, of course. I didn't think he had it in him,' Rachel gasped.

'I've never got flowers as nice at that,' Susan said. 'He must be mad about you. And romantic as well. Lucky you!'

Even Mr Foley himself took a few moments out to bestow Rachel with a benevolent smile as Eve sat with a frozen face. She didn't know which was worse – the realisation that she had almost made a fool of herself, or the cold, hard knowledge that the roses weren't a peace offering from Alex after all.

'I have you to thank for this,' Rachel beamed when the fuss had died down and the bouquet was put safely to one side. Her face was still red with delight.

'Me?' Eve asked hoarsely.

'Yes, your advice. Remember?' Rachel said in a low, conspiratorial voice. 'I thought you might have asked me how I got on last night.'

Eve had completely forgotten. Yesterday seemed like light years away. 'Obviously it worked, what-ever you did,' Eve said grudgingly.

Rachel laughed a light-hearted, happy laugh that Eve suddenly envied. 'I can't thank you enough, Eve. I put on the sexy underwear, ran the bath and it really... well, you know,' she giggled.

No, I don't know, Eve thought hollowly, remembering how she had thrown her new basque into a corner of the wardrobe.

'Anyway, afterwards, long afterwards, by the way, we had a talk, the best we've had in ages,' Rachel continued. 'I told him how I felt and he explained that he's under terrible pressure in work these days and he apologised for neglecting me.'

'So you all lived happily ever after.'

'Yeah,' Rachel winked. 'I had so little sleep last night that I'm totally shattered.'

Me too, Eve thought. But for a different reason.

It seemed that Thursday would never end. She thought she'd never get away from the office with its memories of Alex, away from Rachel with her radiant face, away from the huge bouquet of roses that mocked her every time she caught sight of it. As the hours ticked slowly by and there was no phone call from Alex, no text message, nothing, she just wanted to crawl home and bury herself in bed.

* * *

Paula and Daisy went shopping on Thursday night. They spent the best part of an hour trawling through boutique after boutique, Paula in search of the glitziest party dress for Daisy, Daisy looking for something far more sober.

'Good job I'm with you,' Paula laughed as she replaced one of Daisy's selections on the rail. 'You're going to be the belle of the ball. No half measures.'

'Thanks for coming to the party,' Daisy told her. 'I know it's difficult for you and Tom to get out, but for my mother's sake I want to have a bit of a crowd there.'

'I'm looking forward to it, Daisy. It'll be a great night.'

'It'll do my mother good to have a bit of fuss.'

As they trooped down Wicklow Street, Daisy decided not to warn Paula that her mother might lose the run of herself. There was no point in anticipating trouble before it happened.

'And what about the delectable Sam?' Paula asked with a twinkle in her eye. 'I'm really glad you two have finally got it together.'

Daisy was deliberately nonchalant. 'It's nothing, Paula, just a couple of dates. And I didn't say anything to him. I doubt he'd be interested in coming to a family party.'

Then they found what Paula decreed to be the perfect outfit. 'This is it, Daisy,' she squealed when Daisy emerged from the changing room.

She looked completely different. At Paula's urging she had tried on a black two-piece outfit with a fitted bustier and a calf-length skirt. The cut of the outfit showed off her tall, slender figure to perfection. Strapless and sleeveless, the structured top fitted snugly into her slim waist and skimmed the top of her breasts, tied up along the front with silky black ribbon. The matching skirt hugged the gentle curve of her hips and boasted a side slit that ran midway to Daisy's thigh.

'I'm not sure, Paula.'

Paula was outraged. 'It's perfect, Daisy. You look like a model on the catwalk. It would be a crime if you didn't go for this, it's… it's just fabulous. A little dusting of shimmery powder around your shoulders, a pair of black high-heeled sandals and you're off.'

'It's too….' Daisy hesitated.

'What's the problem? Thousands of women would give their right arm to look just as you look like now. You've got the height, the figure and you're a natural blonde. Daisy O'Neill, you don't know how lucky you are.'

'Lucky?' That was a first. No one had ever told her she was lucky before.

'Yes. You've a figure to die for and skin that's like a baby's bum.'

'I've never been compared to a baby's bum before.' Daisy went back into the changing room and looked in the mirror. She was almost unrecognisable. But that was all the better, wasn't it? The uncompromising Daisy O'Neill had vanished, and in her place was this sophisticated, exotic-looking creature. Wasn't that exactly what she wanted?

* * *

Another Friday, Eve fretted as she swept into the office the following morning. Three weeks since she had met Alex, and almost thirty-six hours since she had said goodbye to him. She completely ignored Daniel and stalked over to her desk. She glared out the window at the bright sunshine and tried not to remember how happy she had felt when Alex had phoned her just the other day.

'Fancy going out at lunchtime?' she asked Rachel as she turned around from the window, forcing herself to behave normally.

'Yeah, we'll give the canteen a miss,' Rachel readily agreed.

They were sitting in a crowded Friday lunchtime pub with chicken salad sandwiches and all the trimmings when Rachel asked, 'I suppose you'll be back out on the razz tomorrow night?'

'Of course,' Eve began, her mouth full of low-calorie coleslaw and chicken. Then she remembered and swallowed quickly. 'Shit. I forgot about this stupid party I have to go to.'

'What party?'

'My mother is organising a birthday party for my mad aunt and I have to go.'

'Family get-togethers are usually good,' Rachel said.

'Not this family,' Eve laughed. 'My aunt is practically an alcoholic, but everyone conspires to ignore it. Her lover deserted her and she never got over it. Pathetic, if you ask me. Then there was an accident, but it was years ago and she.... Never mind, I'm not supposed to be babbling on about the family skeletons.'

'Sounds sad.'

'Believe me, she's a basket case. My mother is always making excuses for her. As for my cousin, she's well and truly stuck up.'

Her gaze wandered around the crowded pub. Her eyes narrowed as she focused on a nearby table, where a group of young lads were enjoying a heated discussion. Students, she thought, casually dressed with a buoyant, carefree look about them as they laughingly discussed some world-weary issue, bursting with testosterone at that age. Pity she couldn't ask one of them to the party. It would be a nice sop to her ego.

'Let's have a drink before we head back to the office,' she suggested to Rachel.

'Okay. I suppose I'm sort of celebrating,' Rachel grinned. 'Romance is alive and well after all.'

'Yes, isn't it,' Eve almost choked.

They had almost finished their lunchtime vodkas when the group of students got up to go, scraping back chairs, hauling bulging sports bags off the floor and jostling between tables. Eve was delighted to catch a few admiring glances thrown in her direction. Then she had a great idea.

'You look happy all of a sudden,' Rachel said.

'I was just thinking about the party.'

'Thought you didn't want to go.'

'I've changed my mind.'

'You never know, you might meet someone.'

'Oh no, I'm going to bring someone.'

'Who?'

'Daniel, of course!'

Chapter Eighteen

Liz stared across the dance floor and frowned. Her elder daughter was an enigma. She had been so sure that Eve was a little bit in love with that tall, attractive guy she had been seeing recently. When Eve had unexpectedly announced that she was bringing a friend to Marina's party, Liz had hoped he was the one. But there she was, out on the dance floor in among the swirl of partygoers and energetic Abba music, dressed in a filmy top and skirt and wrapped around a gangly, sandy-haired teenager who looked as though he had died and gone to heaven.

She would never understand her daughter.

'What's going on?' Harry asked, his voice close to her ear as he spoke above the buzz of laughter and conversation and the sound of Abba's 'Dancing Queen'. He followed the direction of her eyes. 'I thought you said that Eve had found Mr Wonderful. That's scarcely him, is it?'

Liz watched as Eve whispered something to the young lad and flirted outrageously with him. From the look on his face, he was enjoying every minute.

'No, unfortunately,' she said. 'She told me she dumped him, silly girl. Looks like we're back to square one, a different fella for every night of the week.'

Harry curled an arm around Liz's shoulders.

'That's our Eve for you. At least she knows how to enjoy herself. Where's Marina?'

'She's over talking to her neighbours,' Liz said. She looked across the party-bedecked room to where Marina sat chatting to her neighbours. Gold and purple balloons drifted into the air from every table and colourful Happy Birthday banners decorated the walls. Neighbours had turned up as promised, as well as some far-flung cousins. On the surface, it looked like a perfect party scene. 'Maybe if she sees that she can have a good birthday party just like everyone else… who knows?' Liz turned to her husband.

'I hope she appreciates all this.' Harry kissed Liz's forehead. 'Not many sisters would go to all the trouble you have for Marina. You've always been far too good, you know.'

'I think it's the least I could do. Don't you?'

Harry sighed. 'Look, Liz, are you ever going to let go of your misplaced sense of guilt? Or is it going to shadow the rest of your life? The rest of *our* lives?'

'No, of course not,' Liz said firmly. 'I really feel this party is just what Marina needs to help her turn over a new leaf. I'm glad she suggested it. We should have done something like this years ago.'

The mellow sound of 'Fernando' flowed around the hall. 'Come on.' Harry's hand was on her hip. 'Let's give the young ones a run for their money.'

Liz didn't need any coaxing as she followed him out to the dance floor and slid into his arms. She looked over at Marina, half hidden behind drifting balloons, and fervently hoped she was right. And yet, how could a new hairdo, a new outfit and a few hours of food, music and dance make up for years and years of seclusion, never mind blotting out what had caused that seclusion in the first place?

* * *

'You look very stylish, Daisy,' Paula said.

'Don't I just.' Daisy's hand automatically strayed to her glasses, forgetting she was wearing her contacts. She told herself she had to forget about her clothes. She was edgy enough without being conscious of the side slit that ran to her thigh or the soft curves of her breasts rising slightly above her bustier top.

148

'I shouldn't be sitting beside you,' Paula sighed. 'I look fat, plain and dumpy in comparison and it's not fair.'

'You don't look like that to me,' Tom smiled as he reached over and gently patted her waist. He was exactly the kind of husband she had imagined Paula being married to – friendly, easy going and still madly in love with his wife. 'I'm going up to the bar. Same again, everyone?'

'Yes, Tom. Take your time,' Paula told him. 'I want to have a chat with Daisy.'

'Right so, I'll leave you two in peace.'

'You never told me your mother was so glamorous,' Paula began. 'Where on earth did she get that stunning dress?'

Daisy frowned. 'You'll never believe me.'

'Go on.'

'She went out with her sister, my Aunt Liz, during the week and bought it. I thought it looked great on her.'

'Great? It's sensational.'

'That's because she altered it,' Daisy said. 'I've never known her to go near a dress before, she's always worked on curtains and sometimes soft furnishings.'

'Whatever she did, she looks terrific.'

'Yes, she does,' Daisy said. 'She did something to the hem, made it shorter and asymmetrical and added on a small flounce. I had no idea she knew how to do that….' Her voice trailed away as she

149

stared over to where Marina was chatting to their neighbours. Earlier that evening, Daisy had asked her how she had altered the dress so expertly.

'Oh, I don't know,' Marina was vague. Seeing the shuttered look on her mother's face, Daisy hadn't pushed the issue.

'The DJ's great,' Paula said, tapping her feet in time to the music.

'I've asked him to play some David Bowie, my mother's favourite,' Daisy told her. There was quite a good turnout, she realised. Nowhere near the hundred or so that had attended Liz's do, but plenty of neighbours and some relations had turned up. On the outside everything was fine, Daisy had to admit as she sipped her white wine. So why did she have a lingering unease in the pit of her stomach?

'Which is your aunt?' Paula asked.

'She's out on the dance floor, the woman in the red outfit.'

'She looks really fabulous.'

'Liz always looks terrific.'

'And who is that couple?' Paula pointed to a couple wrapped around each other in a corner of the room.

'That's Eve, my cousin.' Daisy forced a laugh. 'I suppose the bloke she's with is her current boyfriend.'

'She seems to be enjoying herself anyway,' Paula said dryly as Tom returned to the table, carrying a tray with fresh drinks.

'Who's enjoying herself?' he asked.

'Never mind, I don't want you getting distracted,' Paula winked at Daisy.

'I'm surprised she bothered to come,' Daisy said. 'I didn't think this was her scene.' She had been half hoping that Eve wouldn't turn up. She knew it would be difficult enough getting through the party without having to contend with her cousin's mocking glances and acerbic tongue.

It seemed, however, that Eve's attention was otherwise engaged, as she had made none of her usual efforts to irritate Daisy. She had, of course, made a grand entrance with her skimpy chiffony outfit and suggestive walk. She had eyed Daisy up and down with the usual disdainful gleam in her mocking eyes and told her she looked very nice indeed, then casually introduced her young boyfriend. Since then, they had scarcely left each other's arms. They were sitting down now in a seat along the wall, wrapped together.

'Not her scene?' Paula laughed. 'She's making enough of a scene all by herself. I don't think that fella has come up for air in the last ten minutes.'

* * *

Daniel Richards could hardly believe his luck. From the moment Eve had wiggled up to his desk on Friday afternoon, leaned over provocatively and asked him in a breathy voice if he was free on

151

Saturday night, he had been totally stressed out.

He had been completely beguiled by Eve ever since he had started in Foley Financials. But she had always treated him like a snotty-nosed kid, strutting suggestively past his desk and teasing him relentlessly. He knew he was too young for her, but that didn't stop him dreaming.

And now she was asking him out.

'Is this another of your jokes?' he had asked, feeling his face burn.

'Of course not. I'm going to a family party, and—'

'Someone else has stood you up,' he suggested, immediately cursing himself. He wanted to go out with her, didn't he? So what if someone else had let her down? At least it opened the door for him.

'Is that what you think?' she teased. 'Seriously, Daniel, I haven't actually asked anyone yet. I thought it would be nice to get to know each other a little better, maybe expand on our working relationship.'

'What's the catch?' he asked. There had to be catch. Why was she asking him out all of a sudden?

Eve leaned a little closer and he caught the scent of her perfume.

'Catch? Do you really think there has to be a catch before I ask you out?'

'No.' He coloured to the roots of his sandy hair. He had definitely blown it now.

'Look, I know I've sometimes been a little hard

on you,' Eve smiled. 'But let's just say I want to make up.'

Right up to the time Eve met him outside the Central Bank, Daniel had been afraid she was stringing him along for one reason or another. He had waited uneasily, self-conscious in his new jacket and jeans, smothered in Eternity for Men cologne, wondering why he had bothered. It was sure to be some kind of a send-up. He would have been better off going for a few pints with the lads and hitting a nightclub later on. He was just about to walk away when he spotted her. She stepped out of a taxi, dressed in some filmy thing that set his pulse racing. It wasn't until she spotted him, greeted him with a wave and tottered across to him, her high heels clicking on the pavement, that he knew all his birthdays had come at once.

* * *

The DJ announced that food was about to be served. After the break, he roared encouragingly, he would expect everyone up on the floor.

'Does your aunt want help with the food?' Paula asked Daisy.

'No, the caterers will look after everything.'

'Good, I'm starving. And by the sound of the DJ we'll soon be working off any extra calories!'

The nagging ache in Daisy's stomach persisted as they joined the queue for the buffet. She told herself there was no need to feel like this, that everything was fine. The night was already half over and her mother was in one piece.

* * *

'Excuse me, Daniel, I'm just off to the loo,' Eve said.

'Aren't you finishing your food?' he asked.

Eve scrunched up her napkin and flung it down on the plate. 'I'm finished. You can dump that if anyone comes around to clear it away.'

She weaved across the floor and came face to face with Marina.

'Hi Marina, enjoying your party?'

'Yes, it's a good night, isn't it?

'Your dress is… all I can think of is the word spectacular. Where did you get it?'

'Liz brought me shopping, remember? But I did a bit of a redesign myself.'

'You're joking!'

'No, I'm not. I seem to have taken everyone by surprise.'

'You certainly have. Let me get you a drink,' Eve offered.

'No, not tonight. I promised Liz I'd behave myself.'

'Don't be ridiculous,' Eve scoffed. 'It's your party, why shouldn't you have a drink to celebrate?'

'Well, Liz asked….'

'Oh, don't mind Mum. Where is she?'

'She's over talking to the caterers.'

'You deserve to celebrate properly,' Eve said firmly, scrabbling in her bag for her purse. 'One drink won't do any harm. Vodka? You like vodka, don't you? Will I get you a vodka and Red Bull? That'll give you enough energy to keep going all night!'

'I suppose just one drink... I *am* supposed to be the belle of the ball.' Marina gave her a conspiratorial smile.

'And I won't tell Mum,' Eve smiled back.

As she checked her reflection in the ladies room, Eve wondered if it had been a good idea to get her aunt a drink. Probably not, but she hadn't really been thinking straight. She flicked her fingers through her hair and sprayed on a cloud of perfume. She looked terrific in her sexy chiffon gear, but it was wasted on Daniel. It wouldn't have made any difference if she had been wearing her oldest jeans. He was slobbering all over her like a hungry puppy, his kisses wet and insistent, his tongue plunging clumsily in and out of her mouth. He probably thought he was putting on a terrific show, but for all his burgeoning testosterone, and no matter how hard she responded, he didn't have an ounce of sex appeal when it came to hands-on performance. Compared to Alex Gallagher... well, there was just no comparison.

No wonder she wasn't thinking straight tonight.

Alex was probably in London by now. He hadn't phoned, the bastard, and naturally she hadn't attempted to contact him. She was well rid of him, damn him to hell. She tried to ignore the hollow ache in her chest as she snapped open her voluminous make-up bag and leaned into the mirror.

* * *

Daisy almost panicked when she saw Marina up at the bar.

She hurried across the floor and scanned the room for her aunt, but Harry was alone at their table and there was no sign of Liz. By the time Daisy reached the bar her mother was moving away with a small tray in her hands.

'Can I help, Mum?'

'Oh, thanks.' Marina handed her the tray. 'I might let it fall.'

'And who are these for?'

'I just went up to get Liz and Harry a drink, and I'm having a diet Coke.' Her blue eyes held Daisy's.

'A diet Coke?' Daisy asked suspiciously as she looked at the drinks on the tray. A pint for Harry, red wine for Liz and a glass of Coke. It seemed okay.

'Harry didn't want me to go to the bar, but I insisted. The least I can do is get them a drink,' Marina said as she kept pace with Daisy. 'And then I'm going to get the neighbours a drink. It was great of them to come, wasn't it?'

'Yes, terrific.' Liz had promised to keep an eye on her, and Marina would scarcely start knocking back vodkas in front of her and Harry. She would have to relax and stop worrying.

She bumped into Liz as she went back to her table. 'Is there anything I can do?' Daisy asked. 'I feel like I'm leaving all the work to you.'

'No problem,' Liz insisted. 'It was my idea to organise things and I just want you to relax and enjoy it.'

Daisy took a calm, relaxing breath. Her mother's party and all was well. There was no need to feel anxious or on edge. Everything was fine. She turned to go back to her table.

And came face to face with Sam.

Chapter Nineteen

Daisy's heart sank. 'Sam! What are you doing here?'

'That's a nice welcome.' Sam looked so taken aback that Daisy made an effort to pull herself together, even though the sight of him filled her with sudden foreboding. 'Sorry, I'm just a little busy right now. How did you know about the party?'

'You don't need to worry about that. I just thought it would be nice to surprise you.'

'I see.'

'Maybe you thought I wouldn't really be interested, but, well, here I am.'

Paula. Paula had asked Sam to come along, no doubt thinking she was doing Daisy a great favour.

'And I'm the one who's surprised, Daisy. I have

to say, you look sensational.' Sam's eyes roved up and down, openly admiring the way Daisy's outfit clung to her slender curves. He threw a casual arm around her bare shoulder and she tensed, moving beyond his reach.

'I was just on my way to say hello to the neighbours. Why don't you get a drink and I'll talk to you soon?'

'So long as I'm not waiting too long....'

* * *

Eve had just decided that she had better get back to Daniel when Marina came into the ladies.

'I'm just finished so you'll have the mirror to yourself,' Eve said.

'Before you go....' Marina hesitated.

'Yes?' Eve paused impatiently and looked at her aunt's reflection in the mirror.

'Do you know if Daisy brought a boyfriend along tonight?'

'What boyfriend?'

'I saw her with someone just now,' Marina frowned.

'Are you sure it was Daisy?'

'Yes, Eve, I'm not that stupid, you know.'

Eve shrugged. 'Well then, obviously she has a boyfriend with her.'

'Obviously,' Marina echoed. 'I just hope she looks after herself.'

'I'm sure she will,' Eve said. Was Marina for real? She tried to keep a straight face at the idea of her cousin having to look after herself. Somehow she couldn't imagine Daisy letting rip in bed. 'Things are different nowadays, Marina. I'm sure even you appreciate that.'

'They're not really, you know,' Marina said, fixing Eve with a shrewd look. 'All you young ones think that, but people and their passions never change.'

Eve edged towards the door. Any minute now, Marina would be giving her a lecture on safe sex. As if she could talk. The vodka and Red Bull must have gone to her head.

'I can't afford to let anything happen to Daisy,' Marina continued.

'I'm sure Daisy can take care of herself,' Eve tossed. 'History is scarcely going to repeat itself.'

'What do you mean?'

There was a sudden silence as their eyes met and held. Eve could have bitten her tongue. She laughed and tried to look nonchalant. 'Nothing really,' she shrugged.

'Come on, Eve. This is interesting. Just what exactly did you mean?'

Bloody hell. Marina was beginning to get agitated. Eve fervently hoped for the best. 'I suppose, well, the way things are nowadays, Daisy's scarcely going to be left holding a baby.'

'Like me, you mean?'

160

'Well, yes, if you want to put it like that.'

'Thanks for being straight with me, Eve. Very few people are, and it's probably my own fault.' Marina waved a dismissive hand. 'Don't mind me, I'm just your nutty aunt. Go on out and enjoy the party.'

She might have guessed that her mad aunt would fall apart under all the fuss and attention. Eve was only too glad to escape back to the function room and leave Marina to her wild imaginings. Not that she was in a hurry to return to Daniel.

The DJ was playing Neil Diamond. She noticed that the music was slightly louder and the lights had been lowered. There was a long queue snaking around the bar and a few couples were entwined on the dance floor. She had a painful recollection of the night in the Burlington, slow dancing with Alex.

Right now, she couldn't wait for this night to be over. She had had more than enough of trying to look as though she was enjoying herself. She was just crossing over to Daniel when she spotted Daisy talking to her friend.

* * *

'No harm done, I hope?'

Daisy shook her head. 'Don't worry about it, Paula.'

'I hope my wife isn't upsetting you, up to her matchmaking tricks,' Tom smiled.

'It's fine, really.'

Maybe it would be okay. The party was half over and her mother seemed to be in one piece. She was just a little uneasy with the look in Sam's eyes, the look that said he wanted to step up a gear with her. But she wasn't alone with him, so there wasn't much he could do, was there? She would have a drink with him, tell him she was busy looking after relatives and neighbours and send him on his way.

'I didn't set out to invite Sam,' Paula was saying. 'He told me he was going to surprise you with tickets for the Gaiety and I had to explain that there wasn't much point on account of the family party. So he obviously decided to turn up and surprise you here instead.'

'It's okay, really.'

'He seems to be very keen on you.'

Daisy smiled. Sam was keen, all right, not that that would get him anywhere. She noticed Eve weaving through the tables towards her.

'Yes?' Daisy asked, turning to face her cousin.

'Where's the boyfriend? Thought you would have introduced us,' Eve giggled.

'He's not my boyfriend,' Daisy said, thinking at the back of her head that it would be a great idea to introduce Sam to Eve. One look at Eve's frothy outfit and the come-to-bed glimmer in her blue eyes and he would surely forget all about Daisy.

'Oh, Marina seems to think you're involved,' Eve tittered. 'She's concerned about you ending up like her.'

'I don't think that's any of your business, Eve,' Daisy said, far more smoothly than she felt.

'Maybe it is, who knows?' Eve shrugged. 'Maybe your mother wants to talk. That's what families are for, isn't it? To be there for one another, to support each other in times of trouble.'

'I don't quite know what you're trying to say.'

'No, of course you don't. That's our family for you. We don't talk, not really. We hide the truth and keep the secrets. Put the best side out.'

'There's nothing wrong with putting the best side out,' Daisy said.

'All depends on what kind of secret you're hiding, doesn't it? Anyhow, I had better go or poor Daniel will think I've abandoned him. I'd keep an eye on your mother if I were you. I don't think parties are her thing,' she said, giving Daisy a knowing wink before she sauntered off.

* * *

'I have a terrible headache,' Eve said to Daniel when she returned to their table.

'That's too bad,' he said.

And it wasn't a lie, for she did have a pounding head, brought on by the effort of trying to look happy. She had to get away, away from the party and from Daniel with his puppy dog adoration, to be home where she could be by herself with her thoughts.

163

'I think I'll have to go home,' she sighed, trying to be casual as she reached for her jacket, thinking that she couldn't bear this for a moment longer.

'Do you want to leave now? Straight away?'

'Yes, I do. Let's just leave quietly, okay? I don't fancy a big goodbye scene with my family.'

'Sure, okay.'

They slipped out into the cold night air and took the short walk to the village and around to the hackney cab office.

'I'll see you home,' Daniel offered.

'Not at all,' Eve said. 'There's no point in me taking you out of your way.'

'I don't like to abandon you like this,' he said.

She could see the disappointment quite plainly in his face and could hear it in his voice. Tough cheese, she thought hollowly. Tough cheese on Daniel *and* on Marina, losers in the swings and roundabouts of love. Tough cheese on Daisy, too. Eve was suddenly tired of them all.

'Don't be silly, I'm a big girl,' she scoffed lightly. She reached up and gave him a peck on the cheek. 'Thanks for a great night.'

'It was a brilliant night, Eve, really terrific.'

'Glad you enjoyed it.' She hopped into a cab, leaving him waiting for the next one, shivering a little in the cold night breeze.

* * *

164

'Daisy, so this is where you're hiding!'

She felt Sam's hand on her bare shoulder and turned around so sharply that it dropped away. 'Hi, Sam. Why don't you sit beside Paula and Tom? They're just over there.' Daisy waved in the direction of their table. 'I'm heading out to the ladies and I'll be back to you in a minute.'

'That's right, run off on me again.'

'Won't be long, I promise.'

Daisy estimated there was about another hour left at the most as she dried her hands under the blast of warm air. She had checked on Marina and she was sitting quietly with the neighbours. She would have to push Eve's disturbing comments to the back of her mind and forget about them for now. She would think about them afterwards, when the party was over and she and Marina were safely home. In the meantime, she just had to go back to the table, have a drink with Sam and then soon the night would be over.

She ran into Liz as she moved through the tables and felt her aunt's shrewd glance looking right inside her.

'Are you okay, Daisy?'

'I'm fine.'

'You look a little pale. Sure everything's all right?' Liz smiled.

She was tempted. Very tempted. All she had to do was ask. So what if it was in the middle of a party and there was noise and babble and music all around? So what if her heart was thumping? She could come straight out and ask Liz if Eve knew something that she didn't, something about… God, what exactly had Eve said anyway? And then her cousin Victoria and her friend Amy danced by, laughing and giggling, and almost bumped into them.

'Hi, Victoria,' Daisy said, instantly glad of the reprieve.

'What?' Her cousin gave her a dirty look and tossed back her long, dark hair. 'Don't you know it's Vikki now?'

'Oh, I see,' Daisy said faintly.

'Don't mind those two giddy goats,' Liz said.

'Mum!' Victoria rolled her eyes.

'I'm looking for Eve. Has anyone seen her?' Liz asked.

'She's already left,' Victoria said.

'Has she?'

'Yeah,' Victoria twirled around. 'She snuck off with Daniel. Bet they're gone somewhere to be alone.'

'That's enough,' Liz said firmly.

'She's mad to be bothering with him. He's not half as sexy as that tall fella she was seeing.' Victoria wheeled across the dance floor with Amy in her wake.

Liz shook her head at Daisy. 'I don't know what I'm going to do with my daughters,' she said with a hint of indulgence. 'Particularly Eve. She was seeing a really lovely chap and then out of the blue she dropped him. Her love life is too colourful by far.' Liz patted her on the shoulder. 'Relax, Daisy. Everything is going well. Marina is enjoying herself and the night seems to be a success, doesn't it?'

'Yes, yes it does,' Daisy replied. She turned and moved back across the floor. Everything was fine so far. She needed to forget about Eve's goading remarks. Marina was enjoying herself. Liz was happy. And it was time she had a drink with Sam.

* * *

It might have been okay, Liz realised afterwards, if the DJ hadn't played the worst possible song. Then again, it might have been okay if she had found out in time that Eve had stupidly given Marina a vodka and Red Bull to start her off. Or if she had known that the few times Marina had gone to the bar for a seemingly innocent diet Coke she was lethally knocking back vodka shots.

It didn't dawn on Liz that things could go so spectacularly wrong when the DJ announced that he had a special request. A special request for the special lady of the moment, he roared into the room. And she wasn't unduly perturbed when he said he was going to slow down the tempo and play some David Bowie.

It was only when she heard the opening sequence to 'Space Oddity' that she suddenly felt weak.

Chapter Twenty

Daisy was pleased. At first. When she heard the DJ's announcement, she searched the room for Marina to see if she was enjoying her special moment in the limelight. Then she spotted her out on the floor. It just took a second for it to register with her that something was wrong, to notice that Marina was far from happy, to realise that far from enjoying the limelight, she was frozen with such a look of horror on her face that Daisy immediately sprang to her feet.

'What's up now?' Sam asked.

'Nothing, Sam, I just need to talk to my mother. I'll be back in a sec.'

Her heart was in her mouth as she threaded through the dancers on the floor. She could see through the weave of bodies that Marina was oblivious to the neighbours and relations shuffling about and throwing her puzzled glances, oblivious to Daisy and Liz hurrying across the room.

Daisy reached her first. Then, slowly but surely, feeling as though she was observing everything from the sidelines like a horrified spectator, her life began to fall apart.

'Mum? What's the matter?' She reached out a hand and touched Marina's shoulder.

Marina recoiled and gave her a look filled with dread. 'Get away from me!'

'Mum!' Daisy looked wildly around and glared at the curious onlookers before turning back to her mother.

'It's okay, Daisy,' Liz said, finally reaching them and taking control.

'Hold on a minute, it's not okay,' Daisy said stubbornly. 'There's something wrong with Mum.'

'Yes, well, I'll look after her. Come on, Marina.' Liz took her sister by the shoulders and began to propel her off the floor.

'Leave me alone,' Marina cried, trying to wiggle out of Liz's firm grasp.

'It's okay,' Liz soothed as she walked Marina out into the corridor.

'What happened?' Daisy demanded, keeping pace with them. 'Everything was fine till a few minutes ago. What's gone wrong?'

'Nothing, Daisy. Nothing for you to worry

about.' They were talking, Daisy realised, as though Marina wasn't there, as though she wasn't standing right beside them in her party dress with Liz's arm securely around her shoulders, tears welling up in her eyes and spilling down onto her cheeks. No way, Daisy thought with grim determination, could Liz pull her usual stunt and gloss over everything as though it was all right. Not this time.

'Of course I'm worried.' Daisy was vehement. 'What's the matter, Mum? You were fine until a few minutes ago. Was it something to do with your special request? I asked the DJ to play that song especially for you.'

'You asked for it? That song? Especially for me?' Marina gave a shrill cry. 'Oh my God! How could you have been so stupid!'

'But you told me you liked David Bowie!'

'You don't know what you've done, you stupid girl. How can I listen to that song when it reminds me of everything I've lost?' Marina collapsed against Liz and began to sob bitterly into her shoulder.

'Everything you've lost?' Daisy spluttered as she looked from her mother to Liz. 'Liz, what does she mean? What's going on?'

'Look, Daisy, there's no need to panic—'

'Of course I'm going to panic. Mum, I'm sorry. I only wanted to make you happy.'

'Happy? Oh, God! How could you possibly

170

make me happy?' Marina lifted her head, drew a ragged breath and continued to weep inconsolably.

'I don't understand. What went wrong?' Daisy asked desperately.

'Don't you know, you silly girl?' Marina wailed.

'Know what?'

'That was our song, me and your father's.' Marina's voice was thick and almost incoherent through her tears. 'And it reminds me of the worst day of my life.'

Daisy felt as though every scrap of air had left her body. 'My father?' She struggled with the strange words on her lips, words that hadn't been uttered for so long.

'Yes, your father,' Marina spat.

'Calm down, Marina,' Liz urged.

'What about him? What's all this all about?'

'Nothing. Everything,' Marina said, shaking her head.

'I want to know what you mean.' Daisy's heart was pounding and there was a pain in her chest, but suddenly she didn't care. In the beat of a moment, the whole falsely constructed fabric of her life disintegrated before her. Years of tiptoeing around Marina, the endless covering up of her endless childhood anxieties, her fake nonchalance whenever her schoolmates asked teasing questions – it all instantly dissolved and was swept away. Daisy felt as though she was stripped to stark, brittle bone.

'You don't want to know, not really.'

Marina looked wounded and her voice was barely a mumble, but Daisy persisted. 'Of course I do. Where is he? My father?'

'Leave it for now, please,' Liz suggested. 'Your mother is upset.'

'What about me? *I'm* upset. Am I the only one around here who doesn't know anything about him?'

'You seriously want to know?' Marina stared at her with unfocused eyes. 'You want to know about the man who took one look at you and... and... ran?' She began to laugh through her tears.

'He what? Liz, is this true?'

'No, well, not quite, but look,' Liz entreated, 'I don't think this is the best time to talk.'

'What do you mean, not quite?' Daisy snapped. 'And I think this is a brilliant time to talk. I'm hearing things I've waited all my life to hear.'

'Then surely we can wait a little longer? Marina is obviously not well.'

'Not well? Say it out straight for once,' Daisy almost snarled. 'I spent a lifetime listening to you telling me that my mother was not well. And I spent a lifetime covering up for her. Go on, say it, describe it whatever way you like. But at least spare me the niceties and tell me that my mother is a drunk.'

Liz hesitated. 'But she's never been this bad before. I don't really know how it happened.'

172

'She is pissed drunk, though, isn't she?'

'You can't blame me for needing a drink,' Marina cried in a ragged voice.

'Marina, please calm down,' Liz said.

'Calm down?' Wild eyed, Marina turned on Liz. 'That's easy for you to say. You have the life you've always wanted. You have everything. But whenever I look at Daisy, I see her father and then I think that my daughter is dead. How would you like to live with that?'

'What? Are you blaming me?' Daisy asked, suddenly chilled to the bone. 'Blaming me because my father ran away? Is this why I had to put up with years and years of making excuses for you, of feeling I had done something wrong? That no matter how much I tried, I could never really please you?' She'd forgotten where she was, that she was out in a corridor while a party was going on just a few yards away. She'd forgotten everything in the heat of the moment until the door at the end of the corridor opened and she heard a sudden blast of music, felt a rush of warm air and just about registered the arrival of Harry.

'I know you all think I'm demented.' Marina's voice was slurred and Daisy could barely make out the words. 'How can I not be demented? Every time I look at you, I'm looking at a ghost. Do you hear me? A ghost! Go away! Leave me alone!' She thrust out a thin arm and looked as though she was about to strike Daisy, but instead she lost her

173

balance so that she lightly tipped her cheek and once again collapsed in hysterical weeping against Liz's shoulder.

Daisy's face scorched where Marina had tipped it. Her mother was mad, well and truly deranged. What the hell had she been drinking? What had happened to cause this disastrous scene? And was it true that her father had walked out when she was a baby? Oh God. She closed her eyes for a moment, as if to remove herself from the entire debacle.

'Harry,' she heard Liz say, 'it might be best to get Marina home.'

'Now? What about the end of the party?'

'Don't be ridiculous. You can see the state Marina's in,' Liz fumed. 'People will be leaving soon anyway. They'll scarcely notice if Marina slips out.'

'What happened? What's wrong with Daisy?'

'We'll talk later,' Liz said grimly. 'Daisy?' She felt Liz touching her arm. 'Are you coming with us? We'll get you home if you want.'

'No. No way.' She shrugged off her aunt's comforting hand. She couldn't face getting into Harry's car and talking to Liz or Harry or least of all Marina, though Marina, clinging to Liz in her alcoholic stupor, now seemed incapable of conversation.

'Daisy, I can't just leave you here like this,' Liz fretted.

She forced a mocking grin, feeling as though her face was going to split in the process. 'Yes you can, Liz. I think it's more important right now to get Mum away from here.'

'Don't worry about what she said, Daisy,' Liz said. 'She's upset and confused. She doesn't know what she's saying.'

'Really?'

'Really,' Liz said firmly. 'We've never seen her quite like this before, have we? Look, will I fetch your friend for you?'

'There's no need. Just bring Mum home and get her away from me. Please.' Her voice caught and Liz shook her head and gave her a small, regretful smile.

'Right so, I'll talk to you tomorrow.'

Daisy heard Liz and Harry talking soothingly to Marina, and through a sheen of tears she saw them gently steer her back into the room, where the music was still blasting, the party banners drifting on the currents of air and the DJ announcing the last dance of the night.

She turned abruptly and pushed against the back door, wrapping her arms around herself as she stood shivering in the chilly night. She looked up at the glitter of stars strewn across the inky sky. Dear God, she fumed, how dare the heavens look so serene, considering the way everything else in her life had fallen apart?

She had no time to think, no time to even try and make sense of what Marina had incoherently spluttered, because as though on cue, Sam appeared by her side.

'What's up? You okay?'

'Yeah, I'm great. Couldn't be better. I just felt like some fresh air.' She felt as though she was in a daze as she put on a fake smile and a tinny, cheery voice, and this time she didn't dislodge the arm he put around her shoulders.

'You're freezing. Come on inside to the heat. Paula asked me to tell you that she and Tom had to leave to let the babysitter go home.'

'That's okay.'

'God, Daisy, you're shivering. Do you want me to bring you home?'

'Home? Not particularly.' She gave him a crooked grin. 'Just get me away from here, please.'

She felt as though she was in a daze as she allowed him to escort her inside, where the party was winding down. All around her, neighbours and relations were leaving. Some of them were melting away, aware that something had happened to Marina, others waved cheerful goodbyes, some of them trooping out with bunches of purple and gold balloons, leaving tables littered with empty glasses and party debris.

She still felt dazed as she collected her bag, threw a jacket around her shoulders and walked out to Sam's Volvo. She was dimly aware of the quiet idle of the engine as the car halted at traffic lights, of a thin draught of heat coming from the car heater, of a stream of streetlights flowing by the window and interrupting the velvety dark of the night. She was aware of Sam talking and herself talking back, although afterwards she couldn't remember any of the conversation.

She was still in a daze when he pulled up outside a two-storey duplex where all the windows were in darkness.

'Where are we?'

'You said you'd like to come back to my humble abode for a drink,' Sam smiled.

'Did I? You live here?' She frowned and tried to recall fragments of their conversation, but her brain felt as though it had seized up.

'Yep. I rent it with a couple of other friends.'

'What friends? I don't—'

'Relax, we each have our own bedroom if that's what's worrying you.'

'That's not what's worrying me.' She gave him a wan smile.

'Good.'

She didn't get a chance to tell him that there were far more important things on her mind than Sam's sleeping arrangements, or that she had no need to know because it wasn't likely to become an issue, because before she had a chance to draw breath, Sam had moved across the narrow confines of his car and was practically on top of her, all hands and mouth and plunging tongue. She could scarcely move or breathe. It was only when his fingers began to delve in under the criss-cross ribbon of her bodice top and his other hand began to slide up past the slit in her skirt along her thighs that she managed to tear her mouth away from his and realised that the nightmarish evening wasn't over just yet.

'Sam!'

'Wanna go inside?'

'Sam, no!'

'Relax,' he said, bending his head so that his mouth trailed along the top of her bodice, across the swell of her breasts.

'Get off me!'

He drew back, looking puzzled. 'What's up? Aren't you enjoying this?'

'Just take me home. Now.'

'But you said you didn't want to go home.' Sam sounded puzzled. 'You agreed to come back to my place for a drink.'

'Did I? This is not what I said... what I meant, Mr Heffernan!' Daisy managed to sit up.

'Aw, c'mon, Daisy. Don't be a spoilsport. And give over with the prim and proper act. We're not in the office now. This is just you and me having some fun.'

'Fun? No thanks!'

'You could have fooled me, Daisy.'

'Just get me home.'

'I don't understand women like you.' Sam looked mystified as he shook his head, ran a hand through his hair and fired the engine. 'You pretend to play hard to get, then when a real man comes along you can't handle it. Prick teaser.'

'What?' Daisy's voice quavered.

'Come on, admit it. All that cool, ice queen pretence is only a front.'

Daisy was speechless. The knot in her stomach tightened. She felt a funny ringing in her ears and she had to hold her hands together to keep them from shaking.

'Or is it?' He threw her a glance as the car screeched away from the kerb. 'Maybe it's for real in your case.'

Chapter Twenty-one

'So are you going to talk about it and tell me exactly what happened?' Harry asked.

It was Sunday morning. Liz had fallen straight into bed the previous night without even taking off her make-up. She had eventually got up later than usual and stood for ages under the shower, as though the cascading water could smooth the edges of her anxiety and somehow cleanse her frazzled spirit. She came into the bright, airy kitchen just as Harry returned from the local newsagent with his Sunday newspapers.

'I don't know what went wrong,' she said as she opened the fridge and took out rashers and eggs.

'You think Marina managed to get some drink into her in spite of us watching her most of the night?' Harry prompted.

'Well, obviously.'

'Maybe it wasn't just diet Coke she was drinking all that time.'

'It was. I tested it when she wasn't looking,' Liz sighed. She opened the grill tray, arranged the strips of rashers and put them under the heat. The reassuring aroma of Sunday morning breakfast began to filter around the kitchen. 'Somewhere, somehow, Marina got drunk last night. Very drunk,' Liz said wearily as she watched Harry fill the kettle. 'All the time I thought she was sitting quietly with her neighbours, she was obviously knocking something back. Then she went off the deep end when that bloody song came on.'

'Don't let it worry you too much, Liz. You certainly did your best to make everything run smoothly.'

'Don't let it worry me?' Liz sighed. At least Harry hadn't said I told you so, she realised, feeling thankful for small mercies. At least he hadn't pointed out that he had been totally against the idea in the first place. She had no idea that the sight of her pale, wan face with not a shred of make-up had silenced any such comment. 'The row with Daisy was the last thing I expected to happen,' she continued.

'What was all that about? Daisy looked completely stunned.' Liz hesitated and in jerky sentences she gave Harry a brief version of events. 'Good lord. No wonder she looked shocked.'

'She was in bits. I told her that Marina didn't know what she was saying. I think we should drop over this evening to see how things are.' Liz turned the heat on under the frying pan and cracked open two eggs.

'You should sit Daisy down and tell her everything. It's ridiculous that she doesn't know.'

Liz shook her head. 'I agree with you completely, Harry, but we promised Marina, remember? And you know how protective she is with Daisy.' She ignored the niggling reminder that she had broken that promise only recently when she had talked to Eve. But Daisy's circumstances were completely different. Her reaction was bound to be appalling. She would want to know every single detail. Marina would never forgive her if Liz went over her head where her own daughter was concerned.

'Protective?' Harry snorted. 'Come on, Liz, more like possessive. Marina was always afraid to let Daisy out of her sight. We couldn't even bring the girl on holidays with us. And now she's rightly terrified of what Daisy will turn around and say. Especially after all this time.'

'I suppose she is.' Liz deftly turned the rashers out onto a warmed plate.

'And what about our wonderful daughter? Any sign of her?' he asked.

'She won't surface for hours,' Liz replied, knowing automatically that he was referring to Eve and not Victoria.

'What's new? That was some exhibition she put

on last night.' Harry carefully arranged the sports supplement on the table so that he could read it and eat his breakfast at the same time.

'Tell me about it.' Liz looked at her orange juice, bacon and crispbread and realised that she wasn't feeling very hungry. She felt disappointed that Eve, her flirty, flighty daughter, could have been so silly as to turn her back on that sexy, intelligent-looking bloke for the sake of a young lad barely out of his teens. And she was furious that Marina had some-how managed to get hold of drink last night and end up in the worst state imaginable.

But most of all, regardless of her disappointment and rage, she didn't really know how she was going to face Daisy. How could she possibly smooth over Marina's harsh words? What could she say to her sensitive niece to ease her hurt?

What was there to say?

* * *

Daisy had tossed and turned the whole night through, eventually falling into a light sleep around six o'clock in the morning. When she finally woke up, sunshine was pressing against the curtains. She stirred in the bed and lay drifting between sleep and wakefulness for a few placid seconds until it all came tumbling back.

She turned over and buried her face into the pillow. She tried to close off her mind, to blank out her thoughts, but nothing could stop images from the previous night from whirling around in her head. She shut her eyes but she could still see Sam Heffernan, feel his mouth on hers, his fingers slithering in behind the material of her bustier. He had driven her home in silence. He had pulled up outside her house and watched with a mocking grin as she fumbled with the seatbelt and got out of his car, confirming that Daisy O'Neill's love life was a permanent disaster zone.

As for Marina, the wounding insults she had hurled at Daisy surged back, taunting her even further. There had been so many questions left unanswered and so many unhappy silences from Marina at various points in time that Daisy had stopped being curious, stopped asking questions and stopped wanting to know. It had been easier to go with the flow, to paper over the confusion, to cover up the tensions in an effort to keep Marina on an even keel.

Until now.

Sam Heffernan had seen right through the armour of her steel-rimmed glasses and uncompromising suits, and with a few savage comments Marina had wrenched away the buffering layers that Daisy had so painfully and carefully constructed around them in order to act out a semblance of normality.

As Daisy lay in bed, she felt angry at the bright sunshine and the cheerful chirp of the Sunday morning birdsong – angry with Sam, but most of all angry with Marina. In a sudden fit of temper, she heaved back the duvet and got out of bed.

As she stood under the warm, soothing shower, dressed in jeans and a jumper, made some coffee and toast and ate it in solitary silence at the kitchen table, the mechanics of going about a normal routine helped Daisy's churning anger to slowly crystallise into a single bright intent.

* * *

Eve turned over in bed, feeling the warmth of the duvet surround her body like a nest of radiant heat. The blessed realisation that it was a Sunday filled her with a wave of unadulterated relief. She waited for her Sunday morning hangover to kick in and was momentarily surprised when there was no sour taste in her mouth, almost no headache to speak of and no queasiness in her tummy.

Of course. She had come home early last night, much to Daniel's disappointment.

Daniel had probably expected great things, things she couldn't possibly deliver considering the way she'd been feeling last night. She tried to relax into the bed and recapture the bliss of semi-slumber, but she couldn't, not when her mind was suddenly full of Alex and the memory of how wonderful it had been to have his arms around her, to smile and laugh into his grey eyes, how exciting it had been to be with him and to feel the warmth of his mouth on hers.

All finished now; all gone.

She closed her eyes and felt slow tears trickling across her face. It was after lunchtime by the time she dragged herself out of bed and went downstairs to make a cup of coffee.

'There you are.' Victoria flounced in from the dining room

'Yeah, so?'

'And where did you disappear to last night?'

'Yes, Eve, how come you left so early?' Liz echoed as she followed her daughter in.

'What's this, twenty questions?'

'I saw you sneaking off with Daniel,' Victoria said smugly. 'You obviously wanted to be home alone with him.'

'Don't be ridiculous,' Eve snapped.

'Bit of a change from your previous boyfriend, isn't he?' Liz remarked blandly as she began to load the dishwasher.

'God, Mum, what's got into you?' She needed this like a hole in the head.

'There was a big row last night,' Victoria told her. 'With Marina and Daisy.'

'There's no need to sound so jubilant,' Liz said sharply.

'Mum and Dad had to bring Marina home,' Victoria said. 'And Daisy was upset.'

'What did everyone expect?' Eve shrugged. 'A

186

birthday party for Marina was bound to end in disaster.'

'What happened, Mum?' Victoria prodded.

'I have no idea.' Liz spun the dial on the dishwasher and turned to face her daughters. 'I don't know what happened last night, but something certainly went wrong and I intend talking to both of you.'

'I have homework to do,' Victoria chirped.

'And I'm busy right now,' Eve tossed as she sailed through the doorway. She decided to go into town to do some shopping. Right now, she needed plenty of distraction.

* * *

She had done something wrong. Marina had felt it in her bones all day as she'd drifted between fitful sleep and a pounding head. She should be used to that feeling by now, she thought, so she couldn't figure out why she was so uneasy.

She'd drunk too much the night before. Looking at the crowd and the birthday banners, she'd felt as though she had wandered into someone else's party by mistake. This couldn't all be just for her. She had done nothing to deserve it.

Anxiety had swept through her when Eve said she had taken everyone by surprise with her dress. It was a mistake to have restyled it and to have disturbed that part of her past. That night, though, she was supposed to be feeling happy and light-hearted, so she gladly accepted Eve's drink, and after that, everything was a comforting oblivion.

Now Daisy was standing in front of her with a funny look on her face and telling her she was going away. Marina still felt so hung over from the night before that the shock barely made an impact. She'd always feared that Daisy would leave her sooner or later. She didn't deserve to have her around, not after what she'd done. She briefly tried to console herself with the fact that if Daisy moved out, at least she wouldn't have to live with a constant reminder of her terrible mistake.

'Away where?' she asked her.

* * *

'London.' Daisy dropped the word deliberately, the long-forbidden word, wondering for a wild moment if the mention of the city after the scene of the night before would suddenly open the floodgates. But Marina's bloodshot eyes remained blank.

'I might have guessed you'd abandon me too,' she muttered.

It was Sunday evening. Marina had got out of bed at four o'clock in the afternoon and come downstairs to the living cum dining room. She made some tea and toast and, looking as though she had a monumental hangover, sat slumped in front of the television. Daisy didn't know what recollection she had of the night before because they had barely spoken. When Liz and Harry arrived after seven, armed with their usual forced cheerfulness, Daisy took a deep breath, ignored her fluttering tummy and made her announcement.

'I'm not abandoning you,' Daisy told her mother slowly and clearly. 'I'm just going away for a while.'

'To that city.'

'Yes.'

Marina's face was so frighteningly empty of expression that Daisy's newfound resolve had almost crumbled. Almost, but not quite. And although she had a sudden urge to pretend that last night had never happened so that they could continue on in much the same way as before, something inside her knew that she could never go back to that false, contrived life, where the ground had so utterly caved away.

Then Marina laughed sharply and looked right through her. 'I won't have a daughter, you know, if you insist on going over there. But don't let that stop you.'

'It won't. And I didn't think you had a daughter anyway,' Daisy retorted, wondering if she would get a reaction. Hadn't she as good as told her she was dead last night? Or didn't she remember?

'Daisy?' Liz suddenly interrupted. 'Why don't we go out for some fresh air? Harry will make Marina a cup of coffee.'

'Whatever you want,' Daisy shrugged. She put on her jacket and followed Liz out into the velvety twilight of the back garden and steeled herself for whatever Liz would say to dissuade her. But to her surprise, Liz was encouraging.

'First of all, I'm really sorry about what happened last night,' Liz began. 'I found out this evening that Eve bought Marina a vodka and Red Bull, of all the bloody drinks. And Victoria admitted that she saw her downing a couple of shots at the bar on more than one occasion. I could cheerfully murder the pair of them.'

'I don't think there's any point in talking about this.'

'Has Marina talked about last night?'

'No. I have a feeling she knows something went wrong, but I don't think she remembers what happened.'

'Has she said anything at all?'

'No, and I haven't brought it up either.'

'I know Marina upset you last night. Believe me, I feel terrible about what happened. All I can say is she really loves you and she didn't know what she was saying.'

'Loves me?' Daisy was scathing. 'Look, Liz, if I remember correctly, she told me I reminded her of everything she had lost. And then she told me I was dead. In other words, she doesn't want to know me any more. What am I supposed to make of that?'

'I know that's what she said, but it's not at all what she meant. Marina was well and truly off her head.' Liz sighed and put a comforting hand on her arm. 'Maybe if I could try to explain a little….'

'Don't bother. It sounded very clear cut to me.' Daisy shrugged off her hand and looked away to where the sky in the west was holding the last glimmers of dark blue light. The sun had long vanished from the horizon and the day was almost over. Soon it would be quite dark and she was glad of that, glad that this day was coming to an end and time itself was moving away from the utter confusion of the last twenty-four hours. 'Anyway, it doesn't matter any more because I'm going to get away from all this,' Daisy finished.

'I think you're perfectly right to go away and see something of the world.'

'But?' Daisy interjected, already anticipating her aunt's objections.

'No buts, Daisy.' Liz looked up at her niece. 'I would just like to think you're going away for the right reasons.'

'After last night, don't you think I've reason enough?' Daisy said cuttingly. 'Who cares about the reason anyway, because I certainly don't.'

Liz sighed. 'Honestly, Daisy, I'd hate to think you were running away for all the wrong reasons.'

'I don't see it as running away, and it's not just Marina—' Daisy stopped short.

'Oh? Is there anything else upsetting you?'

'No, not particularly.' Daisy faced her aunt and Liz looked away.

'Just thought you might want to talk.' Liz shoved her hands into the pockets of her coat and walked down the path towards the end of the garden.

'There's nothing to talk about,' Daisy said, falling into step beside her aunt.

'So you're really going ahead with this?'

'Believe me, wild horses couldn't stop me.'

'I'll miss you. I'll keep an eye on Marina, and better than I did last night.'

'Last night wasn't your fault, Liz. If anyone was to blame for what happened, it was Mum. Anyway, I won't be that far away.'

'Why London, of all places? As you know, it's not Marina's favourite part of the world.'

'All the better. Look, I need to get away, from Marina… from everything. London is the obvious place. I was born there, wasn't I? I'm going back to my roots in a way, back to where my parents met, and if it helps me make sense of who I am, or where I'm coming from, well then, it's a bonus.' She laughed hollowly. 'I might even manage to run into my father and ask him why he abandoned me.'

'I really wish Marina hadn't said it the way she did.' Liz threw a comforting arm around her. 'It wasn't like that, please believe me.'

'Yeah, sure.'

'Look, all I can tell you is that your father was very young at the time.'

'Did you meet him?'

'I did, of course.'

Liz could tell her about him, couldn't she? Everything she wanted to know? Yet Daisy hesitated. She was still bruised from the night before, still angry, and right now she couldn't absorb any more beyond the stark reality that he had walked out when she was just a baby. And from what she had gathered last night, Marina blamed her. Had always blamed her, most likely.

'Maybe I'll finally have the opportunity to meet him myself.'

'I sincerely hope that's not why you're going to London.'

'As I said, I need to get away from Marina for a while and see if I can find my own feet. I'd just like to see where everything started, where I was born.'

'London is very big,' Liz said. 'It's highly unlikely you'd run into your father.'

'I suppose so.' Daisy finally smiled at her aunt. 'Especially as I don't even know his name.'

* * *

Daisy didn't go into work the following day. For the first time in her career, she phoned in sick on a Monday morning. Part of her was filled with a reckless urge to be careless and irresponsible. Another part of her needed to avoid Sam Heffernan and his cronies. There would be plenty for them to snigger about after Saturday night, unfortunately, but she didn't intend being around to witness it. When she met Paula that evening for a drink in a lounge off Dame Street, she was doubly glad that she had stayed at home.

Monday night was quiet enough and Daisy was glad that the few regulars were engrossed in a golfing tournament on the wall-mounted television so that they could chat in peace.

'This has to be about Sam,' Paula said in gossipy tones when they were sitting down with their drinks. 'Otherwise you'd scarcely drag me into town like this.'

'I don't particularly want to talk about Sam,' Daisy said sharply.

'He seemed very happy to talk about you today,' Paula teased.

'I can well imagine.'

'Well, go on, what was he like? By all accounts it was hot and heavy,' Paula grinned. 'He wasn't surprised you were out sick.'

'Sorry, I don't get you.'

'You and Sam. He says you couldn't get enough of him and you were probably still exhausted.'

Daisy almost choked on her glass of wine. 'He what?'

'Don't look so alarmed. I just heard word floating around the factory floor that you two had got it together. Sam seems very proud of himself altogether. He's going around like the cat who licked the cream.'

'The hell he is,' Daisy fumed. 'How dare he!'

'Why, what's wrong?'

'Nothing happened, Paula. He got a bit too touchy feely and I asked him to bring me home straight away. The bastard!'

'You're joking!'

'I swear to God. I can't believe this!'

'Jeez, Daisy. There'll be sparks flying when you come in tomorrow.'

Daisy felt suddenly strong with renewed determination. 'The reason I wanted to see you tonight was to tell you I'm off to London. As soon as possible. And from the sound of what Sam Heffernan is saying, I don't intend to set foot in the office tomorrow, or ever again.'

* * *

'Whatever happened over the weekend, it doesn't seem to have cooled Daniel's devotion,' Rachel said in the canteen on Tuesday.

'Why?'

'He's been looking at you all morning with his usual adoring face.'

'God,' Eve grimaced.

'Maybe he wants to continue where you left off on Saturday night.'

'No way. Daniel needs a crash course in seduction, but I'm not going to be the one to give it to him.' Eve made a face and sipped her coffee.

'Don't be so hard on him. Although I suppose it's difficult for anyone to come up to scratch after Alex,' Rachel grinned. 'Make that impossible.'

'Alex?' Eve said contemptuously, 'He's yesterday's news.' She was secretly horrified at the sudden pang that shot through her. Everyone seemed to be conspiring to bring up his name. She had finished with boyfriends before and they had never rated a second comment. How come Alex was different?

She knew only too well why he was different.

'By the way,' Rachel hesitated. 'What are you doing next weekend?'

'Next weekend? I don't know yet.'

'Fancy coming to an engagement party?' she asked, looking tentatively at Eve.

An engagement party, Alex had asked. She felt a little dizzy as the words echoed in her mind. She could almost see him sitting in the taxi outside her house, his eyes questioning hers and her stomach contracted painfully.

'Whose party?' Eve asked, feeling suddenly and horribly depressed.

Rachel gave her a big grin. 'Mine. John and I... well, we're getting engaged!'

Part II

Chapter Twenty-two

London simmered.

The city baked in searing summer temperatures. Sunshine glinted off the surface of the Thames and bounced off steel and glass office blocks along the serrated skyline in Canary Wharf. It carved across rows of chalk-white Georgian buildings in stately London squares and drenched Kensington Gardens in dazzling heat. Down by Westminster, the pods of the London Eye sparkled and glittered as it quietly revolved.

Alex was glad of the air conditioning as he took up position on the podium and scanned the audience gathered in the conference centre of the hotel. Clear, articulate and impeccably groomed, standing tall and commanding, Alex had the full attention of the capacity audience. His presentation was relaxed yet precise. By the time he was finished, practically every woman in the audience had fallen in love with him.

'You were very impressive, Alex,' Jennie Turner, his personal assistant, said as they joined the delegates streaming into the adjoining lounge.

'We'll see if that translates into a few contracts,' he said, keenly surveying the gathering.

'To judge by the initial level of interest, I think Citimex will need additional staff.'

'Glad you're so optimistic.'

'Here we go,' she said, picking up a folder as two sharply dressed executives made a beeline for Alex.

It was late by the time their business was done. Alex and Jennie left the hotel and stepped out into the cauldron of the warm London evening. Imposing office blocks flanked the opposite side of the street, tall facades rimming the indigo sky. Pavements were filled with office workers going home after a long day and groups of people on their way out for an evening's entertainment, their laughter and chatter echoing in the warm, calm air.

'Are you going straight home, Jennie?' Alex asked, hailing a cab.

'Worse luck,' she said, casting a glance at a group of laughing women clattering by in their evening finery. 'My nights of being out on the town have been sadly curtailed and need advance planning of major proportions.'

Alex held open the door of the cab and Jennie climbed inside. He lifted in their briefcases and laptops and then sat beside her as she gave the cab driver directions.

'You have family?' he asked Jennie.

'Yes, Greg and I have a little girl, Megan. It means we scarcely get out at all, but I wouldn't swap her for the world,' Jennie chatted. 'What about you?'

'Me? I've no ties whatsoever,' he said firmly.

'You should have stayed on in the hotel,' Jennie said brightly as the cab trundled westwards through the busy streets.

'Why?'

'I'm sure there's a number of interested female executives searching the lobby for you at this moment.'

'And that's precisely why I'm sitting here beside you,' Alex clipped, ignoring the embarrassed look on Jennie's face and staring out the window.

* * *

Inside the door of his first-floor apartment in Chiswick, Alex strode down the hall to his home office. He was just about to sit down at his desk and turn on his laptop when he paused. Enough was enough. He turned on his heel and went into the living room, poured himself a generous measure of whiskey, and flicked a switch on the CD player. He sat back on the sofa and stretched out his legs as the sound of R.E.M. belted into the room.

Business in London was booming for Citimex. And that was exactly what he wanted. The relocation to London had stretched his abilities, had widened the scope of his creative talents and had given him no time to think about anything other than work. He supposed he couldn't blame Jennie for being curious. He was a couple of months in London now and since he had taken over the reins at Citimex, all his energies had been poured into his job. Most evenings he worked late, and even at the weekends he spent time in his home office, preparing for the week ahead. His staff were bound to have noticed by now that he had practically no existence outside of the office.

So what, he thought as he refilled his glass. It suited him fine. The last thing he wanted was time on his hands or any complications in his life. Complications like Eve Andrews, for instance. He hadn't been fair to her. Then again, he hadn't been thinking straight. The family birthday party in the Italian restaurant that night had unsettled him and he had automatically responded to her advances, leading her to believe that he felt more for her than he actually did. He sighed and tried to forget her tearful face.

Not so easy to forget, however, was the conversation he had had with his mother before he left for London.

'I'm so glad that you're moving on with your life,' Jane had said as they sat in her kitchen the night before he left.

'What do you mean?'

'You haven't been the same since your father died.'

'How the hell could I possibly be the same?'

'Sorry,' she sighed, 'bad choice of words. None of us will ever be the same, but at least you're picking up your life again. Your father would have been glad of that. I've been worried about you….' Her voice trailed away and she looked unhappy.

'There's nothing to worry about,' Alex said.

'That's the problem, isn't it?' Jane looked at him squarely.

'What problem?'

'You don't want to talk, Alex. You keep shutting me and the girls out.'

'Do I? I don't mean to,' he frowned, a sinking feeling in his heart. He wished he was on the plane to London, miles away. But there was no avoiding his mother's steadfast gaze as she sat across the table from him.

'It's probably me being silly.' Jane summoned a faint smile. 'I just feel you've locked yourself away, somewhere I can't reach. Whenever I mention your dad to you, you always seem to have something urgent to do or an important phone call to make. I even had to twist your arm to persuade you to start driving his BMW.'

'Look, I'm sorry,' Alex began. He stood up and held his hand out to his mother. He drew her to her feet and put comforting arms around her. 'I know it's bad for me, but it must be a hundred times worse for you,' he said into the air above her head. 'Maybe that's why I avoid the subject.'

'I'll get through this,' she said, her voice muffled against his shoulder. 'We'll all get through this. But I'd just like to talk to you now and again.'

'Are you sure you'll be okay when I'm over in London?' He looked at her.

'Of course,' Jane insisted. 'I'm fifty-five, Alex. I'll be fine and I have Aisling and Andrea here, after all.'

'Don't forget to come over and visit.'

'You know me, I'm not exactly the world's greatest flyer. But your sisters will be over as soon as their exams are finished and they have some shopping money saved.'

'And don't forget to take out the BMW from time to time.'

'Didn't I say?' Jane smiled. 'I'm driving you out to the airport tomorrow. It'll give me a chance to have a practice run in it.'

'You'll never go back to the Golf after that!' Alex joked, relieved that the conversation was ending on a light note.

* * *

The CD came to an end, the last guitar chords fading away, and the living room was plunged into silence. Alex yawned and stretched. His body was tired and he had another early start in the morning. His mind was fully alert, though, and he sensed that sleep would elude him.

There had been so much left unsaid between him and his mother. Things that were far better left unsaid, he thought grimly. He tossed the last of the whiskey down his throat and almost hurled the glass across the room. He stopped himself just in time and wondered if the guilt would ever go away.

Chapter Twenty-three

Daisy whipped off her sunglasses as she entered the Underground station. She inserted her ticket into the machine, the barrier snapped open and she hurried through. In her jeans and yellow T-shirt, her blond hair naturally highlighted with the sunshine and a light tan enhancing her soft face, she bore no resemblance to the suit-clad, competent Ms O'Neill who had managed the human resources office in Cardinol Electronics.

She hopped off the escalator and saw she had one minute to wait for her Tube. Right on schedule, it surged into the station with a blast of wind and a disembodied voice telling her to mind the gap. She was several weeks in London now and she liked travelling on the fast, efficient Tube, joining the streams of passengers hurrying through the barriers, travelling on swiftly moving escalators, sometimes grabbing a seat, usually standing while the bowels of London flashed by the carriage window until the bright lights and wall posters heralded another station.

She reached her destination a few stops along the Central line. As she went out through the exit at Notting Hill Gate, a blast of heat ricocheted off the pavements. She strolled past shops, houses and gardens slumbering in the Saturday evening sun, her straw bag swinging against her hip, then walked around the corner and up the laneway to the mews house. She opened the door, dumped her bag in the hall and went through the small, tidy kitchen and out to the tiny patio.

Alison Ryan was sprawled, eyes closed, on a striped lounger wearing a minuscule lime green bikini. A small wicker table beside her held her paperback, her suntan oil and a rapidly warming can of Coors Light. Daisy pulled over a matching lounger and flopped down.

Alison stretched and yawned, opened her eyes and slowly sat up. 'Hi, Daisy. What did you get?'

'I just bought a new top and skirt' Daisy said.

'Let's see.'

'Hold on a sec, I left my bag in the hall.'

'There's plenty of lager in the fridge, help yourself on the way back. And you might as well bring me another. This is thirsty work, this sunbathing,' Alison giggled.

When Daisy returned, Alison was smoothing dollops of suntan oil into already tanned limbs. She admired Daisy's outfit, a lilac crinkle top and matching floaty trousers.

'That's gorgeous, Daisy. You could wear that anywhere,' Alison approved.

'I'll wear it to the barbecue tonight.'

'It'll be perfect. And you've still an hour or so of sunshine to work on your tan. Want some?' She held out the oil.

'No thanks,' Daisy laughed. 'I'm still at the factor thirty stage.'

'Why don't you change into your bikini? If you didn't bring one I can loan you one of mine.'

Daisy didn't hesitate. Back in Dublin she would never have thought of sunbathing in the garden in her bikini. But this wasn't Dublin, and this wasn't the old Daisy O'Neill. 'Good idea,' she said.

'Wow, Daisy, you've a terrific figure,' Alison said when she returned to the patio. 'Legs up to your armpits, smooth skin and curves to die for.'

'Would you go away,' Daisy laughed as she smoothed in lashings of sun lotion. She took a few sips of her beer, perched her sunglasses on her nose and lay back on the lounger. She felt the early evening warmth seeping into her pores and listened to the far-off hum of traffic and the chirp of birds coming from the line of trees that screened the end of the garden, but otherwise all was quiet.

This wasn't Dublin, she reminded herself for the hundredth time, and she was slowly but surely beginning to believe it. Just as she was slowly but surely beginning to believe in the new Daisy O'Neill.

* * *

At first, she had thought that Paula was joking when she told her that her brother and sister-in-law were looking for a lodger.

'They are, really,' Paula had assured her as they sat in the pub in Dame Street the Monday after Marina's party, when Daisy had finally managed to convince Paula that she was serious about going away. 'They have a huge mortgage and one of Alison's friends was renting a room as a bed-sit, but now she's moved in with her boyfriend.'

'Which brother is this?'

'It's Joe. He and Alison got married last year and moved into a mews house ten minutes' walk from the Tube. It would be ideal for you, Daisy,' Paula said enthusiastically. 'Joe and Alison are lovely. You'd easily fit in. And you wouldn't be too far away in case….'

'In case I realise I've made a big mistake?'

'I don't mean it like that,' Paula assured her.

'It's a bit coincidental, your brother suddenly needing a new lodger.' She looked at Paula sceptically.

'Cross my heart, you can phone him yourself.' Paula was earnest. 'He might have already let the room. It's in a good area, so you'd have to contact him as soon as you can. Here, I'll give you his phone number. Think of it, Daisy. You could be over there next weekend if you wanted,' Paula said as she scrabbled in her bag.

'Next weekend?'

'I'll miss you, you know,' Paula continued, giving Daisy a steady look. 'Is there anything I can say or do to change your mind? I feel I can't just stand by and let you throw away your good job on account of that bastard. Running away solves nothing.'

'I'm not running away,' Daisy shrugged. 'I just want a complete change of scene.'

'I don't know what to say. You could have Sam up for sexual harassment, you know.'

'No way, Paula, I just want to forget all about it.'

Paula sighed. 'Personally, I wouldn't let him get away with it. And thanks to you, I'm gasping for another drink. Back in a sec.'

Daisy watched Paula head up to the bar. She couldn't help feeling envious of her, of her happiness with Tom and their two children. She didn't think she would ever fall in love, let alone get married and have a family. Paula thought she was going away purely on account of Sam. Let her think that. And so what if people thought she was running away? So long as there was no Sam

Heffernan bumping into her in the corridor or barging into her office, who cared? She didn't want to work under the same roof as him again. But more importantly, neither did she want to live under the same roof as Marina.

London. Back to her roots. And next weekend, if she wanted. She felt a quiver of excitement. Somewhere away from the likes of Sam and her disastrous love life. Miles removed from Marina, and a place she would never venture.

When Daisy looked back now, from the security of her lounger in a drowsy London back garden, she was amazed that her life had completely changed in a matter of days. She could scarcely believe she had dredged together enough cool composure to meet the managing director on neutral territory, explain that she had no choice but to tender an immediate resignation from Cardinol on account of Sam's insulting behaviour and inform him that Paula would be clearing out her desk.

And it didn't seem to matter that Marina continued to ignore her even as Daisy booked a one-way ticket, sold her car and resolutely packed her bags. In the days before she left, there was no mention made of the party, no apologies of any description and for the first time in her life, Daisy stood her ground and refused to humour Marina.

It was liberating to consign her bullet-proof suits to the back of the wardrobe and dump her glasses in the bin. A façade of tough professionalism wasn't needed where she was going, and anyway, it made no difference, as she had painfully found out. She felt as though she was outside of herself, watching what was going on, almost as though she had erected an impenetrable wall between herself and her emotions and between herself and Marina that helped to catapult her, ever so swiftly, from one life into another.

Little by little, she put Sam and Marina to the back of her mind, quietly amazed at how detached she felt as the days and then the weeks slipped by, pleased at the way her new life was coming together and even more delighted when she settled into a job that was a far cry from the sterile corridors of Cardinol.

* * *

'Hi, girls. It's well for some.'

Joe Ryan was home. Daisy opened her eyes and watched with amusement as he dropped an ice cube on Alison's tummy.

Alison squealed. 'I'll get you for this,' she cried, shaking her can of lager and spraying him with frothy dregs.

Joe ducked. 'Hey, mind my shirt! Daisy, control her please.'

Paula had been right, Daisy thought happily as she watched Joe and Alison play fight on the patio.

212

From the minute she had met them at the airport, she had warmed to their easy friendliness. She had her own comfortable self-contained room in the house so that they weren't treading on each other's toes. Ever since she had arrived, they had included her in many of their invitations. At first Daisy had refused, but Alison had insisted that she join them. So far, Daisy had been to a few parties and out for meals, and that evening they were going to a barbecue.

She looked well in her lilac outfit, Daisy realised later that evening. The shade brought out her delicate tan and she had washed and finger dried her hair so that it softly framed her face. She was casually introduced around to the group of neighbours and friends and a glass of chilled white wine was put into her hand. She felt herself relaxing as the evening drifted by and a whole new life sparkled just within her grasp.

Chapter Twenty-four

Dolan's Bar was located down a side street off Oxford Street. Daisy had been in London three weeks when she and Alison stumbled on it, almost by accident. They were out shopping on a Saturday afternoon, spotted the Irish pub and were about to go past when Alison announced that her feet were killing her and she simply had to sit down.

'That's what you get for wearing those killer heels,' Daisy joked.

'It's all right for you, Daisy. You have the height, but I need a bit of help,' Alison said as she toed off her sandals and wiggled her feet under the wooden table.

'I think Irish bars in London are almost more Irish than the pubs back home,' Daisy commented, looking at the framed pictures and photos on the wood-panelled wall, the piano in the corner, the bar menu with its selection of Irish dishes. 'It's all very cosy and relaxing.'

'I think we should have something to eat with our drinks,' Alison said as she examined the menu. They ordered glasses of lager and roast chicken baguettes. Although their drinks arrived promptly, for a while there was no sign of the food.

'They must be baking the bread from scratch,' Alison lightly moaned. 'I'm starving.'

'That's because you rushed out without any breakfast, isn't it? And all that credit card exercise has given you an appetite,' Daisy grinned.

'God, you're getting very cheeky altogether. When you first came over from Ireland, I thought you wouldn't say boo to a goose!'

'Someone must be having a bad influence.'

'Must be Joe, 'cos it's not me!'

'Sorry for the delay, ladies,' the barman apologised when he hurried across with their food. 'We're extra busy today.'

'Good complaint, I suppose,' Alison said, eyeing her filled baguette with appreciation. 'Looking at this, I'm not surprised you're busy.'

'It can get on top of you,' the barman shrugged. 'Between the restaurant upstairs and the bar food, we could do with an extra pair of hands from time to time.'

'Did you hear that, Daisy?' Alison said with

interest. 'You said you were looking for a job, didn't you?'

'Yes, but… not here.' Daisy looked surprised.

'Why not?'

'I don't think… well, I've never waitressed before.'

'Some of my best student jobs were waitressing.' Alison picked up a fork and began to attack her side salad. 'I was busy, but I had great fun. No real worries or responsibilities. Think about it, anyway. Were you going to look for office work?'

'I'm not sure….'

Office work. Sharp suits. Executive decisions. The cut and thrust of management policies. Running the gauntlet with staff. She had left all that behind, hadn't she? She looked at the shaft of sunlight filtering through the glass in the main door, at the knots of customers out relaxing for the afternoon, some gathered around the bar, others sitting on high stools. She heard the animated buzz of conversation and occasional bursts of laughter. Just outside, London city thrummed with life; she was somewhere new, wasn't she? Somewhere different.

'You can always have a word with Caroline, the boss,' the barman smiled as though he sensed her hesitation.

* * *

The day she started in Dolan's Bar, Caroline welcomed her with open arms. 'You're the answer to our prayers,' she announced.

At that moment, Daisy didn't feel like the answer to anyone's prayers. The angry energy that had galvanised her into changing her life around had temporarily deserted her, leaving her tired and dispirited. She knew she was pale faced and that there were shadows under her eyes, but she also knew she was better off getting some sort of job. Not that she needed the money – she had plenty of savings to keep her going – but she needed to have some useful purpose, to occupy herself.

'We need someone flexible like you to fill in part time. It'll be just four or five shifts a week,' Caroline said. 'Lunchtimes and evening shifts, one or the other, or sometimes both. Last orders are ten o'clock. Sometimes we cater for private parties and we need all hands on deck. It's just a question of ferrying food around, smiling at the customers and clearing the tables. You don't have to worry about anything else.'

Within a week, Daisy knew that the job was perfect for her. She felt a bit strange the first couple of days in her black uniform, but she soon found her way around, moving up and down the wooden staircase between the bar and restaurant as though she had been doing it forever. Her lunch hour shifts mainly involved serving bar food to shoppers and office workers, and in the evening she worked in the restaurant upstairs. It was a big, square, welcoming room, with large windows on two sides giving out onto the busy street below. Vivid scarlet curtains draped the oblong windows with a careless elegance and the walls mirrored the same deep red shade and were hung with an eclectic assortment of pictures, prints and paintings. The ambience was warm, cosy and relaxing, a far cry, thankfully, from the sterile air-conditioned office suite at Cardinol and her professional suits.

She became quite friendly with Caroline, a small, well-rounded woman in her early forties. She was separated, she told her, with a teenage daughter. Daisy soon found out that Peter, the senior barman, regarded Daisy with an almost fatherly, proprietal air, feeling wholly responsible for her recruitment. She soon got to know all of the staff – the other bar staff, Tina and Dave, the chefs, Colm and Marcus, and the rest of the waitressing team, Kim with the dark corkscrew curls and tall, flame-haired Helen. It didn't take her long to find out that Peter fancied Kim like crazy but she wouldn't give him the time of day and that Helen was single and man mad.

Daisy revelled in the pleasant, sociable nature of her job, in the succulent aromas that wafted around the restaurant and the mouth-watering dishes carefully prepared by Colm and Marcus that she in turn served to the customers. The pub was always lively and busy, sometimes jam packed in the early evenings when customers dropped in on their way home from work and always busy at lunchtime. The restaurant upstairs was more relaxed, but just as cheerful.

Sometimes she ate in Dolan's, but other times on her way to and from work she grabbed something in the Tube station. Sometimes she did a quick shop in Boots or Marks & Spencer or she got a bag of fruit from the stall on the corner of Oxford Street. She enjoyed feeling part of the hectic, cosmopolitan melting pot that was London, where no one took too much interest and where she was accepted unquestioningly.

For the present time, she put all thoughts of her London roots, never mind her father, out of her head. It didn't seem to matter much right now. It was enough to be somewhere new and different, miles removed from Marina and her life back in Dublin. It didn't even matter that the occasional time she phoned home Marina continued to act as though she didn't exist, and Daisy was left hanging onto a disconnected line. It made it easier, in fact, to close the door on her old life and find her feet in London, a city that was grander, cleaner, more hurried and far more crowded than she had ever expected.

* * *

'You're what?' Alex thundered into the phone. 'What do you mean, half the staff are firewalled? I thought you were supposed to run enough checks to make sure this wouldn't happen! Get Thomas Scott to phone me immediately.' He glowered as he got up from his desk, strode over to the plate-glass window in his chrome and glass office and stared out.

Citimex Systems had a suite of offices on the tenth floor of a London city centre complex. Down below on the busy street, sunshine glinted off snaking lines of cars and red London buses. Half of Alex's mind noticed the bright blue bowl of the sky and the dazzle of the sunshine on clean white facades. It brought him back for a brief, fleeting moment to the days when childhood summer holidays were always sunny and warm and long. He had a sudden vision of family picnics on Donabate beach and his father building sandcastles on the golden strand. He sighed heavily as he turned from the window.

His phone buzzed and he grabbed it.

'Yes?' he barked. 'What's going on? You should have been out of there by now… I see. In that case, I'll head to Romford myself tomorrow.' He slammed down the phone, strode to the office door and called for Jennie.

'Sorry to hold you back,' he apologised as he swept a hand abstractedly through his dark hair. His tie was loose, the neck of his crisp white shirt slightly open, his dark eyes glittering with irritation. 'I see it's almost five o'clock, but I have to go to

220

Romford in the morning and I need to sort out schedules for next week,' he explained.

'No problem, Alex,' Jennie said, opening the folder with the appointment sheets. 'Are you staying on much longer?' she asked as they completed their work and she switched off her computer.

Alex shrugged. 'Depends.'

'Shame to miss out on that sunny evening,' Jennie said. She gave him a brief grin as she picked up her bag. 'Oops, there I go again with my big mouth.'

'No worries,' Alex said. 'I hope to be finished here by eight o'clock.'

He spent most of Friday in the head offices of the car rental firm in Romford, personally ensuring that the new tracking system was operating correctly, and for the first time ever he fired someone. By the time he started the journey back to Chiswick, Friday evening traffic was bumper to bumper, and as he slowly edged his silver Audi forward, Thomas Scott's words rang in his ears.

'As of now, I'm terminating your contract,' Alex had snapped.

Thomas had blanched. 'You can't mean that. Look, I know I fouled up—'

'Fouled up? That has to be the understatement of the year.' Alex was scathing. 'You're off the team as of now. You can call into the office next week to tidy your desk and we'll arrange to send on whatever is due to you.'

'One lousy mistake!' Thomas said furiously. 'There are always teething problems with new systems. Just because I'm not Mr Perfectionist, like you. We can't all be robots, you know. Sometimes you have to allow for an element of human error.'

'You're fired.'

'Keep your bloody job,' Thomas said contemptuously. 'I don't like working for a heartless machine.'

Lost in thought, Alex almost tipped the family car in front of him and he slammed on the brakes, his hands rigid on the steering wheel. He made a conscious effort to relax, but it was almost impossible. He could hardly believe the brusque way he'd fired Thomas Scott. His total absorption in his career was turning him into a heartless robot.

Then again, he couldn't blame the challenge of London for stressing him out, because no matter how hard he worked, his troubled conscience still simmered away, feeding his anger and fuelling his impatience.

* * *

Saturday brought more warm sunshine, but Alex's dark humour persisted throughout most of the day. He showered, threw on a pair of Levi's and a white polo shirt and after a quick breakfast of tea and toast went into the Citimex office early in the morning to complete an urgent report. By lunchtime he'd had enough. All around him, the building was quiet and mostly empty and the silence pressed in on him. Trust him, Mr Perfectionist himself, to be the only workaholic stuck indoors on a lovely Saturday afternoon. He turned off his computer and took the lift to the ground floor, but instead of heading home to the silence of his apartment, he began to walk.

Pavements were crowded with Saturday afternoon shoppers and traffic was busy, buses and taxis clogging the streets. Alex strode along, weaving through the crowds, heedless of where he was going. He realised he was coming to the end of Regent's Street when he passed Hamley's and he crossed over into Oxford Street, passing the entrance to the Tube station, his progress up the street hampered by the phalanx of afternoon shoppers. He stopped by a stall and bought some fruit, munching an apple as he strode along, and then, when the crowd got a little too much, he ducked down a side street.

The Irish pub on the corner surprised him. In the weeks since he had arrived in London, he had scarcely ventured into a pub. Now, Dolan's Bar, with the Guinness logo emblazoned outside, enticed him in. It suddenly seemed like the most important thing in the world to relax over a pint.

It was packed. What else had he expected, Alex simmered as he looked in vain not only for a seat, but for clear passage to the bar. He felt a flare of impatience. An Irish pub on Saturday afternoon was bound to be jammed. Just because Mr Perfectionist felt like chilling out for a while didn't mean the crowds would suddenly and benignly abate. Nothing for it but to elbow his way through the crush.

Then he almost sent her flying.

She was edging her way back from the bar, a full pint of beer in her hands. She turned and practically cannoned into him, almost spilling the entire contents of the pint on top of herself, but she steadied herself just in time.

He found himself staring into a pair of huge brown eyes. There was something in those eyes that checked his impatience, halting him in his headlong rush. Something vulnerable, a guarded reserve. Then he noticed her face, her fine, high cheekbones, the slim, narrow nose and soft mouth. He saw the way her bright blond hair was styled like a halo around her head and tapered into her delicate neck. She was wearing something black and he caught the drift of her light, flowery scent.

'Are you okay? I'm really sorry,' he began, raising his voice against the babble all around.

'I'm fine,' she clipped as she began to sidle away.

'I wasn't looking where I was going,' he continued.

'Obviously.' Her tone was dismissive.

'Neither were you,' he grinned, intrigued by her slight air of hostility and attempting a joke, but this tall blonde wasn't having any of it.

'I told you, I'm fine.' Her voice was cool, and whatever he had seen in her eyes was carefully shuttered. It certainly wasn't the reaction he was used to getting from women, Alex thought.

'You're Irish, aren't you?' He smiled broadly, suddenly delighted with his discovery, hoping to get a better reaction from this striking girl.

'Maybe I am,' she said, slowly but surely moving past him through the crush of bodies.

'Dublin, I bet, same as me.' He raised an eyebrow. She hesitated, looking poised for flight. 'And what brings you over to London?' he persisted.

'If you'll excuse me.' She looked right through him and turned away. He watched her passage through the crowds as she went over to a table, deposited the drink and then moved across the room. His last view of her was a pair of endless legs hurrying up the stairway at the back of the bar.

Alex shook his head. He was definitely losing it. Definitely working too long and too hard. It was the first time in months he had attempted to strike up a conversation with an attractive girl, and look where it had got him. She had looked at him as though he had ten heads. He was only trying to be friendly, he thought. You'd swear by her reaction that he was about to eat her for breakfast.

He walked out of the jammed pub, out into the heat of the London afternoon and across the road, all thoughts of a pint of Guinness forgotten.

* * *

Standing in the staff toilets, Daisy's face flamed. What the hell had got into her? How could she have been so stupid as to allow a perfect stranger to unsettle her like that? Then again, she didn't want to know about Dublin, and at this point in time she wanted to forget all about her reasons for coming to London.

'Daisy? You okay?' She heard Kim calling to her from the staircase.

'I'm fine,' she said, venturing out onto the upper landing.

'You were tearing up the stairs as though the devil himself was after you,' Kim smiled.

'Maybe he was,' Daisy muttered.

'You don't usually do lunchtimes on Saturday, do you?'

'No, but Caroline asked me to help out today. Tina's away for the weekend.'

'There's a few of us going on to a club tonight, if you're interested.'

'Sorry, not tonight,' she said.

'You're the sensible one, Daisy. I'll stay late and Peter will want to buy me loads of drink and take me home.' Daisy smiled. 'Tell you what,' Kim went on. 'Why don't I fix the two of you up together and get him off my back?'

'No thanks.'

'So you don't fancy Peter?' Kim asked. 'How about Dave?'

''Fraid not.'

'Silly me. You probably have loads of handsome boyfriends running after you, an attractive girl like you.'

'Hundreds,' Daisy said lightly as she went back to the kitchen to collect another order. She told herself to forget all about the man who had completely unnerved her. London was vast. More than likely, she would never see him again.

* * *

Alex threw himself into his work the following week, most nights staying on late at the office. On Wednesday Thomas Scott arrived in to clear his desk and pick up a final cheque, but Alex didn't see him. He was holding a meeting in the conference room and had left instructions that he wasn't to be disturbed.

'What did he have to say for himself?' Alex asked Jennie afterwards.

Jennie shrugged. 'Nothing much.'

'I can imagine,' Alex said dryly. 'You probably don't want to repeat it, thank you.' Her face reddened a little. 'Tell me, Jennie....'

'Yes?'

'Do you think I'm a hard taskmaster?'

'I wouldn't say that.'

'What *would* you say? No, forget it.' He shook his head. 'I shouldn't put you on the spot.'

'Can I just say that I enjoy working for you

Alex,' Jennie spoke up. 'I think everybody else here does, too. I suppose….'

'Yes?'

'I suppose, if anything, that *you* work far too hard.'

'You're probably right.' He gave her a brief grin as he went back into the conference room.

He sat back down at the head of the table where he had spent the best part of the afternoon hammering out different clauses in a contract for a business college. He leaned back in the chair, arms clasped behind his head, lost in thought. His keen concentration had deserted him a little that afternoon, his usual decisiveness blurring around the edges. He had found the bargaining for the contract to be quite tough. His late hours at the office as well as the mountains of paperwork he completed at home were beginning to tell.

In addition to that, paintings of familiar Dublin landmarks placed around the walls of the conference room had unsettled him. Every time the prints caught his eye, whether it was St Patrick's Cathedral or the Ha'penny Bridge, they made him think of a tall, blonde, brown-eyed girl, an Irish girl he had literally bumped into while out in London on a Saturday afternoon.

Chapter Twenty-five

'And how did your weekend go?' Rachel asked.

'How do you think?' Eve grumbled, taking out her mirror. She looked and felt exhausted. She blinked her tired blue eyes and even that action sent shock waves resounding through her head. Her crimson mouth was the only splash of colour in her pale face.

'God, I look awful,' she said, opening up her make-up bag. She looked at the contents and almost picked up her concealer, then changed her mind. She looked up at Rachel. 'D'you think old Fogy would let me go home?' she asked.

'He'd let you do anything, Eve,' Rachel said with a hint of sarcasm.

'Do I look sick to you?'

'At a wild guess, I'd say you have a rotten hangover.'

'So I don't look like I'm coming down with the Asian flu?'

'In the middle of July? I don't think so.'

'You're very sympathetic.'

'Why don't you take two Paracetamol?'

'You don't happen to have any handy, do you?'

''Fraid not. There's bound to be some in the first aid box,' Rachel said cheerfully.

'Do you think I have the energy to make it to the sick room? I just want to sit here and die.'

'What did you get up to this weekend? I hope it was worth it.'

'Are you joking? Spirit was packed on Saturday night and afterwards we were hours waiting for a taxi. Then last night Katie said everyone would be in Café en Seine, but when I turned up they were nowhere to be seen.'

'So who did you meet?'

'Who said I met anyone?'

'You couldn't find your pals but you look as though you've been up all night, so you must have met someone.'

'You're so clever, you're wasted in this job,' Eve huffed.

'Yes, I am,' Rachel said as she tapped at her keyboard quickly and efficiently.

'Show-off,' Eve muttered as she picked up her miniature teddy and began to talk to him. 'Isn't

Rachel a good little worker? Conscientious and motivated, not like couldn't-care-less Eve, who was out all night at a party.'

'Ah ha! A party.'

'So? I bumped into an old friend and we went to a party. Now you know.' Eve put her teddy bear back on top of her computer monitor and glowered at her in tray.

'Anyone interesting?'

'No,' Eve answered shortly.

'So it wasn't worth the hangover,' Rachel said as she continued to type.

'Are you trying to win the typing marathon or something?' Eve asked.

'No, why?' Rachel didn't pause.

'There's no need to show off your Monday morning sparkle. Your speedy fingers don't impress me. And the clatter you're making is going right through my head. What has you so busy, anyway?'

Rachel lowered her voice. 'I'm doing something for Daniel.'

Eve automatically looked across to Daniel's desk, but he wasn't there.

'And where is the number-one stud this morning?' she asked.

'He's gone to his grandmother's funeral down in Cork. He'll be back tomorrow. As a matter of fact,' Rachel lowered her voice even further, 'I'm updating his CV.'

'You're what?' Eve's raised voice attracted plenty

of attention. Katie and Susan smirked at her from down the floor and Mr Foley appeared from nowhere and made his way over to the workstation.

'Thanks a bunch, Eve. I'm doing my best to avoid detection,' Rachel snapped as she saved her work and hurriedly opened a spreadsheet.

'Is everything okay, Eve?'

'Yes, Mr Foley,' she said as demurely as possible. Eve smothered a giggle and made a face at his retreating back. 'Fogy the bogey. There are times when he gives me the creeps,' she said.

'If that's how you feel, maybe you should look for another job,' Rachel said blandly.

'What's up with you?' Eve said, tossing her dark hair, which made her head pound all the more. 'I was only having a laugh.'

'I didn't find it very amusing.'

'You're great fun altogether,' Eve said, feeling miffed.

She didn't know what had got into Rachel. Lately she seemed more impatient with her, quicker to side with Daniel, and even now, picking up on what she had said about old Fogy. If that's what getting engaged did to you, you could forget it, Eve thought as she stabbed at her keyboard. She managed to look busy for an hour or so in spite of her pounding head and eventually Rachel waved a hand at her and asked her if she was going to take a break.

'Are you still talking to me?' Rachel asked, a

friendly smile on her face.

'I suppose I've no choice,' Eve said grudgingly.

'C'mon,' Rachel encouraged. 'You need a caffeine injection. You'll feel better afterwards.'

'Okay,' Eve sighed as she rose to her feet.

In the canteen, Eve made a beeline for Katie and Susan. 'And where were you lot?' she asked, putting down her cup of coffee and drawing up a chair. 'I made a right fool of myself, wandering around Café en Seine all by myself.'

'Sorry, Eve, there was a change of plan. But don't blame me, it was Susan's fault,' Katie laughed, nodding across the table.

'As far as I'm concerned it was everybody's fault,' Eve said, taking a tentative sip of her coffee.

'We left a message on your mobile,' Susan looked contrite. 'Didn't you get it?'

'How could I when my battery ran out?'

'How were we supposed to know?' Katie shrugged. She tore the wrapper off a cereal bar and looked at Eve curiously. 'It seems to me like you managed to make a night of it anyway.'

'Yeah, Eve,' Susan joined in. 'What did you get up to?'

'Nothing very exciting,' she began nonchalantly.

'She bumped into an old fan of hers,' Rachel said. 'I have never, ever seen her in such a state on a Monday morning.'

'Start at the beginning,' Katie invited, moving her chair in a little closer.

Eve brightened up as she looked around at the interested faces. She soon had everyone laughing as she described meeting up with an old boyfriend and heading off to a party with him. This was more like it. Eve Andrews, social butterfly. Back to her normal self.

* * *

Rachel suggested they go out to lunch. 'You'll need a decent portion of calories to get through the day,' she said.

'The thought of food!' Eve groaned. 'You're right, though. I'll never make it to half past five feeling like this.'

They went to the restaurant nearest the office. Rachel ordered a huge salad but Eve had chicken and chips. Comfort food, she said to herself as she dipped a chip in tomato sauce and popped it into her mouth. And who cared? It was only Monday, after all, with a whole boring week to get through. She deserved some pampering.

'You look a bit better,' Rachel said after a while.

'I needed something like this,' Eve grinned. She nibbled on a piece of chicken and looked out the window onto the busy street. Pedestrians were scurrying by, jostling with umbrellas, and the sky was overcast with low, grey clouds. 'Not looking too good, is it?'

'No,' Rachel agreed. 'I heard there's a heat wave

in London. I hope it's heading this way. It's about time.'

London. Eve's heart jumped and she barely heard anything else. London. Alex. But then, there were so many things that brought Alex to mind. A whiff of familiar aftershave, the sight of a tall, dark-haired man striding down Grafton Street, the spicy aroma wafting out from pizza restaurants, Friday mornings at half past ten....

She had only gone out with him four times, five if you counted the very first night in the pizza place. Yet even though she hadn't seen him in almost three months, every moment they had shared was printed indelibly on her mind. Alex Gallagher, the sexiest man on the planet.

After Alex, all the other guys she dated seemed dull and boring. They just took her mind off things for a few short hours, helping her to forget for a little while that everywhere she looked she searched in vain for a pair of dark grey eyes. A pair of eyes that had looked at her dispassionately as he told her she had been a mistake, she firmly reminded herself.

She forced her attention back to Rachel.

'So long as it's nice on the sixteenth of September, I don't care,' Rachel was saying.

Eve sighed. Here we go again, back to the wedding. She already felt bored. Nowadays she couldn't have a conversation with Rachel without some mention being made of it. If it wasn't the hotel it was the wedding dress, the honeymoon or the number of guests being invited. Eve was amazed at the range of topics that could be used to generate wedding talk.

The day that Rachel had come into work bubbling with excitement and flashing her engagement ring, Eve had felt physically sick. Still raw in the aftermath of Alex, she was appalled at how resentful she felt.

'I thought the party was next Saturday,' she had said in a strangled voice.

'It is,' Rachel had giggled. 'But we couldn't wait. John officially proposed last night! Go on, make a wish.' Rachel thrust her ringed finger at Eve.

Eve put the diamond solitaire on the third finger of her left hand and turned it towards her heart, once, twice, three times. Alex, Alex, Alex.

They were getting married this September, Rachel had said, almost delirious with excitement. They had been extremely lucky to get a hotel cancellation. They planned to honeymoon in Italy on the Amalfi coast and stay on in the apartment for a while. Eve wanted to shut her ears. The less she heard of wedding talk, the better. Then Rachel had asked her to be her bridesmaid.

'You know I've no sisters,' Rachel said. 'And only for your help and advice along the way I don't think I'd be walking up the aisle with John.'

'I'm not sure if I'm the bridesmaid type. I'd be more comfortable in a slinky black number than trussed up in a candy floss dress.'

'We'll go shopping together,' Rachel said. 'I won't buy anything without your approval. Anyway, Eve, I'll need your advice on *my* dress!'

Rachel had looked so eager that Eve hadn't had the heart to refuse her, even though the last thing she wanted was to trail Rachel around bridal boutiques as she prepared for her wedding. And as she had feared, she was already bored silly and there were still two months to go. How on earth would she survive it, she simmered as she picked at the last of her chicken and listened to Rachel prattling on about her hotel venue.

'What's happening with Daniel?' she interrupted. 'How come you're doing up his CV?'

'Nosy, nosy,' Rachel teased. 'Do you want any dessert? The pavlova looks delicious.'

'No thanks, I think I've had enough calories for one day,' Eve said.

'Me too. I can't afford to put on an ounce before the wedding. My dress—'

'You're going to be beautiful,' Eve said firmly. 'Now tell me what's up with Daniel.'

'He's getting a new job,' Rachel confided. 'He was never the same after that date with you. Mr Foley thought that his output had gone out the window and his concentration had seriously lapsed.'

'You're not serious!'

'No, of course not,' Rachel joked. 'He's hardly leaving on account of you. He was employed on one of those temporary contracts and he's due to go on Friday week. He's hoping to land a great job in one of the banks.'

'Thanks for telling me.'

'I only found out the other day,' Rachel said. 'I asked him if there was anything I could do, so he asked me to update his CV.'

'You always had a soft spot for him,' Eve said.

'I suppose he reminds me of my kid brother. And I'm trying to make up for all the aggravation you've caused him.'

'Aggravation?' Eve looked innocently at Rachel.

'You know what I mean,' Rachel said crisply.

* * *

'You're not really leaving, are you?' Eve teased as she leaned over Daniel's desk the following day.

Daniel flushed to the roots of his sandy hair. 'I am. I'm finishing up on Friday week.'

'Friday week?' Eve pretended to be surprised. 'We'll have to make the most of it, won't we?'

'What d'you mean?' he suddenly confronted her, giving her his full attention.

Eve was caught unaware. Surprise, surprise, Daniel had balls after all. 'Oh, well, you know,' she smiled, suddenly at a loss for words.

'Sure I do, Eve.' He looked directly at her, a challenge in his hazel eyes.

Eve went back to her desk, feeling suddenly

piqued. The prospect of a new job had given Daniel a burst of confidence. Pity he hadn't displayed some of his newfound assertiveness before now. It made him a far more interesting proposition.

As the days dragged by, Eve was appalled to discover that she would miss him. It seemed crazy. Had anyone told her a couple of months ago that she would miss Daniel, she would have laughed. But somewhere during the past few months, she had got used to being the focus of his attention. She had enjoyed teasing him, baiting him, watching for his reaction. It was meaningless fun, something to help brighten up an otherwise dull and boring day. More importantly, something to get her through the first few miserable weeks after Alex. Daniel's infatuation hadn't diminished after their date; if anything he seemed to be even more besotted with Eve. She was horrified to realise that she would miss all that.

'What are the plans for Daniel's booze-up?' she asked Rachel, forcing a casual note into her voice.

'What booze-up? I didn't hear of any.'

'Surely he's going out for a drink with the guys he hangs around with?'

'Ronan and Conor? I don't know. Maybe Daniel doesn't want a fuss.'

'They'll have to have *something*. They usually go out for drinks after work on Friday, don't they?' Eve asked, but Rachel shrugged. 'Maybe we could join them?' Eve suggested.

'How come you're so interested in Daniel all of a sudden?' Rachel asked.

'You know me, any excuse for a night out,' Eve grinned.

'Daniel mightn't want to have you there. Have you thought of that?'

'Of course he'd want me along. I have to buy him a farewell drink.'

'I'll talk to Conor. I wouldn't mind going along myself, but just for a couple of drinks because—'

'I know, I know,' Eve threw her eyes up to heaven. 'You're saving for the wedding.'

Chapter Twenty-six

Alex felt slightly uneasy as he nursed his pint. He had spent the morning fidgeting around the apartment, tidying an already tidy kitchen, switching on Saturday morning television and flicking impatiently between channels. He had gone into his home office, taken one look at his bulging briefcase and walked straight out again. Early in the afternoon, he had come in town. Into Dolan's Bar, to be precise.

But what exactly did he think he was doing here? How come he had had such a yearning for a pint? And now that he was here... the pint was lovely all right, yet he drank it very slowly, reluctant to be finished, reluctant to leave the premises, but not too keen on ordering another.

After all, it was rather early in the afternoon.

He swallowed the last of his drink till there was only froth left in the glass, yet he stalled, lingering in the bar, taking up a table all to himself, wondering if by any chance he might spot a tall, blonde Irish girl. He was mad, he told himself, quite mad.

And there was no sign of her whatsoever.

'Excuse me,' he said to the young lad who was collecting empty glasses. 'I'm actually looking for someone. A tall, blonde bar girl?'

'That must be Tina,' the young lad said. 'She's over there.' He nodded his head towards the back of the bar, where Tina was serving a customer.

'No, that's not her,' Alex said.

'There's no one else,' the young lad told him.

'I saw her here, oh, about two weeks ago,' Alex said firmly.

'I'm sorry, sir, but Tina's the only bar girl here who's tall and blonde,' the young lad said, equally firmly. 'Can I get you another drink?'

Alex was surprised at how disappointed he felt. He shook his head, got off his stool and headed for the door. He was just about to open it when he felt a hand on his arm.

'Excuse me, sir, I've just realised there's been a mix-up.'

'What mix-up?' Alex asked impatiently, suddenly short tempered. He wanted out of there and now, but this lad was in his way, barring his exit.

'When you asked me about the bar girl?'

'Forget it,' Alex said crisply. He had made a right fool of himself, chasing after someone who didn't seem to exist.

'It's just that she's not really a bar girl.'

'I'm in rather a hurry.' Alex made to move past him.

'She's one of the part-time waitresses, the girl you were asking about. Tall and blonde?'

'A waitress?'

'Like yourself, she's Irish, and she'll be here tomorrow evening,' he volunteered.

'Ah. And does she have a name, your Irish waitress?'

'Don't you know? I thought Daisy was a friend of yours and that's why you were looking for her.'

'Daisy?'

'Yes, Daisy O'Neill.'

* * *

Alex scarcely noticed the Saturday afternoon shoppers as he caught the Tube back to Chiswick. Daisy O'Neill. The name ran around and around in his head as he thought of the brown eyes that had tugged at an answering chord deep inside him.

He felt ridiculously pleased as he got off the Tube and walked the mile or so to his apartment block. He was glad he hadn't been mistaken, that his eyes hadn't been playing tricks, that she did exist after all. She was a part-time waitress in

Dolan's Bar. He knew where to find her now, and better again, he had a name to put to her lovely face.

* * *

Paula phoned Daisy that night. 'I'm coming over next weekend,' she said, 'so roll out the red carpet! It's all arranged,' Paula went on enthusiastically. 'And it's minus Tom and the kids! So tell that brother of mine to expect me.'

'Sure! It'll be great to see you,' Daisy said.

'I can't wait. A weekend of freedom.'

It would be lovely to see Paula again, Daisy thought as she put down the phone. She went out occasionally with Joe and Alison and sometimes with the girls in Dolan's Bar, but Tina and Helen invariably ended up chasing men and Daisy usually came home early. It would be fun to catch up with Paula and have a laugh.

* * *

When Daisy walked into Dolan's on Sunday for the evening shift, the pub was packed to capacity and the restaurant was fully booked for the night. She was just about to go upstairs when Dave, the young barman, called her over.

'Daisy! Before I forget, there was a man in look-ing for you on Saturday afternoon.'

'What man?' Daisy's stomach automatically clenched.

'An Irish man. Sorry, I didn't get his name.'

'He was scarcely looking for me.'

'He was too. He seemed very sure of himself. Said he saw you here a couple of weeks ago. He's tall, and I suppose,' Dave grinned, 'you'd say he was a fine thing.'

'I don't know anyone who fits that description,' Daisy said coolly as she marched up the stairs.

Calm down, she told herself as she checked her reflection before she went on duty. There was no need to reach for the lavender scent. She was somewhere new, somewhere different, where the old Daisy O'Neill didn't exist. And right now, the new Daisy O'Neill was going to be busy. She had six tables and almost fifty covers to look after this evening, and that was all she had to concern herself with.

But the night hadn't even begun, the first customers hadn't even arrived, and Daisy was just laying out cutlery on the tables when she sensed someone looking at her. Even before she looked up she felt a slow blush creep across her face.

He was standing by the reception desk at the doorway, hands in the pockets of his jeans, and he looked very confident as he flashed Daisy a huge grin.

For a breathless moment she felt suspended in time and then there was the sound of knives and forks slithering through her fingers and clattering across the polished wooden floor. Daisy's face was scarlet as she bent down, gathered them up with shaky hands and hurried into the kitchen.

Caroline was busy checking condiments and sauce boats. 'Everything all right, Daisy?' she asked.

'Sorry, I let these fall… em, I think there's a man outside looking for a reservation.'

'We're fully booked tonight, so whoever he is, he's out of luck.'

There was no choice but to face him again. Wearing her coolest expression and feeling as though she was stepping onto a tightrope without a safety net, Daisy strode back out onto the restaurant floor and over to the reception desk. He hadn't moved. He was still waiting and wearing that amused look on his face.

'I'm afraid we're fully booked tonight,' she said, managing to avoid his eyes.

'Who said I was looking for a table?' he grinned. 'Maybe I want to make amends for almost knocking a pint of beer over you.'

'There's nothing to apologise for.'

'Then perhaps, Daisy….' Their eyes connected. He smiled at her and continued in a friendly tone of voice, 'I hope you don't mind, but the barman downstairs gave me your name. My name is Alex, by the way, and in case you're interested—'

'I'm not interested,' Daisy said curtly as she turned on her heel and sought the sanctuary of the

246

kitchen. She busied herself checking plates and glasses and the next time she ventured out onto the floor, the space where he had stood seemed absurdly empty.

'Who was your man?' Kim asked.

'I haven't a clue,' Daisy shrugged.

'God, Daisy, the sexiest thing I've seen in ages and you don't know his name? Did you see the way he was smiling at you? Made me go weak at the knees. Why didn't you take a booking from him?'

'He didn't want food.'

'No? What was he after?'

'Search me,' Daisy fobbed her off.

'He must have been after you. Caroline, you should have seen him. Sex on legs if I ever saw it. Wow!' She rolled her eyes appreciatively. 'If you're not interested, Daisy, you need your head examined. The next time he comes back, I'll personally look after him.'

'Hopefully there won't be a next time.' She was glad she was rushed off her feet serving soups and Atlantic oysters, Irish beef sausages and treacle tarts. Glad, too, that the restaurant was full to capacity and the empty space by the reception desk wasn't so noticeable as the night went on.

* * *

'Is everything going well?' Jane asked.

'Busier than ever, to be honest,' Alex said.

'I don't just mean work, you know, but are you too busy for visitors? The girls are thinking of going over for a few days. If it's too short notice….'

'Not at all, I'd love to see them,' Alex said.

'You don't have to take time out to entertain them. They'll be doing their own thing.'

'I'm sure that includes plenty of retail therapy,' Alex joked.

'Why not? They both did well in their exams. I'll phone you with the flight details,' Jane said.

It would be good to have his sisters over, Alex decided as he relaxed with a glass of whiskey. A bit of life around the apartment might help him to forget the brown eyes that interrupted his train of thought far too often for comfort.

Chapter Twenty-seven

'I'll be late home tonight,' Eve said as she gulped down a cup of coffee.

'Doing anything exciting?' Liz asked.

'Nothing special,' Eve said. 'One of the lads is leaving and... for God's sake!' She went over to a pile of laundry that Liz had just taken out of the dryer and pounced on a black Lycra top. 'What the hell is this doing in the wash?' Eve erupted. 'I presumed that it was safely upstairs in my press. Has that bitch sister of mine been at my clothes?'

'For God's sake, calm down.'

'No, I won't calm down. She has no right to take my clothes behind my back.'

'Look, Eve—'

'This top cost me an absolute fortune and not only did she wear it but she put it in the washing machine. The washing machine!' Eve shrieked. 'Wait till I get her.'

'That's enough!'

'I was going to wear that top tonight,' Eve continued heedlessly. 'How dare Victoria take it without asking me!'

'She must have asked you. She'd scarcely take it otherwise,' Liz pointed out. 'You've been going around with your head somewhere else, so you probably didn't hear her.'

'No way,' Eve bristled. 'Not in a million years would I have given her a loan of it. I was going to wear it tonight, I want to look my best.'

'I thought tonight was nothing special,' Liz eyed her.

'I might have known you'd take her side,' Eve fumed.

'God, I wish you'd realise how ridiculous you sound,' Liz finally snapped. 'I don't know what's got into you these past couple of months, or why you're sounding like a hormonally crazed teenager. I'll talk to you tonight.'

'I won't be home tonight,' Eve said on the spur of the moment. She stomped up the stairs to her room and fetched another clingy top to change into after work. She knew she was behaving ridiculously and she felt as though she was fourteen again, full of rioting emotions. But somehow she was unable to stem the black tide of anger that ceaselessly churned inside her.

She thumped down the stairs and as she opened the hall door, she remembered. She had worn the top last Sunday night. Too lazy to hand wash it during the week, she had flung it into the washing machine yesterday evening.

She slammed the hall door with a satisfying thunk.

* * *

'Can I get you another drink, Eve?'

'Don't tell me I'm empty already,' she giggled, lifting her glass and squinting inside. 'Oh look, no vodka for Eve,' she hiccuped.

'Are you okay?' Rachel looked at her quizzically. 'Take it easy.'

Eve eyed her belligerently. 'Are you counting my drinks or something?'

Rachel rolled her eyes. 'Don't be silly. You've been knocking back vodka like there's no tomorrow.'

'Tomorrow, tomorrow, you're only a day away,' Eve began to sing, completely out of tune.

'Stay quiet or you'll have us thrown out,' Rachel shushed her. 'At this hour on a Friday, we'll never get a seat in another pub.'

'I don't know why you're so worried,' Eve sulked. 'It's so packed and noisy that no one can hear me.'

The pub was jammed, music and laughter cascading around them in relentless waves. A gang from the office had started out in Grafton Street and had commenced a pub crawl, working their way down to Temple Bar. Pub by pub, their numbers had dwindled and now there were only four of them left – Eve, Rachel, Conor and Daniel. Rachel should have already gone home, she had said, but she wasn't leaving Eve at the mercy of herself.

'We haven't got enough room here anyway,' Eve grumbled. 'We should have stayed in the last pub.'

'I was perfectly comfortable. You were the one who wanted to leave,' Rachel pointed out.

'Was I?' Eve frowned. 'Why was that?'

'How am I supposed to know? Here comes Conor with your drink. Maybe you do need another one.' Rachel shook her head.

From the depths of Eve's fuddled brain, something began to emerge. She recalled a terrible urge to leave the earlier pub they had been in. Someone had come in, yes, that was it, someone who had reminded her of Alex. The same height, same dark hair, same look of cool authority. And she had felt suddenly bleak.

Was this going to be the story of her life? Looking for him everywhere she went, seeing reminders of him almost every day, feeling her heart clench and her mouth go dry when she caught sight of someone similar? She had gulped down her drink, picked up her jacket and suggested that they carry on down to a pub in Temple Bar.

Eve picked up her glass, forgetting it was empty. All of a sudden she felt stone-cold sober. As Conor returned from the bar with more drinks, Eve moved around the table into his empty seat.

'Now I'm right beside the man of the moment,' she giggled, sitting beside Daniel, rubbing her bare shoulder against his arm. Conor passed over her vodka and Red Bull and she drank half of it in one go.

* * *

Daniel shifted a little in his seat. Eve had been acting the flirt with him on and off during the evening. To anyone watching, it would have looked like she fancied him like mad, but by now he knew her only too well. It was all a game with Eve, and now she had just taken it one step further as she moved into the seat beside him and pressed her body against his. He knew it meant nothing. She was just building him up for another hollow let down, another hurried goodbye at the taxi rank.

He was glad he was leaving his job, glad he was getting away from her and his hopeless, stupid infatuation. Over the last few days as he had tidied his desk, he had been relieved to notice that he already felt a little differently about her, as though she already belonged to his past. Now, right up to the end, she was still toying with him, still trying to provoke him, but he let it all wash over him. He checked his watch. In another hour, they would all be heading home, the night over, and he would never see her again, he hoped.

So he thought he was hearing things when she leaned very close to him and asked him if she could stay the night.

'What?' he spluttered, almost choking on his pint.

'Don't look so shocked,' she said, putting her hand on his thigh. 'You've a place of your own, haven't you?'

'It's nothing much, just a tiny bed-sit,' he said.

'Is there enough room for two? I don't mind squashing into a single bed, all the better….' Her fingers were gently scratching against his thigh.

'I – I wasn't expecting this,' he stuttered, thankful that he hadn't had too much to drink. He tried to ignore the sliver of excitement that stirred inside him. Eve was obviously pissed. She didn't realise what she was saying.

'Don't you want me to stay?' she murmured.

'Oh yes, I do.' He squirmed at how eager he sounded and tried to recover his composure. 'It's just….'

'Just what?'

'Hey, you two, try and keep your hands off each other till afterwards,' Conor joked. Daniel sat up as though stung.

'I can't help it if I find Daniel very sexy, can I?' Eve said, her fingers continuing to trail against his thigh.

'Guess you're all set for the night,' Conor laughed.

'Are you feeling okay, Eve?' Rachel asked, concerned.

'Course I'm all right.'

Daniel felt like telling them that there was nothing to worry about, it was just Eve playing games. Even when she insisted on getting into a taxi with him, he thought she was just teasing him all the more.

She was so quiet on the journey home that he thought she had fallen asleep. Any minute now, he told himself, she'll wake up and demand to be brought straight home. She'll give him a quick peck on the cheek and say goodbye in her mocking tone of voice. The nearer the taxi got to Rathmines, the more he strengthened his resolve not to care when she finally woke up and cried abduction. He wondered if she would be too drunk to remember that it was she who had insisted on going back to his bed-sit. Then she surprised him by stirring against his shoulder and telling him that she liked his aftershave.

So she wasn't asleep after all.

And when they reached his bed-sit in Rathmines, she got out of the taxi with him.

He apologised for living on the second floor as he led the way up dimly lit stairs, convinced that she was about to turn and run. Even when he opened the door to his bed-sit and she followed him inside, he told himself that this was surely as far as it went. He went over to the tiny kitchen area and plugged in the kettle.

'What are you doing?' she asked.

'I'm making some coffee,' he said.

'Have you anything else to drink? Bud? Heineken?'

'Eve, d'you not think you've had enough to drink?'

'I'm not drunk, if that's what you think,' she pouted. She took off her jacket and threw it on the back of a chair. Then she went over to his bed.

'Eve,' he hesitated, torn between desire and anxiety, 'I'm not sure if this is a good idea.'

'Don't you want me to stay?'

'It might be best if you went home.'

'Daniel, don't be such a spoilsport,' she cooed as she opened her top and took it off. 'Don't you want me?'

'I do—' He tried in vain to look away from her lacy black bra and the twin curves of her breasts.

'Don't you find me attractive? Do you think I'm sexier than the girls in Cork?' she asked in a husky voice, trailing a crimson-tipped finger across the top of her breasts. 'Would you call making love to me a mistake?'

'God no,' he said, his voice suddenly thick with want. 'But I can't take advantage of you like this.'

'Take advantage? Don't be ridiculous,' she laughed. 'I'm not drunk, if that's what's worrying you. I know exactly what I'm doing.' She stood up and walked towards him and pulled off her bra. 'I'm spending the night with you. In your bed. One night only. No strings, okay?' She stood close to him and began to open the buttons of his shirt.

Daniel couldn't take his eyes off her breasts. She moved closer, opened his shirt, pushed her nipples against his chest and brushed her hand against the hardness in his groin.

'Eve.' He tried one more time, his voice hoarse. 'I'm afraid you might regret this in the morning.' He could barely get the words out and his hazel eyes clouded with desire.

She looked up at him and smiled. 'Are you afraid *you* might regret it in the morning?'

'No, how could I?' he lied, knowing even as he bent his head to those soft breasts and felt her hand on the zip of his trousers, his groin straining with excitement, that it would be worse than ever now and almost impossible to forget her.

* * *

It was late when Eve woke up the following morning. She lay cramped in Daniel's single bed and listened to the sound of traffic thrumming on the road outside. She was turned away from him, but she sensed him breathing beside her. And then she remembered.

The look on his face in the lamplight, a mixture

of excitement and nerves as he told her haltingly that he didn't have a whole lot of experience; his face when she encouraged him to take off the rest of her clothes; the way she felt suddenly warmed by the look of awe he gave her when she finally lay naked in his arms.

She told him not to worry, that she would show him everything.

Which she did.

And she remembered the tentative, almost solicitous feel of his hands and mouth on her body; the gratitude in his hazel eyes when he told her that he had always fancied her and that this was the best night of his life. As she lay quietly in the narrow bed and listened to the muted roar of Saturday morning traffic, she wondered what she had done.

Given him the best night of his life, of course, she told herself firmly, which was a helluva lot more than Alex Gallagher had ever given her.

Daniel made some coffee as she quickly dressed. 'I don't suppose....' he began hesitantly. His sandy hair was rumpled and he looked about sixteen.

'No, Daniel,' she said lightly as she gave him a peck on the cheek. 'No strings, remember?'

He smiled ruefully and her last view of him was the sight of his young, vulnerable face as he stood at the hall door and watched her taxi join the stream of traffic on the Rathmines road.

Chapter Twenty-eight

Paula's weekend in London started off quietly enough. Daisy, Alison and Joe met her at Heathrow on Friday evening and the four of them sat up drinking wine, eating pizza and exchanging family gossip until late. Daisy was content to sit quietly, laughing at some of Paula's escapades with her children.

It was after eleven when Paula came downstairs on Saturday morning.

'Uninterrupted sleep is a luxury I don't have too often,' she said when she eventually joined Daisy in the kitchen, 'never mind a long soak in the bath. It was so relaxing. Pure bliss!' She sighed contentedly.

'All set for some shopping?' Daisy asked.

'Of course! Lead the way! D'you know, you're

259

looking really terrific. I don't think I've ever seen you look as well.'

'I think London agrees with me,' Daisy smiled.

'What happened to the glasses?'

'I wear contacts most of the time now, especially since I'm not using a computer for work.'

'You look different, softer somehow. And I'd forgotten how slim you are, you lucky divil.' Paula shook her head. 'Did you get highlights in your hair?'

Daisy ran a hand through her spiky blond hair. 'This is just from the sun.'

'People pay a fortune to get that sunkissed look and you have it for free.'

They spent most of Saturday afternoon on Oxford Street, Paula diving in and out of shops, almost running under a bus as she dodged across the street, telling Daisy she could live happily ever after in Selfridges, she'd had no idea how immense it was. She was struggling with half a dozen carrier bags by the time she was finished.

* * *

Unexpectedly, Daisy had to work for a few hours that night as Helen had sprained her ankle, so it was decided that Paula, Joe and Alison would come into town and book a table in Dolan's.

'We can't have you slogging away all by yourself,' Paula said. 'We'll come and watch.'

'Thanks a bunch!'

'I promise I'll behave. No sending the soup back.'

'You wouldn't dare!'

Halfway through their meal, when Daisy pulled over a chair during her break and sat down for a quick chat, Paula admitted that the food was gorgeous.

'Those cheese fritters – mmm – and as for the sirloin, it just melted in the mouth.'

'Glad you enjoyed it,' Daisy smiled. 'Can I recommend the chocolate and Baileys mousse for afters?'

'I'm stuffed, but go on, it sounds delicious. It's really lovely here,' Paula approved. 'No wonder you look so happy. It's homely and relaxing. And a radical change from Cardinol.'

'That's the general idea,' Daisy grinned.

'Speaking of which….'

'Yes?' Daisy tensed and immediately chided herself.

'I've left,' Paula said airily. 'I'm starting a job in Ballymount after the summer holidays.'

'I thought you were happy in Cardinol.'

'I was, once upon a time.'

'What happened?'

'I got sick of looking at Sam Heffernan,' Paula admitted.

'What's he been up to now?' Daisy asked casually.

'Oh, nothing much,' Paula dismissed. 'I just got

261

sick of the sight of him, swaggering into the office every day, knowing how badly he treated you.'

'It's over and done with,' Daisy said, her eyes stony.

'You should never have let him get away with it,' Paula pointed out.

'I dunno,' Daisy sighed. 'Maybe I was partly to blame.'

'What? Are you mad? No way!' Paula gave her a thunderous look. 'Don't even go there. I much preferred it when you were angry. Now go back to your lovely food and forget all about your crazy notions!'

When she was finished serving for the night, Daisy joined them at the table for a few drinks. Then Kim joined in and Caroline said she couldn't possibly miss the party, so she produced a bottle of wine on the house, pulled over a chair and sat down as well. Daisy sat back, sipped her wine and watched her friends laughing and chatting in the mellow atmosphere.

She felt as though she had moved mountains since the last time she had seen Paula. Her life had changed forever, thanks to Marina's party. Changed for the better. This was her world now, the busy melting pot of London, the easy ambience of Dolan's Bar, her relative independence with Joe and Alison. No spending her working day in a veritable straitjacket or coming home to walk on eggshells around Marina.

Then she realised that Kim was talking to her. 'I didn't see Mr Sex on Legs in this evening, Daisy. I hope you haven't chased him away for good,' Kim said with a knowing glint in her eyes.

'What's this?' Paula jumped to attention.

Daisy shrugged and fervently wished that Kim had kept her mouth shut. 'It's nothing, Paula.'

'Nothing?' Kim shook her dark curls indignantly. 'Paula, he was the most fabulous man you can imagine and you should have seen the way he was looking at Daisy! Believe me, this guy chatting her up was seriously to die for.'

'Who is he? What's his name? Where did you meet?' Paula fired off a volley of questions.

'There's nothing much to tell,' Daisy said dismissively.

'You can at least explain what Kim is talking about. Have you gone out with him? What's he like in bed?'

'Paula! I scarcely know him. I just know his name is Alex.'

'Not bad,' Paula approved. 'Did you like the look of him?'

'I was only talking to him for a minute. But I'm not in the least bit interested.'

'What was your first impression?'

'I suppose he seemed okay.' Okay? She thought of his dark grey eyes, keen and intelligent. She remembered his friendly smile. And she had liked the sound of his voice…. 'He seems okay,' she elaborated. 'Considerate, I'd say, probably clever.'

'You've left out all the good bits,' Kim said wickedly. 'Magnetic, sexy, probably brilliant in bed… and on that note, I have to leave you and love you, girls. I have a hot date tonight, although he couldn't hold a candle to Alex.'

'But I don't understand.' Paula turned to Daisy when Kim had left. 'Why aren't you interested? He sounds great.'

'I'm having a break from men for the moment.'

'Don't be ridiculous,' Paula scoffed. 'Just because you had one bad experience with Heffernan doesn't mean you have to live like a nun.'

'I don't really want to get involved,' Daisy said. One bad experience? If only. Little did Paula know that Sam had been the latest in a long line of disasters.

'I'm disappointed in you, Daisy,' Paula ploughed on. She lifted the bottle of wine and drained it into Daisy's glass. 'I can't believe you'd turn down a man like Alex all because of that prick Heffernan.'

'Well, I doubt if he'll be around this way again.'

'Then Sam's having the last laugh. I wouldn't let that slimy bastard get the better of me. Anyway, come on. It's early yet. Let's get one more bottle of wine….'

* * *

Alex was delighted to see his sisters. The girls loved his apartment, taking over the spare bedroom and proclaiming it as theirs for whenever they needed it, and their lively company cheered him up. During the daytime they shopped and went sightseeing. He brought them out for meals in the evenings, delighted with their company, and his sisters told him off in no uncertain terms for working far too hard. They couldn't believe that they saw more of London in a weekend than he had seen in all the months he'd been living there.

Their visit flew by and all too soon it was Sunday evening and he was back out at Heathrow seeing them off. That was when he spotted her again. Ahead of him, up near the top of the straggling Aer Lingus queue, he caught sight of a tall girl with short blond hair. Then she turned sideways to talk to someone next to her and he knew for sure.

Daisy. Just when he had decided to put her out of his life, here she was turning up once more. He had stalked out of Dolan's the previous weekend feeling like a fool. This girl didn't want to have anything to do with him. For one reason or another, she had decided that he wasn't worth the effort of basic courtesy. That was her problem, he'd fumed.

And now, almost as though fate had decreed it, in the middle of the seething crowds in Heathrow she was standing ahead of him at the queue for the check-in desk, possibly the only woman in London who seemed to consider him some kind of monster.

The queue shuffled forward a little and he edged his sisters' cases along with his foot. Andrea and Aisling had left him holding their place in the queue while they went looking for some magazines. It dawned on him then, as he watched her approach the desk, that Daisy was possibly going back to Ireland. He felt an immediate pang of regret and wondered why all his critical faculties seemed to have deserted him where this girl was concerned. By the time Andrea and Aisling returned, complete with staple airline necessities of glossy magazines and bumper-sized chocolate bars, his mind was made up.

'Back in a minute, girls,' he winked at them before striding off. Daisy and her companion had finished checking in and were heading towards the boarding gate. He hurried through the crowds, slowing to a casual pace as he finally caught up with them.

'Why hello, we meet again,' he said.

Daisy stopped in her tracks. He couldn't help but notice the pink blush that crept across her face. Annoyance? Embarrassment? Was it possible that she was shy? He couldn't say. Her brown eyes were wary when they met his.

'Well, Daisy, aren't you going to introduce us?' her friend said, giving him a warm, appreciative glance. She seemed much happier to see him and he could have sworn that she leaned over and gave Daisy a gentle pinch.

'Perhaps I should introduce myself, as Daisy scarcely knows me,' he said, proffering his hand. 'Alex Gallagher.'

'I'm Paula McCullagh and this is my brother, Joe,' Paula said, shaking his hand firmly and indicating the man beside her.

'Daisy, why don't we say our goodbyes now, and you can talk to your friend?' Paula suggested. 'I need to get some goodies for my holy terrors and Joe will lead the way, won't you, Joe?'

'I thought you had plenty,' Daisy began.

'Not enough for my lot,' Paula laughed. She leaned over and hugged Daisy and Alex noticed that she whispered something into her ear, making Daisy look even more embarrassed.

'Right so, we're off,' Paula said cheerfully as Joe led her in the direction of the concourse shops.

* * *

'Don't run away, not this time,' Alex said.

He needn't have said anything because Daisy felt as though she couldn't move. The further away Paula walked with Joe and her trumped-up excuse of buying even more treats, the more vulnerable Daisy felt. Alex's grey eyes seemed to look right inside her. Her stomach felt fluttery and her mouth was dry.

'He's bloody gorgeous,' Paula had whispered in her ear. 'Forget about Heffernan and get a life!'

She wished she was wearing her armour-plated glasses. They would have been some kind of a defensive prop.

'First of all, I presume it's Paula who's heading off?' he asked.

'Yes, the eight o'clock flight,' Daisy found her voice.

'Good.' He looked happy with himself. 'That's the same flight as my sisters,' he went on. 'Speaking of the devils, here they come.' She watched as they approached, laughing and chatting, two tall, attractive, confident girls. 'Daisy, meet my sisters,' he said as they drew close, 'Andrea and Aisling.'

Daisy smiled and nodded.

'I'll be back in a sec,' Alex said. 'I just want to put them through the departure gates, make sure they go home!' They grinned at Daisy as Alex ushered them in the direction of the gate and they all threw their arms around each other, hugging one another closely. Finally Alex stood back and watched as they passed through the barrier, waving furiously at him.

Then he turned and walked back to Daisy.

Chapter Twenty-nine

'Have you ever been to the zoo?'

'The zoo?'

'You know, monkeys and elephants.'

'No, not for years.' Here they were, standing in the busiest airport terminal in the world, people streaming all around them, struggling with baggage, waving goodbye, hugging and kissing. The tannoy was loud and disembodied, the departure screens flickering with information. It was noisy and clamorous and Alex was standing in front of Daisy and calmly talking about the zoo. The same man she had walked away from in Dolan's, Dave's 'fine thing', Kim's 'brilliant in bed', Paula's 'bloody gorgeous'....

Alex smiled. He really was gorgeous. Daisy

noticed that his eyes crinkled attractively at the corners. Although she was tall, she had to tilt her head slightly to look up at him. One thing was for sure, he was way out of her league.

'Do I look as though I bite?' He seemed amused at her obvious scrutiny.

Daisy blushed. 'No, not at all.'

'I meant the London Zoo, of course. Have you ever been?'

'London Zoo? No,' she answered truthfully.

'My sisters were over with me for a few days and they raved about it,' he said.

She liked his voice. Kind of gravelly, with a crisp bite to it. Attractive and sexy, like the man himself.

Definitely way out of her league.

'They said I was mad not to have visited it before now,' he continued.

'Really.' She felt tongue tied and awkward and couldn't think of a better response.

'They've done more sightseeing in a few days than I've done in a few months. They gave me quite a rough time and told me I was working too hard.'

'Are you?'

'Yes, I suppose I am. I don't seem to have much free time. And you know what they say about all work.'

'Yes, I do,' she smiled.

He was wearing a light blue top, open at the neck, and she could see the taut column of his throat and the firm line of his jaw. She was startled to realise that there was something very attractive about his mouth. Her heart was pounding and she felt as though her skin was on fire, but Alex looked relaxed and happy, as though he had conversations like this every day of the week. Then she spotted Joe out of the corner of her eye, hovering uncertainly.

'I have to go now,' she said, feeling instantly relieved. 'Joe is waiting for me.' She nodded across the busy concourse.

Alex frowned. He wheeled around and stared over at Joe and then looked back at Daisy. She was completely unprepared for the look of disappointment that swept across his face. For a moment he seemed to be lost for words. 'I assumed that Joe was travelling with his sister,' Alex said, sounding tense. He raked long fingers through his tousled hair. 'I was obviously mistaken. I didn't realise… that you and he….'

'Oh, no,' Daisy said, feeling a little shocked at how important it was to explain. 'I stay with Joe and his wife. His wife Alison. I rent a room in their house….' Her voice trailed away as his eyes caught and held hers and somehow she couldn't look away. Then he suddenly relaxed and laughed.

'Daisy O'Neill, what will I do with you?' He shook his head and looked amused. 'Do I look like a monster?' he asked, changing tack out of the blue.

'No, of course not.'

'Do I look like I'm going to eat you for breakfast?'

'No….'

'Well then, will you come to the zoo with me some Sunday afternoon? I think it's about time I caught up with a bit of sightseeing. It wouldn't be much fun to go on my own, so I was wondering if you would care to join me?'

Sightseeing. The zoo for a couple of hours. Lions, tigers and elephants. No big deal, surely. Even though she was finished with men, the zoo on a Sunday afternoon wasn't really a date. In a voice that didn't seem to belong to her, Daisy heard herself saying yes.

'I'm glad that's settled,' Alex grinned. 'Would next Sunday suit?'

'Yes, I think so.'

'I'll collect you where?' He pulled out a pen and wrote her address and phone number on the back of a business card. 'That's not too far from my apartment,' he told her. 'I'll collect you around two o'clock?'

'That's fine.'

'Good.' He gave her another devastating grin and she almost changed her mind. 'In the meantime, off you go. Joe's been waiting patiently.' He tipped her lightly on the shoulder and she felt like she was on auto pilot as she moved through the busy crowds, meeting Joe near the exit doors.

272

Before she left the concourse she quickly glanced behind her, but she couldn't see Alex, even though she could still feel his eyes on her, still feel the imprint of his light touch on her shoulder.

* * *

Paula phoned her the minute she arrived back in Dublin.

'I haven't even unpacked yet,' her excited voice floated down the line. 'What happened with Mr Sexy?'

'Not much,' Daisy said.

'C'mon, Daisy. Don't let me down.'

'We're going to the zoo next Sunday.'

Paula squealed. 'He looks fabulous, you lucky thing. I bet he has a big fancy car. Those whiz kids have everything.'

Whiz kid? God, what was she letting herself in for? More grief? Hold on, it was only a trip to the zoo on a Sunday afternoon. Nothing major. And that's what she kept telling herself. There was no need to be nervous, no need to go rushing for the lavender scent or practise what she might say in advance. It was only an afternoon, just a few short hours. All week she was half expecting him to phone to say he couldn't make it, to tell her politely that something else had cropped up. She was half convinced that he would realise they were worlds apart and change his mind.

But he didn't.

* * *

Alex turned from the doorway. He had rung the bell twice and there was no sign of Daisy. Maybe she had changed her mind. Maybe he was mad to be pursuing her like this. Then the mahogany door opened as she stood in the doorway, tall and slender, dressed in lilac and cream and sunkissed hair, and he realised that no, he wasn't mad at all. He felt like taking her into his arms and slowly kissing away her vulnerable look, but that would have to wait for now, he decided. Daisy would surely bolt. Instead he smiled and asked her if she was ready. She smiled back and pulled the door closed behind her. He caught her light flowery scent as she joined him on the path and they walked down to his car.

She had trouble fixing her seatbelt and he had to lean over a little, his face so close to hers that he could see the fine sprinkling of freckles on her nose. He was only inches from that soft mouth. He noticed her eyes darkening slightly and he could have sworn that she flinched a little, so he drew back and started the engine.

'What do you normally do on a Sunday?' he asked casually as he put the Audi into gear and drove off.

'It depends,' she replied. 'Sometimes I go for a walk or out for lunch. Usually I have to catch up on some phone calls and laundry. Then every second Sunday I'm usually on the evening shift in Dolan's.'

'So you don't mind taking this afternoon off and

traipsing around the zoo with a confirmed work-aholic like me?'

'It makes for a change,' she said.

'I suppose it does,' he grinned. He was a change from phone calls and laundry. That was something new.

He slotted in a Coldplay CD and music filled the car as they journeyed through the London streets, heading off the A40 and out onto the Marylebone Road. He talked about the glorious weather and said he was happy to be taking an afternoon off and he sensed Daisy relaxing a little.

Something had obviously put that guardedness in her eyes, he reasoned, and had given her that slight air of hostility he had sensed at the outset. And it was nothing he had said or done, he realised. Otherwise she wouldn't be sitting here beside him as he drove towards the car park and the zoo.

* * *

Daisy put on her sunglasses. Not quite armour plating, but it was some modicum of defence. It was going to be fine. There were throngs of people out enjoying the sunny afternoon, all strolling around the grounds of the zoo. There were couples too, some entwined, others holding hands. The sun sparkled, filtering through the trees. A light breeze ruffled her hair and tickled her neck.

Alex was attractive in a pair of jeans and a short-sleeved white shirt. She noticed the way his casual hairstyle tipped at the collar of his shirt. She saw how his eyes crinkled attractively in the sunshine. She decided not to think about that. There was no need to concern herself with how sexy he looked. She was only his companion for the zoo. Nothing else.

'There's about five thousand animals in the zoo,' he said conversationally.

'That sounds like a lot,' she smiled.

'We may not get around to everything and I think we've already missed penguin feeding time,' he continued.

'That's too bad. I was really looking forward to that.'

It was easy then, as they strolled around, to make light conversation, to compare the antics of the flamingos and the pelicans, to joke about the spider monkeys and the chimpanzees and Daisy pretended to be scared as they watched the Asian lions.

'You don't fancy them?' Alex joked.

'Ugh. No way.' Daisy laughed and shook her head as they moved on.

'What about the reptile house? Want to have a look? Snakes? Alligators?'

'No thanks.' Daisy wrinkled her nose. 'They're a bit too slimy for me. I'll wait, though, if you want to have a look.'

'I don't really want to go in either, and anyway,

276

I wouldn't dream of abandoning you to the mercy of the animals,' he teased. He touched her lightly on the arm as he looked at her, an amused grin on his face, and she had the suddenly uncomfortable feeling that he could see right through the barrier of her sunglasses.

Alex bought ice cream and bottles of water and they went over to a bench under the shade of a tree and sat down. Alex chatted about his sisters, their recent visit and the amount of shopping and sightseeing they had fit into a few short days. 'Whirlwinds, they were.' He shook his head. 'Constantly on the go, packing every day with activities. Then they turned around and told me I was working too hard! I was certainly busy, I usually am, but I don't think even I could have covered half of London on foot the way they did!'

Daisy knew by the tone of his voice that he was very fond of his sisters. 'Will they be coming over again?' she asked.

'They both have summer jobs so I'm not sure if they'll manage another visit before they're back in college.'

'What are they studying?'

Alex told her that Andrea was going into the final year of a business and marketing degree and that Aisling was studying communications.

'Don't know why,' he joked. 'My sister has no trouble communicating. She could lecture on it herself, never mind study it!'

'They seemed very nice,' Daisy said, recalling the attractive girls she had seen at Heathrow, oozing with confidence, sure in the knowledge that the world was at their feet. 'Very good looking,' she added.

'It's a family trait,' Alex grinned. He looked suddenly boyish and mischievous and for a moment Daisy was tempted to give him a playful thump. She stopped herself just in time and took a large gulp of water to hide her confusion.

'C'mon,' Alex said, rising to his feet. He took careful aim and lobbed his empty bottle of water into a nearby bin. 'That's enough about my family. I don't want to spend the afternoon boring you completely. We still have time to visit the bugs.'

'The what?' Daisy frowned and stayed put.

'The giant anteaters… joke, joke,' he teased. 'I didn't really think that would interest you. Let's try the camels instead.' He held out his hand but Daisy pretended she didn't see it as she rose to her feet. They walked down the path towards the aviary, Alex with his hands now stuffed in the pockets of his jeans.

'I think that's it,' Alex said eventually when they arrived back at the point where they had started out from. 'I don't think there's many more animals lurking in the jungle. I think we've seen most of them.'

'Except for the snakes,' she said, a smile playing on her lips. She was surprised at herself. Was she teasing him? Flirting with sex-on-legs Alex Gallagher?

'We can always go back, if you like,' he suggested.

'No thanks.' She smiled and shook her head and turned towards the exit.

It seemed a pity to leave Regent's Park bathed in August afternoon sunshine all the same. It would have been lovely to take a stroll down by the lake with Alex… Daisy's thoughts ran away unchecked until she firmly reined them in.

Alex led the way over to his Audi. 'I like to keep my promises,' he said. 'I told you a couple of hours and then home, didn't I?'

'Yes, you did,' Daisy smiled, keeping step with him. It was almost as though he could read her mind, she thought, as though he, too, regretted leaving the dazzling park and the warmth of the London summer sun and the endless blue skies.

Who was she kidding? No doubt he had a date on for tonight with someone glamorous. The likes of Alex would always be in demand. Even if he worked long hours, his social life was bound to be exciting and every bit as hectic as his career.

They drove home with the windows zapped down completely, the breeze running through Daisy's blond hair, ruffling it at the edges.

'Thanks for a lovely—' she began.

'What about next Sunday?' he asked at the same time.

'Next Sunday?' she faltered.

'I have a lot of catching up to do,' he smiled. 'My sisters have given me a long list of places I have to see. And it beats spending a Sunday afternoon chained to my laptop. Have you done much sight-seeing yourself?'

'I've been around a bit.' Her hand went auto-matically to her sunglasses. Her heart was beating somewhere in her throat.

'Perhaps you could show me around London a little? Sorry,' he gave a half laugh. 'I shouldn't be trying to monopolise your Sunday afternoons. I'm sure you've plenty of better things to do.'

Sure she had – laundry and phone calls and walks in the park. What could possibly be more exciting?

'I'm just a workaholic who's trying to reform by taking a couple of hours away from the laptop at the weekend,' he continued. 'It would be nice to have some company.'

'Maybe.' She bit her lip.

'Believe me, my staff would thank you for it. They think I'm turning into a proper slave driver.'

'Yeah, well….'

'Good. How about two o'clock next Sunday?' he suggested. 'I'll leave the car and collect you in a cab,' he went on. 'That way we won't have to worry about parking.' He gave her a friendly grin as she picked up her bag, opened the passenger door and smiled goodbye.

Chapter Thirty

Rachel's prayers were answered. The sixteenth of September was a lovely Indian summer day. An early morning haze persisted until midday, then dispersed so that by one o'clock the sun was gleaming in a flawlessly blue sky.

'After weeks of dull weather, this has to be a miracle,' Rachel's father said over and over.

You'd think he was personally responsible for the good weather, Eve huffed. And not just the weather, but the entire wedding. She had arrived at Rachel's thronged family home to find him already dressed and strutting about the busy house as proud as a peacock in his wedding finery. 'The best day of my life,' he said, his voice progressively louder and louder as he splashed generous measures of spirits and handed them around. Pompous ass, Eve decided crossly as she escaped upstairs to get dressed.

She was just jealous, she admitted to herself as she watched Rachel having her make-up professionally applied while her mother fluttered about, full of tiny anxieties – jealous of all the fuss being made as Rachel was transformed into a beautiful bride.

Eve tried to squash her envy as she lifted her bridesmaid dress off the hanger. She was glad that the wedding day had finally arrived. Okay, she would have the next few hours to get through and when Rachel returned from honeymoon she would have the post-mortem to contend with. And last but not least, the photographs and video to drool over and admire.

But after that, Eve fervently hoped life would get back to normal. There would be an end to wedding talk. Rachel would come into work each day much as usual and go home to the apartment she shared with John. All the planning, the excitement, the anticipation would be over.

And some hidden, nameless anger deep in Eve's heart might quieten.

She had got disgustingly drunk at the hen party. It wasn't so much a hen party as a hen weekend. A gang of them from the office and some of Rachel's cousins had gone down to Limerick on the Friday evening, returning home on Sunday afternoon. They had organised a minibus to ferry them down and back. Eve remembered driving down the N7 in the drizzly rain, stopping for something to eat in Portlaoise, then hitting Limerick town as dusk was falling. After that she remembered precious little else, except on the way home when Katie had to ask the long-suffering minibus driver to pull onto the hard shoulder outside Nenagh so that Eve could get sick by the side of the road.

'Eve, it's time to go.' Rachel's voice was quietly excited.

'Rachel, you look absolutely stunning,' Eve said with genuine emotion. Her friend was dressed in a pale ivory sheath, beautiful in its simplicity, her hair caught up and studded with tiny fresh flowers. She carried a matching sheaf of flowers on her arm. Her green eyes were shining with happiness and she took Eve's breath away.

'I can't believe it's finally happening,' Rachel's voice trembled. 'You don't think – oh Eve, you don't think anything could go wrong at the last minute, do you?'

'Stop worrying,' Eve told her, putting a reassuring hand on her arm.

Rachel smiled at Eve. 'I'm so happy you agreed to be my bridesmaid.'

'Why wouldn't I be your bridesmaid?' Eve said. 'The very least I can do is make sure you get up that aisle in one piece.' She would have to put her jealousy on ice for now, she decided firmly. This was Rachel's day. There would be plenty of time afterwards for Eve to cry into her pillow.

'You look lovely in that dress,' Rachel said. 'No candy floss dress for my bridesmaid.'

Eve ran her hand across the skirt of her lilac damask dress. There was a thigh-high slit in the long, pencil-slim skirt and a fitted bodice just modest enough to cover her curvy breasts; Eve felt she was acceptably dressed. She had objected vehemently to the large bow embellishing the back of the dress and Rachel had immediately offered to have it removed. Eve's dark hair was styled in its usual smooth, silky bob, a small arrangement of fresh flowers secured on top.

Clutching her dainty bouquet, Eve went out past hordes of admiring neighbours into the bright September sun. There were more neighbours spilling out on the pavement and a large limousine drawn up against the kerb. Eve climbed into the limousine and waited for Rachel's mother to join her.

She shouldn't begrudge Rachel her happiness, Eve told herself sternly. She would have to pull herself together, put a huge smile on her face and look as though she was perfectly happy to be the bridesmaid.

Eve had never thought of herself as sentimental, but the sight of Rachel gliding up the aisle on her proud father's arm brought a lump to her throat. John and his brother Robert, the best man, waited patiently at the foot of the altar, immaculately turned out in charcoal grey suits.

The ceremony proceeded without a hitch, the priest happy and relaxed, putting Rachel at ease. Long afterwards, Eve still remembered the quiet, intimate smiles that Rachel had shared with John, the scent of the flowers, the evocative singing and the sudden, unexpected prickle of tears at the back of her eyes as Rachel and John promised to love each other for the rest of their lives.

As hard as she tried to hold her envy in check, Eve couldn't help feeling it spill over as the day advanced. It was strange playing second fiddle to a luminous, happy Rachel, watching her friend at the centre of everyone's attention and, what's more, enjoying every minute of it. Rachel flirted unashamedly with the photographer and flitted around groups of wedding guests, laughing and joking. She graciously accepted the congratulations of the hotel manager when she and John arrived at the reception and was quite the assured bride when she asked to see the beautifully decorated dining room for a final check. When the wedding guests were all finally assembled inside and it was time for the meal, she and John made a triumphant entrance, Rachel's head held high as they took their places at the head table.

Gone was the bundle of nerves that had turned to Eve in the bedroom just a few hours previously, worrying in case something went wrong. If there were any minor hitches, Rachel dismissed them with a laugh. Of course, it helped that she had

John's ring on her finger, Eve realised as she watched them laughing together over a private joke. And it also helped that he had quietly declared his love for her in front of a hundred or so wedding guests.

'You look like you're enjoying yourself,' she said to Rachel as they waited for the soup dishes to be cleared.

'I can't describe how I feel today, Eve,' Rachel said, her eyes alight with happiness. 'It's just brilliant. Everyone should get married and have a wedding day like this!'

'It helps if you're in love,' Eve said dryly, picking up her abandoned bread roll and absently chewing on it.

'Of course,' Rachel giggled. 'And someone has to love you enough to want to marry you.'

'That stands to reason.'

'Don't worry, Eve, your time will come,' Rachel smiled. 'Sooner or later you'll get fed up with meaningless relationships and you'll fall in love!'

Eve felt a momentary flash of anger with Rachel and her condescending advice. Just because all was well in her little world, she was suddenly the expert. She hadn't a clue, of course, that Eve was already fed up with meaningless relationships and her aimless social life. She was glad when the meal was over and the band arrived to set up their equipment. The wedding was half over and she wouldn't be on show for much longer, so she could relax a little. Not that she wanted to get drunk. She was going to behave herself tonight. A crowd from work was arriving for the afters and she was fed up being gossip fodder for the Foley Financials gang.

But when John swung Rachel out onto the floor for the first dance of the evening, Eve thought her heart was going to burst. Her thoughts had raced automatically to Alex and the ill-fated night she had tried to seduce him with the sound of Robbie Williams on the stereo. Through a mist of pain, she noticed Robert, the best man, heading in her direction and she knew that in keeping with wedding protocol he was going to ask her to join the happy couple on the floor. She forced yet another smile onto her frozen face, promising herself that this was her last bridesmaid duty. When the ordeal was over she smiled her thanks and made her way outside to the terrace.

The evening air was cool and redolent with scents drifting up from various shrubs and bushes. She could hear the noise of the band and shrieks of laughter above the babble of conversation. In the western sky, the sun was sliding behind a drift of clouds.

'Hi, Eve.'

'Daniel! You startled me!'

'Sorry, I've just arrived and, well, I saw you heading out for some fresh air, so I followed you.'

'Are the evening crowd here already?'

'No, not yet. Guess I got here a bit too soon.'

She had completely forgotten that Daniel had been invited to the afters of the wedding along with the gang from Foley's. She hadn't seen him since the night they had spent together. Now it looked like she would have to put up with his glances of adoration for the rest of the evening.

Although maybe that might not be so bad after all, she suddenly realised, remembering the touch of his hands and the way he had made her feel. She remembered, too, how poignantly grateful he had been. She could do with some more of that, some more balm on her wounded soul.

'So what? All the better if you're early,' she grinned as she began to walk down the terrace and he fell into step beside her. 'How's the new job?'

'It's going great, Eve. I'm really enjoying it,' he answered.

'We miss you in the office,' she told him.

'I'm sure you do, all right!'

'We do, really. Foley's hasn't been the same.'

'I have to say, I was glad of the chance to get out.'

'Were you?'

'Yeah.' He looked away, then turned back to her and gave her a lopsided grin. 'I made a right fool of myself with you, didn't I?'

'I don't know what you mean.'

'Come on, it was perfectly obvious what you thought of me. I was better off getting away from all that.'

Could this be Daniel talking, with his puppy dog adoring face and his tentative hands? Eve felt chilly all of a sudden.

'Sorry, Daniel, I don't understand.'

He stopped then and turned to face her, and she saw him clearly in the light spilling out onto the terrace from the hotel window. He was wearing a casual light grey suit and a black shirt open at the neck. His sandy hair was spiked with gel and his hazel eyes were full of something she couldn't really fathom.

'I was mad about you, you know that.'

'Was?'

'Was, is, who cares?' he shrugged. 'It was obvious, though, that you only saw me as a bit of diversion, someone to tease and mess with on boring days in Foley's.'

He was so close to the mark that she felt stung.

'That's not true—' she began.

He shook his head. 'Forget it. I feel as though I've moved on from all that.'

'And what about the night we spent together? Are you going to tell me it was a mistake?' she shot out.

'A mistake? God, no, Eve. That was… a special night for me. I'm still trying to figure out if you were drunk, or if you were just using me. But whatever it was, idiot that I am, I'll never forget that night. You looked beautiful. You still look beautiful tonight.'

'We could have more of those kinds of nights,' she smiled at him, feeling a peculiar ache in her tummy. Other wedding guests strolled out onto the terrace and an echo of laughter floated across the air, so they were no longer alone.

'Thanks but no thanks. I've been doing my best to forget you these last few weeks and I couldn't go back to square one again.'

She suddenly remembered the defenceless look on his face the morning she had walked out of his bed-sit. 'I guess that's it, then, isn't it? Time to go back to the party,' she said as she smiled at him mockingly. She turned and swept back up along the path, her high heels clicking on the flagstones.

The music and dancing were in full swing. Evening guests had arrived and platters of sandwiches and cocktail sausages were being handed around. The gang from Foleys had all arrived and had commandeered two of the tables. Katie and Susan were there along with Ronan and Conor, and Eve sat down beside them.

'Where were you?' Katie demanded. 'I wanted to get a photo of you with Rachel.'

'I just went out for some air,' Eve explained. She saw Daniel coming in from the terrace and he joined the group at the next table, sitting down beside Lucy, one of the girls from the accounts department.

Rachel whirled by their table in the arms of her father.

'She's in great demand on the dance floor,' Susan said. 'Isn't she absolutely gorgeous? She certainly trimmed down to fit into that fabulous dress. I wish I had half her willpower.'

Funny to think of Rachel having willpower, Eve thought, watching Rachel throw back her head and laugh at something her father said. It wasn't something she would have associated with her unassertive friend. Up till now, that is, she corrected herself.

'And get a look at John,' Katie said. 'He never struck me as the handsome type, but he looks downright sexy in that suit. Rachel's doing all right for herself. You're not looking too bad yourself, Eve. Nice dress.' Katie gave Eve a patronising glance.

'Thanks,' Eve answered curtly. She was already fed up with her dress. She felt as though she had been wearing it forever. When she saw the others all glammed up in slinky black, spaghetti-strapped, cleavage-revealing concoctions, she felt decidedly dull. She should have brought a change of clothes. She would have given anything to wipe that look off Katie's face. She downed a couple of vodkas in quick succession, despite her resolve to go easy on the booze. The others chatted away but she let the conversation flow over her head, not inclined to join in.

'C'mon Eve.' Conor was beside her. 'If I can't get a dance with the bride, maybe the bridesmaid will give me a twirl.'

'Thanks, Conor,' Eve smarted, rising to her feet. 'Sorry you're stuck with the leftovers.'

'Sometimes the leftovers can be very tasty,' he said, grinning at her as they went out onto the dance floor. The band was playing a Westlife ballad. Conor wasn't bad, she supposed, if you liked them tall and gangly. Not her type, though.

'Didn't think I'd see Daniel here tonight,' he said.

'Why not?'

'I thought he'd want to avoid you,' Conor teased.

'That's ridiculous. He's hardly afraid of me.'

'No, I think he was more afraid of himself. But what d'you know, he managed to turn up. And he looks as though he's enjoying himself.'

'You know how it goes,' Eve said. 'You move on, new people, new places.' She lifted her chin, making herself believe, at that moment in time, every word she said.

'Yeah, right. Daniel didn't waste any time.' Conor jerked his head and motioned to where Daniel was up on the floor with Lucy. Arms wrapped around each other, they moved slowly together and when the song came to an end, Daniel bent his head and kissed her.

As soon as there was a break in the music, Eve stalked out to the ladies room and chatted to Rachel's mum, looking as though she hadn't got a care in the world, and returned to the reception room just in time to see Daniel and Lucy slip out onto the terrace. Good riddance, she decided, knocking back her vodka. She was just going to get very quietly drunk and to hell with everyone else.

Chapter Thirty-one

A couple of weeks later, Daisy found herself in Harrod's trying on a pair of pale pink jeans and a sleeveless white top. She examined her reflection and wondered what Alex would think. Then she stared at her face, her brown eyes suddenly bright, her cheeks slightly flushed.

Since when had she ever dressed up for a man?

But Alex was different. She was really enjoying her Sunday afternoons, meeting him and chatting about her week and the comings and goings in Dolan's. She liked his friendly, undemanding company, the way he made her laugh and the way his grey eyes softened whenever he smiled at her. So far, they had been to the Tate Modern and Madame Tussauds. They had spent an afternoon strolling around Covent Garden and last Sunday they had travelled around on an open-topped bus. Even though it began to rain and they had to share Daisy's umbrella, they spent most of the journey sitting at the back of the bus, joking and laughing.

'I feel as though I'm a teenager again, on a school tour,' Alex had said. 'Only this is far more enjoyable.' He didn't look far off a teenager, she'd realised as they sat close under the umbrella. He looked youthful and almost mischievous with a roguish grin on his face.

Calm down, she admonished herself as she stood in front of the mirror in Harrod's and remembered that grin. She was only a Sunday afternoon diversion. She didn't have to worry about how stunningly attractive – correction, how downright sexy – he was. It was beyond the scope of their easy friendship. After all, he was way out of her league, remember? Besides which, he was bound to have loads of sexy girlfriends with whom he romanced away the night-time hours.

* * *

The Sunday afternoon they went to see Buckingham Palace, they approached it from the direction of St James's Park.

'The views from the lake are lovely,' Daisy said as they got out of the cab at the pedestrian lights on Birdcage Walk. 'And the park itself is worth a look.'

'Lead on, you're the boss,' Alex smiled.

Daisy looked at him out of the corner of her eye and grinned. He looked great, and she knew she looked good in her new jeans and top. Hand in hand they strolled down a path that cut through the park. It was a warm afternoon towards the end of September and the sun was high in a cloudless blue sky.

'There's a bridge further up that we can cross,' she said, feeling suddenly light hearted and happy, as though the afternoon was bursting with promise. She led the way and Alex followed, and standing on the bridge over the lake in St James's Park, they had their first view of the palace. They stood side by side, leaning against the white railings as the lake waters rippled beneath them and Daisy could feel the heat of Alex's arm against hers. Birds wheeled and flapped lazily in the air. Behind them someone was feeding the ducks and she could hear children's excited cries and the cackle of the ducks. Up before them, parkland trees drowsed on lawns that swept down to the water's edge, and further along, beyond a row of glistening fountains where sun-drenched spray glittered in the afternoon, the white façade of the palace shimmered in the sunshine.

'Lovely, isn't it?' she said, turning to face him, forgetting how close they were standing, so close that she could see herself reflected in his dark eyes.

'Yes, it's really beautiful,' Alex agreed, but she

felt disconcerted when she realised that he was looking steadily at her and not the view.

'I was born in London, you know,' she blurted in an effort to distract him. She was immediately sorry she had spoken. Up to now, she had deliberately steered clear of the subject of families with Alex, and beyond his occasional reference to his sisters, it had never come up for discussion.

'Are your parents English?' he asked.

Daisy smiled ruefully. Here goes. 'I never knew my father,' she admitted. That was easy enough. She had spent the best part of her life getting used to various reactions. There was no point in adding that she had recently discovered he had done a runner when she was a baby.

He shot her a look of concern, but his voice when he spoke was calm and matter of fact. 'Is that so?'

'Just one of those things,' she shrugged.

'And what about your mother?'

Daisy looked away. Marina still stubbornly and hurtfully refused to acknowledge her existence. So in this different world, with the new Daisy O'Neill, it was far easier to act in turn as if Marina, and the ghosts of the past, didn't exist. She couldn't possibly go there, she couldn't dim the glorious sunlight of this moment or blur the incandescent beauty of the park. And she couldn't lose the warm layers of the afternoon that held her in thrall. So she turned to Alex and told him in a small voice that her mother was dead.

'Do you want to talk about it?' he asked, his eyes full of solicitude.

'No,' she answered curtly. She was horrified with herself, belatedly realising exactly what she had done, but knowing in that split second that she couldn't possibly take it back, couldn't possibly explain. So she blanked it out of her mind and focused on Alex by her side, the warm sunshine, the children's laughter, the glittering lake and the lazy patterns made by the circling birds.

This, now, was her life at the present moment.

Afterwards they sat on a wooden bench under the sweep of trees and he kissed her and held her close. His mouth was tender, his hand on the curve of her face was a warmth she welcomed and the touch of his lips reached a place inside her that somehow made everything feel all right.

* * *

'And how's the great romance?' Paula asked.

'It's not a great romance,' Daisy objected.

'You sound out of breath. Is he there now?' Paula lowered her voice. 'Were you having a passionate snog?'

'Don't be daft! I had to rush to answer the phone. Right now I'm standing with a towel around my shoulders and globs of conditioner in my hair.'

'Getting yourself glammed up?' Paula teased.

'No. Anyway, I only see Alex on Sunday afternoons. It's nothing special. Just a couple of hours away from his laptop.'

'Nothing special? C'mon, Daisy, you must have seen the whole of London two or three times by now.'

'Not quite.'

'Well, it's more than a couple of hours away from a laptop. Is that really what he told you?'

'It's one of the reasons,' Daisy admitted.

'Ah ha! I can guess the rest. But what's going to happen when winter arrives? Where are you going to bring sexy Alex when the weather is cold and damp? Let me make a suggestion….'

'I won't be bringing him anywhere,' Daisy said firmly. 'I'll definitely be finished with my tour guide duties by then. And I'm sure Alex has loads of equally sexy girlfriends who'll be only too delighted to keep him occupied during the winter!'

Daisy rinsed her hair, watching the suds swirl down through the plughole and feeling the spray of warm water on her head. In her bedroom, she switched on the hairdryer and began to dry her hair, directing the heat away from the roots like the hairdresser had shown her. She was letting her hair grow a little, the style still layered but longer and more feathery around her face. And even though it was early October, her sunkissed highlights were as blond as ever.

Alex had said her hair was lovely the day they

were in St James's Park. The day she had told him her mother was dead.

What the hell had possessed her to come out with such a blatant lie? She had thought about it over and over afterwards, trying to recall exactly how she had felt. She remembered the beauty of the park, sunlight dancing on the rippling lake, the green sweep of the lawns, the overhanging trees drenched in sunshine. The quiet presence of Alex by her side as they leaned over the railings, the feel of his arm against hers. She had felt suddenly enclosed in a warm, peaceful calm unlike anything she had ever known before. Then he had mentioned her mother and it had seemed easier to let the lie slip out rather than try to explain. After all, Marina and the shadows of the past had no place in that magical, shimmery afternoon.

They had no place in her life right now.

Chapter Thirty-two

Eve was in her element. Versace, Chanel, Gucci, Karen Millen, all practically within a stone's throw of each other. What more could a serious shopper want? All this, and Alex too. Heaven on earth. She just couldn't understand why she hadn't come to London sooner.

Months after he had walked out of her life, Eve still found herself thinking of Alex at odd times throughout the day. She still searched for him in city centre pubs and nightclubs with a hopeful heart. One sunny autumn day when she was alone at her workstation, she had even gone so far as to phone Citimex in a fit of desperation, just hoping against hope that she might hear his voice. She had been informed by the plummy tones of the receptionist that he was currently working over in the London branch.

She had replaced the receiver with a hammering heart, and looking out the window at the riot of autumnal colour on St Stephen's Green, she wondered if life would ever go back to the way it had been before Alex. And then she had thought of a weekend in London. Katie and Susan had been only too pleased to go along with her. It was one of her better ideas, they agreed, a weekend in the Mecca for shoppers.

'We can shop till we drop and then hit the nightclubs!' Eve had brightly suggested.

'Yeah, it's about time we did something different and got away from the Dublin scene,' Katie agreed.

'You can count me in,' Susan said.

So they had brought their weekend cases into Foley's on the Friday and made a pretence at work all day, much to the annoyance of everyone else on the third floor. They had got a taxi out to Dublin Airport on Friday evening, flown to Heathrow, checked into their hotel and sat drinking in an English bar until Susan reminded them that they needed their energy for the next day's shopping. Now it was Saturday afternoon and they were sitting at a sushi bar in Soho with a mass of shopping bags sprawled at their feet and Eve had lost count of the number of her credit card transactions. Who cared? She was having a ball.

On top of all that, Alex was here, somewhere in

the middle of this vibrant city. Maybe he had strolled along these streets, ducked in for coffee here or here, perhaps he had got off the Tube at Knightsbridge and taken the exit for Brompton Road. Perhaps he had sat eating sushi here…. In the bar last night, all glass-backed shelves and huge, squashy couches, she'd had to forcibly remind herself that the odds were one in a million that he might just happen to drop in. But even the thought that he was here somewhere, that she was walking streets where he might have walked, was enough to infuse everything with a magical aura.

'Hey girls, what are we doing for food this evening?' she asked, suddenly recalling a conversation she'd had with her mother earlier that week.

'Who said anything about wasting money on food?' Katie retorted. 'I'm more interested in the night life.'

'Yeah, but we'll have to eat at some stage… and the thing is,' Eve pulled a face, 'I'm half supposed to be meeting up with my cousin.'

'What cousin?'

'She's over here for a while, working in a restaurant or something, and you know what mothers are like. Mine thinks it would be a great idea for us to get together. But if Daisy's working tonight, all the better.'

'Don't you want to see her? Maybe she could show us around.'

'I somehow doubt very much if Daisy is clued in

303

to anything decent in the London scene. Just let me make a phone call,' Eve said, pulling out her mobile.

Daisy answered immediately. Eve in London? Yes, unfortunately, she happened to be working that evening. Yes, she supposed if they were looking for somewhere to eat, the Irish bar where she worked served lovely food and was right in the centre of everything. There might be a table free in the early part of the night and they could all say hello.

'You'd have to vacate the table by nine o'clock,' Daisy told her.

'So early?' Eve cooed. 'I'm only joking, Daisy. That's perfect. It gives us plenty of drinking time. Now tell me exactly how to get there.'

Eve frowned as she broke the connection.

'Well? Are we sorted?' Katie asked.

'Yeah. We can have something to eat and say hello to my cousin all at once....' Her voice trailed away.

'Is there a problem?'

'No... it's just that my cousin sounded different.'

'In what way?'

'Dunno, really.'

She not only sounded different, she looked different, Eve acknowledged as later that evening they sat at a table by the window, enjoying pan-roasted fillet of salmon and a bottle of Chilean Sauvignon Blanc. She watched Daisy jot down orders, carry plates heaped with food and smile and joke with customers. She even popped the cork on a bottle of champagne and poured snipes with an easy confidence.

Her blond hair was slightly longer and softer about her face and she had ditched the prim and proper glasses. But it was more than just that. She looked less uptight, even relaxed, almost as though she was at home in these surroundings and happy and casual in a way that Eve had never seen her before.

'What happened to you?' she asked when Daisy took a quick break to talk to her.

'What do you mean?'

'You look different or something.'

'Do I?'

Eve narrowed her blue eyes speculatively and took a sip of her wine. 'Who is he?'

'Who's who?'

'C'mon, Daisy, you're looking terrific. There has to be a man in your life,' she stated.

Daisy's smile was offhand. 'Not necessarily. But I have some friends, I suppose.'

'Male?'

'Perhaps.'

'Aren't you going to elaborate?'

Daisy shrugged. 'There's nothing much to tell.'

'You can trust me, I'm very good at keeping secrets,' Eve said, injecting her words with meaning.

Daisy didn't appear to be the least bit fazed. 'No doubt you are,' she said calmly. 'But I don't have any secrets to share, Eve.'

'Really?' Eve raised her eyebrows.

'Really.'

Her cousin certainly wasn't giving anything away. Eve went on, 'You seem to have settled in over here very well.'

'Yes, I have.'

'Of course, you were born in London, weren't you?'

'That's right.' Daisy's face was bland.

'It must be like your second home. Does Marina mind you being over here? Somehow or other, I can't imagine her ever coming to visit.' She thought she finally saw a reaction, just a flicker of anxiety in Daisy's eyes, but it was rapidly extinguished.

'No, Marina hasn't come to visit,' Daisy said smoothly, avoiding the question.

'Probably not. After all, whatever about you, she'd scarcely have great memories of London, would she?' Eve laughed carelessly. Daisy's face was deadpan. 'No worries. I'm more interested in what happened to you in the last few months. Because if she did manage to make it over, she'd scarcely recognise you. Would you get many Irish in a place like this?' Eve innocently tossed, and unless she was very much mistaken, her cousin's face went slightly pink.

'Yes, of course you would.'

'So he's Irish, is he?'

'I never said that.'

'You don't have to say anything, Daisy,' Eve laughed. 'I know by your face. I hope he behaves himself, or as Marina would say, I trust you're looking after yourself.'

They left the restaurant by nine o'clock. Daisy was busy at a table and just said a quick goodbye. As she clattered down the staircase en route to a night out in London, Eve couldn't help but be intrigued. Not only had Daisy looked happy, but she looked good in a way Eve had never noticed before. She would almost go so far as to say that Daisy looked pretty.

Definitely a man.

Chapter Thirty-three

Daisy struggles for breath. She knows she's in the grip of the nightmare. This time it's worse than ever, and the crashing sound is so loud that it frightens her. She feels an all-consuming terror and her heart is thudding so hard that she thinks it's going to burst.

Even in her sleep she tries to make sense of it before the nightmare turns the corner and mockingly evaporates. She sees herself looking down at her dress, as one drop, then two, then a quick succession of drops fall darkly onto the material, so rapidly that the drops join and spread. Her finger traces the ever-widening pattern, and when she lifts her hand to her face she catches the heavy smell.

She hears someone scream, but she doesn't know where it's coming from. The little girl dressed in white is dancing right in front of her, smiling as though she's very happy, but when Daisy tries to follow her, she disappears from sight. Even though she senses she can't be very far away, Daisy feels abandoned and desolate. She hears the sound of glass smashing, catches sight of Liz's anxious face and then she sees a baby being lifted into the air. Someone tries to pull her up but she struggles and kicks out because she is afraid.

Daisy awakes with a strangled sob. She leaves the lamp burning until dawn's welcoming brightness breaks against the curtains.

Chapter Thirty-four

She had thought her life had changed forever, but that had been a silly misconception. For the past was here, it was all around her, and more potent than ever before. It was the second time she'd had the nightmare this week, waking in the middle of the night frightened out of her wits. Although she put it off for as long as possible, eventually she had to ask, had to find out, had to know if there was any reason why occasional nightmares in Dublin had followed her across the Irish Sea. And not only had they followed her, but they were clearer, sharper, more focused and more frightening.

'Liz?'

'Hi, Daisy, everything going well over in London? I must say, Eve thought you were looking great.'

'Everything's fine. How's Mum?'

'She's okay, so don't be worrying.'

'She still won't talk whenever I phone.'

'She'll come around in time when she gets used to the idea, I promise.'

'God, Liz, how long is that going to take? Or is she still pretending that I don't exist any more?' Daisy's voice hardened.

'I know it's difficult for you, but let's just say I'm working on it.'

'It doesn't matter,' Daisy sighed. 'I phoned to ask you something about London.'

'Oh? Have you done anything about looking for…?'

'No, not yet,' Daisy said quickly. 'I kind of left all that to one side for now.'

'That's no harm. You don't have to do anything, just for the sake of it.'

'I'll see. I was just wondering, well, did anything in particular happen when I was over here years ago?'

'Like what?'

'That's the thing, I don't know. That's why I'm asking you.'

'Sorry, Daisy, I can't really help you out there. What do you mean, exactly? What do you think might have happened?'

'Nothing. I'm not sure… don't mind me.' Was she imagining it, or had Liz's voice sounded strained? She told herself to forget all about it as she put the phone down. Her nightmares had started again just after Eve's unsettling visit. She didn't have a clue what they meant, beyond leaving her with a feeling of terror and desolation. If there was anything she needed to know, Liz would surely have told her. But in one sense, she didn't want to know.

Life was opening up for her now in a way she had never thought possible. She had found a new side to herself when she had come to London, away from Dublin and Marina. And now she was too busy enjoying her new life, her job in Dolan's and her friendship with Alex.

She certainly hadn't wanted to hear from Eve, much less set eyes on her, stalking back into her life, strolling into Dolan's with her blue eyes full of amused speculation, shooting ripples of unease across the smooth surface of her new existence. Filling her with reminders of everything she had left behind. She shouldn't have to be haunted by the fact that her father had abandoned her, or alarmed by the fact that Marina couldn't bear to discuss it or that now she couldn't even acknowledge Daisy's existence. No thanks. The past was in the past and she didn't want to visit it any more. She didn't want to give it any breathing space in her mind.

But then, as though it was determined to leap up and grab her attention, Alex suggested a trip to London Bridge.

* * *

'The bridge?'

'Don't look so nervous, I'm not dragging you to the dungeons in the Tower.'

'I hope not,' she faked a smile.

London Bridge, a place she had deliberately avoided. But perhaps it would be as well to get it over with and test the water, so to speak, see how she felt when she was up close. And if she went with Alex and treated it as though it was a normal, touristy visit, surely that should be easy enough?

So on a dry, dullish Sunday, when the sky was dappled with varying shades of grey, they took a cab to Tower Hill. They walked across to the Thames, joined the tourists leaning against the black railings and Daisy made herself look down to the left to where London Bridge spanned the river. She had seen it in the distance, of course, hovering on the horizon in her trips around London, much as it had always hovered at the back of her mind, but until now she had never ventured anywhere close.

In real life, it was a lot bigger and far more beautiful and elegant than it looked in her old, well-thumbed photograph. The first thing that struck a strange note with her was the traffic – cars, vans, all manner of vehicles gaily surging across the bridge.

'I think modern-day traffic looks funny on such an old bridge,' she said in an effort to be upbeat.

'I suppose it does. Especially when you realise that it's centuries old, after all, and full of history.'

'Full of history, and full of ghosts.' She unexpectedly shivered.

'Daisy, you look pale. Will I get you a coffee?'

'Sure, thanks.'

He bought two cups of coffee at a nearby kiosk and they sat down at a wrought iron table. Daisy's chilled hands hugged the hot container. She sat quietly lost in thought as the breeze wafted in off the glinting river, a tugboat chugged by and pigeons scurried underfoot as they pecked for crumbs on the uneven flagstones. Overhead, an aircraft slowly drifted through the clouds and she could hear the restless hum of distant traffic. She realised that the scene probably hadn't changed much since Liz and Marina had stood and been photographed, besides one or two new buildings on the far side of the river and the fact that tourists now had camcorders and digital cameras for instant memories. She shivered again.

'Daisy? Hello? You're miles away. Everything okay?' Alex asked.

She pulled herself together and grinned. 'Yeah, of course.'

'Will we stroll down nearer to the bridge? We can walk out onto it if you want.'

'Let's go down a bit further anyway.'

She took a deep breath and got to her feet, sending the pigeons scattering as she went over to the bin and dumped her unfinished coffee. She felt as though she was stepping out into an unknown space as they strolled further down towards the shelter of trees. Perhaps it had been here. She paused, looking at the angle of the bridge, the foliage overhead and the metallic sheen of the Thames in the background. She tried to remember the way Liz and Marina had leaned against the railings as they laughed into the camera. Yes, definitely here, she realised with a painful sense of shock. And coming fast on that realisation was the bone-chilling awareness that all those years ago, maybe her father had held the camera….

She suddenly felt weak.

'Daisy! Good grief, are you all right?' Alex's eyes were full of alarm.

'I'm just a bit dizzy,' she said, gulping air into her tight chest.

'What's wrong?'

Alex put his arm around her and she had no choice but to grab hold and lean into him. He felt solid and strong and somehow reassuring. 'I'm okay, really. It's nothing.'

'What's up? Do you want to walk out onto the bridge? Or should we head back?'

'No, I can't go out there,' she gasped. 'Sorry about this.'

'No prob. Forget about the walk, I'm more concerned about you. Can't afford to have my best tour guide falling down on the job.' He tightened his hold a little.

'I'll be fine in a minute. Really,' she smiled.

He didn't look entirely convinced, but he didn't push it any further and he kept his arm rather comfortingly around her as they retraced their steps. She snuck a look back just before they turned at the corner, but the bridge looked much the same. It hadn't suddenly crumbled into the Thames because Daisy and her ghosts had decided to visit. It still spanned the river with an imperious grace, stalwart and invincible, as it had been for centuries.

If only she could tell Alex she was at a place that had haunted her childhood and was even now causing her flutters of anxiety. But that, of course, was out of the question.

* * *

He phoned her unexpectedly on Thursday evening. 'It's about next Sunday.' He paused, sounding regretful.

'What about it?' She was conscious that her voice was a little sharp. Alex wanted out, more than likely after her silly behaviour last Sunday.

'I have to go to Birmingham on urgent business this evening,' he explained. 'It's an upgrade in a busy hospital, so unfortunately I'll be gone all weekend.'

'Oh. I see.'

'What did you think I was going to say?' He sounded as though he was smiling.

316

'I thought you were going to tell me you had booked the London Eye,' she joked.

'One of these days I'll drag you up in it.'

'God, no, I've no head for heights.'

'Is that why you almost collapsed on me last Sunday?' he asked sternly.

'Yeah.' She said it with such relief that it was obvious she was fibbing.

Alex paused, then said, 'No worries. I'll see you the following week, okay? I'll call for you early, I'd like to go to Windsor.'

'Good, that's great, thanks. And Alex?'

'Yes?'

'Safe journey.'

* * *

Alex gunned the Audi down the M40. He checked the speedometer and braked slightly when he hit over eighty miles an hour. Penalty points on his licence was all he needed. A blood red sunset was staining the sky and an unending chain of lights pinpricked the motorway as dusk approached. He had been afraid he would find the journey long and tiresome, but he felt fully alert.

He hoped there weren't any major problems in Birmingham. If time permitted, he had one or two questions of his own he wanted to put to the doctors. Questions he had been afraid to face, but were now important.

And then his thoughts turned, quite naturally, to Daisy. He was spending a little less time in the office in recent weeks, going home at a more reasonable hour, feeling less inclined to take work home at the weekends, less inclined to push himself into the ground to complete projects in double-quick time. Thanks to Daisy, the focus of his life had shifted completely. He thought of the soft mouth he wanted to kiss forever and the brown eyes full of friendly laughter that were playing havoc with his heart strings. And hidden behind her laughter, the air of vulnerability that checked his impatience and gave him pause.

Difficult though it was, he forced his concentration back to the wide grey ribbon of motorway that rolled unceasingly as he swept along. For the first time in his life, he had met someone special, someone who meant the world to him. He longed to spend more time with her, to find out everything about her, to crush her in his arms and make love to her properly. But although every other woman he had gone out with would have been hinting at bed by now, Daisy showed no such inclination. He would just have to be patient. At least he had discovered the reason for that air of guarded reserve.

She had never known her father. And he would never forget the look on her face the day she told him her mother was dead.

Chapter Thirty-five

The phone directory was thick and heavy and it didn't help that her fingers felt as though they were suddenly made of butter.

Daisy took a deep, calming breath and steadied her hands.

Chris Hyland, Liz had said. The name of her father. She had told it to Daisy the evening before she had left for London. Just in case.

'It's highly unlikely you'll find him,' Liz had paused. 'London's huge and he did say something to Marina about moving away, maybe heading to Canada.'

'I really appreciate that you've told me, Liz.'

Daisy had tucked the information away all those months ago, but she hadn't forgotten it. Only now did she feel ready to check it out a little further and see what she could find. Because something very subtle, almost intangible, had happened to her after her trip to London Bridge with Alex.

Yes, it had been upsetting. Yes, she had thought at the time that she was going to faint. But she had arrived home in one piece that day, feeling a little embarrassed but comforted by Alex's kind attention. And as the days went by and her routine of going in and out to Dolan's continued and life in London trundled on much as normal, she realised that she felt stronger in herself, even a little calmer. It was as though she had reached out and touched the bottom and it wasn't quite as bad as she had feared.

And in hitting the bottom, she had touched something solid inside herself. She had visited the place that had haunted her for years and she had survived. Survived quite well, to judge by the way she jostled cheerfully for the Tube, chatted and laughed with customers in Dolan's and slept right through the last few nights. So surely she could take another step forward and maybe confront more of her ghosts?

That was why she was sitting here now in a London library, sifting through some phone books, looking up the surname Hyland, C for Chris, Christopher, Christy....

If she had expected one of the entries to jump out at her or one of the names to be more meaningful than another, she was sadly mistaken.

Looking at the extent of the listings, she realised that she was on a hiding to nothing. And there was only an outside chance that one of them just might happen to be her father. For starters, he could be ex-directory, but it was more likely, as Liz had suggested, that he wasn't even living in London.

The other avenue she could explore was the Internet. There were websites dedicated to tracking down people, weren't there? She had discounted any enquiries into the register of births and marriages. She had already seen her birth cert, years ago, and she knew where she had been born. That had never been a secret. But the section for her father's name was, of course, blank. And she knew he and Marina had never married.

So her first line of enquiry was the phone books, just to get an idea of what was involved, but the printed names meant nothing to her. Nothing whatsoever. There was no surge of recognition, no lightning bolt of knowledge.

But supposing one of the entries had meant something to her. What then? If she did manage to track her father down, what next? Did she intend to turn up on his doorstep and introduce herself? What sort of conversation could she have with him? What might she say, what might he say in self-defence?

Would she rebuke him for all those years of neglect, all those childhood years without a father? When Eve had looked down her nose and Liz had tried to compensate and Marina had quietly turned to drink? Would she berate him, tell him he was a selfish bastard for running away? If she gave it enough thought, there were lots of things she could say and none of them were pretty.

And what good would it do? She would be turning up on a stranger's doorstep. He could be married with children of his own. Either way, it was bound to be a humiliating, embarrassing experience. Did she really want to put herself through that?

No thanks. Daisy closed over the books with a snap. It was suddenly very clear to her that she was worth far more than an undignified episode on a stranger's doorstep. Why waste her time and energy, never mind sleepless nights, fretting about someone who had never wanted anything to do with her? He was no part of her life now, and never had been.

She stood up and walked out into the sunny London afternoon.

The following day, with Alex still in Birmingham and determined to see things through to the end, she got the Tube to Belsize Park. She walked up the slight incline and, heedless of the drizzly rain, stood across from the Royal Free Hospital in Hampstead. She tried to picture a young Marina coming out with a baby in her arms, all those years ago. These were the streets Marina had frequented on her antenatal visits and this was the place where Daisy had caught her first glimpse of the world. She felt sudden tears in her eyes, but told herself it was nothing but the rain.

She stalled for a while and watched as traffic trundled by, taxis pulled up and disgorged passengers and patients, ambulances drove to and fro. There was an endless stream of activity. It had probably continued like this all day, every day, for the last twenty-six years. And would continue on into the future. Plenty of human drama, life and death, and a mother leaving the hospital with a newborn baby, miraculous though it was to the individuals concerned, was rather an everyday occurrence, a small microcosm that constituted no major significance in the grand scheme of things.

Afterwards she strolled around by Camden town. The other piece of information she had requested off Liz was that Marina had brought Daisy home to a ground-floor flat somewhere in the vicinity of this sprawling area. However, Liz had also told her that the terrace where they had lived had been demolished to make way for a shopping centre soon after their return to Dublin, so there was nothing much to see.

Nonetheless, Daisy thought, these were the streets where Marina had pushed her in a buggy. They were damp now and slippy with rain, but they meant nothing to her. She might as well have been anywhere in the world.

Anywhere at all.

* * *

'And what did you get up to last weekend when I wasn't around?' Alex asked. He collected her the following Sunday and now they were sweeping down the motorway to Windsor.

She was so pleased to see him again that she momentarily let down her guard. 'I was tracing my roots,' she said lightly.

'Wow. Sure, of course, you were born here. Find out anything interesting?'

'The main thing I discovered is that I'm not so concerned with ancient history.'

He smiled across at her, a warm, friendly smile, and she longed to tell him that she had faced her demons, literally retraced the steps of her past, and came to the startling realisation that they meant nothing any more. She wanted to tell him that she had faced the shadows that had dogged her childhood and discovered that they had no real substance, but that was out of the question.

'Why not?' he asked. 'History can be very interesting. Why don't I give you a hand with charting your family tree?'

'God, no, not my family.' Her brusque retort slipped out automatically and he shot her a glance of surprise.

'Do you mean they're not interesting, or don't you want me to go there?'

'Both, I suppose,' she tentatively said, wondering how he would react, but he just gave her a shrewd smile and said, 'No worries.'

She enjoyed Windsor. Out on high battlements, where the Berkshire countryside was spread like a map before them, she stood beside Alex, leaning companionably over the edge of a parapet warmed by the sun, and Daisy noticed that the trees of Windsor Park were turning vibrant shades of golden and russet. She realised with a start that autumn was well advanced and she was almost five months in London. As they stood there, together in the moment, she felt a measure of calm stillness flowing through her and soothing her.

She wanted this moment to go on forever, but all too soon they were driving back to London. She sat back and relaxed as the powerful car surged along, eating up the miles to London. They were cruising towards the outskirts of the city before she realised that something was wrong.

'Alex, I think you must have missed a turn.' She struggled to sit up straighter, searching for familiar landmarks as they slowed at a roundabout.

'No I haven't,' he said, his eyes flicking in his mirrors before he took the third exit.

'But this isn't the way to—'

'I know. Didn't I tell you? You're coming back to my place for coffee,' he said in a crisp, firm voice.

What the hell was this about? Alex's place for coffee? Daisy sat rigidly until he pulled up outside a modern, three-storey block. The gleaming kitchen was small and tidy, the last yellow rays of October sunlight slanting in through the window and sparking off the stainless steel taps. Daisy watched as Alex filled the kettle and took blue mugs out of the glass-fronted wall press.

He wheeled around and caught her staring at him. 'Milk and no sugar?'

'Yes, please.'

'Go on through to the living room,' he suggested.

She wandered around the living room, unable to sit still or relax. One part of her darting mind noticed that the walls were washed in an off-white shade and that the floor was covered with an amber carpet. Wooden blinds screened the window, which looked out onto a private patio. There was a TV and CD player in one corner of the room and a pile of CDs on a shelf in the alcove. A coffee table was drawn up in front of the sofa and Daisy idly picked up that morning's newspaper. Alex's newspaper. She put it back again as though it was on fire when he came into the room.

'You're welcome to have a look around if you like,' he said pleasantly as he put the mugs down on the coffee table.

'No thanks.'

'Relax, Daisy. I only brought you here to show you something. I'm not about to whisk you off to bed, if that's what's worrying you.' Daisy felt the colour sweep across her face. She obediently perched on the edge of the sofa and sipped at her coffee. 'I wanted to show you this,' Alex said. He went over to the windowsill and returned with a photo in a wooden frame. 'Here, have a look.'

It was a photo of Alex and his two sisters, alongside an older couple who had to be his parents, his mother blonde and smiling, his father not unlike Alex, the same intelligent, dark grey eyes, his hair edged with silver.

'That was taken in our family home last Christmas,' he said, sitting down beside her on the sofa. 'It was the last photograph taken of us together like that. A few weeks later, my father was dead.'

There was a moment's silence before Daisy eventually found her voice. 'God, Alex – what can I say – I'm really sorry.'

'I didn't show you this to extract a dose of sympathy,' he said gently. 'It was very hard, but I'm over the worst of it now. I threw all my energy into the job and I have to admit that I turned into a right old hermit. I was scarcely interested in life outside the office, until I met you.' She tried to ignore the significance of his words. He was upset, wasn't he? 'So I just wanted you to know that I understand what you're going through,' he continued softly.

It took a full, charged minute for the penny to drop. Something lurched inside Daisy's stomach and formed itself into a painful knot that spread around inside so that she could scarcely speak. She tried to take a gulp of air and correct this appalling misunderstanding before things went any further, but to her consternation, Alex took her hand in his and began to tell her of the day his father died.

'I didn't particularly want to talk to you about Dad until now. It's something I've never really spoken about. Maybe it's harder for men, I dunno. I know my mother and sisters wept buckets in the first weeks after Dad died, and they talked and talked, but I just felt kind of blank and empty.'

Blank and empty? 'Yes, I know that feeling,' she admitted.

'I knew you'd understand.' His dark eyes slowly scanned her face. She had to let him talk. For now. Anything else could surely wait, so she sat still, his hand in hers as the mugs of coffee grew cold and light seeped from the October sky outside. She listened as he hesitantly began to tell her in a jumble of words and half-finished phrases about the Wednesday morning when he got a phone call in work and life as he knew it altered forever.

'I got to the hospital, but it was too late.' Alex paused. 'It was instant. A brain haemorrhage. He had collapsed just as he arrived at his desk in work.' He shook his head slowly. 'I don't think I'll ever forget the look on my mother's face. She arrived at the hospital just after me. Then – then I had to tell my sisters.'

'God, Alex. How terrible,' she whispered, forgetting her own confusing thoughts in the face of his anguish.

'It was a nightmare. But that wasn't the worst,' he said, his hand gripping hers firmly, looking at her with shadowed grey eyes. 'Because throughout the awful nightmare, I blamed myself.'

'Why?'

'D'you know, it's such a relief to talk. I've never told a soul until now. Not my mother, and certainly not my sisters. I avoided any talk of my father. And all this time, I held myself responsible.'

'But why?' she repeated softly.

'I had called to the house to watch a football match with him the night before, and we ended up having an argument. We were on our own in the house. The girls were out and my mother was at her aerobics. We'd had this argument before, just after I came home from America,' Alex told her in a subdued voice. 'But that night it was worse. Dad thought I should start my own business, and he offered to fund me. I refused. I said I would make it on my own and without the benefit of his hard-earned money. He said I was being ridiculous and things got a little heated. I walked out and that was the last time I saw him.'

'Alex,' Daisy began, desperately hoping she'd find the right words. 'I'm no doctor, but I doubt very much that a brain haemorrhage can be caused by a row.'

Alex raked a hand through his hair and slowly nodded. 'When I was in Birmingham I had a chat with one of the neurosurgeons. He went through a few things with me and I know now that I had nothing to do with my father's death. In one sense

I feel relieved, but in another I don't. The fact remains that we had a row the night before he died.' He looked away, but not before Daisy caught sight of the bleakness in his eyes.

Silence fell and stretched between them and the shadows in the room lengthened. Daisy sat still, conscious of the warmth of his hand in hers, and she automatically tightened her grip. She forgot about her muddled thoughts, her lies and the misunderstanding that lay between them. She forgot about herself sitting awkwardly on the sofa. Alex seemed to fill her mind and he was the only person who mattered at this moment in time.

She moved first. She leaned towards him, sensing his silent distress, trying to ease it, hoping to soothe it. 'Alex?' She lightly touched his arm and instinctively touched her lips to the side of his mouth. She felt his arms around her, hugging her close to him, and he kissed her back, his lips lingering on hers so that by the time they finally stopped for breath, Daisy's legs were so weak that she couldn't possibly have stood up.

'You don't know how much I needed to hold you tight, you beautiful girl,' he murmured. He smoothed down her hair and touched her face with his fingertips and she felt as though she was glowing inside.

'And you're far too lovely to keep just for Sunday afternoons,' he continued. She couldn't read the expression in his eyes due to the shadows stealing across the room. She just felt the almost hypnotic movement of his fingers against her skin.

'So I think it's time we took things a little further. What do you think?' he asked, his voice still a murmur.

Something caught in her throat. 'What are you suggesting?' she croaked.

'Did I say something wrong?' His hand suddenly stopped its gentle movement. 'I was only suggesting that maybe we could see more of each other,' he said. 'Why wait until a Sunday afternoon? I'd love to see more of you, Daisy. Like, for instance, a Friday or a Saturday night? If you're not working, of course.'

'Oh, I see.' She tried in vain to mask her evident relief.

'Why, what did you think I meant?'

She gave him a nervous smile. Alex reached behind him and switched on a lamp so that the room was bathed in soft yellow light.

'Daisy.' He shook his head and smiled at her. 'I told you that I'm not about to whisk you off to my bed, didn't I? I'll make you a promise,' he continued. Once more he took her hand in his and his thumb rubbed against the soft underside of her palm. 'I'm going to wait until you ask me. And don't think it's because I don't want you,' he said. 'I do want you, Daisy. I'd like nothing better than to make love to you right now, but I can see that you're not entirely comfortable with the idea. Not yet, anyway. I know it will be something special, so I don't mind waiting.'

'What about....'

'Yes?'

'Your other girlfriends?' Her voice was almost a whisper.

'What other girlfriends?' His eyes locked with hers and he smiled a steady smile and she thought she was going to get weak all over again. Later, when he brought her home and kissed her thoroughly once more in the quiet of the porch, she couldn't believe how easily she went into his arms.

Over the next few weeks, as she began to see more of Alex, Daisy felt as though she was living some kind of double life. On the one hand, she was relieved that she had followed in the footsteps of her past and discovered that it held no terror for her. But much as she wanted to, she couldn't very well share this news with Alex. And when she was with him, it was all too easy to live in the moment and enjoy his company, to continue to blot out the past, especially when she had little or no communication with Marina. She kept Alex away from Joe and Alison, just in case. It was easy enough to be ready when he called, to say to Alison that she wasn't serious about him and didn't want to start asking him in for meals or get involved in foursomes.

So although life was a little more complicated, she didn't have to worry about Alex finding out the truth. She reminded herself of this as she sat close beside him in the cinema or theatre, or when her eyes locked with his across a restaurant table or as they laughed and joked over a few drinks on a Friday night. Alex never referred to her family, probably expecting that she would raise the subject when the time was right.

But that time would never come, she assured herself. For although she barely recognised herself as she melted into his arms at the end of an evening, bed wasn't on her agenda. And their relationship would eventually fizzle out, for Alex would surely get tired of her, tired of waiting.

Wouldn't he?

Chapter Thirty-six

'We should do this more often,' Liz suggested brightly as she picked up a menu.

'Yes, we should,' Marina said.

'And it's nice to have a midweek treat like this, isn't it?' she continued in a cheerful tone and smiled encouragingly at Marina. She was rewarded with an answering smile.

'Mmm, it is,' Marina agreed as she relaxed against the banquette.

Liz sighed with relief. She watched surreptitiously as Marina studied the menu. She looked better than she had in ages. Thanks to Harry's advice, Liz silently admitted. Though at the time it hadn't seemed such a good idea, coming as it did almost on the heels of Daisy's departure.

'Daisy's gone,' Marina had flatly said the week after Daisy had left when Liz had popped in to make sure her sister was alive and well.

'Yes, it's just for a while, remember?' Liz said brightly, deliberately masking her annoyance at the mound of washing up waiting to be done. At least Marina's floaty black trousers and light grey kaftan were freshly laundered. Her face was devoid of make-up and her hair was neatly tied back.

'No, she's gone for good.'

Liz had looked at her sister's devastated face and had quietly washed up and tidied the kitchen. By the end of the third week after Daisy's departure, Liz had called into Marina almost half a dozen times. She had washed up, cleaned and tidied and coaxed her into her workroom as though she was a recalcitrant child.

Then Harry had turned around and asked if she intended looking after Marina for the rest of her life.

'What do you mean?' she had replied. Suddenly she didn't like the way he was looking at her, his light blue eyes distinctly challenging.

'You're not doing Marina any favours, you know,' Harry was blunt. 'She needs to stand on her own two feet and take responsibility for her life.'

'Yes, but—'

'No, Liz. It's about time you stopped nourishing your survivor's guilt. Marina is quite capable of look-ing after herself. She certainly doesn't need you

335

running after her. At least Daisy managed to break free, even if the circumstances were questionable, but that doesn't mean you have to try and make up for it.'

'Look, Harry, I told Daisy I'd keep an eye on her and I thought that you of all people would understand.'

'There's a big difference between keeping an eye on her and pandering to her moods. You're not personally responsible for Marina's happiness and the sooner you understand that, the better.'

'I don't like what I'm hearing.' Liz's eyes flashed.

'I wish you'd face the fact that as long as you continue to mollycoddle Marina, things will never change.'

It was the first time in years that they had had a major row. Liz told Harry he was being heartless and he told his wife that she was being taken for granted. They slept as far away from each other as possible in their bed, the rift between them far greater than half the width of the mattress.

His words echoed in her head a couple of weeks later when she stood in Marina's kitchen and saw the usual pile of dirty dishes on the worktop.

'You're late,' Marina said, an accusing note in her voice.

'What do you mean, I'm late?' Liz asked, suddenly sharp.

'I thought you weren't going to come this week,' Marina said fretfully. 'I thought you had left me, like Daisy.'

'Daisy hasn't left you, Marina,' Liz tried to sound patient.

'Yes she has.'

'Don't be silly,' Liz said, placating. 'Daisy's just gone away for a little while to find her feet, like most young people do.'

'No, she's not my daughter any more.' Marina didn't care if Liz looked unhappy with that last remark. Daisy hadn't just gone away to find her feet – she'd gone to *London*, of all places. Liz knew that she'd already lost one daughter to that city. Now she had lost another. Although she had always known her daughter would move out, she had never envisaged her going to London.

The day she left home, Marina felt as though something had died inside her all over again. When Daisy phoned occasionally, she couldn't even bring herself to talk to her.

'Of course Daisy is still your daughter, and she'll be back in time,' Liz said. 'The best thing you can do is keep busy. I wish I had some of your talent.'

'Talent?' Marina scoffed. 'Don't make me laugh.' What good was talent? It couldn't compensate for an empty life. She felt Liz's arm around her shoulders.

'C'mon, I'll give you a hand,' she said as she steered Marina towards the front room.

'Leave me alone,' Marina snapped, irritable that Liz was standing close enough to catch the whiff of her afternoon vodka. 'You know I can't manage without Daisy.' She felt a surge of rage and with a sweep of her hand she sent the pile of dirty crockery clattering into the sink. 'Now look what you made me do,' she said as she faced her sister.

'I didn't make you do anything,' Liz coolly pointed out. 'You did that all by yourself.'

'It's easy for you to talk, but you don't know what it's like for me.' Marina felt tears in her eyes as she dragged up her usual defence, fully expecting Liz's typical sympathy.

Liz wavered. Was this the way it was going to be? A wounded Marina unable to get on with her life, dependent on vodka to get her through the empty nights, dependent on Liz to pick up the pieces? An acquiescent Liz, full of survivor's guilt, like Harry had said, fearful of upsetting Marina, always pussy-footing around her? Even now, she was afraid to tell her that Daisy had fled to London mainly on account of Marina's bad behaviour on the night of her birthday, an episode Marina seemed to have conveniently blanked out.

She looked at the dirty crockery that Marina had sent crashing into the sink. She looked at her sister's face, set in its usual pitiable mode. She thought of the way she had been rushed off her feet in the office all morning and the pile of ironing waiting at home. Then Liz did what she should have done years ago. She finally lost her cool.

'That's it, Marina. I've had about all I can take,' she snapped, the blood rushing to her head.

Marina stared at her. 'It's about time you began to pull yourself together,' Liz ploughed on, ignoring her sister's astonishment and her own accelerating heartbeat. 'Yes, I know things have been difficult, and I know you're missing Daisy. But that doesn't mean you can expect me to come around here to pick up your dirty dishes and empty your waste bin and hold you by the hand and coax you, pretty please, over to your sewing machine. If you want to drown your sorrows in a bottle of vodka, that's your business. But I'm not about to spend the rest of my life propping you up!' Liz finally stopped to draw breath, secretly horrified at her outburst.

'That's not fair,' Marina gasped, eventually finding her voice.

'Yes it is,' Liz said firmly as she tried to collect her whirling thoughts. 'I'm merely pointing out that you're quite capable of looking after your house and you don't need me running after you.'

'But I do need help.'

'Help for what?' Liz's tone was a little softer. She wondered if she was about to make some kind of breakthrough with her sister. She had gently hinted at counselling on more than one occasion in the past, only to be instantly rebuffed. 'What kind of help, Marina?' she repeated.

'Don't get any of your funny ideas, Liz. It's just, you know, the house gets on top of me... sometimes I can't really cope,' Marina said.

'You're well able to cope,' Liz scoffed. 'You

339

coped before, didn't you? And you're also well able to run up a few pairs of curtains without me holding your hand. For God's sake, Marina, with a talent like yours you could do them in your sleep.'

'Hang on, Liz,' Marina was scathing. 'Your life has turned out just as you always wanted. You don't know how lucky you are. But how can I ever hope to have a normal life?'

'Believe me, I do appreciate my life. But what's a normal life?' For the first time ever, Liz didn't give in to her sister's self-absorption. For the first time ever, she held her ground and challenged her. 'Marina, take off your blinkers. There are thousands of people out there who are going around their daily business and they have any number of problems and heartache,' she said. 'People you meet in the supermarket or at the bus stop. People who have to get up every morning and get on with things, no matter what their difficulties are—'

Marina suddenly interrupted. 'Why are you so cross and angry with me?'

'I'm cross with you because you're wasting your life,' Liz said, struggling for calm, wondering where the words were coming from, all those words she had been afraid to say. Until now. 'I'm cross because you're clinging to the past and using it as an excuse to sink your head into a bottle of vodka.'

'Can you blame me?'

'And what about Daisy?' Liz suddenly changed tack, again refusing to go down the same old worn, familiar path of self-pity with her sister. 'You have a beautiful daughter. She's intelligent and sensitive and kind. Don't you care what she thinks or how she feels? Have you ever thought of what it's like to be saddled with a mother who's riddled with alcohol most nights?'

'How dare you talk to me like this!'

'It's about time someone did. But don't worry, I'm going now,' Liz said, picking up her handbag and taking out her car keys. 'You could have a good future with Daisy,' Liz called over her shoulder as she stalked out into the hall and headed for the door. 'She won't stay away forever. In time she'll get married, maybe have children. Think about it, Marina. You could have grandchildren to look forward to.'

'Grandchildren?'

In spite of her consuming anger, Liz heard the shake in her sister's voice. 'Yes, grandchildren,' she repeated as she halted at the door and looked back steadily at Marina. 'But you know something? It's entirely up to you what kind of a granny they'll have. It's your choice.' And with that, Liz went out the door and closed it firmly behind her.

She didn't shed a tear until she reached home. Harry took one look at her and folded her into his arms. Later, he cuddled her in the warmth of their bed and told her she had done the right thing. She didn't believe him, of course. She didn't believe him until the following week, when she called in again and the kitchen was neat and tidy and a slightly defensive Marina informed her that Liz would be pleased to know that her work was up to date.

There were no instant miracles, but little by little, as the months went by, Liz encouraged her sister to get out more often. She brought Marina to the hairdresser again. She made an appointment for her in the local beauty salon for an aromatherapy massage. She brought her shopping to Liffey Valley and one night they went to the cinema together and ogled Brad Pitt. It was so nice that they went again. It also had the bonus of being a drink-free night, as Liz pointed out to Harry.

And now, for the first time in ages, they were meeting for lunch in town.

Lunch first, followed by Christmas shopping, Liz had suggested.

'But it's only the beginning of November,' Marina had said. Liz didn't bother to explain that she had most of her Christmas shopping already done. She guessed correctly that Marina had usually left all of that up to Daisy, not that Marina had ever celebrated Christmas to any great degree.

And this time she didn't bother to collect Marina. She let her make her own way into the city centre on the bus. She was relieved when she spotted Marina coming towards her, looking a little lost, perhaps, but there nonetheless.

'I can't believe how busy it all is,' Marina said as they sat in the restaurant in Wicklow Street and gave their order to the waitress. 'Town is jammed. Where on earth is everyone coming from?'

'It's the start of the Christmas rush,' Liz explained. 'It gets earlier every year.'

'It'll be great to have Daisy home,' Marina said wistfully.

Liz was momentarily startled. 'Did she say she was coming home for the holiday?' she asked, wondering if by some miracle her sister and niece had at last made up. Maybe Marina was doing even better than she had thought.

'She'll hardly stay away for Christmas.' Marina fixed Liz with a surprised look.

'When were you talking to her?' Liz asked directly.

'Well, I wasn't really, not yet,' Marina hedged. 'I know she'll ring again soon and I'll ask her then. As you said yourself, she won't stay away forever, and most people come home for Christmas, don't they?'

Liz hurriedly decided it was best to change the subject and avoid all mention of Daisy and London and Christmas. Marina still had her mind completely closed to the remarks she had hurled at Daisy before she left for London. Was it possible she had suffered some alcohol-induced memory loss? It did happen, and she had probably had a lot more to drink on the night than Liz realised. There was no point in reminding her at this moment in time, just when Liz was trying to help her get a life for herself. In all likelihood, Marina would go completely off the deep end.

Though how she thought Daisy was coming home when Marina still refused to talk to her was something else entirely.

'Guess where Eve's going tonight?' Liz said. 'La Stampa. I don't know who she's going with, but apparently he's loaded.'

'Trust Eve to get lucky. I always knew she'd land on her feet,' Marina said with a wry smile.

'Knowing my daughter, it won't amount to any-thing,' Liz shrugged, wondering what had got into Eve in recent times. For although she was twenty-four years old, lately she was carrying on like a truculent teenager. Sometimes, much and all as she loved her, she felt like giving her a good shake, Liz thought as she picked up a piece of bread and tore it into bite-size lumps.

* * *

At that moment, unaware of her mother's agitation, Eve was in Grafton Street, finishing her Christmas shopping. She was already well prepared for the season. She had checked out her favourite boutiques as she put together her seasonal wardrobe. Short slinky dresses, stylish skirts, velvet slash-neck figure-hugging bodices, voile tops, black and more black, with a little silver and gold thrown in.

All that remained was to select her perfumes and

run through her cosmetics. Some new shades had been introduced in the Mac range and she looked forward to testing them out. She had just had her hair trimmed and deep conditioned, but it would probably need a further trim and treatment the week before Christmas.

She just hoped her credit card would stand up to the strain. This year she had spared no expense, splashing out as much as she could afford and more in a frenzy of retail therapy, in a final, last-ditch attempt to put Alex Gallagher firmly out of her mind.

Not that she was succeeding very well. She had felt depressed after the weekend in London. Naturally she hadn't bumped into him. It would have been a minor miracle to run into him in a city of that size. But she had been disgusted all the same at her sudden reluctance to board the plane that was taking her home, away from any possibility, however remote, of seeing him.

And as much as she hated her job in Foley Financials and longed for a change of scene, she couldn't bring herself to leave, not if there was the slightest chance that he might walk in through the door again. She'd found out that Citimex Systems was contracted to maintain the upgraded computer system for two years, so she lived in the hope that one day he might appear at her desk, asking if he could check her access in that gritty, sexy voice of his.

Eve joined the queue for the checkout, paid for her glitzy evening bag and strolled back to the office in thin November sunshine. The worst thing of all was the fact that she had to make out as though everything was great in her world. For how could she possibly admit to anyone that social butterfly Eve Andrews couldn't stop thinking about the one man who had told her quite cuttingly that making love to her had been a mistake?

Sometimes she longed to confide in Rachel, but that would never do. Rachel usually cried on her shoulder when her love life was on the blink. It was never the other way around. Eve's love life was never on the blink.

Nowadays she didn't even have the slim satisfaction of blithely dishing out advice to Rachel, not when Rachel was so ecstatically and joyfully sparkling with wedded bliss, so smugly confident and secure in her world of perfect marital rapture.

'We've put a deposit on a house in Clonee,' Rachel had said only that morning. 'It's perfect, just what we wanted. We were supposed to go out and celebrate last night, but we ended up having a private celebration,' she continued, bubbling with excitement. 'I never thought I could be so happy. I can't believe I deserve all this!'

'That's great news, Rachel.' Eve plastered a smile on her face.

'I was wondering….' Rachel hesitated.

'Yes?'

346

'John's working late tonight, so I was wondering if you'd like to come over to the apartment to see the wedding video? I can't believe you haven't seen it yet!' Rachel looked at her hopefully.

'I'm afraid I can't make it tonight,' Eve said, glad for once that she had a genuine excuse. 'I'm going out for a meal with the chap I met last Saturday night.'

'Who knows? This could be the start of something.' Rachel looked pleased.

'Somehow I doubt that,' Eve said flippantly. 'I'm just going out with Tony because I deserving a little spoiling.'

'A little spoiling?' Rachel had looked amused. 'Eve, your entire life has been spent in pampered luxury. You've always had everything you ever wanted.'

That was part of the problem, wasn't it, Eve thought bleakly as she left the November lunchtime sunshine and marched into the heated foyer of the office. She had been brought up to believe that she could have everything she ever wanted in life.

And that belief had served her well, until now.

Chapter Thirty-seven

Daisy opened her wardrobe door and hesitated. She sifted through her clothes, her fingers stalling when they brushed against a long black skirt and matching bustier. She took down the hanger and held the outfit against herself, turning to examine her reflection in the mirror. Her brown eyes looked back at her, startled and unsure.

Memories crowded in of the night she had put on the stunning creation, but there were no butterflies in her tummy, no quickening heartbeat. It was almost as though time and distance had somehow managed to erase everything.

When Alex called for her at seven o'clock, he was carrying a huge back umbrella angled against the slanting rain. Daisy saw his eyes widen as she opened the door and stood in the spill of light coming from the hallway.

'Daisy! You look… you look really lovely,' he finished, his grey eyes admiring.

She felt a little flustered as she grabbed her coat and hurried with him down the rain-washed driveway out to the black cab, his arm around her holding her close under the protection of the umbrella. But when she turned to him in the back seat of the cab, she was glad she had dressed up for the occasion. They were going to see *The Phantom of the Opera* and Alex had never looked more handsome. Under his overcoat, he was wearing a dark suit that contrasted sharply with his white shirt. Daisy felt a heightened awareness of him sitting close beside her as the cab swished though the busy London streets on that Saturday night in mid-November.

There was an air of expectation in the theatre. Daisy was oblivious to the heads that turned as they made their way in through the tiled foyer and up the carpeted staircase to their seats. She didn't realise the attractive couple they made – Alex, tall and handsome, and Daisy, her hand tucked into his as she kept pace with him.

The orchestra tuned up, the lights dimmed and the story unfolded of the Phantom that stalked the opera house in Paris and of his love for the young singer. The music was overwhelming, song following song, and it captured Daisy in its evocative, spellbinding weave so that emotion clogged the back of her throat.

At one stage she realised that her hand was tightly clutching Alex's, her nails digging into his palm. She tried to relax her hold but he just smiled at her in the darkened auditorium and drew her hand forward so that he could interlace her fingers with both of his hands.

And then it was over, the whole theatre gripped for several moments in silent, stunned appreciation. In the flurry of the final tumultuous applause, Daisy caught Alex's eye and hurriedly looked away. Her emotions were very near the surface and she felt as though they were reflected in her eyes and laid bare to his gaze. She knew he had spotted something when he leaned across and kissed her on the forehead. Daisy's legs were shaky as the house lights sprang on, and with Alex close beside her, they joined the throng of people heading for the bar.

'I don't need to ask what you thought,' he said as Daisy perched on a stool. She still felt disorientated after the flood of music and emotion. She shook her head and laughed shakily, her eyes slightly dazed.

'It was very moving… the music… just out of this world.'

'I knew you'd enjoy it,' Alex smiled.

'The whole experience was just….' Daisy was lost for words.

'You don't need to say anything. What would you like to drink?' he asked as the queue for the bar thinned a little.

'The usual, please,' she replied, her mouth curving in a smile.

'One white wine coming up,' he said as he turned and joined the queue.

She watched him as he waited, knowing that at any moment he would look back as though to check that she was still there. And sure enough, as he edged forward towards the counter, he turned and gave her a glance that made her breath catch in her throat.

She looked away and suddenly caught sight of her reflection in a large mirror on the wall and her heart skipped a beat. Her blond hair was gleaming in the spotlight, her black bustier clung to her curves and showed off the creamy skin of her shoulders and neck to perfection. Was this really her, this glamorous-looking creature? Was this the new Daisy O'Neill? If so, she was a far cry from the tough, uncompromising Ms O'Neill of before. She laughed quietly to herself, a tiny bubble of happiness welling up inside her.

'You look really lovely tonight, Daisy,' Alex said as they sipped their drinks companionably.

'Thank you,' she smiled across at him, then added, flirting openly, 'just tonight?'

He threw back his head and laughed. 'You always look lovely, Daisy. Tonight, though, you

351

look….' Their eyes locked and Alex looked away. Daisy waited, holding her breath. 'You look wonderful,' he finally said.

* * *

Alex wasn't fooled by her false nonchalance. Daisy was still a little nervous around him – nervous of accepting a compliment, nervous of the signals she read in his eyes.

And she was right to be nervous, he ruefully admitted, considering the urge with which he longed to sweep her off to his bed and the way he wanted to make love to her over and over. Once he had her in his bed, he didn't think he would ever let her go. He longed to taste her creamy skin and once and for all banish that vulnerable look from her eyes and make up for the absence of parents in her life. He sipped his glass of whiskey, wondering how much longer he could hold out. For however long it took, he grimly reminded himself. Daisy was far too special. He wasn't going to rush her and he wasn't going to upset her in any way. It was difficult, though, to put a lid on distracting thoughts when she was sitting right in front of him and looking so beautiful. Very difficult, considering how much he loved her.

'Do you want to go for something to eat?' he asked, hoping to prolong the night.

'No thanks,' she smiled. 'The way I feel now, I

couldn't possibly eat a thing. I'm still full up with all the wonderful music. Unless you…?'

'No, I'm fine,' he said. He didn't think he'd be able to eat a thing either, not with Daisy sitting across the table looking so desirable.

It was still raining when they left the theatre and headed up the street and into the Saturday night bedlam of Piccadilly Circus. Alex opened the umbrella and curled his arm around Daisy's shoulders, drawing her close so that they were cocooned together under the wide brim.

The pavements were crowded with pedestrians scurrying through the wet night. A jumble of neon signs screamed from huge high-rise buildings, the slick, shiny streets throwing up distorted reflections, lighting up the area as far as the eye could see. Traffic trundled by, cars honking at dashing, wayward pedestrians. Cabs screeched to a halt, disgorging laughing passengers, collecting others anxious to get out of the rain. It was a busy, vibrant scene that was utterly discordant after the night of enthralling music.

'Let's get out of here,' Alex said, noticing the expression on Daisy's face.

She clung to Alex and he hailed the next cab. As they drove home, Daisy sat quietly beside him, her head on his shoulder, her hair tickling his chin. He didn't move a muscle, loving the feel of her so close to him, unwilling to break the spell. When they reached Joe and Alison's house, he was more than pleasantly surprised when she asked him to come in.

The night wasn't over. Not just yet.

* * *

Daisy asked Alex in entirely on impulse. Joe and Alison were at a party and not due home until the early hours, and, still feeling raw and emotional after the uplifting experience of the music, she suddenly felt that she didn't want to be alone with her thoughts in the silent, empty house.

She wondered what she had done when she saw him standing in the soft lamplight of the living room. Alex had taken off his overcoat and jacket and had removed his tie.

'Do you want some coffee or tea?' she babbled as she edged towards the living room door.

'No thanks.' His grey eyes were intent upon her, calm and imperturbable.

'Or I think there's a bottle of whiskey some-where….' By now she was almost out the door, looking for an excuse to bolt.

'No, nothing thank you. Nothing to drink, I mean.' He looked across the room at her, steadily and patiently. Daisy stood still, unable to break contact with his eyes. 'Come here,' he said quietly.

She didn't move.

'Come here,' he said again and held out his hand. She could almost taste the tension in the air and she felt her heart beating wildly in her throat. Then Alex moved across the room and wrapped his arms around her.

He kissed her as he had never kissed her before. Slow, sensual kisses, his tongue teasing the velvety inside of her lip, causing her heart to leap. She felt his hands on the curve of her chin, in her hair, on her shoulders as he drew her closer still. Her heart was hammering so loudly she was sure he could hear it, and she felt the heat of his skin through the fabric of his shirt.

Up to now he had been playing with her, she thought. He'd been holding back. For this was real, this was Alex, this passionate, sensual man. A spark of fear darted somewhere inside her, but she had to ignore it.

Daisy lost all track of time. There was only Alex and the feel of his mouth on hers and his arms fusing her tightly to him. He eventually broke contact with her and lifted his head, but only for the moment it took to move over to the sofa, and then she was sitting beside him and he was kissing her again. He shifted slightly and she felt as though she was in a trance as he gently pressed her back so that she was lying along the couch. He lifted a cushion and placed it under her head. His fingers trailed along the curve of her cheek and the outline of her lips and his warm mouth followed, kissing her deeply again.

She felt his hands on her body, stroking her

shoulders and the curve of her waist, pausing for a moment before moving up to cover her breasts. And then she felt a fluttering panic. She sought to control it as Alex continued to stroke through the fabric of her bustier, his hands gently trailing around the top, where the material met the gentle swell of her breasts. Deep inside, she felt something spark. She shuddered.

Alex stopped.

The first thing she noticed was the air. It was suddenly cold around her as Alex moved away and she struggled to sit up. She felt a sense of shock and her mouth still quivered where his had been, her body tingled where his hands had touched. Silence painfully stretched between them.

He was sitting watching her, his eyes dark with a passionate intensity that almost frightened her. 'I think I'd better go,' he suggested softly.

'Go?' she echoed. She had failed him somehow, gone wrong somewhere. What else had she expected?

'Yes,' he sighed. 'If I stay any longer I might do something I'd regret.' He ran a hand abstractedly through his hair.

Regret? What did he mean? 'I'm sorry if you regret it, Alex,' she said stiffly. She swung rubbery legs out onto the floor and tried to sit up straighter.

'No, Daisy, don't misunderstand,' he said swiftly. 'I don't regret anything – far from it. You're beautiful, so very desirable, but there's only one place this is heading.' Somewhere it registered at the back of

356

her mind that Alex Gallagher had told her she was beautiful. And even now, he was watching her and waiting. 'You haven't asked me yet,' he murmured. 'Remember? I said I'd wait until you asked. Well?' he persisted, his voice soft and hypnotic. 'Are you going to ask me upstairs? Would you like to spend the night with me?' He reached towards her and Daisy involuntary flinched, which she immediately regretted. 'See? You're still a little nervous of me, Daisy. And I haven't even got to the ribbon of your top.'

'Look, Alex—' Tell him! her mind shouted. He'll surely understand.

'It's okay.' He gathered her close and this time she went into his arms. She leaned into his shoulder and listened to his murmuring voice. 'That's why I'd better go home now. A few more minutes here with you and… God, I may not even get as far as your bed. That's what I would regret, because I don't want it to be like that with you.'

'What *do* you want it to be like?' she whispered.

'Don't tempt me.' He drew away from her. 'And now I'm definitely going.' He gave her a final hug, a last gentle kiss and then he rose to his feet. He pulled on his jacket and slung on his overcoat. He walked out into the hall and picked up his black umbrella.

It was only when Daisy followed him out and felt the cold tiles that she realised she was in her stocking feet. Somewhere, somehow, her shoes had been removed. Then she remembered Alex taking them off as she sat on the sofa. It seemed a suddenly intimate gesture, and now he was a tall, daunting figure as he strode to the door.

'Can I call a cab?' she asked, wrapping her arms around herself and feeling at a loss. He opened the hall door and a rush of cold air swept in, making her shiver.

'No thanks,' he said. 'I'll walk down to the corner. I'm bound to catch one there. Anyway, I could do with some fresh air.'

And with a final wry smile he was gone, out into the dark, drizzly London night.

* * *

Her tears came at last in the quiet of the pre-dawn. She had lain awake dry eyed for what seemed like an age. She heard Joe and Alison come home and go to bed. Then the house settled into quietness again and eventually the tears trickled, running down her nose, seeping into her pillow, dampening her hair where his hands had soothed and stroked.

She thought of the events of the night: the wonderful music, the spellbinding singing, Alex, handsome in his suit, catching her eye across a busy bar. The journey home through the wet streets, her head on his shoulder. The passionate Alex, kissing her so sensually, the look in his dark eyes and the way she'd felt, as though she was drowning in it all.

And then she had ruined everything.

He had said she was beautiful. And desirable. But he didn't know what she was really like, under her sexy outfit. Had she worn it on purpose? Had she wanted to see what kind of reaction she'd get? If so, she hadn't been disappointed. For a few minutes she had felt beautiful and desirable. She'd felt so close to Alex, closer than she'd ever felt to anyone before.

And then, in spite of everything, the old familiar Daisy had returned. Alex had sensed it immediately and he had stopped. Nothing had really changed, had it? She might have tried to turn her life around, but the Daisy of the passionate disasters was still alive and well. She wondered what would have happened had he not behaved like a gentleman. Supposing his hands had strayed to the ribbons on her bustier? She shut that thought away. No way did she want to imagine the scene that surely would have followed.

* * *

Work was a blessing the following week. Kim was out sick with a bad dose of the flu and Caroline asked her to do some extra shifts.

'No problem,' Daisy told her. 'Just tell me when you need me.'

'Are you sure?'

'Positive.'

When Alex phoned her that evening, she had her excuses ready. She didn't know if he believed her when she explained that she would be working late all week. There was silence on the line for a moment and then he spoke, his voice warm and concerned, telling her to take care and not to work too hard. Sounding, she thought as she broke the connection, as though nothing had gone wrong the previous Saturday night, as though he still felt she was beautiful and desirable....

Later that week, Caroline began to talk about Christmas. They would be run off their feet with office parties, she explained. It was their busiest time of the year, they would be taking on seasonal staff, and it was a case of all hands on deck.

'We're usually very well organised,' she told Daisy. 'We have an excellent Christmas menu and everything is booked and ordered in advance, right down to the wines. It's good fun and the atmosphere is brilliant, even if you're frantically running around the tables!'

Christmas. She didn't want to think about it, didn't want to know. Even as boxes of Christmas crackers, balloons and festive napkins arrived into Dolan's and as London's streets and shops were transformed into a virtual fairyland and the Tube was jammed with Christmas shoppers, Daisy wished she could just ignore it in the hope that it would go away.

But, of course, it wouldn't.

She was astonished when Marina asked outright if she was coming home.

Chapter Thirty-eight

She had begun to talk in the last couple of weeks.

Liz had been right. In time, Marina had come around enough to talk to Daisy. And even if she spoke as if Daisy was in the next room and not on the other side of the Irish Sea, even if she still seemed to be ignorant of the ugly scene that had precipitated Daisy's departure and although the phone calls were usually stilted, at least it was a step in the right direction.

Then she asked, 'When will you be home, Daisy?'

'I'm not sure, Mum. I'll be home, but not for a while yet.'

'But what about Christmas?'

Daisy gripped the phone. 'I'm afraid I won't be

home by then,' she said stiffly, glad that she was on the other end of a phone line and not face to face with Marina.

'Is this some kind of a joke?' Marina sounded puzzled. 'I'm talking about Christmas. Of course you'll be home.'

'Sorry, but I only have a couple of days off work and it's scarcely worth my while.' Lies. Mother of God, more lies, as if there weren't already enough. Caroline would have given her more time off if she wanted, but she couldn't go back to Dublin, not yet. She still felt a basic need to keep a distance between herself and Marina.

'I see,' Marina answered coldly. 'I suppose I should have expected this.'

Had she really forgotten the insults she had hurled at Daisy? It seemed so. Daisy felt angry and sad at the same time – angry that there was such a rift between them and sad that right now she couldn't see any way across it.

Then the nightmares returned, two nights in a row. She had confronted her past, she reminded herself as she groped for the lamp, but it hadn't quite gone away. She told herself she was upset on account of Marina, for there was nothing else she had to face. There were surely no other secrets or shadows to be dispelled.

* * *

She hadn't been out with Alex for almost two weeks. Her extra hours in Dolan's had kept her busy and Kim was no sooner back in work when Daisy was laid up with the flu. A few days in bed was far too long to have time to think, she realised. She wiped her streaming eyes and went through tissue after tissue, the memory of that Saturday night chasing around and around in her head. She was almost glad when she was up on her feet and back in work, even if it did mean she had no excuse not to see Alex.

He turned up with a bouquet of winter flowers.

'For the recovered patient,' he joked, standing under the light of the hallway in his overcoat. An image of him standing in the hallway on a previous occasion suddenly flashed, when cold tiles had chilled her stocking feet and her heart had fluttered in distress.

'You shouldn't have,' she said, embarrassed.

'Why not, don't you deserve it?' he smiled.

Daisy felt a sudden rush of happiness. She had missed him, his company, his easy laughter, the feeling of his arms around her, the warmth of his kisses…. She buried her head in the sweet scent of the flowers and muttered something about putting the flowers into water as she hurriedly escaped to the kitchen.

He brought her to a restaurant in Chiswick. It was cosy and intimate, with flickering candlelight dotting the tables and miniature flower buds unfurling perfect petals in tiny crystal vases. He

364

was sitting across the table, relaxed and friendly, and he wasn't looking at her as though she was an ice queen. He didn't seem to think she was the untouchable one, as she had once been called. He didn't seem to think she was unable to cut it, as she had also been cruelly told.

Then Alex began to talk about Christmas, about the gifts he was buying for his sisters and mother. 'Maybe we could go shopping together?' he asked. 'Up Oxford Street, under the festive lights?'

'I'd like that,' she smiled in return.

'And if you behave yourself, I might even bring you to see Santa,' he joked.

Liz had brought her to see Santa in Clery's Toy Shop, with Eve. Daisy had been half afraid of the bearded man, whereas Eve had confidently rattled off a long list of requirements. They had both received parcels appropriate to their age and Eve had had hysterics because she thought Daisy's parcel was better than hers. Then Liz, naturally, had gone back to the grotto and paid for an additional, more grown-up parcel for Eve.

The following year, Eve had scornfully announced that there was no such thing as Santa, it was only daddies dressing up. So whatever about Daisy, who had no daddy, she, Eve, was sure to get lots of toys anyway.

'There you go again.' Alex's voice broke into her thoughts. 'You're a million miles away,' he smiled across the table.

'What do you mean?'

'Sometimes you just look as though you're somewhere else entirely.'

'Really? Sorry, Alex, I was just thinking that it's been a long time since I've been to see Santa.'

'Childhood memories?'

'You could say that,' Daisy said lightly, ignoring the spasm in her heart and the sudden urge she had to tell Alex everything. She looked at his face and tried to imagine what it would be like to rest in his arms and pour everything out.

And then he asked her to fly home with him for Christmas.

'I'm going back to the family home for Christmas, especially as it's the first Christmas without Dad, so wouldn't it be an idea to fly home together? Dublin Airport looks great at Christmas and it would be lovely to come through together, don't you think?'

'That won't be possible,' Daisy began, putting down her fork.

'Why not? I was even hoping that maybe we could see each other in Dublin? Talking about childhood memories, I'd love to meet your friends and whatever family you have, see where you grew up, where you went to school….'

See each other in Dublin? Friends and family? No chance, never, ever. 'You see, Alex, I'm not going home,' she shrugged casually.

'You're not going home?'

'No.' Another shrug, but this time she added a bright smile as though it was the most natural thing in the world to want to stay in London for Christmas.

'Why not?' He frowned at her and for a moment she caught a glimpse of Alex Gallagher the authoritative, dynamic executive, and she almost lost her breath. Then he suddenly smiled apologetically and shook his head. 'Sorry, I didn't mean to pry. I automatically assumed you'd be going home to family… aunts? Cousins?'

'I don't have any family that I'd particularly want to go home to,' she blurted. It was partly the truth, wasn't it? Only a little white lie. Only more complications.

His next words sent her into a tailspin. 'Then it's very simple, really. Why don't you come home with me? My mother and sisters would love to have you and there's plenty of room.'

Daisy struggled to keep her composure. So much for the new, improved Daisy O'Neill. She had already found out that the desirable Daisy in the sexy black bustier didn't really exist. She was only a sham. Now it seemed that everything else about her was a sham too.

My mother is dead… I don't have any family…. The words echoed in her head. Little white lies? God.

'Daisy?' His hand reached across the table and captured hers. 'You haven't answered my question.

There's a guest room you could use,' he continued, his hand warm around hers. 'Think of it, a family Christmas. Then on St Stephen's Day, a long walk in Marlay Park. It's a family tradition, and I'd love to share it with you,' he said.

It sounded wonderful, she thought. It sounded perfect. What could be better than strolling in Marlay Park with Alex on a calm St Stephen's Day? But thanks to her stupidity, Alex and Daisy, together in Dublin, was a non-runner.

'Look, Alex.' Daisy swallowed her disappointment and in desperation she seized on the one sure thing that would get her off the hook. 'I don't feel like celebrating Christmas. Not this year. I just want to get it over with, put it behind me. I'm sure you understand.' He could interpret that any way he liked, she thought anxiously, knowing that she had enmeshed herself even further in a web of complicated lies and deceit.

'I see,' he said, giving her a thoughtful look. 'Yes, of course I understand.'

'Thanks for the invitation.' She smiled a false smile and her stomach churned at the thoughts of her deception and how glibly she had trotted out the lie.

Daisy was tense for the rest of the night. She picked at her cheesecake and wondered what kind of a monster she had become. An unfeeling, callous monster. And that was just for starters. Heaven help her if Alex ever discovered the truth, although that would scarcely happen, her mind churned. After all, he surely wouldn't be sticking around very much longer. And they would never be back in Dublin together.

When she asked him in for coffee, he refused. He walked her up to the hall door as the cab idled at the kerb. She felt a sudden stab of loss as he took her keys, opened the door and pushed her gently into the hall. He kissed her softly, touched her cheek and backed away. She watched as he strode down the driveway, missing him already, missing the warmth of his arms around her, the feel of his mouth on hers.

What had she expected, she asked herself crossly as the cab purred away. She'd made a mess of things the last time she'd asked him in. Alex was hardly interested in picking up where he'd left off. She looked up at the sky, but all was inky black, not even a glimmer of a star or a curve of the moon in sight. She shivered in the cold night air, all quiet now that the thrumming of the cab had receded into the distance.

* * *

The music thundered around her in rolling waves, the floor jammed with bodies moving in the limited space. Eve was poured into a silvery Lycra top and a short velvet skirt. Her eyes were half closed and her hips moved sensuously as she danced.

369

She was out with Katie and Susan and it had been a rather dull Saturday night, not helped by the fact that she had bumped into Daniel Richards, who was arm in arm with Lucy, waiting to cross at the traffic lights on O'Connell Bridge. She had been rather piqued to see that he looked as though he was really enjoying himself. When she had called out a cheery hello, he had stared right through her.

'That's okay, pretend not to see me,' she called out, slightly surprised that he continued to ignore her, feeling a grim sense of satisfaction at the startled look on Lucy's face.

The nightclub had been fairly uneventful until she had decided to pretend that Alex was there; then it became full of magic. She threw herself into the music and closed her eyes momentarily and she could almost feel his grey eyes burning into hers, the heat of his body close to hers, and when someone tipped her on the shoulder she jumped, thinking it was him.

It was Tony.

'So this is where you get to on a Saturday night.' He leaned closer and shouted at her above the noise of the music and she made an effort to mask her sharp disappointment. She tossed back her hair and laughed.

'How did you manage to track me down?' she shouted at him.

He put his hands possessively on her hips and

drew her towards him. 'I started at the top of Harcourt Street and worked my way across the city,' he said, his mouth close to her ear.

'Yeah, sure!' She laughed again and out of the corner of her eye she caught Susan and Katie throwing envious glances in her direction. So far, they were still on the prowl with not a man in sight. She leaned in towards Tony and caught his husky male scent. 'You're very persistent,' she teased, resting her french-manicured fingers on his chest, feeling the hardness of his body through his shirt.

She hadn't seen him since their meal out a couple of weeks ago. She had enjoyed the night in the discreet, moneyed ambience of La Stampa, and afterwards, his smooth kisses. At the end of the night, though, she had casually told him that she might see him around and he had replied that she could count on that.

'Let's dance,' she invited, moving back a little and throwing herself into the music once more, this time dancing for him.

'I prefer it like this,' he said, reaching for her hands. Without taking his eyes off her face, he placed one of her hands on his hip. He took her other hand and looped it around his waist and holding her close, he began to move. 'That's better,' he said. Even though everyone around them was throwing shapes in time to the disco beat, Tony moved ever so slowly with Eve in his arms.

She'd had too much to drink, Eve realised, because it was all too easy to pretend that Tony was Alex. She closed her eyes and rested her head on his chest and relaxed into him as the music flowed around them. She didn't care if she was sending out all the wrong signals. For the moment, just now, it filled an urgent need that nothing else seemed to heal.

It was only when he lifted her chin and began to kiss her that she felt empty inside all over again. But she gave it everything she had, moving her tongue against his, arching her body, closing her eyes and pretending it was Alex's mouth on hers, Alex's hands on her body.

'Eve?' Tony asked eventually when they had come up for air. 'Can we go now?' he murmured, his arms still wrapped around her, his mouth inches from hers.

'Go where?' She feigned stupidity, suddenly reluctant to be alone with him.

'Back to my place?'

When she saw the expectant look on his face, she realised belatedly that she had indeed been sending out the wrong signals. The last thing she wanted was to go back to his place. It only meant one thing, and there was no way she could go to bed with him and pretend it was Alex.

'No, sorry Tony, I'm... look, let's just leave it for now.'

'There's someone else, isn't there?' Tony said unexpectedly.

'What do you mean?'

'You're not really with me, are you?'

'Of course I am,' she insisted. 'I'm here right beside you, aren't I?'

'You don't need to let on, Eve. Call it instinct if you want, but I know when I'm not wanted. He's a fool, whoever he is, for leaving you free to roam around.' Then he was gone, melting through the crowds on the dance floor.

She left before the night was over, going out into the cold night air with Katie and Susan. Dublin city centre was alive with groups of Christmas revellers roaring Christmas songs, couples clinging together at taxi ranks, colleagues and friends in glitzy clothes pouring out from Christmas parties, all against a myriad of festive, glittering lights twinkling from shop windows, offices and street decorations.

She would have to pull herself together and put Alex out of her mind once and for all. She decided to relax and enjoy the season. There was something about Christmas that she loved, she thought as the taxi drove through Rathmines. Even here, lamp-lit streets were thronged with revellers on their way home, couples walking arm in arm, groups of friends steering along the pavements and singing, framed by shop windows full of twinkling Christmas lights.

Eve suddenly thought of Daniel Richards.

It seemed as though he had managed to forget all about her and erase Eve Andrews from his life.

She wondered where he had been going with Lucy and if he had brought her back to his bed-sit at the end of the evening. Maybe even now he was making love to her with the same careful attentiveness that he had shown to Eve.

She felt a sudden lurch in her heart as she recalled how deliberately she had used him. What was the point, though, in recalling her ruthless dismissal of him, or the way he had looked at her as she left his bed-sit? She had told him no strings; she had made that perfectly clear. And whatever he had felt for her at the time, he was quite clearly over her by now.

In much the same way, she told herself firmly, that she was over Alex.

Chapter Thirty-nine

Eve threw herself into the Christmas whirl. Behind her silvery laughter was the decision that she had banished all thoughts of Alex from her head for good. She revelled in the glitzy run-up to Christmas like she never had before. She floated into Foley Financials each morning, feeling as though the clouds had lifted and all she could see ahead were sunny blue skies. Life had moved on at last.

And it didn't matter that Daniel's eyes had suddenly begun to haunt her as she remembered with uncomfortable clarity just how much she had taunted and teased him all those months in Foley's. It didn't matter that his face swam into her dreams as she recalled just how easily she had walked all over him.

Her only regret was that it had taken her so long to get over Alex, she thought as she got ready for the office party. Why the hell had it taken her so much time to forget that bastard? And she hadn't even gone to bed with him. Eve shook her head as she took out her make-up case and selected her eye liner. She must have been mad, stark-raving mad. At the office party in Jury's Hotel, she flirted frivolously with every male in sight, laughing a little louder than usual, showing the world that she was having the time of her life. But for the first time ever after a Christmas party, she went home on her own.

* * *

'Guess what?' Victoria said the week before Christmas.

'What?' Eve asked irritably as she spooned instant coffee into a mug.

'Guess who Mum invited for Christmas dinner?'

'She's invited someone?'

'Yeah, Marina.'

'You're joking. Not mad Marina.' Eve winced as she dropped the spoon and it clattered onto the counter.

'Who's taking my sister's name in vain?' Liz breezed into the kitchen. 'God, Eve, you look bad,' she continued unsympathetically. 'Late night?'

'It wasn't that late. I got in around four.'

'An early night for you.'

'What's this about Marina?' she asked as she poured boiling water into her mug.

'I've invited her for Christmas,' Liz said crisply.

'That's just terrific,' Eve snapped. 'What about Daisy?'

'Daisy's staying in London.'

'What? She's not still over there, is she?' Eve asked, mentally blocking out any reaction to the mention of London.

'Yes, she is and Marina's very upset. So don't go aggravating her, Eve. I just want a peaceful family Christmas,' Liz said meaningfully.

'I have no intention of aggravating Marina. I'm just amazed that Daisy's managed to duck out of Christmas. I never thought she'd have the guts to stay away this long.'

'Marina thinks she's pregnant,' Victoria suddenly announced.

'Victoria!' Liz gave her a look of outrage.

'I heard you telling Dad,' Victoria said defensively.

'Don't you dare attempt to repeat that.' Liz was furious.

'That's the funniest thing I've heard in years,' Eve laughed. 'Daisy, pregnant! What a ridiculous idea. I think she did have a fella the time I was over there, but she'd probably run a mile if he came onto her.'

'That's enough,' Liz rebuked. 'I want no mention whatsoever of London or Daisy when Marina is here.'

'How come we have to put up with her?'

'I'm hardly going to leave her all alone on Christmas Day.'

'Don't see why not,' Eve said sulkily.

'That's quite enough, Eve. You'd better see to it that you make Marina welcome.'

'I hope you have plenty of vodka in stock.'

'I don't think Marina will be drinking much,' Liz said.

'I'm not worried about Marina,' Eve scoffed. 'I'm thinking of me. I intend to get well and truly plastered.'

* * *

Daisy met Alex after work on Christmas Eve. Although Dolan's Bar was staying open until the usual time, the kitchens closed up soon after lunch and Alex met Daisy for a quick meal before he left for Heathrow. In the restaurant he surprised her with a small package, sliding it across the table towards her. 'Christmas pressie,' he said.

She opened it to reveal a CD of *The Phantom of the Opera.*

'And that's not all,' he said, handing her another gift-wrapped package, a bottle of perfume. And later, when he left her home, Alex insisted on coming in and dropping something else under the Christmas tree.

'That's your real present,' he said. 'Not to be

opened until Christmas Day,' he cautioned. Then he wrapped her in his arms and kissed her slowly and lingeringly.

'That will have to last me all the way into the new year,' he said, his voice husky as they drew apart. 'And maybe then, Daisy…?'

The unspoken question shivered in the air. Her mouth trembled and her face burned where he cradled it in the palm of his hand. The front room was lit only by the fairy lights on the Christmas tree. She looked at his face in the semi-darkness and what she saw there made her heart leap. Alex wanted and desired her. She saw the need in his dark grey eyes and she ached inside with a strange kind of longing.

'Don't go away,' he murmured, pulling her into his arms. 'I'll be back to you.'

She watched from the doorway as he jumped into the driving seat. Impulsively she went after him, shivering in her thick knit jumper in the chilly December air, and Alex got out of his car and there, on the pavement, began to kiss her again. Eventually he pushed her gently away and told her he would miss his flight if he didn't get a move on. 'Although maybe Christmas in London would be an excellent idea,' he said, his eyes searching hers.

She shook her head. 'Your family is expecting you,' she told him. 'You can't let them down.'

'I suppose not,' he smiled. She waved as he drove away, watching the red tail lights as he went down the road, hearing the beep of his car horn before he turned the corner and disappeared from sight.

* * *

'You're happy over in London?' Jane asked.

'Very,' he agreed.

'Come on, spit it out. Who is she?'

'What do you mean?' Alex lightly quipped.

'You're in love.'

'How did you know?' He didn't bother to deny it. There was no point, especially when he couldn't stop the wide grin from spreading across his face.

'It's obvious,' Jane smiled.

'Her name is Daisy and let me tell you all about her,' he began as they headed into the copse.

It was St Stephen's Day and they were strolling in Marlay Park. Jane was muffled up in a suede jacket, jeans and walking boots. Alex strolled beside her, his hands in the pockets of his fleece-lined jacket. He had arrived into a chaotic Dublin Airport at eight o'clock on Christmas Eve, and so far he hadn't had much of a chance to talk to his mother alone.

Marlay Park was dotted with walkers and joggers enjoying the crisp, fresh air. The day was cool and dry, the light breeze invigorating. Rising up beyond the green expanse of parkland, the Dublin Mountains were a blue-grey backdrop. In the stretches of woodland, denuded tree branches laced together against a cool blue sky. Forgotten leaves, a legacy of autumn, lay in crumpled drifts against the edges of the track where they strolled.

Alex missed Daisy. He wished she was here now with him, her arm in his as they walked together in this fresh, calm morning. Pale sunshine filtered through the bare-branched trees and he could just imagine the way it would shine on her hair.

'I asked her to come home with me for Christmas. I knew you wouldn't mind,' he finally explained.

'And?'

Alex shrugged. 'You know how it is. She just wanted to forget Christmas for this year, on account of her mother. She felt she wouldn't be good company.'

'I understand,' Jane agreed. 'Didn't you tell her that we all felt like that this year? I was dreading Christmas without Brian. But we managed to get through the day unscathed, didn't we? Having you home, and so obviously happy, was a great boost. Anyway, Daisy sounds lovely. I can't wait to meet her. Maybe you can persuade her to come over early in the new year.'

'I hope so. She's very special.'

'I'm sure she is.'

'I'm just sorry that Dad never had the chance to meet her.'

'No regrets,' Jane said, putting her hand on his arm. 'Your dad was very proud of you and he would have been delighted to see you so happy. That came first with him, you know. Your and the girls' happiness.'

'Was he really so proud of me?' Alex paused on the winding track.

'Of course. Never, ever doubt that, Alex,' Jane said firmly. 'Even the night before he died….' Her voice wavered a little. 'Even that night, he was talking about you before we went to bed. He admired your determination and independence, your self-reliance.'

'Really?'

'Yes, and why wouldn't he? Don't look so surprised,' Jane said. 'I know about the proposal he put to you, the start-up funding he offered.'

'You do?'

'Of course. We talked about everything. That's why I miss him so much. He told me about your decision to turn him down and he admired you for that, for having the guts to want to make it on your own.'

Then Alex asked her the question he had longed to ask her, but couldn't up to now give voice to. 'Dad wasn't angry with me, then?'

'Angry? What gave you that idea?' His mother stopped and looked at him.

'Well, we had some words the night before….'

Jane shook her head in disbelief. 'Oh, Alex, you mad thing, I hope to God you haven't been beating yourself up over that,' she scolded. Alex remained silent. 'Have you? Why didn't you talk to me sooner?' she demanded, putting her hand on his arm. 'Brian thought he had been a little impatient with you. But you know what Brian was like! Sometimes *you* can be very impatient, Alex, but Brian was ten times worse. There was no stopping your dad. He wanted to sort out everyone's life. He wasn't the least bit angry with you, so get that idea right out of your head.'

Impatient, not angry. His father had been impatient. That was all. No big deal. It certainly didn't sound like the scene that Alex had carried in his head for the best part of a year. Maybe, just maybe, the awful events of the following morning had coloured his thinking, had distorted his version of events. Whatever. The main thing was that his father hadn't been angry with him. As Alex realised this, he was aware of a great sense of relief.

They continued walking and after a while he said in a light tone of voice, 'I'm not always that impatient, by the way.'

'No?'

'I think it's fair to say that I've shown remarkable restraint over the last few weeks. And sorry, but no,' he grinned. 'I'm not going to elaborate.'

Again he wished Daisy was here. He wished he could conjure her up so that he could tell her how happy he felt and how much he loved her.

And then, perhaps, show her exactly how much….

Chapter Forty

Daisy went to Alison's family for Christmas dinner at Joe and Alison's insistence. There would be fourteen at the table and she was more than welcome to join the gang. No way were they leaving Daisy out of the celebrations.

Caroline invited her over on Boxing Day. She was dying for Daisy to meet her daughter, Sharon. Besides, she had a huge hen turkey she just had to get rid of and she was hoping she could tempt Daisy with some of her homemade trifle. After all, it wasn't fair that she had such a slim figure. Before Daisy realised it, Christmas was over and she was back in Dolan's, only this time they were catering for the shoppers who were battling the post-Christmas sales.

Then it was New Year's Eve and Alison was having a party. Daisy had covered the lunch hour and the early evening shift in Dolan's, and once again she found herself being the one who was calm and in control while Alison was having a major panic attack.

'I must have been mad! What made me invite the gang from the office? As if I haven't got enough people coming!' Alison fluttered around the kitchen in her dressing gown, a towel wrapped around her hair. She dove into one of the kitchen presses, rummaging around for glasses.

'Relax, Alison, we'll manage,' Daisy soothed, looking up from the table where she was arranging finger food.

'Oh God, look at the time!' Alison wailed as she went over to the freezer and began to pull out the contents. 'Where the hell are the ice bags? I'll never be ready.'

'Of course you will,' Daisy said. 'Go upstairs and get changed. I'll make more ice and finish off the food.' She was glad to be able to make herself useful. She owed so much to Joe and Alison, as much for their unconditional acceptance of her as well as their friendly hospitality. They hadn't been the least bit curious when she told them she was staying in London for Christmas, and she was grateful for that.

Paula, on the other hand, was convinced she intended to be tucked away somewhere with Alex for the Christmas break. 'An intimate hotel in the Cotswolds, I'd guess,' she had purred down the phone. 'I can just see the four-poster bed and the log fires burning. From what I remember of Alex, I bet they won't be the only fires!'

'Get lost, Paula,' Daisy had frowned, feeling suddenly irritable. 'Alex is going home to his family.'

'And you're not?'

'No.' It was far too complicated to explain, Daisy thought. She wouldn't even have known where to start. And she didn't want to talk about it anyway. She was relieved when Christmas was over. She was even more relieved that she was busy now on New Year's Eve and hadn't got a spare second to think.

Alison went over to the oven and pulled out a sizzling tray of chicken wings. 'The vol-au-vents have to be done, and the salsa bites,' she gabbled. 'And I completely forgot to chill the white wine. Why on earth did I say I'd have this party?'

Joe came into the kitchen and took one look at his harassed wife. 'For God's sake, Ali, relax. You're not going to be awarded extra brownie points for the chill factor of the wine.'

'Everything is under control, Joe,' Daisy told him. 'Alison is going upstairs now to get ready, aren't you, Alison?'

'There. You heard what Daisy said.' Joe waggled a finger at his wife. 'Just follow her example and calm down.'

Daisy smiled in the direction of Alison's retreating back. It was easy for her to be calm in the midst of all the party chaos, for all this was nothing compared to the usual chaotic state of the thoughts churning around in her mind.

* * *

The night was a great success. Daisy was rushed off her feet, ferrying drinks and food to and fro, dodging balloons and party poppers as well as one of Alison's work colleagues who showed more of an interest in her than Daisy would have liked.

Drink flowed and the music throbbed and towards midnight Joe tuned into BBC1 and they watched the countdown from Trafalgar Square. Joe popped the cork on bottles of champagne and someone else released the party streamers and began to burst balloons, so mad confusion reigned for several minutes.

Daisy was hugged and kissed and hugged again and wished all the best. Party streamers fell from her hair as Joe gave her a big bear hug and said that he hoped all her wishes came true. Then she spotted Alison's colleague making his way purposefully towards her, so she escaped upstairs to her room.

She pulled back the curtains and opened the window so that a chink of cool air flowed into the room. The house was warm and stuffy and she welcomed the breath of fresh air. She had time to think then, of Alex. Her hand automatically went to the delicate gold bracelet she was wearing. The package he had left under the Christmas tree had been opened as ordered on Christmas morning.

How could they possibly continue like this? The kisses she offered were nothing in response to the need she sensed inside him, a need she sensed he was barely keeping under control. Her past failures in the bedroom stared her in the face. No way could she inflict that kind of disastrous scenario on Alex, of all people, never mind the ghosts she continued to conceal from him.

Surely it would be best to finish things now, while they were still friends? She couldn't really see any way out otherwise. She shivered and reached for the handle of the window. Down in the garden, someone opened the patio door and a column of light poured out across the garden, along with the noise of the party. She closed the window and drew across the curtains.

* * *

'I never really liked New Year's Eve,' Marina said, her voice wobbling a little.

Here we go, Liz silently braced herself. She could hear the commotion from the neighbour's house two doors down as the party burst out the front door and a gang of revellers started to do the conga on the quiet, tree-lined avenue.

Why wasn't she out there with them, cheering in the new year? What had made her decide to be the sacrificial lamb and invite Marina not only for Christmas Day but also New Year's Eve? Christmas Day had gone smoothly enough, she supposed, but earlier tonight, when she had collected Marina, she had noticed straight away that her sister was already drunk.

She exchanged a look with Harry but he just gave her a non-committal shrug. 'Don't know why people make such a fuss of it myself,' Liz said mildly, breaking her own golden rule and pouring more drink for Marina as well as herself.

'It's a bad night to be alone with your thoughts,' Marina went on.

'I think it's the same as any other night, really,' Harry said.

Marina smiled at him. 'Easy to see, Harry, that you don't have any unhappy memories.'

He smiled back. 'No I don't, and I consider myself to be a very lucky man.'

'And you're lucky too, Liz,' Marina said. 'You have your two daughters. I don't have anyone left now.'

'You have Daisy.'

'She's deserted me, just like her father did.' Marina began to cry harsh, wracking sobs that shook her small frame.

In the end Harry reluctantly agreed that they couldn't very well send Marina home to an empty house, considering the state she was in. Maybe she could sleep in Eve's bed, Liz suggested. Victoria was out and due home at one o'clock, but Eve had mentioned something about staying over in a friend's house.

It wouldn't kill her to lend her bed to Marina, just this once. Eve didn't even have to know, she decided as between them she and Harry got Marina up the stairs.

Chapter Forty-one

The gang from Foley's had all met in a city centre bar earlier that evening, prior to going out to Conor's new apartment in Dundrum for a housewarming cum New Year's Eve bash. Rachel and John had joined them for a couple of drinks in the bar but had then gone home for a private celebration.

No one could attempt to leave before six in the morning, Conor had warned in advance. He only had two bedrooms, but he had borrowed sleeping bags and duvets for anyone who wanted to crash out on the floor. The kitchen was stockpiled with drink and everyone would have to help themselves as he was going to be far too busy enjoying himself to do barman. The only things his guests weren't allowed to touch under pain of death were his precious collection of CDs and his high-tech music centre.

Eve, Susan and Katie were very impressed, and not just because they were wrapped in a warm alcoholic glow after the earlier session in the pub. The living room of the apartment was lit with a disco light that Conor had 'borrowed' from his younger sister. There were balloons and party poppers and Conor had carefully planned the music in advance so that a succession of disco beats, party songs and the occasional smoochy ballad blasted the air.

'I'm taking a fresh look at Conor,' Katie said, her eyes roving appreciatively around the apartment.

'So am I,' Susan admitted. The three of them sat slightly squashed on a two-seater sofa in a corner of the living room. Midnight had come and gone and had been duly celebrated with the fizzing champagne that Conor had surprisingly produced. Maybe not so surprisingly after all, Eve thought, considering that Conor, flush with property ownership, seemed to have discovered a whole new persona. She turned around on the sofa and asked Katie if she really fancied Conor.

'Maybe I do. And remember that I saw Conor first, cos I'm longer in Foley's,' Katie grinned.

'Well, neither of us will stand a chance if Eve decides to move in for the kill,' Susan pointed out.

'How about it Eve? Fancy Conor, now that he's a man of substance?'

Eve took a gulp of her Smirnoff Ice and wrinkled her nose. 'No thanks, girls. Conor is nice and all that, but….'

The door to the living room opened, and in walked Daniel. Eve looked past him, expecting to see Lucy on his heels, but he appeared to be alone. She watched him for several moments as he circled the edge of the room, joking with Conor and the lads from Foley's, draining a bottle of beer and going into the kitchen to fetch another. He made no move in her direction.

'Excuse me a minute,' she eventually said as she rose a little unsteadily to her feet. She pushed through the crowded room until she was standing in front of him and he broke off his conversation with Conor and turned to face her.

'Hi Eve.' He made a move back towards Conor, but Eve put her hand on his arm, holding his attention.

'Hi Daniel. All alone? Where's the lovely Lucy tonight?' she asked.

'Didn't you hear? We split up before Christmas.'

'That's too bad. Would you like to cry on my shoulder?'

'Not really.' He sounded down, she realised, taking little notice of his negative answer. Probably upset and depressed at getting dumped just before Christmas.

'Lucy's an awful silly girl,' Eve tittered, trying to make light of things but suddenly conscious that she had had quite a lot to drink. 'You should never break up with a boyfriend just before Christmas. You should wait till afterwards, when your Christmas pressie has been safely delivered!'

'You have it wrong. I broke up with Lucy. And before you jump to conclusions, I gave her a present anyway.'

'Well, I'm really sorry you've split up, whatever the reason. Why don't I give you a consolation kiss for New Year's Eve?' She put her arms around him and lifted her face. She pressed her body against his and backed him into the dimly lit corner.

'I don't particularly want to kiss you, Eve.'

'What's wrong? Am I that bad that you can't face a teeny weeny kiss?'

He jerked away from her and her arms fell to her sides. 'I shouldn't have come here tonight,' he said. 'I thought by now that I could have sat in the same room as you and not feel anything. But I was wrong.'

She flinched. 'What's that supposed to mean?'

'I don't want to talk about it.' His voice was slightly harsh.

'No, I'd like to know. What exactly have I done wrong?' she challenged.

'Nothing, Eve.' He gave her a half smile that suddenly went right to her heart. 'Except you've spoiled me for everyone else, haven't you?'

What the hell did he mean? Maybe he couldn't quite get it together with Lucy, but there was no need to blame her. 'That's not my fault. I didn't do it on purpose.'

He looked at her shrewdly. 'Of course you didn't. It was just a laugh, wasn't it? No strings. Ha! I thought I could have made a go of it with Lucy, but….' He shrugged.

'Why don't we go somewhere quiet and talk about it?' Eve suggested. 'There's a spare bedroom next door, we can have a chat in peace and, who knows,' she gave him a knowing look, 'maybe I could help you forget all about Lucy.'

'No way. I want you out of my life. The last thing I need is the two of us alone in a bedroom.'

'Not even for old time's sake?' she said in a soft voice, trying to win him around.

'Don't be ridiculous.' Daniel was coolly casual. 'You're not playing with me any more, Eve. Why don't you just get lost!' He abandoned his bottle of beer and marched out of the apartment.

She was relieved that no one had taken much notice and that there were no witnesses to her humiliation, because Conor had started to play a silly party game with the balloons and everyone seemed to be shrieking and clowning around. She went into the kitchen, grabbed some more bottles of Smirnoff Ice and squeezed her way back to the corner of the sofa she'd been sitting on.

Daniel seemed to think she had wrecked his life. He was being totally ridiculous, she assured herself. He would just have to grow up. Silly fool that he was, he had turned down a chance to go to bed with her again. Who knows, it could have been a very good start to the new year. As for the way he had stalked off on her... good riddance. She finished one bottle and reached for another, feeling a mounting anger at the ease with which he had casually told her to get lost.

In the end she left early, slipping out without Conor seeing her, phoning for a taxi from the foyer of his apartment block. She couldn't face staying on until the following morning, trying to keep a happy face in the drink-fuelled, jovial atmosphere. She felt tired all of a sudden, tired of life and complicated love lives. Then halfway home in the warm, stuffy taxi, as if things weren't bad enough, she was overwhelmed with painful waves of nausea. She began to breathe softly through her nose and tried to relax, praying she would make it home in one piece.

She crept into the house in Templeogue and headed straight for the downstairs loo, making it just in time. After a while she felt a little better. Her stomach settled down when it was finally empty and the trembling eased. She still had a peculiar ache in her chest and she wondered if she had finally managed to poison her system with an excess of alcohol. She groaned aloud and looked at her pale face in the mirror.

She rinsed her face with tepid water, not caring that her mascara was smudged, and went into the kitchen to get a drink of water. She ignored the main light and switched on the recessed lighting in the wall presses so that the room was filled with a soft glow.

'Eve!'

She whirled around and almost dropped her glass. 'Mum! You gave me a fright!'

'What are you doing home?' Liz asked. She was standing in the doorway, wrapped in a silky dressing gown.

'Why shouldn't I be home?' Eve frowned, wondering why her mother looked so nervous.

'I thought you were out for the night.'

'I was. Now I'm home.'

'No, I meant staying out for the night.'

'Yeah, well,' Eve shrugged, 'I thought I'd come home and wish you all a happy new year, but it seems the party's over.'

'The party never even got started,' Liz said, moving into the kitchen and closing the door quietly behind her. 'Marina was very upset so I couldn't send her home, so, well... I didn't think you'd be home,' she said sheepishly.

'What's the problem?'

'There isn't really a problem,' Liz began. 'It's just that, well, I gave Marina a loan of your bed.'

'You what?'

'Look, Eve,' Liz began. 'She was very distressed. I couldn't possibly send her home.'

'Distressed?' Eve echoed. 'I don't care how

distressed she was, you'd no right to give her my bed just like that.'

'She was really in a bad way.'

'You're always making excuses for her,' Eve fumed. 'What about me? Maybe I'm in a bad way tonight. Maybe I need my bed.'

'Keep your voice down,' Liz ordered.

'No, why should I?' Eve huffed. 'I'm tired and upset and I can't even get into my bed because mad Marina is hogging it!'

'Look, I'm sorry about this,' Liz began.

'Oh, forget it, Mum!' The edge of alcohol had worn off and now Eve just felt downhearted. What a crappy start to the year. Somehow or other, Daniel had upset her and now she hadn't even got the privacy of her bed in which to have a good bawl.

'How come you're upset?' Liz suddenly asked. 'Is anything the matter?'

'If you must know, I had too much to drink,' Eve shrugged. 'Nothing new, you'll probably say,' she laughed hollowly.

'Happens to us all,' Liz said, giving her an indulgent smile. 'Are you okay now?'

'Yeah, of course.'

'Any particular reason why you had too much to drink?' Liz asked casually.

'No, not really.'

'You don't want to talk, I suppose.'

'My main problem right now is that I'm short of a bed, thanks to you!'

'I'll make up the futon in your dad's study,' Liz suggested. 'I'm really sorry about this, Eve, but I didn't think you'd be home.'

Neither did I, Eve silently fretted. I should have been out enjoying the night and not standing in the kitchen with a sour taste in my mouth, an achy tummy and the beginnings of an unmerciful hangover. 'And what was wrong with Marina?' she asked, wondering why she was having this conversation with her mother at… was it only two o'clock in the morning? Somehow it felt much, much later.

'She's missing Daisy,' Liz said. 'And I suppose New Year's Eve just got too much for her.'

'Don't say it – Marina's unhappy memories.' Eve shook her head. 'You've told me already, Mum. What she needs is a man in her life, then all her problems would be solved. She'd be only too glad to have Daisy out of her hair.'

'I wish it were that easy,' Liz said. 'She was really upset when Daisy's father went off. She was madly in love with him, you know. And she always said he was the only one for her, the only man she would ever love.'

'That's pathetic. She should have got over him years ago. It's total madness to decide that only one person can be the love of your life,' Eve said scathingly. 'And she could only have been, what, twenty-four? My age….' Her voice suddenly trailed away.

'She was very young, all right, when her life completely fell apart. Poor Marina. We were the lucky ones, Eve, you and me. We survived intact, didn't we?'

An icicle of alarm began a slow glide down Eve's backbone. 'Sorry, Mum, I don't get you.'

'We walked away from the whole thing without so much as a scratch,' Liz said, staring into space, looking as though she was miles removed.

'What whole thing?'

'The accident, of course.'

'What do you mean? You don't mean to say… I was there? *We* were there? When the crash happened?'

'Yes, of course, didn't you know?' Liz looked confused.

'No. How could I have known?' Eve's voice was shrill.

This was a nightmare. Not even a nightmare – worse than that. This was actual reality. No longer was the accident something vague that had happened in the dim and distant past, an impersonal statistic. She had been there, at that time, in that place, when her small cousin's life had been snuffed out. Probably beside her in the car, even as it happened. Good God.

She was wide awake now, with a hangover beginning to pound away inside her head. 'You didn't talk about the details, Mum,' Eve said shakily. 'The gory details, I seem to remember you calling them.'

'We were all in the car together,' Liz sighed. 'You, me, Daisy, Marina and of course Jessica, coming back from the park. Marina was driving, you see, and to this day she's always blamed herself for what happened.'

Chapter Forty-two

Forever afterwards, Liz is there in that long moment of silence in the warm London street, a silence followed by the sound of running footsteps and doors slamming. She doesn't want to open her eyes, afraid of what she might see. She sits in the passenger seat of the car and holds her breath as though she can hold the moment in check.

She opens her eyes to brilliant sunlight. It dazzles off the bonnet of the car and reflects a thousand times over in the shattered windscreen. She looks across to where Marina is slumped across the wheel of the car, her dark hair swinging forward and hiding her face.

There are urgent cries outside on the London street. Liz moves delicately in her seat and looks behind her. Nestled securely in a Moses basket, swathed in soft pink cotton, a starfish hand lying against her translucent face, Eve is sound asleep and a silent, thankful tear slips down Liz's face.

Then she looks beyond her daughter to the twins. She sees immediately that Jessica is dead.

And Daisy begins to scream.

Chapter Forty-three

'Did you miss me?'

'Of course I did, and thanks again for the beautiful present,' Daisy said.

'You're very welcome,' Alex said, accelerating smoothly out into the flow of London traffic.

He had arrived into Heathrow the night before and had phoned her immediately. 'Dinner tomorrow night?'

'Lovely,' Daisy had said. 'I'm covering lunchtime tomorrow and I should be finished after four o'clock. But why don't I cook us something?' she suggested on the spur of the moment. She was still flushed with the success of her New Year's Eve party food and it would be nice, she thought, to have a welcome back meal for Alex. 'Nothing too exotic,' she hastily added. 'Just your favourite steak and chips.'

As soon as Daisy's shift had finished she had changed out of her uniform into a pair of jeans and a pink cotton jumper. She had waited for Alex, feeling suddenly shy. Kim was polishing glasses when Alex came into the bar and she pretended to swoon. Caroline jumped immediately to attention. He had almost caused Daisy to turn and run in the face of his air of authority, until he had smiled at her with his dark grey eyes and given her a conspiratorial wink behind Caroline's back. Hand in hand, dodging the rain, they had hurried out to his car.

It was a wet evening in early January. It was somehow comforting to be sitting in the passenger seat, out of the driving rain, even if her proximity to Alex was a little unsettling. She looked out the window instead and watched the windscreen wipers swish to and fro.

'Are you sure about this?' Alex asked as they halted once more in the heavy traffic. Daisy focused on the red taillights shimmering ahead, piercing the gloom of the evening.

'Of course,' she said. 'Don't you trust my cooking?'

'I'm sure I'll love your cooking, but I don't want to put you to any trouble. We can just pick up a Chinese if you want.'

'Not at all, I want to do this,' Daisy insisted.

'Besides, I have everything bought.'

'If you're absolutely certain….'

'I am. Maybe I'm dying to show you what a great cook I am.'

'Big head,' he teased.

'Is that what you think?'

He caught her hand briefly and brought it to his lips. 'Sorry, darling, I couldn't resist.'

Darling. He had just called her darling. Had he missed her as much as she had missed him? Daisy snuck a glance at his profile, but he was giving his full attention to the traffic.

Alex drove right up to the door of his apartment block, jumping out of the Audi and ushering Daisy in out of the teeming rain. He dashed back out to his car and parked it while Daisy hung up her coat and went to the kitchen. The central heating had already come on and the apartment was warm and welcoming. Daisy switched on lights and went over to the kitchen worktop with her shopping bag. She tipped out steaks, onions, mushrooms, the makings of a salad and a bag of oven chips.

She wondered what the hell she was doing.

It was one thing to plan a nice meal for Alex in her head. Even to go out and shop for ingredients and join an impersonal supermarket queue. So far, so good. But it was a different thing entirely, an intimate thing, to be here now, in his kitchen, opening his presses and drawers, looking for his cutlery, olive oil, preparing his grill….

'Don't turn that on. Not just yet.'

Daisy whirled around. He had come in quietly. His dark hair was beaded with rain and the shoulders of his coat were speckled with drops. He walked across the kitchen towards her, his eyes so tender that her throat went dry.

'Your coat, it's wet….' Her voice faded away.

'Then I had better take it off,' he smiled as he shrugged out of it and threw it across a chair. He took off his jacket and loosened his tie and tossed it in the same direction. Her eyes automatically closed as he reached for her and wrapped her in his arms.

'Daisy, I missed you so much,' he murmured, his fingers threaded in her hair, his mouth inches from hers.

'Did you?' She was dizzy.

'Did I, you ask.' She could hear amusement in his tone. 'How dare you sound so surprised,' he teased, his hand cradling her face. 'I missed you from the time I boarded the plane, and I missed you the moment I landed in Dublin. I wanted to see your face on Christmas morning, I wanted to walk with you in Marlay Park and I wanted you with me on New Year's Eve so that we could see in the new year, us, together, so that I could hold you close and kiss you… just like this….'

She felt on fire as she waited for a long, endless moment, and she kept her eyes closed for fear of what he might see there, and then his mouth was on hers. This was fine, this was easy, she told herself, and he deepened the kiss gradually until Daisy was slowly swept away. In a far corner of her mind she suddenly realised that she was kissing him back almost as passionately as he was kissing her. Any strangeness she had felt after his absence seemed to have dissolved. The scent of him, the touch of his mouth and feel of his arms around her seemed so sharply familiar that she was momentarily startled. She thought her knees were going to give way, so she leaned momentarily against the length of his body.

She heard his quick intake of breath and then he pushed her gently away, telling her that he dare not continue, at least for the moment. 'We have some food to cook,' he smiled. 'Then I want to talk to you and I need a clear head.'

'What about?' she asked, feeling wobbly inside and embarrassed at her unexpected show of passion.

'Later,' he said, patting her pink cheek. 'Let's see to those steaks.'

It was better when she was occupied. She relaxed a little and found that it was fun to be standing side by side in his compact kitchen, watching the steaks sizzle under the grill, frying the mushrooms and onions, heating the chips in the oven. Outside the night was cold and wet and flurries of rain beat against the window, but inside it was cosy and warm, the aroma of cooking food filtering around and Alex at her elbow, teasing and joking.

'Who's cooking this food?' she asked him sternly as he made a comment about the mushrooms.

'Sorry, sorry.' He held up his hands in mock apology. 'I'll set the table and keep out of your way.'

They ate side by side at his small kitchen table and she listened carefully as he told her about the chat he'd had with his mother.

'I'm glad we had the chance to talk about Dad,' he said, confiding in her. 'It was a weight off my mind to know that he wasn't angry with me the night before he died. I feel... I feel a great sense of release, a letting go.'

'I'm glad,' Daisy smiled. 'I told you you were being far too hard on yourself.'

'I should've talked to my mother months ago,' he said, shaking his head. 'It would have saved me a lot of angst.'

'At least you feel better about things now,' she said softly.

'Yes, I do. And what about you?' he asked, concern evident in his glance. 'Did you get through Christmas all right?'

'Me?' She was startled for a minute.

'Yes, you know....'

'Oh,' she said faintly. She had completely forgotten about the lies and deceit and it all came back to her now, washing over her in a cold, hard wave, sweeping away the sense of joy and happiness that had swelled in her heart.

For a moment she longed to tell him the truth

and beg his forgiveness, tell him she was truly sorry for deceiving him. She was tempted to suggest that they go back to the beginning and start all over again. She stole a quick glance at his face as he sat across the table from him and her heart bled.

Not all the lavender scent in the world would relax her enough to be able to admit the truth to Alex. It was unthinkable, so she swallowed hard and told him in a flat tone that she had got through Christmas in one piece.

'My mother was disappointed that you didn't join us.'

'Was she?'

'Until I told her that I would bring you home soon.'

'Did you?' Her voice was high and tight. She sensed a change in him, and she tried to lighten the atmosphere, to return to the jokey banter they had earlier exchanged. 'That was delicious,' she said, pushing her plate away. 'My compliments to the cook.'

'And mine too,' he said, taking the plates over to the dishwasher. Daisy offered to help clear away but he wouldn't let her. 'I'll leave these for now,' he said. 'Come over to the sitting room. I want to talk to you about something.'

It was only a short walk, just a few paces, yet even then Daisy had the sense of something about to happen. She sat on the edge of the sofa as he handed her a glass of wine.

'I don't know where to start,' he said, running a hand through his dark hair, leaving it tossed and untidy.

'I suppose the beginning would be as good a place as any,' Daisy said lightly, trying to ignore the slither of alarm that uncoiled in her stomach.

They had come to the end. This was it. Alex wanted out.

He sat down beside her and took her hand in his.

Definitely over. She braced herself for the bad news and forced her trembling mouth into a smile of acceptance. Just as well to have it over and done with now. They couldn't have continued the way they were.

'I have to go back to Dublin,' he told her. 'For good. Promotion, believe it or not.'

'Dublin?'

'Yes, well, I was only over here on loan. You know that, don't you?'

'That's right.' Another fib. She'd forgotten completely.

'I had a meeting with my boss, Mark, the day before yesterday. He's taking over another company and I'm going in as one of the directors.'

'That's great news, Alex. I'm really happy for you.'

'And that's not all.'

'Yes?'

'Well, you see, Daisy, I want you to come home with me.'

411

Dear God. Funny how things could hit like a bolt out of the blue. At the back of her mind, she had always pictured a scene where Alex was telling her that it was time for him to move on, that their relationship had run its course. She had even imagined what she might say in reply to ease things for both of them, to send him on his way with the minimum of fuss and embarrassment. Never in her wildest dreams had she imagined this.

'Sorry, Alex, I'm afraid I can't,' she began, dragging her chaotic thoughts together.

'Can't? What do you mean, can't?'

'I just can't.' She shook her head, appalled at this turn of events.

'It's very simple, really,' he went on. 'I have to go back to Dublin and I need you to come with me. I can't bear to leave you behind.'

Daisy's heart turned over. He couldn't possibly need her. He didn't know the real Daisy O'Neill. Kissing him was easy. Going to bed with him would be a disaster.

'Going back to Dublin doesn't suit me at all,' she said, trying to sound firm. 'It's out of the question right now.'

'So it's Dublin, is it? It's not just me,' he looked at her thoughtfully.

'That's right.'

'Then there's only one thing for it,' he said. 'I'll have to call Mark and tell him I'm refusing his offer.'

'I can't let you do that!'

'Daisy, you mean far more to me than any offer of promotion. If going back to Dublin means losing you, then I'll stay put.'

'No way,' Daisy was horrified. 'You can't possibly turn down an opportunity like that on account of me. I won't let you.'

Alex grinned. 'You can't stop me.'

Daisy's heart raced. 'Yes, I can,' she said in a resolute voice. 'I think you'd be mad to turn down a promotion because of me,' she said, taking the only way out that she could find. 'Who knows how long we'll be together, anyway?'

Alex looked puzzled. Daisy would rather have died than watch the uncertainly sweep across his face. She had no other option, though, so she steeled herself and tried to stay cool and calm.

'Sorry Daisy, I don't get you.'

His eyes. Suddenly she couldn't bear to look at them. 'Let's face it,' she shrugged. 'We're not exactly committed or anything like that. It was nice knowing you, but I think that this is as far as things are going between us, so you'd be far better off going home to Dublin while you have this golden opportunity.' She drained her glass of wine and hated herself.

'I'm finding this rather difficult.' Alex's voice was charged with emotion. 'Do you have any idea what I'm trying to say to you?'

She nailed a smile to her frozen face. 'Are you listening to what I'm telling you?'

'Don't you care for me? Even a little bit? Look at me,' he ordered. She turned to him and concentrated on a spot in the middle of his forehead. 'Tell me you don't like this.' His fingers traced a path around her burning face. 'Or this.' He entwined his fingers in her hair and drew her closer. 'Or how about this.' He ran a finger down her forehead, over her nose and stopped at her upper lip. Daisy's mouth automatically opened in response and his finger slipped inside to the velvety warmth. Their eyes locked and Alex moved towards her until they were only inches apart.

'Tell me you don't like this.' He took his finger away from her mouth and replaced it with his lips. She felt hot tears clog the back of her throat and she kept her eyes firmly closed lest they spill out. His kiss went on forever, and by the time he was lifting his mouth off hers, she felt completely devastated. 'Tell me you don't care for me even a little bit, and you're a rotten liar,' he said, looking at her evenly.

Liar? Oh God, little did he know, she thought desperately. Another reason why Dublin was a no-go area.

'Look, Alex, it's no use,' she said.

'No use? Would you mind explaining that remark?' he asked.

'We have no future together, you and me.'

'Says who?'

She tried to think of something that would once

414

and for all make him go home to his brilliant new job in Dublin and forget all about her.

'You see….'

'This had better be good, Daisy,' he said, a slight edge to his voice.

'Well, I've always wanted to travel,' she began.

'Travel?' His eyes narrowed in confusion.

'Yes, travel the world. I've only really begun, Alex, and there's so much out there. I have it all planned in my head.' She tried to keep her voice calm. 'Six months in London, six months in America, and after that, who knows?'

'You can't be serious.'

'I am.' She met his gaze head on, feeling hot and cold all over, and he looked so disappointed that she could have wept.

And later she did.

After he had driven her home, so stony that his face looked carved from granite, accelerating down the road as soon as she had got out of the car, Daisy crawled into bed and turned her face blindly into her pillow.

Chapter Forty-four

When the nightmare grips her in the middle of the
dark hours, she's almost glad of its distraction.
Daisy tenses at the sound of smashing glass and
once again she hears the high-pitched scream.

She automatically looks for the little girl. This
time, she's going to follow her and see the shadowy
nightmare through to the end. When she gets to
the point where the little girl usually disappears,
she calls to her and begs her to stay.

The scene suddenly changes. Daisy shifts in her
sleep. Everything is blurry and indistinct. She sees
Marina crying again, and Liz's arm is around her.
There are strange people everywhere and even though
the sky is blue and the sun is shining and there are
bright flowers all around, everyone looks sad.

Then she sees the girl, but now she isn't dancing. She's dressed all in white and lying in a little white box. She's still and cold and seems frighteningly familiar. Daisy awakes in a sweat.

Chapter Forty-five

'You're looking pleased with yourself,' Eve said.

'Oh, is it obvious?' Rachel glowed.

'You'd want to be blind not to notice that grin on your face,' Eve said a little more sharply than she had intended.

'You don't sound too happy.'

'This place is doing my head in,' Eve huffed, sifting through her in tray, picking up statements at random and letting them slew across her desk. 'I never thought I'd be stuck in this stupid job for so long.'

'It's not that bad.'

'Yes it is. It's mind-numbing, ridiculously boring.' She threw a scowling glance around the office.

'Wow. You're in a bad way.'

'I've just about had enough.'

'I'd really hate to see you go,' Rachel said earnestly. 'But if you want me to do up your CV, just say the word.'

'Maybe I'll take you up on that. I feel I really need a change of scene. I'm just fed up with the same old thing, week in, week out. Anyway, what's your news?'

Rachel gave her a huge grin. 'John surprised me last night. We're going skiing at the end of January! Imagine, me, skiing! I thought it was only for the rich, but John insists we can afford it. I deserve a treat, he says, what with all the saving for the house. I've scarcely bought any new clothes in ages.'

'That's great,' Eve said woodenly. She tried hard to feel enthusiastic for Rachel, but she failed dismally.

'I hope I'll be able to ski and that I don't make an eejit of myself.'

'There's nothing to it. After the first day you'll feel you were always at it.'

'I hope so. I don't want to let John down. What about you? You usually head off to the slopes, don't you?'

'Not this year. I didn't have it organised in time.'

'Maybe next year?' Rachel smiled.

'Yeah, maybe.' She looked out the window at the leaden January sky and tried not to think about the thrill of skiing down the slopes, the crisp snow underneath, the sun glinting on it to form a million dazzling gems. And the nightlife, partying until dawn, falling into someone's arms at five in the morning, back out onto the slopes the next day and the feeling of freedom as she careered down the piste with the air rushing past....

It seemed like a long time, Eve thought as she turned back to her computer, since she had felt quite so utterly, mindlessly free.

The new year had got off to the worst start possible. She had left Conor's party early, feeling out of sorts and expecting to huddle under her cosy duvet and sink into oblivion. Then she had crawled home only to discover that Marina was in her bed. She could have coped with that, though, and bunked down on the futon in her father's study. She could have said goodnight to her mother and tried to grab some sleep, only Liz had unwittingly turned around with her startling news. And out of nowhere they ended up having a huge row in the kitchen at half past two in the morning on New Year's Day.

Even now, days later as she sat at her desk, Eve remembered every word.

'You never told me I was in the car,' she had said to her mother, speaking very slowly as if to try and understand the words.

'I told you the accident happened when we were over in London,' Liz frowned.

'Yes, but I thought you meant we as in you and

Marina. I didn't think you meant you and me.'

'I brought you over to London when you were about two months old so that I could show you off to Marina and the twins. We went to the park and you were tucked quite safely into Daisy's Moses basket. We were just on our way home when a car crashed into the side of us, where Jessica happened to be strapped into her car seat, the opposite side to where you were.' Liz shrugged and tears glimmered in her eyes.

'In other words, I could have been killed,' Eve said baldly.

'Please don't say it like that, it doesn't bear thinking about. But yes, if you had been on the other side of the car, you could have been killed. You've no idea how grateful your dad and I were that you survived. Not only did you emerge without a scratch, you slept throughout the whole episode. So you see, we were lucky, the two of us.'

'This is crazy,' Eve said. 'I feel kind of shaky all of a sudden.'

Liz continued as though she hadn't spoken. 'And to me and your father, you were always extra special. We were so thankful that you were safe and alive… so eternally grateful.' Liz closed her eyes for a moment.

'You put me on a pedestal, didn't you?' Eve said tremulously. 'You've always treated me as though I was some kind of precious… being….'

'Well, naturally we adored you,' Liz smiled. 'How could we not?'

'I always wondered why I was different, why you, well, spoiled me so much. Was this why? Because I survived and Jessica didn't? Because I could easily have died?' Even to herself, Eve's voice sounded querulous.

'We were mad about you anyway, our first child. Then after the narrow escape… you've no idea, Eve, how glad we were that you were still with us, safe and well.'

'You know, Mum, maybe I would have preferred a little less of the idolisation,' Eve said slowly. 'Maybe I would have preferred to have been treated like everyone else.'

'I don't understand.'

She could see that her mother looked totally lost, but it didn't seem to matter, what with the weird way she was feeling right now. 'Is that why I got far too many presents for Christmas and birthdays?' she suddenly asked. 'Why you always gave me far too much pocket money? Why you didn't turn a hair when I barely scraped a pass in my exams and decided not to bother with college?'

'What's got into you? You're beginning to sound as though you've had far too much to drink.'

'Yes, I did have too much to drink, but so what? Maybe I didn't like feeling as though I was different from anyone else. Did you ever think that I might have had problems with this as I was growing up?'

'You were different in the nicest possible way.'

'You're wrong, Mum.' Eve felt close to tears. 'I'm not nicer or better than anyone else. And I never really wanted to be all that different. I just wanted to be the same as everyone else. You obviously have no idea what it's been like for me, growing up under the weight of all your adoration.'

She could see by the anger on Liz's face that she had finally hit home. 'Kindly explain that remark!' Liz snapped. 'Would you mind telling me what's wrong with being cherished and loved?'

'There's nothing wrong with being cherished and loved. But there *is* something wrong with being spoiled rotten. Maybe it wasn't good for me to be told that I could always have everything I ever wanted. Because that just doesn't happen. Real life isn't like that, and it's only now that I'm finding that out. And thanks to you, I'm finding that out the hard way.'

'Eve! All we ever did was love you to bits.'

'No, Mum, all you ever did was indulge me to bits. There's a big difference,' Eve cried as she flounced out, slammed the door and strode into her father's study.

She had hardly spoken to her mother since and the atmosphere at home crackled with tension. Her father had tried to talk to her the other night, but she'd cut him short. And somewhere along the line between New Year's Eve and returning to work she had lost her mobile. Normally that would have been a major disaster, but suddenly it was the least of her worries. She was still coming to terms with the fact that when she was just a baby, her life was almost over before it had begun. That if Eve had been strapped into the other side of the car, it could have been Liz and not Marina who hit the bottle, Eve dead instead of little Jessica. And as a result, she had been spoiled all her life. Her mother had told her she was lucky to have emerged from the car unscathed. But she was wrong. She had emerged in one piece, perhaps, but she had not escaped unscathed.

* * *

Daisy twisted her striped woollen scarf around her neck and pulled on a pair of gloves as she and Alex began to walk down Oxford Street.

It was a week since Alex had told her of his impending return to Dublin, a week of sleepless nights, silent tears, of avoiding Caroline's puzzled glances and trying to pretend that all was well in front of Joe and Alison. She had suggested to Alex that perhaps they shouldn't see each other again, that after all, there wasn't much point if he was leaving soon. She had tried to make her voice sound casual and matter of fact when he had phoned during the week.

'If you think I'm giving up that easily, Daisy, you're mistaken,' he had briskly told her. 'I'm busy in the office this week, clearing things up, but I intend seeing you on Saturday afternoon.'

'I'm doing two shifts on Saturday,' she hedged.

'Lunchtime and evening.'

'In that case, I'll meet you during your break.' His voice was clipped. 'We need to talk.'

He met her at four o'clock outside Selfridges. It was sunny, the sky unexpectedly bright for a January afternoon, and the slight breeze was cool. Oxford Street was swarming with shoppers and she was glad of the crowds, that she wasn't alone somewhere with Alex. She huddled into her scarf and shoved her gloved hands into the pockets of her corduroy jacket and wished with all her heart that she could find the right words to send him on his way with the minimum of hurt.

'Let's talk about this again,' he said.

'There's nothing to talk about.'

'I don't happen to agree with you,' Alex said as he walked alongside her. 'As far as I'm concerned, there's everything to talk about.' He halted in his stride and turned to face her, his eyes searching hers. 'I don't care that we're standing in the middle of Oxford Street. I have to tell you that you mean the world to me,' he said, putting his arm around her shoulder and, heedless of the crowds, drawing her close. 'I can't let you slip out of my life. Don't I mean anything to you? Anything at all?'

Daisy couldn't look at him. She couldn't possibly answer that question.

'Just as well we're out in a public street,' he said. 'Otherwise I'd be sorely tempted to show you exactly how much I love you.'

'Don't say that. Please.'

'Why not? It's the truth.' He put his hands on her shoulders. 'Daisy, look at me.'

'Oh, Alex, it's no use. I'm very fond of you, yes, we've had some good times together. I think you're a great guy – yes, really – but it's me. I've always had a grand ambition to travel around the world before I hit thirty.' She forced her mouth into the ghost of a smile, wondering how she had managed to formulate the words.

Much easier, all the same, than saying hey, guess what, my mother's not dead after all, she's alive and well and living in Dublin. I came over to London to face my past and I didn't get very far. Apologies for the lies and deceit. And didn't I mention, you'd get fed up with me pretty quickly, as I'm not much use in bed.

'How come you never talked about this before, this burning desire to see the world?' he asked, looking at her keenly. She flinched under his gaze, knowing that she was enmeshing herself in further complications.

'I suppose it didn't really come up in conversation,' she shrugged.

'It certainly didn't. And where exactly were you thinking of going?'

'London was just my first stop, then after that America, maybe Canada.'

'I see. Well then,' he surprised her with a sudden smile, 'that only leaves plan B.'

'Plan B?' her voice quavered.

'You scarcely think I'm giving up that easily, Daisy.' He threw a casual arm around her shoulders as they continued walking along the street. 'Ah yes, plan B. How do you feel about having a travelling companion?'

'A what?'

'You heard,' he grinned. 'Maybe I'd like to see something of the world too. Wouldn't it be a good idea to travel together?'

'No way, Alex, you're joking!'

'I'm deadly serious.'

'You can't just up and leave your job,' Daisy floundered.

'Why not? I could take a sabbatical, tell Mark I need to recharge the batteries. I couldn't tell him the real reason, of course.' She looked at him sharply. 'He mightn't be too happy if I explain that I've fallen in love and it's the only way I can be close to you.'

'Forget it,' she babbled as she shook her head. 'It's just not on. No way. It's totally out of the question.'

He stopped and faced her once more. 'I absolutely love you, Daisy. And I thought you felt something for me. Would you mind telling me where I went wrong?' he asked in a quiet, carefully controlled voice.

'You didn't do anything wrong.' She looked away, at a line of red double-decker buses and small children eagerly scrambling along the street with their parents. It seemed very important to follow their progress up the street and watch them swarm around a souvenir stall as she told Alex calmly and coolly that she wanted to be a free agent and she wasn't interested in taking any travelling companions on board.

'I think that's a fairly definitive answer.' He gave her a smile that cut straight to her heart, a crooked smile she would have given anything to wipe away, but it was too late now. She couldn't possibly come clean with the stark, unvarnished truth.

* * *

'Heathrow, please, terminal one,' Alex said as he settled himself in the cab.

'Sure thing.' The driver swung out into the traffic. Alex looked back and watched as the apartment block he had lived in for the past few months gradually receded into the distance. Then he turned his face resolutely to the journey ahead.

It was less than an hour's drive to the airport. The boot was crammed with his luggage and he would probably have to pay an excess fee at the check-in desk. No matter. He was bringing home the sum total of his London life – suits, shirts, casual clothes, books and CDs. Everything.

Everything except the one thing he wanted above all else.

Daisy.

He had eventually given up trying to talk to her. He couldn't persuade her to come home with him any more than he could persuade her that they go travelling together. Staying on in London to be near her wasn't an option. What was the point if she was going away, she repeated with an obstinate look on her face. So he had accepted Mark's offer, tidied his desk, packed his belongings and said a heartbreaking goodbye to her on a cold, damp January night.

At the check-in desk in Heathrow, the young female clerk tagged his luggage and waved him through with a big, bright smile. He tried to summon an answering smile, but it was impossible. He headed for the departure area, remembering the Sunday evening he had unexpectedly bumped into Daisy. He looked around, even stalled for several moments, just in case she might, by some miracle, appear beside him.

But there was no sign of her, no sign anywhere of a tall, slender girl with bright blond hair and brown eyes. He felt angry as he stalked across the concourse towards the boarding gate. Angry with Daisy for being so stubborn, but most of all angry with himself for grossly misreading everything.

He could have sworn she was falling in love with him, that he meant something to her, something special.

How had he let the one woman he truly loved slip through his fingers so easily?

Chapter Forty-six

Why hadn't she gone to America instead, Daisy fretted as the long week following Alex's departure finally drew to a close. If she had gone to America, she wouldn't have met Alex and she wouldn't be sitting in the kitchen in Dolan's on a Friday after a hectic lunchtime, wondering if her heart would ever mend, with a horrible, bleak feeling that was like a physical ache in every part of her body.

She would get through this, she told herself firmly as she took off her uniform and got ready to go home. There had been times before, many times, when life had been difficult and challenging, like coping with Marina and feeling out of synch with her brash, confident schoolmates and college pals and getting over some of her disastrous dates.

She had somehow survived, hadn't she? This would be the same.

And who did she think she was kidding, she thought as she reached into her bag for her lavender scent. Nothing she had experienced so far came anywhere near this raw, aching hurt. No wonder her nightmares had taken on a new and disturbing dimension.

'Still here, Daisy?' Caroline breezed in.

'I'll be off in a minute,' she answered.

'Anything exciting on for the weekend?' Caroline asked.

'Not much.'

'Not much?' Caroline's eyebrows rose in disbelief. 'I wouldn't call seeing Alex Gallagher "not much".'

'Well, the thing is… actually, Caroline, Alex has gone back to Dublin,' Daisy said, forcing her voice to sound matter of fact. 'He was offered a great job. A promotion.'

'Don't tell me he's left you behind, or are you….' Caroline's face was perplexed.

'Not exactly.' Daisy's voice trailed away. How could she continue this conversation? She was mad to think she could have brought up Alex's name and talk normally.

'Sorry, I didn't mean to pry,' Caroline said hastily.

'No, it's okay.' Her voice was choked and her throat was about to close over. She swallowed hard

431

and clenched her hands so that her nails dug into the palm of her hand. She made a monumental effort to pull herself together.

'He did ask me to go with him, but I turned him down. I'm not really into long-term relationships.'

She had thought in the long and empty night-time hours that this was the best explanation, since everyone was bound to ask her where Alex had got to. She felt so broken hearted that she had been tempted to pretend he had dumped her. Then maybe she wouldn't have to put on a brave face in front of everyone. She could cry all she liked and they would understand.

But she had dismissed that idea straight away. It wasn't fair to Alex, and everyone would behave as though she was the innocent, injured party, whereas instead she had brought it all upon herself. She, Daisy, was the guilty one – guilty of lies and deceit, of going so far as to actually deny her mother's existence, and the most upsetting thing of all, guilty of hurting Alex.

Caroline gave her a strange look. 'I see,' she said, but by the expression on her face, Daisy realised that she didn't see at all. Caroline's confusion was the least of her worries. She was just wondering how she was going to get through this evening and tomorrow, and the next day, and the day after that.

* * *

'Will you be much longer in there?' Eve blazed as she banged on the bathroom door.

'About ten minutes.'

'Ten minutes? You've been in there almost half an hour already! What on earth are you up to?'

'Never mind.' Victoria's voice was muffled.

'You'd better get your ass out of there soon. I'm going out at eight and I have to get a move on.'

Eve flounced back into her room and began to sort through the clothes scattered on the bed. It was Friday night, the start of the weekend, and if the last couple of weekends were anything to go by, it would be hectic. She had reached an uneasy truce at home without any mention being made of the row on New Year's Day. She was talking civilly to her parents, though Liz was still going around with the slightly fragile air of the injured martyr.

She had come right out and asked Eve what had gone wrong in her life, what sort of lesson she was learning the hard way, that she thought her daughter was perfectly happy and if she ever wanted to talk, or if there was anything Liz could do…?

Eve had firmly shaken her head and told her she was fine.

And she *was* fine, she told herself firmly as she sorted through her slinky tops. After the lull of early January, her social life had picked up again and it was brilliant and everything she had hoped for. She caught sight of her reflection in the mirror. Her blue eyes stared back at her expressionlessly.

* * *

Daisy lifted the phone. The house was quiet with Joe and Alison out for the evening, and the Friday night stretched emptily ahead. It seemed important all of a sudden to phone Ireland, to hear someone's voice, to wallow in the normality of it all, to reassure herself that life was still going on much as usual in Dublin. She needed to establish some kind of connection, to touch base with the real Daisy O'Neill. Funny that she needed to phone Ireland in order to do that, the thought struck her, considering she had travelled over to London to find herself.

She was almost to the point of phoning Marina when she changed her mind. It would be much easier to phone Liz. Even a chat about the weather would help, Daisy thought as she began to dial. Any communication at all would do, once it pulled her back on track, and talking to her aunt might be better than talking to her mother.

After all, she had nothing to feel guilty about where Liz was concerned.

* * *

At first Eve wasn't going to answer. She was coming out of the bathroom wrapped in a bath sheet when the phone rang and she frowned irritably.

'Eve, get the phone!' Victoria yelled as she ran back into the now-vacated bathroom.

'You get it,' Eve said crossly.

'I can't! I have to rinse the colour off my hair this very minute!'

'You're too young to be messing with your hair,' Eve sighed as she went into her parents' bedroom. She sat down on the edge of their bed and picked up the extension.

It was Daisy.

'Is that you, Eve?'

'No, it's a burglar,' she replied, wondering why her cousin still managed to irritate her.

'Is your mother there?'

'No, she's out with Dad and Marina. Believe it or not, they've gone to something in the Gaiety.'

'Really?'

'Yes, really,' Eve said. 'How are things over in wonderful, exciting London?' she asked, quite unprepared for the ripple of unease that surged through her at the mention of London. She gripped the phone tighter as she realised that it seemed ridiculously important to know what the weather was like, the traffic perhaps, if the sun was shining... anything, any minute detail would do. She sensed disturbing thoughts unravelling at the back of her mind, Alex thoughts, and she tried hard to focus on Daisy in an effort to ignore them.

'They're not all that exciting,' Daisy said flatly.

Her dull, boring cousin hadn't changed, Eve thought, trying to give Daisy her full attention. 'You seem to be finding it very interesting,' she said. 'You've been over there for months now.'

'Yeah, well,' Daisy hesitated.

'You probably feel you belong there now,' Eve continued, anxious to prolong the conversation, hoping it might help to rid her mind of suddenly dangerous thoughts.

'No, not really.'

'Well, seeing as how you lived there already,' Eve chatted away.

'I know, but I was only very young.'

'Yes, you were. Hard to believe Marina was the same age as you when the accident happened,' Eve prattled on, realising her mistake too late. She wasn't supposed to mention it, especially not to Daisy. Daisy was bound to get upset, Liz had said. It was best for all concerned, her mother had insisted, to keep quiet about the whole sorry episode. 'Sorry Daisy, I forgot I wasn't supposed to talk about it.'

'About what?'

'The accident.'

'What accident?'

'The car crash. Look, there's no need to pretend with me. I know I should have kept quiet about it, but Mum has told me everything. Between you and me, I really feel sorry for Marina. No wonder—'

'I don't know what you're talking about,' Daisy interrupted, her voice suddenly edgy across the phone line.

'You don't know?'

'No, I don't.'

'But surely—' Eve was suddenly aghast. She sat on the edge of the bed in her bath sheet, the phone gripped in her hand, her night out with her pals momentarily forgotten.

'Yes?' Daisy was terse.

'Surely you remember Jessica?'

* * *

In the end Eve cut short her shopping trip on Saturday afternoon.

'What are you doing home this early?' Victoria asked when Eve sailed through the hall door. 'Credit card maxed already?'

'Don't be ridiculous,' Eve brushed past her. 'Where's Mum?'

'She's out in the conservatory. What's up?'

'Nothing.' Nothing except for a sudden flash of understanding in the cold light of Saturday morning. Nothing except for the memory of Daisy's sudden gasp on the phone the previous evening and the silence on the line when she had quietly hung up. Nothing except for the uncomfortable realisation that Daisy didn't seem to know about the accident. Shopping or no shopping, Eve's conscience finally got the better of her.

'Mum?'

Liz was misting her arrangement of plants. She turned around at the sound of Eve's voice. 'What's up?'

'I'm not sure,' Eve began hesitantly, grateful for once that her mother was such a calm, take-charge sort of person. 'I think there's something you should know....'

* * *

The phone rang out in London, and Daisy's mobile was switched off. Liz sat on the side of her bed, the exact same spot where Eve had sat the previous evening. She tried the house in London one more time before putting down the phone, then stared into space.

It wasn't Eve's fault. Liz had asked her not to talk about it, of course, but she had stopped short of coming right out and warning her that Daisy was unaware of the tragic events that had soured her childhood. Her life, more accurately.

She had stopped short because spoiled and all as Eve was, she could usually be trusted to keep a confidence. As well as that, the two cousins hardly ever saw each other. She couldn't bring herself to admit to Eve that Daisy hadn't been told the full story. After all, it was a bit much to be keeping the whole sorry episode strictly under wraps at this stage.

Daisy deserved to know. In fact, she should have been told long ago.

It had been all too easy though, when Daisy was a child, to follow Marina's wishes and ignore the whole thing, especially when Daisy didn't seem to have any recollection of the event whatsoever. But it was entirely different now that she was a grown woman. She had a right to know the truth.

Liz sighed heavily. She realised with a sliver of anxiety that she was rehearsing all her arguments in order to talk to Marina and prepare her for Daisy's alarm and confusion. Yet why should she be trying to soften the blow? Why did she have to come to the rescue once more? It was Marina's own fault that she was now in this position.

Liz felt suddenly defeated. Maybe if she had been less concerned about Marina down through the years she could have paid more attention to Eve's genuine needs instead of constantly showering her daughter with expensive presents and unlimited pocket money. Because somewhere along the line, she had got it wrong.

The row with Eve still stung badly, still hurt. She loved her daughter unconditionally. She had always thought you could never spoil anyone with too much love. Where had things gone wrong? How had that love translated into an adoration that had somehow oppressed her daughter? And what had gone wrong in Eve's life that she had found difficult to handle?

The zoo was quiet. Rainy Saturday afternoons at the end of January were scarcely peak visiting times, Daisy thought as she strolled down the damp path by the camels' enclosure. A lot of the animals were still indoors, and there was nothing like the lively activity that hallmarked the summer season.

Earlier there had been a shower of rain, but it had cleared now and overhead the blue sky sparkled. Daisy felt the slight breeze cool on her face and she took measured, calming breaths of the thin, crisp air. She meandered around, automatically putting one step in front of the other, not caring where her footsteps led and only realising after a while that she was following much the same track that she had followed with Alex, all those months ago.

Alex. She hadn't thought about him in a while. In fact, she hadn't thought about him for the last eighteen hours. There was no room to think about him in her head right now, because her mind was full of Eve's remarks and her own shadowy memories.

Jessica.

It was a whisper, something that trembled at the edge of her mind, a name that danced like a leaf in the breeze, unfurling strands of forgotten memories, a name that laced her dreams.

Who was Jessica? And what the hell had happened? How come she had felt a sudden jolt of recognition as Eve had said the name? How come it was as though she had always known her, across a distance of space and time?

* * *

Liz reached her at eight o'clock on Sunday evening.

Daisy had spent that afternoon down by London Bridge. It had seemed the obvious place to go. She had actually walked out onto the bridge, and then she had strolled along the embankment by the Thames. She had idly watched the fast-flowing movement of the grey, flinty river, the tugboats churning the water, and looked at the glimmer of buildings on the other side of the river. She felt blank, almost lifeless, as though her mind had shut down and she had retreated to an empty space inside. She wished she could go on feeling like this forever.

Back in her room in Notting Hill, she switched on her mobile and waited for it to ring. She didn't have too long to wait until Liz finally made contact with her. Funny how she had guessed it would be Liz who phoned and not her mother.

'Daisy? I've been trying to reach you since yesterday evening.'

'I was out.'

'So I gathered,' Liz said.

Daisy finally knew for sure that something was amiss when Liz didn't even question the fact that she had kept her mobile switched off. She began to shake.

'You were talking to Eve?' Liz said.

'That's right.'

'Daisy, I'm sorry, she had no right to talk to you like that.'

'Like what?'

'You see, she didn't realise that you didn't....'

'Didn't know?' Daisy prompted.

'Exactly.' Liz's voice was clear and calm.

'In that case, would you mind telling me who exactly Jessica is?'

'Certainly,' Liz said purposefully. 'But not on the telephone.'

Daisy slowly let out her breath. 'Then I suppose you're not going to tell me about the accident, either.'

'Not tonight, no.'

So there had been an accident, and it seemed to involve someone called Jessica. But Liz was still smooth and unruffled. She sounded much the same as ever, and her aura of calm control somehow communicated itself to Daisy. Her shaking gradually stopped. 'I see,' she said.

'I think you should know what happened,' Liz went on, still in that imperturbable tone of voice. 'I can come over to London if you want, perhaps next weekend?'

'Just to tell me?'

'Well, yes, to have a chat about it.'

'What about Mum?' Daisy blurted. I feel sorry for Marina, Eve had said. No wonder.... 'Was she... had she anything....'

'It involves Marina. And you. And me.'

'And Jessica?'

'Yes, Jessica as well.'

'I think then... it might be best if I came home. I want to see Mum. To talk to her.'

'I think that's a very good idea. Marina will want to talk to you as well. You haven't phoned her yet, have you?'

'No.'

'It might be best, then, if you let me talk to her and tell her why you're coming home. Will you leave that to me?'

* * *

'I'm glad you're seeing sense at last,' Caroline said on Monday afternoon.

'What do you mean?' Daisy threw her a confused glance.

'I'll be sorry to lose you, but if I were in your shoes, I'd do the same thing.'

'You're not losing me, Caroline, I'm just going home for a long weekend,' Daisy told her. 'I'm flying back next Wednesday. And I'll be back in Dolan's on Thursday evening, just in time for the rush.'

443

'You really think Alex will let you out of his sight?'

'Alex? I'm not going over to him,' Daisy firmly explained. 'I'm just seeing my family.'

'Aw, Daisy,' Caroline smiled. 'You don't have to keep it a secret. I don't blame you for running after him, not one bit.'

'Look Caroline, I don't even know where Alex lives,' she said crossly as she picked up a cloth and began to wipe down the pile of trays.

This was all she needed, Daisy fretted as she worked methodically. She didn't want to be reminded that she was returning to Alex territory. She didn't want to be reminded of him, full stop. She had cried all her tears and locked away her aching heart and told herself that in time she would forget all about him.

Anyway, she had other things on her mind right now, and she would scarcely bump into him over the course of a long weekend in Dublin.

* * *

'I knew it!' Paula squealed.

'Don't you start, Paula. This is not about Alex,' Daisy said grimly.

'What?' Paula's shrieked across the telephone line.

'You heard.'

'Daisy, are you mad?'

'No, I'm only sorry that I told you I'd be home.'

444

'Okay, calm down. We'll get together at some stage and you can tell me exactly why you turned him down. And you'd better have a good reason.'

'Sorry, Paula, if I meet you for a drink, I won't be discussing Alex Gallagher, because he's out of my life.'

'Funny all the same how you're landing home just a couple of weeks after him.'

'It's purely coincidence. And I mean it, Paula. No questions.'

Even Joe and Alison thought she was going home on account of Alex. Alison gave her a knowing grin and asked if she would have to put the room up for rent again.

'I'll be back. I'm only going to Dublin for a long weekend.'

'I see.' Alison hesitated. 'If you don't mind me saying, you haven't been yourself since he went home. Are you sure you're all right?'

'Of course,' Daisy lied automatically. At least she wouldn't have to worry about pointed remarks from her family, Daisy thought with relief as she packed some clothes into her weekend case. Thankfully, none of them knew she had been seeing Alex.

They weren't even aware of his existence.

* * *

On Friday night, Liz met her at the airport.

'Where's Mum?' Daisy asked immediately as she

came through to the busy arrivals hall and gave her aunt a brief hug.

'We'll be seeing her later,' Liz said. 'I have to say, you're looking great!'

Her aunt was telling lies or else she badly needed glasses, Daisy decided as she picked up her small case and followed Liz over to the car park. No way could her pale face or the dark circles under her brown eyes be classified as looking great. And Liz looked nervous. Her aunt was slimmer than she remembered. Her trouser suit was feminine and elegant and her hair was its usual dark sleek bob, but there was an air of anxiety about her and a troubled look in the depths of her blue eyes.

'I thought we'd go back to my place first,' Liz said smoothly as she sped home in Harry's Mercedes along the southbound M50. 'Then after that, I'll bring you home to Marina.'

After that? After what, Daisy frantically wondered as she stared ahead at the line of red tail lights moving along the motorway. Daisy tried to stay calm, but it was impossible. Her aunt's smooth voice did nothing to quench the anxiety that had been bubbling up inside her since the previous weekend. What was so important that Liz had been prepared to drop everything and fly to London? Why had she insisted on collecting Daisy from the airport and bringing her to Templeogue first instead of home?

And who was Jessica?

Daisy's unease mounted when they reached Templeogue and she realised that the house was empty. 'Where is everyone?' she asked as she stood in the quiet of the living room, ignoring a dart of alarm.

'Oh, you know, it's Friday night,' Liz laughed as though that explained everything. 'The girls are out, of course.'

'And Harry?'

'He's at an after-work party, one of his colleagues is retiring,' her aunt said, far too nonchalantly. 'Normally Harry doesn't bother with these things, but....'

'You wanted him out of the way?' Daisy hazarded.

'Well, yes, to be honest, I did,' Liz told her.

'I think it's about time I knew what was going on,' Daisy said firmly.

'Of course, but first I think you should sit down.'

Liz sat down beside her and put an arm around her, and Daisy listened as she talked about Marina, her stylish, ambitious younger sister, moving to London straight after school in order to study fashion design. 'She was – *is* – very talented.'

Then Liz talked about Marina falling in love. The excited phone calls from London. Marina sounding ecstatic. He was wonderful. He was terrific. Marina was madly in love.

'Was this my father?' Daisy asked.

'Yes. They lived together for almost two years. And then he broke her heart.'

'I know some of this,' Daisy said impatiently. 'He walked out when I was born, as my mother was only too kind to explain, remember? You were there. You heard her. And that's why she never spoke to me about him. I was the cause of him running away, wasn't I?'

'Not quite,' Liz stalled her. 'There was more to it than that, Daisy. It wasn't just you. Chris walked out when Marina gave birth to twins.'

'My mother had twins?' Daisy erupted. 'What twins?'

'Jessica and you. Her twin baby girls.'

Jessica.

Jessica and you.

'Is this some kind of joke?' Daisy asked heatedly. 'I don't think it's very funny.'

'I know it's a bit of a shock, but please let me explain. Marina had no idea she was expecting twins until you and Jessica were actually born.'

'I don't believe you.'

'It's true, hand on my heart.'

'Are you telling me that I have a twin?'

'Yes, you did.'

'Did? And where is she now, my twin sister?'

'Daisy, look.' Liz gave her a sympathetic glance. 'Just let me tell you exactly what happened.' Daisy's heart was thumping erratically and she felt as though she couldn't breathe. She gripped her hands and tried to focus on Liz's words. 'Your father was younger than Marina, barely twenty-two, and he just couldn't cope. He just told her he couldn't deal with it. He might have managed one baby, but not two. And she never heard from him after that. He had cleared out of their London flat by the time your mum came out of hospital. But believe me, Daisy, she did fall in love again.'

'She did?'

'Yes, with you and Jessica,' Liz smiled.

It was crazy. It was too much to take in. And where was Jessica now, Daisy fretted as a splinter of unease embedded itself in her stomach.

'You were identical twins,' Liz was saying. 'Tiny little babies, with just a wisp of white blond hair and big dark eyes. Marina decided to stay on in London. It was her home now, she insisted. She threw all her energies into you two and was determined to carve out a name for herself so that you would never want for anything.'

Liz talked about the brilliant, creative Marina O'Neill, who fit her career in around the needs of her babies and who was beginning to raise a lot of eyebrows in the top echelons of the fashion world. 'She was really going places,' Liz sighed, her eyes reflective and thoughtful. 'Celebrities were queuing up to have a Marina O'Neill original. Then just before you were two years old, I went over to visit. Eve was just a baby and I brought her with me… and then… you probably don't remember, Daisy, although I'm sure it's buried somewhere....'

Liz turned and gave her a look that turned Daisy's insides to ice.

Part III

Chapter Forty-seven

London, a sunny afternoon in the middle of August.

Aunt Liz is over for a visit. She's brought sweets and presents and a tiny little baby with fluffy black hair who mostly sleeps. Daisy and Jessica proudly show off their new identical gingham dresses. Aunt Liz tells them they are ever so lucky to be wearing Marina O'Neill originals. Most London women would give their eye teeth for such a creation. Daisy doesn't understand what Aunt Liz means, but Mummy smiles and looks very happy, so it's okay. She turns on the music and Jessica and Daisy twirl around the kitchen, taking turns to dip in and out of the shaft of sunlight that slants across the floor.

Daisy looks at Jessica. She is laughing and giggling. The sunshine turns her fluffy blond hair into a golden light around her head. She looks beautiful, but not as beautiful as Mummy.

Mummy is always beautiful. She smiles down at Daisy and it makes her feel warm inside. Mummy's dress is soft and floaty. Daisy reaches out dimpled fingers and tries to catch the hem as she joins them in the dance. She takes Jessica by the hand and they all dance together.

Mummy tells them that they are her pretty things. She says it all the time. Sometimes she puts on the song and every time she hears the words it makes Daisy feel light and happy. They play ring a ring a rosy and when they all fall down Mummy pulls them into her arms and gives them a big hug.

Then she says it's a perfect day for a picnic....

Chapter Forty-eight

'And that, Paula, is more or less the story of my life,' Daisy finished, her eyes bright with unshed tears. 'I'm still finding it hard to understand.'

'I don't know what to say. This is hard to believe,' Paula said. 'You had no idea at all?'

'Nope, no idea whatsoever. But somehow, when my aunt was talking, it made a strange kind of sense, as though I had always known deep down inside. Does that sound weird?'

'No, not at all.'

'Liz said I didn't seem to remember anything, and they thought it was best, her and Mum, to leave it at that because I was so young. And Mum, of course, couldn't think straight anyway. She was in tatters.'

'I'd say she was,' Paula sympathised.

'You see, she blamed herself.'

'But surely it was the other driver's fault.'

'Of course it was. He came out of nowhere,' Daisy told her. 'But Mum felt that she was the one behind the wheel. If only she had been driving a little slower, or faster, or if she had seen him coming in time to jam on the brakes… God.'

'If only,' Paula sighed. 'The most useless words in the English language.'

'She's never driven since,' Daisy said. 'I thought she just couldn't drive and never bothered to learn. And of course, that was when she stared to drink. When Liz brought me home last night, I had a long talk with Mum.'

'It'll take time for you to get your head around it all.'

'I still can't believe it. I feel as though I'm talking about someone else and not me. The whole thing seems unreal. Sorry, Paula, this is turning out to be a great Saturday night for you. But I had to talk to someone, a friend… I thought it might help to straighten things out in my mind.'

'You must have got an awful shock,' Paula said. She leaned across the couch and gave Daisy a warm, reassuring hug. 'I'm glad you felt you could turn to me. As far as I'm concerned, you can spend the whole night talking if that's what you feel like. I think you're still in a state of shock, if you don't mind me saying so. Have another glass of wine, it might help to relax you a little.' She refilled their glasses and stuck the bottle of white wine back in the cooler.

'Where's Tom?' Daisy suddenly asked, looking around the living room as though she expected to find him hiding behind a piece of furniture. 'Don't tell me. I suppose a colleague of his has retired and he's gone to the farewell party.'

'He's gone to a stag night. He'll probably fall in the door at three in the morning. And the kids are sound asleep, so we won't be disturbed.'

'Just as well. I really don't feel like facing anyone right now.' Daisy's voice suddenly wobbled. She sipped her wine and quickly pulled herself together.

'How's your mother tonight?' Paula asked.

'She's okay, I guess,' Daisy sighed. 'We had another long chat today. Liz had talked to her earlier this week and they agreed that she should be the one to tell me. My mother just couldn't face it.'

'I suppose she couldn't,' Paula said. 'It must've been very tough on her.'

'She couldn't stay in London after that,' Daisy explained. 'She couldn't stand it, so she packed everything up and came home to Dublin. She packed everything except Jessica's stuff. She didn't keep anything of hers, not even a photograph.'

'It must have been her way of coping.'

'It was the only way she could survive, she told me. And she never had the same interest in her career,' Daisy continued. 'She could have been a brilliant fashion designer. Instead she's doing boring piece work just to pay the bills.'

'That's a shame,' Paula agreed.

'I asked her about it, but she said she just never had the passion for creative design, that it was as though it had died when Jessica died.' Daisy's voice faltered.

'If it's too difficult, you don't have to talk about it.'

Daisy shook her head. 'I still can't believe that I had a sister, a *twin* sister. Luckily my aunt had put some photos away and she showed them to me. It was crazy, really. It was like looking at two of me.'

'You don't have any memories of her at all?'

'That's the strange part,' Daisy shivered. 'I've no memories, but for years I've been having dreams – no, nightmares – and I've seen her in them. I've been there, in the car, waking up in a state of terror. And all the time I was growing up, there was always an emptiness at the back of my mind that I never properly understood. It's hard to explain, some sense of loss, a void, nothing I can pin down,' Daisy shrugged. 'The more I get my head around it, the more things are making a strange kind of sense to me.'

'God, Daisy. As if it wasn't bad enough when your father upped and left.'

'According to Liz, Mum was devastated when he walked out. Then she felt angry. But after a while she felt more sorry for him than anything else, because he would never have the joy of knowing us.'

'Is that what she said?'

'Yes.' For the first time that evening, Daisy smiled. 'D'you know, the one thing that has come out of all this is the fact that I know for sure that my mother has always loved me.'

'Of course she loves you,' Paula chided.

'I didn't always know that,' Daisy explained. 'Deep down inside, I was afraid that I had done something wrong. I mean, how come Mum wouldn't talk about my father? How come she drank too much? I always had this sense of unhappiness about my mother, even when she wasn't drinking, and I thought I was partly to blame.'

'Were you annoyed with her when you discovered the truth?' Paula asked gently.

'God, no.' She stopped for a moment, lost in thought, trying to understand what she had felt and make some sense of it. It had been late on Friday night by the time Liz brought her home and Marina was still up waiting, with such a look of dread and anxiety on her face that in spite of feeling as though she was in a strange dream, Daisy had immediately put her arms around her and soundlessly hugged her. 'My mother was petrified,' she told Paula. 'She didn't know what to expect when Liz brought me home. I was more shocked than anything else, but no way angry.'

'I think that's just as well. Your mum has been through more than enough.'

'Thing is, it didn't seem to matter after all. I was so glad in a way, to know the truth, that the fact she had kept it from me all this time didn't really seem to matter,' Daisy said. 'The most important thing is that she's always loved me and we have each other. What happened was dreadful for both of us. I should've been told years ago, certainly, but that doesn't seem to count. Not now.'

'That's good,' Paula smiled. 'I think it's important for you and your mum to move forward and not look back.'

'It is, isn't it?' Daisy smiled again, then said, 'Hold on a minute. What did I just say? The exact words?'

'I can scarcely remember the exact words,' Paula grinned. 'I'm on my third glass of wine.'

'It's important, Paula.' Daisy looked at her earnestly. 'I'm just trying to get my head around something.'

Paula frowned. 'Let me see… something about knowing you didn't do anything wrong and your mother has always loved you… and it doesn't matter now that she kept the truth from you all those years?'

'Yes, I did say that, didn't I?' Daisy gave her a startled glance full of confusion.

* * *

Once more, Daisy lay sleepless until dawn. She felt as though it was months and not weeks since she'd had a proper night's sleep. Everything had taken on an air of unreality. The whole shape of her life had been hurled into the air and turned on its head. No wonder she was lying here at two o'clock in the morning, staring at the familiar shadows of her bedroom, while her thoughts flitted endlessly in her head. Thoughts of Marina, who had been younger than her giving birth to twins and around her age when the accident had taken away one of her beloved daughters, who had used drink as a crutch to help her blot out the tragedy and couldn't help but see memories of the past every time she looked at Daisy.

She thought of Jessica, the little sister she had never really known, who had flitted through her dreams and eased her nightmares, the nightmares she instinctively knew were gone for good. No wonder her thoughts were in a whirl. It had nothing to do with the fact that Alex Gallagher was out there somewhere within a three-mile radius, so near and yet so far. And it had nothing to do with the fact that she could still hear his voice in her head as he told her that he loved her. She dared not think of him. Most of all, she had to forget the sudden flash of clarity that had rocked her to the core as she had talked to Paula earlier that night.

* * *

Liz invited Daisy and Marina for dinner the next day. 'Nothing too fancy, it'll just be the four of us,'

Liz said. 'Eve is gone away with her pals for the weekend and Victoria is sleeping over in her friend's house so she won't be home until this evening. You might as well come over, seeing as you're home for a few days.'

No Eve or Victoria, just Liz and Harry – that suited Daisy. She didn't particularly want to see her cousins. She still felt bruised and vulnerable and she needed more time to sort out her head and get used to everything before she faced sharp-tongued Eve and Victoria and their blatant curiosity. 'Right so, we'll see you later,' she answered.

'Are you sure it's okay with you, Daisy?' Marina asked.

'It's fine, don't be worrying.' Daisy gave her shoulder a quick squeeze.

'We don't have to go to Liz's if you don't want to.'

'We might as well go.' Daisy tried to sound cheerful. 'No point in turning down a roast beef dinner with all the trimmings.'

The meal was excellent. Liz was a great cook and she fluttered around her niece as though she was made of glass. Harry also bent over backwards to make sure that Daisy felt comfortable and at ease. They had always been extra solicitous with her, and now she knew why. It was amazing how everything seemed so different, Daisy thought, feeling giddy for a moment. It was almost as though she was viewing her entire life through a side window and

462

it all looked so totally changed.

They were sipping Irish coffees when they heard a key scrape in the lock and the snap of brisk footsteps in the hall, then Eve swept through the dining room door.

Chapter Forty-nine

'I didn't realise we had visitors,' Eve said. Bloody hell. She had completely forgotten that Daisy was home for the weekend. Had she realised that Marina and Daisy were here for dinner, she would have slipped quietly up to her room and avoided them completely. But it was too late now. She stood transfixed in the doorway as four pairs of eyes focused on her.

'You're home early,' Liz said.

'I wasn't feeling too well.'

'Sorry to hear that. I wasn't expecting you home until tonight, so I haven't kept you any dinner.'

'Oh, don't worry, I'm not a bit hungry,' Eve tossed. 'By the way, Daisy, about that phone call... I didn't mean to upset you,' she said, her blue eyes taking in her cousin's pale face and puffy eyes. She suddenly felt sorry for Daisy – what a raw deal she'd had. After all, it wasn't every day that you discovered you had a twin sister who had died in an accident years ago.

'Doesn't matter,' Daisy shrugged.

'It must have been a helluva a shock and all that,' Eve babbled. 'I didn't realise that I was putting my foot in it. I assumed you knew all along. I mean, I can't believe it was kept from you all this time….' Her apologetic laugh trailed away as everyone continued to stare at her.

'That's enough, Eve,' Liz said curtly.

'It's okay,' Daisy said. 'No harm done.'

God, she looks woeful, Eve thought, and like she hasn't slept in a fortnight. How pathetic. 'No harm done?' she echoed, 'I'm not so sure about that. You're very forgiving, Daisy. I'm not sure if I'd be quite so obliging if I were in your shoes.'

'I think that's enough, Eve,' Liz repeated firmly.

'I'm going now, up to bed. I just wanted to apologise to Daisy.' Eve looked evenly at her mother. 'After all, I was the one who let the cat out of the bag.'

'And I'm glad you did,' Marina suddenly spoke up. 'I'm so relieved that everything is out in the open at last. It was foolish of me to think that I could spend the rest of my life ignoring it. So thank you, Eve, you've done me a great favour.'

She was good for something, wasn't she, Eve

fretted as she finally escaped to the sanctuary of her bedroom. Good for doing favours for her mad aunt who, according to her mother, had been besotted by one man, so besotted that all others paled into insignificance by comparison. Her mad aunt who had turned to drink as an antidote to her shattered, empty life.

Just like me, Eve silently sobbed as she locked her bedroom door and flung herself across the bed. There must be something in the genes, she realised dismally. Right now, she needed a stiff drink, because right now she felt as though her life was empty and shattered. And like Marina, she was beginning to think there was only one man who existed in this world for her.

* * *

She had bumped into him at lunchtime on Friday.

Late back to the office, as usual, and laden down with cumbersome carrier bags from her lunchtime shopping spree, the main thing on her mind was the weekend ahead with the girls. She had just passed the reception desk and had sailed through the doorway of Foley's when she met him coming out.

Alex Gallagher.

Every bone in her body seemed to melt.

'What are you doing here?' she croaked. Once upon a time she had longed for this moment with all her heart. Now that it had finally arrived, Eve felt like crying. Why the hell did he have to surface in her life right now, just when she had finally managed to forget all about him?

Alex stared down at her, causing her heartbeat to accelerate. God. She needed this like a hole in the head.

'It's me. Remember? Eve?' Her breath was ragged. A million questions swarmed in her head. Was he home now? Back from London? Back in his old job? What was the name of his firm? Why couldn't she remember it?

'Eve?' He frowned, his glance cold as he looked right through her. He seemed distant and pre-occupied. At last his face cleared. 'Eve – of course.'

'You were in the office?' she asked, clutching her carrier bags in a painful grip in an effort to focus on anything except her turmoil.

'I was, yes,' he replied.

'Don't tell me we're getting another new system,' she said, her voice amazingly light considering that her heart was thumping like a trip hammer.

'Good grief, no,' he said. 'I was just over to discuss a maintenance bug with Mr Foley. It was causing a few problems, but it's cleared now.'

Eve smiled at him as though she was an expert on the system. 'Glad to hear that. You're going back now, to your… office?'

'That's right,' he said.

He looked thinner, she realised, now that she was over the initial shock of seeing him again, and his face was slightly haggard. He even seemed to have lost some of his edge, that confident authority. If anything it made him more attractive, she thought. He was as sexy as ever, but in a brooding, soulful kind of way.

'So you're home now, directing important operations?' she smiled.

'You could say that,' he said.

'Did you have a good time in London?' she asked, wondering why he still had the power to reduce her attempts at conversation to nothing better than innocuous comments.

'London?' He gave her a chilly glance.

'Isn't that where you were?' she smiled encouragingly.

His face was grim. 'That's right.'

'You didn't like it?' she asked tentatively. If the look on his face was anything to go by, London had been a disaster. Something had gone wrong over there. The job, perhaps? Why else would he be back home? Whatever had happened, he looked as though he was badly in need of some tender loving care.

He shrugged. 'I'm holding you up. Better let you get back to your work.'

'Yeah,' she smiled, 'only another few hours to go before the weekend.'

'Ah. Your favourite time of the week.'

'Of course,' she grinned. This was more like it. Now they were on familiar ground.

'I suppose you have an action-packed weekend lined up?' he asked.

'I'm heading down to Kilkenny with the girls, so it'll be busy enough,' she said. 'Every so often we take a break from the Dublin scene and try out somewhere different.' She almost told him they had been over in London last year, but remembering the expression on his face, she stopped herself just in time.

'Good idea,' he said. He nodded at her shopping bags. 'You look as though you're well prepared.'

'You know me,' she smiled.

'Enjoy your weekend,' he said as he headed toward the doors.

'Oh, I will. And by the way....'

'Yes?'

'We must get together for coffee some time?' She let it hover in the air, not quite an invitation, more the hint of a suggestion.

'Sure, Eve, any time. You can fill me in on the hottest action spots.'

With a nod of his head he disappeared. Eve had to call on every ounce of self-possession in order to stroll back to her desk, sit down and open her computer files. Never before had it taken so long for five-thirty to arrive.

The weekend had been a disaster. She had tried hard. In the swirl of Friday and Saturday night, in the mad frenzy of Kilkenny's best nightclubs, she had laughed and joked and overindulged with a fierce determination. They had planned to stay on through Sunday and watch a hurling match on the extra-wide screen in the hotel bar then travel back to Dublin later that evening, but suddenly Eve had had enough.

'I've decided to get the early bus home,' she announced to her pals as she came out of the en-suite bathroom of their hotel room, all dressed and ready to go.

'God, what's up, Eve?' Katie's voice was muffled as she rolled over in bed and hugged her pillow.

'You can't go home now.' Susan propped herself up on her elbow and shoved her blond hair out of her face. 'We'll have great *craic* this afternoon watching the match with the natives. Think of the atmosphere. You can't miss that!'

'I don't feel good,' Eve told them. 'I think I'm getting a chill on my kidneys and it's no joke. I feel really crap and I just want to get home. Believe me, you'll have much better fun without me sitting around with a mopey face.'

'I suppose that's what's been bugging you since Friday?' Katie said from under the duvet.

'What?' How did Katie know something had been bugging her? She thought she had hidden it very well with her careless laughter.

'I have some great cure-all tablets,' Susan suggested. 'They'll soon sort you out.'

'There's no way I can take anything at the moment. I have so much alcohol in my system that

I'd probably explode.'

It was the first time she'd ever cut a weekend short and travelled home alone on a Bus Éireann coach. And she could have done without running into Marina and Daisy, but she badly needed to be on her own and she was utterly relieved when she escaped upstairs and reached the privacy of her bedroom. She lay on her bed, ignoring the muted sound of laughter and conversation coming from the dining room. Since she had bumped into Alex on Friday afternoon, her heart felt as though it was mangled in a vice grip and every nerve in her body was throbbing with pain. One look at him and everything he had put her through, everything she had felt for him, came flooding back.

After a while, she heard Marina and Daisy getting ready to leave. She stayed on her bed, staring at the ceiling and deliberately ignored the calls of goodbye that floated up the stairs. It was later again before she got up, looked at her haunted blue eyes in the mirror and fervently wished that Alex Gallagher would go to hell.

Chapter Fifty

'Hello? Eve? Is someone there? You're miles away this morning,' Rachel said, waving a file in front of her.

'Not quite,' Eve snapped. She was about as far away as the doors at the end of the corridor.

It was a drizzly Monday morning, and for once in her life Eve had been almost glad to go into work. She had even welcomed the light rain as she stepped off the bus in St Stephen's Green because it was such a relief to have some kind of normality about Monday morning after her head-wrecking weekend. Better again, her in tray needed urgent remedial attention after time lost on Friday afternoon, so thankfully there would be no time whatsoever to think about Alex.

But the minute she had passed through the doors where she had bumped into him, her brain had gone into overdrive once more. She sat at her desk, automatically moving her mouse, and everything that had tormented her during the weekend went around and around in her head.

So what if she had called Alex a bastard? So what if he had let her down? The sexiest man on earth, who threw everyone else in the shade, was finally home from London. He had remembered her, remembered things about her like her busy social life, and he had sort of agreed to coffee. He had even asked her about city centre nightspots. What did that mean? For starters, he was surely unattached. Further than that, she was afraid to think.

'Is everything all right?' Rachel asked. 'I don't mean to pry, but you were really quiet on Friday afternoon. And now this morning, you seem as though you're on a different planet.'

'Maybe I am,' Eve sighed abstractedly as she picked up her teddy bear and twiddled its ears.

'The planet of love, I bet,' Rachel smiled triumphantly. 'At long last.'

'Don't be ridiculous.' Eve's blue eyes flashed.

'Well, I've never seen you like this before.'

'Like what?'

'Kind of moody and preoccupied.'

'What's that got to do with love?'

'Everything.'

'That's daft.'

'It's not all sweetness and light,' Rachel insisted. 'It can be heart thumping and knee trembling, and lots of sleepless nights. Not to mention being unable to eat and feeling headachy.'

'That's pure crap,' Eve snorted. She tried to ignore the spasm in her stomach as Rachel described exactly how she had felt since Friday afternoon. Oh God, how come her life was getting so complicated all of a sudden? 'Who'd want to fall in love at that rate?' she said scathingly.

'Sometimes you have no choice,' Rachel grinned.

'Oh, so you're forced into this, are you? That's even better again.'

'It can happen like a bolt out of the blue and often there's no rhyme or reason,' Rachel said. 'Before you know it, your life has no meaning without him.'

'Is that the way you feel about John?'

'Of course.'

'And tell me, how did you know it was the real thing? Apart from all the ridiculous knee trembling?' Eve did her best to sound nonchalant.

'Don't tell me you're asking *me* for advice?'

'Just curious,' she shrugged. This was crazy. She didn't really want to know, did she?

Rachel hesitated. 'Promise me you won't laugh?'

'I promise.'

'Without sounding too slushy, every single thing

revolves around him and he's the most essential person in my world,' Rachel said in a dreamy voice. 'I would do anything to make him happy. Anyway, I'm dying to know. Who is he and where did you meet him?'

'There isn't anybody.'

'Come off it.'

'Honestly, there's no one on the horizon,' Eve lied glibly. 'Aren't you going to ask me about Kilkenny? We had a mad time....'

Later that morning, as she followed Rachel up to the canteen, Eve tried to ease her turmoil. She reminded herself that she hadn't seen Alex for months and they had only gone out together a few times. They hadn't even got as far as the bedroom. Okay, bumping into him by chance had thrown her completely off balance, but it didn't really mean anything. She had just reacted automatically to his sexy good looks, as any woman would.

Look at the cruel way he had dumped her. She was stark-raving mad to have suggested coffee, and he was only up to his usual tricks when he had asked about Dublin nightspots. Okay, so maybe it meant he was still available, but that didn't cut any ice with her, not now, and by the time four o'clock came she had convinced herself that Alex had just caught her off guard. She was mad to have allowed him to upset her weekend.

Rachel stood up and put on her coat.

'Where are you off to?' Eve asked.

'You're not with it today,' Rachel grinned. 'I told you I'm going to the dentist.'

'Ugh. Best of luck.'

'See you tomorrow.' Rachel picked up her bag and slung it over her shoulder. 'Oh, and happy dreams! At least try and get some sleep, because you look like you need it!'

'Thanks a bunch,' Eve said. She stared blankly at her computer screen as the germ of an idea hovered in her mind. Now that Rachel had left the office and the immediate coast was clear, there was a simple way to put an end to the confusion that had gripped her since Friday afternoon. A quick phone call and she could prove to herself that Alex meant nothing to her. She could tell him to forget about the coffee and any ideas he might have for a personally guided tour of Dublin's A-list venues. Then she could get him out of her head once and for all.

In a sudden burst of determination, she lifted the phone, dialled the Citimex main switch and asked to speak to Alex. He answered immediately.

'Alex Gallagher speaking.' Eve froze. 'Hello? How may I help you?' he repeated, then after a long moment's silence, hung up.

Eve sat at her desk, heedless of anything going on around her. She had been kidding herself all along. He still meant everything to her. She only had to hear his voice again to realise that she had never forgotten Alex. Not for one minute.

* * *

Alex replaced the phone on his desk and stared into space. He had had a moment's wild hope that it might have been Daisy on the line, but no such luck.

Daisy! There was no forgetting her eyes and the way they lit up when she smiled, the sound of her laughter, the feel of her in his arms and the touch of her velvety lips. He wondered if he would even hear from her again. By now she was probably over in Boston or New York or wherever and had forgotten all about him.

He had only himself to blame. Why hadn't he just gone ahead and swept her into bed? Sometimes, maybe, it was right to behave like a gentleman. But there were other times, surely, when it was far more important to follow all your instincts and show someone how much you loved them? Yes, Daisy had been nervous of him for quite a while. But towards the end, she had melted into his arms with remarkable ease.

He got up from his desk, left the office and walked over to the water cooler, passing Julie, his PA. The wary expression on her face didn't escape him. He had been like a bear with a sore head since his return from London. At least with the merger he had plenty of work he could bury himself in. Most nights he stayed late in the office, trying to ignore the ache that simmered away just below the surface. He hadn't even bothered to unpack properly and his apartment was still upside down.

Of course, if he was really stuck for some frivolous, social chit chat, he could always meet up with empty-headed, fun-loving Eve. She certainly didn't seem to have changed in the months he'd been away.

In spite of his heartache, he laughed.

'Everything okay, Alex?' Julie asked.

'I was just thinking of something funny,' he admitted. Funny? Meeting Eve? How hilarious could you get! If he had any sense at all, he would avoid her like the plague.

Chapter Fifty-one

'Caroline?'

'Daisy, hi! How are things?'

'Fine. Em, I'm thinking of taking the rest of the week off, if that's okay? I'm hoping to stay on a bit longer.'

'No problem,' Caroline said breezily. 'Everything all right in Ireland?'

'Yes, great,' Daisy said as she pulled abstractedly at the phone cord. 'I just need some more time over here.'

A long weekend, she had realised, wasn't anywhere near long enough to catch up on everything with Marina, to get used to the strangeness of talking to her about long-forbidden topics, never mind become accustomed to the new shape her life had suddenly taken. Thankfully she was over the initial shock, but she needed time to adjust, to absorb this new and unfamiliar territory of her early childhood, to let everything sift through her mind and settle into her consciousness.

'Are you sure you're coming back?' Caroline asked, a teasing note in her voice.

'Of course. I'll be flying back next Sunday afternoon.'

'With or without Alex?'

'I told you already, this has nothing to do with Alex,' Daisy said firmly.

'Whatever you say,' Caroline said cheerfully. 'I'm sure you'll come to your senses before long and you can tell him I was asking for him.'

'You'll have to tell Alex yourself, because I have no intentions of contacting him.'

'Aw, Daisy, give yourself a break. The man's crazy about you!' Daisy was silent. 'Okay,' Caroline said, breaking the silence. 'Just enjoy your few days off and we'll see you next Monday.'

'Who's Alex?' Marina asked as she came down the stairs.

The phone clattered onto the hall table. Daisy turned around and silently cursed her reddening face. 'Just someone I met in London,' she shrugged and gave her mother an embarrassed smile.

'A friend?'

'No one important.'

'Are you sure?'

'I'm positive.' Daisy lifted her chin.

'Hmm,' Marina looked at her thoughtfully. 'It would be nice for you to have a boyfriend. Don't let what happened to me put you off.'

'Don't worry, Mum, everything's fine. I can look after myself,' Daisy said.

'I know you can. But don't….' Marina hesitated. 'Don't be afraid of love.'

Daisy laughed hollowly. 'What makes you think I'd be afraid?'

'I had plenty of time to think in the last few days,' Marina slowly began, 'and one of the main things I realised was that I haven't been fair to you.'

'It's okay, Mum.' Daisy cut her short. 'You don't need to apologise. You had enough stuff on your mind.'

'No, Daisy, I need to say this,' Marina insisted. She sat down at the bottom of the stairs and looked up at her daughter earnestly. 'I'm sure some things I said in the past may have put you off men. I suppose I was partly afraid you'd end up like me. Well, it was wrong of me and unfair to you. You're so precious to me, but life itself is precious and it's important to get out there and live it. Unfortunately, I haven't been a great example of that,' Marina continued. 'But I just wanted to make sure you knew that for the time we had together, I was very happy with your father.'

'Even though he broke your heart?' Daisy asked her directly.

Marina nodded. 'What we had was special. He was young, though, and immature. In a way I can't blame him for running off. And then I was so delighted to have you and… and Jessica that my life was full again. But after… the accident, between everything that had happened, I was very bitter and I was afraid to love again. And I don't want that happening to you,' she smiled. 'I'd like to see you having the same kind of happiness that I had with your father. And I'm hoping….'

'Hoping for what?'

Marina stood up and gave Daisy a hug. 'I'm hoping that there'll be grandchildren to look forward to. In time, of course. Wouldn't that be wonderful?'

Daisy hugged her back. Grandchildren? Not much of a chance. Her mother was going to be sorely disappointed.

As for Alex, she had told Caroline she had no intention of contacting him and had told her mother he was no one important. Yet he lingered constantly at the forefront of her mind, even in the midst of coming to terms with everything, even as she tentatively felt around the new frames of her life.

At odd times during the day and in the middle of long, sleepless nights she remembered the look of devastation in his eyes as she had coldly said goodbye. He deserved to know the truth, to know that he had done nothing wrong. She ached to feel

482

his arms around her, to confide in him and share her startling news. Most of all, she desperately wanted him to hold her tight.

Yes, it would mean admitting to a patchwork of lies. But he had said he loved her. Maybe, just maybe, he would understand.

* * *

'You were different, you and Jessica,' Marina said.

'Were we? How?' They were sitting in the kitchen having coffee on Tuesday morning. On impulse Daisy had bought two of the gooiest cream cakes imaginable to have with their coffee, and now she was slowly picking up crumbs of icing sugar off her plate and licking them off her finger as she talked to Marina. They were still catching up with everything, feeling their way slowly around painful topics, coming to terms with the events that had shaped their lives.

'She was the elder by twenty minutes,' Marina smiled, remembering. 'And from then on, she was always the boss, the one in charge. You were the quiet one, happy to follow in her wake.'

Daisy smiled. 'And did we really look exactly the same?'

'You were identical. In looks. But it was easy enough for me to tell you apart.'

'It's hard to picture it all. You were younger than I am now, and yet you had twins and a great career.

That took some guts.'

'You could have all that too,' Marina pointed out. 'Certainly the career, and hopefully some day you'll meet someone you love, and in time,' she smiled, 'you might have twins? They're hereditary, you know.'

'Hereditary?'

'Yes, on your father's side, actually.' She paused. 'I don't blame him, you know.'

'So you said.'

'And he didn't really abandon you,' Marina said gently. 'I wish I could explain it better, but on balance, it was more a question of rescuing himself from something he couldn't possibly handle.'

'I see.'

'If you had known him, you'd understand. He was far too young, a bit of a dreamer. He didn't really understand himself or what he wanted in life,' Marina continued. 'He wasn't cut out for domesticity, let alone twin babies. He was mad about motorbikes and David Bowie.'

'Oh?'

'You're the image of him, Daisy. You remind me of him, but only in looks, of course. Your father was blond with brown eyes, tall and long legged. He introduced me to Bowie's music. He played it non-stop in our London flat – I think I know the lyrics to almost everything – and we had our favourite song….'

'What song?' Daisy faltered, suddenly realising with a painful clarity what was coming next.

"Space Oddity', of course,' Marina smiled ruefully. 'It was on the radio, you see, the afternoon we were in the park, just before I drove home. I was distracted by it, remembering Chris, and perhaps not concentrating enough… that was why I held myself responsible….'

'Don't even go there, Mum. Liz told me exactly what happened. She's even shown me the official report. She kept it all this time.'

'Has she?'

'Yes, and I know there was nothing you could do.'

'I might have a look at it. I never actually read it.'

'You should. It would give you some peace of mind, I think.' Then Daisy brought up the subject they had so far avoided. 'Talking about your song, is that what went wrong the night of your party?'

'I'm really sorry about that… that night, Daisy. I'm ashamed to say that I don't even remember any of it. Liz only told me what happened last week, when she explained why you were coming home. She was afraid to tell me sooner in case I completely went off the rails. Which I would have, of course. I couldn't believe the hurtful things I said to you. And I'm really sorry. I must have been off my head that night.'

'Yes, you were.' Daisy suddenly grinned. 'It's okay. I was upset, but now I understand.'

They sat quietly for a moment, Marina lost in thought. Outside the kitchen window, a watery sun struggled to break free from the clouds and

485

Daisy followed its progress as it sent a prism of pale yellow light across the room. She felt lighter inside, as though something constricting that she had carried around for years had finally dissolved.

'I was almost going to look for him in London,' her voice spilled into the silence.

'Were you? How?' Marina looked at her with surprise.

'Liz told me his name. But I realised that I might as well have been looking for a needle in a haystack. And then I discovered that it wasn't really important after all.'

'I don't know if he even stayed in London. He was talking about going to Canada.'

'So Liz told me. Anyway, it doesn't matter any more.'

Somewhere out there was a tall, fair-haired dreamer called Chris who had loved Marina long enough to give her twin babies, but not long enough to stay around. And it wasn't necessary to come face to face with him. Not now.

'We would never have made a go of it, not in the long term,' Marina said. 'I was relieved in a way that he left. It would have been like caging a butterfly. I was just sorry that he never had the happiness of knowing you. He would have loved you, I know that for sure.'

Daisy smiled. 'Tell me more about him.'

* * *

They went out for a meal on Tuesday night and Marina stuck to mineral water and announced that she was taking on new business. 'I was thinking I might experiment a little,' she said. 'There's always a huge demand in the neighbourhood for debs and bridesmaid dresses.'

'That's a big decision for you,' Daisy said, eyeing her mother. Was this Marina? The Marina who for years had stuck rigidly to curtains and soft furnishings?

'Liz suggested it,' she said. 'I suppose it's only now that I feel as though I want to do more with my life. You really did me a big favour when you went to London.'

'Did I?'

'Yes. I had to learn to cope by myself and I did. About time, too. Mind you, I did get a bit of shock treatment.' Marina looked slightly bashful as she told Daisy about the row she had had with Liz. 'I'm not saying I've completely reformed,' she continued with a spark of mischief in her blue eyes. 'But I do feel as though a fog has been lifted and I'm determined to make a fresh start. I'm not letting the rest of my life pass me by.'

'That's very brave of you,' Daisy approved.

'Oh, I don't feel in the least bit brave,' Marina laughed. 'But I'd like to give it a try. I've already been asked to have a look at a bridesmaid pattern.'

'You definitely have the talent.'

'So I've been told. And I'm not wasting any

more of my life,' Marina smiled. 'You've been marvellous over the last few days, and very supportive. Eve did me another big favour. I suppose, deep down, I was always afraid of you finding out the truth. The longer it went on, the worse it got. There was never the right time. And I was terrified this last week, wondering how you'd react. But the roof hasn't fallen in, has it? We're still talking, aren't we? Talking now more than we ever did.'

'When I think of what you went through, how could I not be supportive?' Daisy smiled.

'So I suppose you've given me a certain confidence,' Marina said.

Confidence. That was all *she* needed, Daisy thought. The spark of confidence to phone Alex, to make the initial call and take it from there. The days were running out and she was due to fly back to London on Sunday afternoon. She had his mobile number – she knew it off by heart, as it was seared into her brain. All she had to do was punch it in and start talking.

Easy. Oh yes, easy peasy.

Chapter Fifty-two

On Wednesday afternoon, Alex slammed his desk drawer shut so hard in a fit of temper that a pile of discs clattered across the desk. Damn and blast. He didn't realise he had cursed aloud until Julie's nervous face appeared in the doorway.

'Alex? Everything okay?'

'Yes, thank you, Julie,' he snapped as he gathered up the discs and shoved them to one side.

Only it wasn't, was it? Nothing was okay. Nothing had been right since he had come home from London, particularly since the silent phone call on Monday afternoon. What had made him think it was Daisy? Why had he let it unsettle him so much? His mood was black and his decision-making skills had degenerated to the degree that work was almost impossible. He would have to pull himself together, and sharpish, or he would find himself on the receiving end of his P45, with his name blacklisted in every major firm in Dublin.

When his mobile rang shortly before four o'clock, he snatched it up and barked, 'Alex Gallagher.'

There was silence for a moment and he was beginning to wonder if he was the victim of another crank caller, when the voice came through as though from very far away.

'Alex?'

The one softly spoken word was enough to send the blood pounding to his head, enough to make him rise hurriedly to his feet, stride across the floor and close the connecting door to the outside office.

'Daisy!' He told himself to calm down. She could be phoning from Outer Mongolia for all he knew. 'Where are you? Or is this just a call to tell me how lovely the Canadian Rockies are? Because if it is, I really don't want to know.'

'Well….'

'What is it?'

'It's just that, you see, I'm in… I'm in Dublin.'

'You're what?' A ray of hope gleamed for a long, endless moment. 'You're home?'

'Yes… and I'd like to….'

'And you'd like to see me?' he hurriedly finished her sentence.

'Yes, I would. There's something I want to talk to you about.'

He shook his head as though to clear his brain. He had to get this straight. Daisy was in Dublin and she wanted to see him.

'Maybe it doesn't suit,' she sounded apologetic. 'I'll understand if you don't want—'

'Where are you?' he demanded. 'I can collect you.' He glanced at his cluttered desk and deliberately looked away again. 'Tell me where you are and I'll be there as soon as possible.'

'Now?'

'Yes, of course now,' he said impatiently. He had waited long enough and he wasn't about to wait a second longer than necessary now.

'Well, I'd prefer to meet you, em… are you in your office in town?'

'Yes.'

'Could I meet you somewhere in the city centre?'

'Perfect. How about five o'clock?'

'You're sure that's okay with you?'

'Of course it is,' he assured her. It was more than okay. It was splendid. It was everything he wanted.

* * *

Daisy disconnected the call, feeling like jelly. Five o'clock. She hadn't expected to be seeing him quite so soon. He could have been in a meeting or away

491

on business. And after the way they had parted, he may not even have wanted to see her.

She didn't know how she had finally plucked up the courage to call. She'd been sitting with the phone in her hand for almost half an hour, feeling as tense as a coiled-up spring, then in spite of her thumping heart, her wooden fingers seemed to act of their own accord. But as Marina had said, you didn't necessarily have to feel brave in order to give it a try.

She went into the front room, where Marina was working on a piece of pale pink taffeta that flowed from her fingers like watered silk.

'I'm off out,' she said, hoping Marina wouldn't make a fuss.

'Doing anything nice?'

'Just meeting… a friend of mine,' she smiled nervously.

'Oh? A friend?' Marina gave her a look that was alive with interest. 'He's not called Alex by any chance, is he? Although he's over in London, isn't he?'

Daisy gave her an embarrassed grin. No more secrets. No more lies. 'Well, he's back in Dublin right now.'

'Well, enjoy! And don't rush home.' Marina gave her a meaningful look. 'I'll expect you when I see you.'

Daisy flushed scarlet. 'Oh, I don't think I'll be that late.'

'No worries,' Marina said brightly. 'I won't be waiting up!'

Daisy's hands were shaking so much when she got on the bus that she could barely push the coins into the slot and she sensed the bus driver's impatience as she held up the queue. When she sat down, she automatically reached into her bag for her lavender scent. She scrabbled around for furious minutes until it gradually dawned on her that she must have left it at home. She sat in stunned dismay for several moments, then smiled to herself.

She would just have to jump into the deep end without her safety net. Then again, there was no need to feel too rattled. Trinity College was a handy place to meet. She could mingle with the students and tourists, and if she changed her mind at the last minute, she could duck inside the grounds of the college and leave by another exit.

As it happened, she had no time to change her mind. Alex was already there, waiting. He saw her immediately and strode towards her, almost lifting her off her feet as he swept her into his arms.

* * *

'You'll never guess who I saw in town,' Victoria said as she burst into Eve's bedroom, dressed all in black, her eyes heavily ringed with kohl.

'Who?' Eve asked, bored and disinterested. She was having a night in, doing her nails in front of the telly in her room, but there was nothing decent on save for a rerun of a *Sex and the City* episode she had already watched twice.

'Guess,' urged Victoria.

'Give over the drama.'

'Go on, I'll even give you a hint, because you'll never believe this!'

'Victoria, you're beginning to annoy me.'

'What's wrong with this family? How many times do I have to tell you?'

'Okay – *Vikki* – cool it.'

'Anyway, I think you'll be deadly interested,' Victoria said, her eyes alight. 'It concerns a certain ex of yours and one of our relations.'

Eve reached for the cotton wool and nail varnish remover. 'Get real. I'm scarcely interested in any of my exes.'

'Just as well, because he was all over Daisy.'

'Daisy?'

'Yeah, they were even kissing in the middle of everyone outside Trinity College. How mortified can you get? And they didn't even notice me.'

'And what on earth were you doing in town dressed like that? Weren't you supposed to be at supervised study?' Eve asked archly.

'None of your business. Don't you want to know about Daisy?'

Eve shrugged. 'Not really. She's very welcome to any of my cast-offs. He must be a right sap if he's interested in her!'

'No way, Eve! I can't remember his name.' Victoria's brow crinkled. 'He's tall and really sexy. Even Mum thought he was a fine thing. We thought you were mad to dump him.'

'Who are you talking about?' Eve was suddenly alert.

'The fella that Daisy was with.'

'I know, silly, but who was he? What did he look like?'

'I thought you weren't interested.'

Eve shrugged and tried to sound casual. 'I might need to talk to Daisy about him. Give her some advice. Compare notes, you know.'

'No, I don't know yet.' Victoria gave her sister a meaningful look. 'But I can just imagine the kind of notes you'd be comparing. Anyway, I don't think Daisy will need any advice. He was all over her like a rash.'

'So, who was he?'

'Hmm, can't think of his name. He called here a couple of times in a big swanky car....'

'Yes?'

'It was that chap you dumped last year – Alex.'

Eve threw back her head and laughed. 'You must be mistaken. You couldn't possibly have seen Daisy with Alex Gallagher.'

'If it wasn't him, then it was his double,' Victoria said stoutly.

'No way. And him all over Daisy like a rash? Get real.'

'Well, don't believe me if you don't want to, but I'm not that stupid,' Victoria huffed. 'They were wrapped around each other and then they walked off practically glued together. They looked very well, they're both so tall. I hardly recognised Daisy, she looked so happy. And he's dead sexy,' Victoria rolled her eyes.

'And what time did you see this… this apparition at?' Eve snapped.

''Bout five o'clock.'

'Well, that's all it was. An apparition.' She found it hard after that to concentrate on her nails. She almost knocked over her bottle of nail varnish remover and even her new cuticle-softening serum failed to impress her. She caught herself thinking of Alex again and wondering where he was tonight, if he might be out on the town.

He was scarcely with Daisy, after all. Victoria was mad.

* * *

She had thought that they might go for a drink, to have a chat. There were plenty of pubs and hotels in the area where they could have sat and talked.

But Alex had other ideas.

'I'm taking you home.'

'Home?'

'Yes,' he said in a decisive tone of voice. 'You see, I think I'd be arrested if we didn't go somewhere private.' He smiled at her, his face full of warmth, and her heart overflowed. With his arm firmly around her, he steered her through the crowded streets. How lovely to see him again! How perfect to feel his arms around her! She scarcely remembered the walk to his car or the drive to his apartment, caught up as she was in a blur of heady emotion.

'You don't mind putting up with an untidy apartment?' he asked.

'Of course not.' Daisy was puzzled. 'Why?'

'Believe it or not, I've been so busy since I came home that I haven't had much chance to sort out all the unpacking.'

'No problem. Once there's somewhere we can talk,' she said, vaguely aware that they were driving towards the outskirts of Rathfarnham.

'Talk?' He shot her a look of surprise. 'Maybe I had better warn you, Daisy, that I don't have much talking in mind. I let you slip through my fingers before. I have no intention of letting that happen again.'

She heard what he was saying, but it didn't worry her unduly. When they reached his apartment, they would talk. In the quiet of his living room, she would explain everything to him; she would sit him down at arm's length, if necessary, and make him listen. He deserved to know the truth. And she longed to pour out her heart and tell him everything.

But when they reached the quiet of his living room, he slung off his jacket, pulled off his tie and drew down the blind against the gathering February dusk. She barely noticed the marbled fireplace, the jumble of CDs in the corner, the expensive-looking sound system. All she saw was Alex. He turned to her and gave her a look so full of love and longing that her knees trembled. She felt his arms around her, his fingers threading through her hair, and then his mouth on hers as he began to kiss her, slow, melting kisses that met an answering need in her soul. Soft, lingering kisses, touches like a butterfly on her forehead and cheek that made her heart pound and robbed her of breath.

She hadn't realised how much she had missed him, or how much he had invaded her heart and nourished her soul. She needed this, to feel him close, his mouth on hers, his arms around her. She felt like someone who had been starved, and now she inhaled the crisp, masculine scent of him and put trembling arms around him as though it was critical to her very survival. She closed her eyes and all thoughts of talk were abandoned as she clung to him and kissed him back.

He stopped kissing her for a moment. 'Daisy? I'm about to break my promise to you. I know I promised to wait until you asked,' he murmured. She felt his hands gently sifting through her hair. 'But right now, I'm a very impatient man and I can't wait a moment longer. Do you understand?'

Oh my God, she shuddered, he meant every single word.

'My bedroom is across the hall and that's where I'm bringing you. Right now. And if you have any objections, well, too bad.' He gave her a lopsided grin.

She struggled for the words to explain, but she could scarcely speak. 'First I need to tell you….'

'You don't need to tell me anything.' He shook his head and held her close. 'I'm not even going to ask you why you're back in Dublin. We've waited too long for this.' She felt his breath against her hot face as he murmured against her ear.

'There's something… it's important,' she whispered.

'We have the rest of our lives to talk. Nothing is more important than you and I showing how much we love each other. You do love me, don't you?'

'Yes.' Her voice was the merest whisper. 'That's why I need to … to explain….'

'We'll have plenty of time to talk later,' he murmured.

'But you need to know….' Her eyes shimmered with sudden tears.

Finally he asked, 'What is it, love?'

'Some stuff will keep for now,' she said, 'but Alex… you need to know that… in bed… I'm not much good.'

'Not much good?' He looked so astonished that she was momentarily surprised.

'Alex, don't be cross....'

His voice was suddenly very calm. 'I'm not in the least bit cross. But I don't understand. Is there a problem? Trust me, tell me.' He waited quietly, took her hand in his and interlaced their fingers. The contact soothed her enough to continue.

She swallowed. 'It's just that....' She shrugged and looked down at the knots in the wooden floor. 'You see, I've never....' There was no easy way to tell him, no easy way to explain. And without the benefit of her calming lavender scent or even a deep breath, as normal breathing was impossible, Daisy looked at him evenly. She lifted her small, determined chin and taking a leap of love and faith she put her heart and her soul on the line. 'I've never, well... slept with... that is, not completely....'

They stared at each other.

He didn't laugh or look at her as though it was ridiculous. Instead his grey eyes locked with hers in electrifying silence for several long moments and his grip on her hand tightened. And then he smiled.

'Daisy, love,' he murmured. Very slowly, he lifted her hand to his mouth and kissed it, then tenderly said, 'Would you like to, now, with me?'

Would she like to? With Alex? She thought she was going to faint with longing.

'Yes, but I've had disasters in the past and I don't want to make a mess of things, not with you.'

'A mess?' He grinned suddenly, a boyish, light-hearted grin that made her heart soar. 'I sincerely hope we're going to make a mess – of the bed. Think of the fun we're going to have. And trust me, you'll be brilliant. Although maybe I should warn you….'

'What?' she croaked.

'I'm afraid you won't be getting much in the way of sleep. Okay?'

Her reply was so faint that she didn't think he heard it, but he must have, because he took her by the hand and led her across the hall. He switched on lamps on either side of the bed and the room was suddenly cosier, more intimate. He pulled back the duvet and her mouth felt as dry as a bone.

'We should really have champagne, or at the very least some music or candles,' he smiled, his eyes warm and tender. 'I could get a bottle of wine.'

'No, it's okay.' It was difficult to talk, but she couldn't bear to let him out of her sight now that she had come this far.

'Sure?'

'Sure.'

'Stop me at any time, Daisy, if you change your mind.' His eyes held hers as he slipped off her wrap cardigan and opened the buttons on her blouse. He teased it off her shoulders and he bent to kiss the nape of her neck.

'Do you like this, darling?'

'Yes.' Yes, she most certainly did.

'Do you like this?' He placed his hand on the curve of her breast, over her white cotton bra.

'Yes.' Oh, God, she did.

'I can feel your heartbeat,' he said. She smiled tremulously, feeling her skin burn where he touched it. She could scarcely believe this was happening, that she didn't want to pull her clothes together and run away. Far from it. It felt so right to be here now, with him. She watched as if mesmerised as he pulled off his shirt and tossed it to one side and she swallowed hard when she saw the firm planes of his chest and the fuzz of dark hair covering his skin.

'Well then, okay so far?'

'Yes, more than okay,' she breathed. Alex began to kiss her again and her arms stole around him, and she felt the taut cords of his back under his warm skin. His hands stroked her over and over and ever so slowly he pushed down the strap of her bra.

'Are you still with me, Daisy?'

'Y-yes....' She felt dizzy for a moment, but she realised in a rush of scalding heat that she didn't want him to stop as he dropped butterfly kisses in the hollow beside her collarbone and along her creamy throat and as his skilful hands removed her bra.

And she didn't want him to stop as he lowered his head to her breasts, sending shock waves rippling inside her. Somehow she was lying on his bed without knowing how she had got there. Then, stopping every so often to stroke and kiss her quivering skin, he was carefully removing her ankle boots and socks, then her jeans were dropping on the floor. Only when he had taken off his own clothes and made her start as she looked at his hard, lithe body and kissed every inch of her long legs and slender thighs did Alex finally slide away her lace-trimmed panties.

'Okay, you brilliant, beautiful girl?'

'Okay,' she whispered.

He kissed her deeply and they lay close together for several moments while he murmured to her. Her senses leapt with the feel of his hard body next to hers and the touch of his hands sent quivering ripples deep inside her.

Ah, God, she had never thought it could be as good as this.

And then Alex began to tickle her.

Her eyes were bright with joyful surprise as he tickled her softly, mercilessly, making her giggle and gasp. She tickled him back and he sent her rolling across the bed with him so that they were a tangle of limbs, sheets and laughter.

Dear God, she had never thought it could be such fun.

Daisy paused and locked with his grey eyes in mid-laugh, and then she was lost. Her impish grin quickly vanished as he began to touch her again and his mouth swooped on hers, his tongue teasing, his every movement drawing her deeper along with him and torching her senses. She was lost somewhere in a mindless, glorious heat that started and ended with the touch of his hands and the scorching feel of his skin on hers.

She didn't want him to stop, she never wanted him to stop; she lost herself in the moment, in the heat of his body, in the tenderness of his hands as Alex led her slowly and sensuously and hotly into a dance that was older than the stars glimmering one by one in the night sky outside.

Chapter Fifty-three

'You're not with it today,' Rachel said mildly.

'So what?' Eve snapped, inputting data at a furious speed.

'You must have it bad.'

'Have what bad?'

'Well, whoever you're in love with, of course.'

Eve turned her attention from her computer screen long enough to give Rachel a glacial look. 'I'd prefer if you kept your ridiculous comments to yourself.'

'Sounds bad. I know exactly how you feel. Are you sure you don't want to talk about it?'

'Look, you haven't a clue how I feel, and anyway, there's nothing to talk about.'

'You know what they say about the path of true

love,' Rachel said sympathetically. 'When I think of all the times I sat crying into my keyboard....'

'That's enough,' Eve fumed. 'I'm not in love, I have never been in love and I don't ever intend to be. Right?' She saved her work, pushed back her chair and, ignoring Rachel's look of surprise, strode down the office floor to the ladies room.

She had to get away from the desk because any minute now she was going to start crying into her keyboard.

I am not in love. I have never been in love. Once she kept saying it, things would be okay. It didn't matter that she couldn't get Alex out of her head, or that try as she might, she couldn't get Victoria's words out of her mind. And it didn't matter that late into the night as she had tossed and turned, she had suddenly remembered with a painful jolt of alarm that Daisy had just recently come home from London. Almost hot on Alex's heels.

I am not in love, she repeated as she rinsed and dried her hands. And Daisy and Alex together was too absurd by far. She was going to put her mad ideas out of her mind and concentrate on more important things. Her hair, for example. She leaned forward and examined her dark, glossy hair in the mirror and decided that it badly needed a deep conditioning treatment, probably a trim as well. She tried to remember the last time she had been to the hairdresser and was horrified to calculate that it had been over six weeks. She strolled back to her desk and wondered how she could have been so forgetful.

Somehow she got through the day and put up with Rachel's sympathetic and infuriating glances, but the last straw came shortly after four o'clock when Susan stopped by her desk.

'Fancy going for a drink after work?'

'Tonight?'

'Yeah, an early start to the weekend.'

'Hmm, maybe.' Her glance strayed to Rachel just in time to catch the look of complicity she exchanged with Susan. 'On second thought,' Eve said frostily, 'no thanks.'

'Eve, it'll do you good.' Rachel gave her a worried look.

'I said no,' Eve repeated. 'Anyway, I already have plans made,' she added on the spur of the moment.

'Oh?'

'Yes, I'm seeing my cousin.'

It was a brilliant idea. Eve turned back to her keyboard and congratulated herself on her lightning decision. She couldn't very well phone Alex and find out what, if anything, was going on, but she could certainly phone Daisy. She could see how Daisy was getting on, maybe have a chat, and ask her about her future plans. And at the very least put an end to the silly ideas chasing around in her head.

* * *

'Hi, Marina, it's Eve.'

'Hello Eve! What can I do for you?'

'I'm looking for Daisy. Is she around?'

'Well, no, she's not at home.'

'Oh. I lost my mobile along with her phone number just after Christmas. Could you give it to me again so I can ring her? I'd love to have a chat with her.'

'It's very nice of you, but there's no point in trying to have a chat with her this evening. Daisy's meeting a friend in town.'

'Is she?' Eve felt her voice cracking. She held the phone in her left hand and stared out the window. She focused on a knot of trees in St Stephen's Green, still a dark wintry fuzz against the clear February sky, as Marina's voice chattered on, the words crashing like boulders into her mind, sending a hot, electrifying wave of anger that ripped through all her senses.

'I'm sure she won't mind me telling you, but she's meeting her boyfriend at five o'clock. Two nights in a row! And I think it's serious.' Marina's tone of voice lowered significantly. 'She met him in London, you know.' Before Marina said anything else, Eve instinctively knew. 'I don't really know much about him except that his name is Alex,' Marina continued. 'I'm sure Daisy will tell me more in her own good time.'

Slowly and carefully, Eve turned from the window, said goodbye to Marina and put down the

508

phone. Any sudden movement was impossible because her whole body felt seized up. There had to be some mistake. Daisy and Alex? It wasn't possible. Her cousin and the sexiest man on the planet? No way. Worse still, her cousin and the one man who seemed to have taken up permanent residence in Eve's head? What kind of ridiculous joke was this? 'What time is it?' she asked Rachel.

'Half past four. Why?' Rachel threw her a puzzled glance.

'I'm not feeling well. I have to go home. Tell old Fogy.' Eve began to scrabble her files together. She didn't realise that her face was flaming until she was outside and felt the cool February air on her cheeks. There was a funny mist in front of her eyes and even though she blinked rapidly, she couldn't really focus on anything as she stalked along. She was heedless of the heavy traffic and she almost walked under a taxi as she crossed the road at Nassau Street. When the driver blasted the horn she jumped out of her skin, but recovered enough to salute him mockingly with one finger.

She waited outside the railings by Trinity College. They may not even be meeting here, but it was worth a try.

And then she saw Alex striding through the crowds and her heart dropped like a stone.

* * *

509

It was like being enveloped all over in a warm glow, Daisy thought. But it was more than that, much more. It was like being wrapped in some kind of glittering radiance. And even though the February sky was overlaid with a thin palette of clouds, Daisy felt as though she walked in a pool of dazzling sunshine as she hurried to meet Alex.

He had dropped her off in the city centre that morning on his way to the office.

'I hate leaving you like this,' he said as he turned to her in the car park and kissed her again. 'Already I'm dead late, and I have urgent meetings on today that I can't afford to miss, but after that….' His eyes were full of promise as he searched her face.

'I'll meet you?' she offered, scarily amazed at her newfound confidence, amazed at the way her life was suddenly full of new meaning, even more amazed at the way her body had ignited at the touch of Alex's hands. Although looking at him now, with his dark hair slightly tousled, it was scarcely any wonder at all.

'You don't have to do that,' he grinned. 'I'll collect you and save you coming into town. Besides, I want to see where you live.'

'I'd prefer to meet you in town,' she smiled, glossing over her sudden disquiet. 'You can see where I live another time.'

'So long as it's soon,' he said. He lifted her hand and kissed her fingers one by one.

'It will be,' she promised. 'Same place, same

time tonight?' she asked as they hurriedly got out of the car.

'I can hardly wait,' he said, kissing her goodbye.

She would have to talk to him tonight, Daisy decided as she quickened her step. She would have to tell him firmly that she had something important to say before they got as far as his bedroom. He would surely understand. He loved her, didn't he? He had already shown her how much.

There had been no time for talk last night. Last night had been so special that whenever she thought about it as she went through the day, she felt as though she was moving in a sunburst.

Even her mother seemed to sense that something significant had happened. Daisy was relieved that Marina had said very little to her, giving her much-needed space of her own, chatting about the bridesmaid dress she was designing for a neighbour's daughter instead of Daisy's arrival home at almost ten o'clock in the morning. She had passed little comment when Daisy informed her that she was going out again that evening. She had just told Daisy that she looked lovely.

Daisy crossed at the pedestrian crossing and her heart leapt when she saw Alex waiting for her, handsome as ever. Memories of the previous night sparkled like fireworks. Already her body was anticipating his touch.

Then she noticed that he was talking to someone. He was talking to Eve.

Eve? No, not Eve. Anyone in the whole wide world but Eve. She almost turned and ran but they had already spotted her, Alex smiling warmly, Eve looking at her with narrowed, curious eyes, and she had no option but to join them.

Then, slowly but surely, everything started to go wrong.

'Hi, Alex. Hello, Eve,' Daisy said, and even his arm curling around her shoulders and drawing her close couldn't prevent an icy numbness from taking gradual hold of her limbs.

'Hello, Daisy.' Eve gave her a challenging stare with her blue eyes, a look Daisy recognised of old. Eve turned to Alex, raised her pencil-slim eyebrows and said, 'So this is who you're waiting for? What a surprise!'

'You know each other?' Alex looked from Daisy to Eve.

'We're cousins,' Eve told him. 'Fancy that.'

'Cousins?' His face registered disbelief. 'I had no idea.'

'Hard to believe, isn't it? We're not the least bit alike, Alex, I can assure you. I believe you two met in London. Quite an amazing coincidence,' Eve gurgled, looking at Daisy as though it was a huge joke.

Daisy stood motionless, feeling totally helpless as the glow that had surrounded her all day slowly fragmented. She heard the words coming out of Alex's mouth, heard what Eve was saying and tried to grasp the significance of it all. They knew each other, that much was patently obvious. How well was anyone's guess. Or was it, knowing Eve's reputation?

Dear God, this was beyond belief.

He was talking again to Eve. 'Yes, we met in London,' he was saying. 'The day we met I almost sent Daisy flying, didn't I, love?'

Daisy felt his eyes on her and his arm gently squeezing, as though fully expecting her to agree with him, but she felt so frozen that she couldn't even nod her head. She saw by Eve's calculating eyes that she had taken everything in.

'So you decided to get together now that Daisy's home for a few days?' Eve said.

Alex looked at Daisy. 'A few days?' he frowned, and again she refused to acknowledge his glance.

'I suppose coffee with me is off the agenda. For the moment, at least.' Eve sounded amused. 'And I take it you'll want to postpone our trip around Dublin's hippest night spots?' Her words ricocheted around Daisy and she wanted to run and hide, but Alex's arm around her shoulders had her firmly anchored. She saw the blank stare that Alex gave Eve.

'Forgotten already?' Eve laughed. 'Oh, Daisy, you'd want to watch your step with this one. He's a real charmer, aren't you, Alex? Only last week he was asking me to show him the best fun spots in town.'

Once again, Daisy felt Alex's eyes on her as though trying to connect with her. 'I knew Eve before... before I went to London,' he was saying.

Eve gurgled. 'We were, what shall I say... good friends? After all, we were scarcely good lovers.'

'It was only a couple of dates,' Alex said with a hard edge to his voice. 'Now if you'll excuse us.' He began to move away, propelling Daisy along with him.

Eve put her hand on Daisy's arm, stalling her. 'A couple of dates? Alex told me he loved my sense of fun, didn't you, Alex? You'd want to be careful with him, Daisy. I wouldn't trust him if I were you. He's quite capable of loving you and leaving you. And he's very fussy about his lovemaking, aren't you, Alex?'

'That's enough, Eve.'

Daisy couldn't shake off the grip of Eve's fingers on her arm. 'I just think that Daisy should know what you're like,' she said scathingly. 'I wasn't enough for him, you see. He had the balls to say that making love to me was a mistake. A mistake! Now you know me, Daisy, so what the hell would you make of that?'

'C'mon, Daisy, we're out of here.' Alex's voice sounded stiff and quite unlike his usual tone, Daisy thought, feeling as though she was in the middle of a bad dream, a dream she couldn't hope to stop from coming to its cruel, nightmarish end.

'I must meet you for a drink, Daisy,' Eve said petulantly. 'It looks like we have quite a lot to catch up on. I asked your mother for your mobile number, but guess what, she was so keen to tell me about your new boyfriend that she forgot to give it to me.'

Daisy turned to stone. She sensed Alex's total bewilderment as he halted in his tracks, stared at Eve, then finally stared at her.

'Daisy?' Mutely, she shook her head. 'What's going on?' Alex questioned, his dark eyes puzzled. 'Talk to me, Daisy.'

'Did I say something wrong?' Eve tittered. 'Don't worry, Marina sounded very happy. She seems to be pleased that you have a boyfriend. And you needn't worry, Daisy. I won't tell her that you're following in my footsteps. It can be another one of our family secrets.'

'Who's Marina?' Alex asked in a dangerously quiet voice.

Now it was Eve's turn to look surprised. 'Daisy's mother, of course.'

'Your mother?'

Daisy stared at him in silence.

'So your mother isn't….'

She gulped and gave a tiny shake of her head.

'I thought your mother….'

She felt her heart shattering piece by piece as his eyes narrowed in disbelief. He stared wordlessly at her for long, interminable seconds. She felt his arm disengaging and saw him back away. Then he turned and strode off, cutting a swathe through the swarming crowds, leaving her bereft.

'What's up with him?' Eve asked. Daisy shook her head. 'Why did he walk off?'

'Leave it, Eve.' Daisy's teeth were chattering and her lips barely moved.

'What's wrong with you? I told you you couldn't trust him. And you needn't look so shocked.' Eve sounded scathing. 'Alex Gallagher isn't worth a damn. You're better off without him.'

The pain in Daisy's chest was so sharp that she had to struggle to control her breathing and she fought down a sudden urge to lash out at her cousin.

'Besides,' Eve's laughter tinkled, 'you scarcely think you'd manage to keep a man like Alex happy, do you?'

* * *

Eve was just about to add on some further biting comments, but Daisy looked so stricken that she decided to hold her tongue for once. Worse again, her cousin looked as though she was about to faint. What the hell had all that been about? What had happened just now? Daisy's normally cool composure had vanished and she looked lost and vulnerable in a way Eve had never seen before.

'C'mon, maybe we'd better go and sit down somewhere.' Eve took her by the arm and steered her back towards the railings. 'I haven't got a clue what's happened. Let's go somewhere and we can talk.'

Daisy was staring at her as though she had suggested a trip to the moon.

'How about some coffee? Or a drink?' She tugged at Daisy's arm. 'You look like you could do with one. Don't worry about Alex. You're well rid of him. You'd never be able to keep up with him anyway. He's sexual dynamite.'

And Eve was left staring after her as Daisy gave her a bleak look, turned on her heel and strode away into the dusky February evening, where the cool breeze ruffled her blond hair and played with the ends of her scarf.

Chapter Fifty-four

'Do you think you might tell me about it some-time?' Jane asked.

'Tell you about what?'

'Whatever demon has been driving you for about the past twenty-four hours?'

'You don't want to know,' Alex snapped. He reached for the bottle of whiskey. 'And don't say anything.' He shot her a grim look before he poured himself another glass.

Jane shrugged. 'You can drink until the cows come home if that's what you want. I presume you're staying here again tonight?'

Alex glanced around at the familiar comfort of the living room of his childhood home – the upright piano in the corner, the framed photographs on the sideboard, the painting of Marlay Park over the mantelpiece. 'Yes, if that's okay with you?'

'Of course it's okay. Anytime. Some of your clothes and stuff are still here since Christmas. And your bedroom will always be upstairs. I have no plans to turn it into a mini-gym or haven of pleasure. And if you feel like talking....'

'I don't.'

'Whatever.'

'There's nothing you need to worry about.'

'Sure,' she replied. 'I'm just a little concerned, though, as to why my son is sitting here for the second night in a row propped up with a bottle of whiskey. That's all.'

'Will the girls be home tonight?' he asked, refusing to be drawn.

'They've gone to a party. Andrea's friend is twenty-one. They'll be late home, and I'm off out to my Friday night bridge, so you'll have the place to yourself.'

'Fine.'

The house was quiet after Jane left. Alex slumped on the couch and closed his eyes. He hadn't been back to his apartment since he had walked away from Daisy. He couldn't bring himself to return to where they had spent the night together. He couldn't possibly walk back into his bedroom, where white sheets were still rumpled and pillows were strewn after they had made love almost all night and then in the morning before they had hurriedly left, laughing as they rushed out to the car, him dead late for work – just yesterday morning? It couldn't be. He shook his head. It seemed like a million years ago.

But even here, in his childhood home, there was no getting away from her. Even now, with his eyes closed, he could still catch the scent of her and feel the softness of her hair where he had threaded his hands as he kissed her. He still saw her face, the flush of her cheeks as he touched her, still saw the quickening desire in her eyes, heard her sighs of pleasure, felt her silky limbs entwined with his and tasted the warm moistness of her mouth….

In desperation he seized the remote control and turned on the television, tuning into a silly game show, adjusting the volume so that the canned laughter drowned out his thoughts. He poured himself another glass of whiskey.

By the time Jane came home at eleven o'clock, he had fallen asleep.

'Alex, wake up.' He felt her hand on his shoulder as she nudged him into wakefulness.

Reluctantly he forced his eyes open, sat up and rubbed his face. Jane picked up the remote control and turned off the television. 'Are you okay?' His mother's face was etched with anxiety.

'Of course I'm okay,' he growled.

'You don't look it,' she sighed. 'Alex… I'm not going to pry, but please don't let whatever it is eat away at you,' she began. 'And for heaven's sake, don't bottle it up.'

Like the last time, the unspoken words hung in the air between them. For a moment he saw himself as she could see him, unshaven, his dark eyes bleary, his hair sticking up in spikes where he had run his agitated fingers through it, his mouth set in sharp, obstinate lines. He remembered the long, lonely months after his father's death when he had refused to unburden himself, and the relief when he had finally spoken about it.

'Would you like a drink?' he asked.

'Okay, I'll have just one,' Jane said. She fetched a glass from the sideboard and handed it to him. 'Lots of tonic, please.'

He poured a whiskey, added plenty of tonic and passed her back the glass. 'I think that should be okay.'

Jane sat on the adjacent armchair and began to talk about her bridge. She chatted away for several moments until Alex suddenly interrupted.

'It's Daisy.'

'I see.'

'She's in Dublin. Tell me, what would you do if you discovered that someone you loved had told you a pack of lies?'

'God, I don't know,' Jane hesitated. 'I suppose it would all depend.'

'Depend on what?'

Jane gave him a sympathetic glance. 'There may be a good reason.'

521

'The hell there is,' he said savagely as he tossed back his drink. 'Give me one good reason for pretending that someone is dead.'

Jane's eyes widened. 'Oh… I see.'

'Well, I don't,' Alex erupted. 'In fact, I haven't a clue why Daisy O'Neill told me that her mother was dead. And it wasn't just a once-off thing. It was a pretence that she kept up, all the time we were in London, even Christmas… God.' His voice was suddenly muffled as he slumped forward on the couch and rested his face in his hands. He felt Jane's hand on his arm.

'You know, I thought she was hurting on account of her mother, especially after what we went through with Dad… I thought I knew exactly what she was going through.' He began to laugh and then he shook his head as though in disbelief. 'It was all lies. Lies! What the hell do you make of that?'

Jane sat quietly for a moment, then said, 'I don't make anything of it. It's got nothing whatsoever to do with me. What do *you* make of it?'

'What?'

'Well? Why do you think Daisy told you some untruths, if that is the case?'

'Oh, it is indeed, very much the case. Her mother is alive and well, as I found out yesterday evening.'

Jane frowned. 'You must have got quite a shock.'

'That's one hell of an understatement.'

'Why do you think she would go to those drastic extremes?'

'I told you, I haven't a clue.'

'Well then, it seems to me that something must have happened to drive her to such lengths. And maybe the first thing you should do is find out what happened.'

'Maybe I don't want to see her again.'

'Really? You told me that Daisy was very special. Don't you think that at the very least you deserve some kind of explanation? And that you might also give Daisy a chance to justify herself?'

* * *

An explanation, that was all. He tossed and turned long into the night. Just an explanation, nothing more. For how could he ever trust her again?

Trust me, he had asked as he had taken her into his arms on Wednesday evening. And at that moment in time, he had trusted her implicitly. Yes, she had asked to talk to him. Yes, she had said there was something he needed to know. But the lies and deceit had started long before then and she had had plenty of opportunity in London to explain. No wonder she had refused to come home with him to Dublin. She must have realised that the truth would have come out at some stage.

Although she had come home after all, and she had taken a chance on seeing him, hadn't she? She had tried to talk, in spite of everything. What exactly did that say?

To hell with her. Explanation or no explanation, he didn't think he could bear to look at her again. He lay sleepless in bed listening to the rumble of occasional traffic, watching the movement of car headlamps throw slanting shadows across the bedroom ceiling. He was still wide awake as dawn light stretched tentative fingers along the eastern horizon and pressed against the outline of the window. He lay on his back and stared at nothing, trying not to think of her face or her brown eyes.

Chapter Fifty-five

Eve stretched her limbs and blinked at the clock face. Ten o'clock. She lay there puzzled for a moment, then with a sigh of satisfaction remembered that it was Saturday morning. She resumed a more comfortable position under her duvet. A long lie-in, a soak in the bath, then into town for her hair and facial appointment. Bliss.

But she couldn't quite relax or return to that delicious state of tranquil inertia. Once again, it all came flooding back.

Daisy. And Alex. And the scene on Thursday evening. She had thought about little else since.

What the hell was going on? Apart from the incredible fact that those two seemed to have met up in London, nothing else made much sense. For example, when she had bumped into him in Foley's, Alex had made it very clear that London was an episode he wished to forget. And it was his suggestion that Eve reacquaint him with Dublin nightlife. Not exactly the kind of thing you'd be interested in, surely, if you had a girlfriend in the wings.

Eve plumped up her soft pillows and snuggled under the duvet in a vain attempt to relax. He had looked very happy when she met him on Thursday evening. He had told her that he was waiting for someone and her heart had felt like lead. She had refused to believe that he was waiting for her cousin until she'd actually seen Daisy walking through the crowds. Then she had almost gasped with the hot flash of jealousy that consumed her.

Yet Daisy had obviously considered her a threat. Her face had looked suddenly alarmed as she spotted Eve. Maybe she knew in her heart of hearts that there was no way she could expect to hang on to a man like Alex, especially with the likes of Eve on the scene. Could it be that Alex had already mentioned her to Daisy, the girlfriend he had said goodbye to before he left for London, the girlfriend he intended to see again?

All she could really grasp at the moment was the fact that Daisy and Alex couldn't have known each other very long – after all, Alex didn't seem to know anything about Marina. And it was quite obvious that he'd had some kind of falling out with

Daisy, right in front of her on Thursday evening, but she couldn't begin to imagine how it had happened or what it was about. The main thing was that he had left Daisy high and dry. She didn't understand why he had stalked off with that ferocious look on his face. It didn't make any sense.

And she couldn't help thinking that she had played it all so totally wrong.

Eve forgot about her lie-in and sat up in bed. She groaned aloud, remembering the sarcastic comments she had made to Daisy in front of Alex. Surely she had blown any chance she might have had with him with those catty remarks? What had possessed her to be so silly and childish? She had been upset, of course, and who wouldn't be, with the man she fancied above all others, apparently seeing her cousin? And this time, she couldn't very well stamp her foot and expect Liz to sort it out.

Was there any chance that her jealous behaviour had caused Alex to march off in a huff, any chance at all that maybe he was annoyed with himself because he knew he had upset Eve? And last but not least, Eve pondered as she slowly got out of bed and pushed her feet into her fluffy slippers, the important thing to remember was that Daisy was only home for a week, wasn't she? In fact, she was probably even now packing her bags....

* * *

'Why don't we go to the cinema tonight?'

'The cinema?'

'I've sometimes gone with Liz and it's been fun. Just an idea for your last night?'

'Sure, okay.' In spite of her aching heart, Daisy gave her mother a little grin. She couldn't remember the last time they had gone to the cinema together.

'There now, I finally managed to make you smile,' Marina observed.

'I'm fine, really,' Daisy insisted.

'Well, I'm not sure about that,' Marina's voice was gentle. 'Then again, I'm the last person on earth who can afford to be inquisitive after the example I set!'

Daisy forced a smile. 'It's cool, Mum.'

'Cool! What's that supposed to mean?'

'It means everything's okay.'

'Is it really? No matter. I can see you don't want to talk.'

Talk? She couldn't possibly talk. No way. Maybe she was more like her mother than she realised, because the only way she could put up with the terrifying emptiness in her heart was to lock it away and act normal on the outside, to act as though Alex had been nothing more than a casual acquaintance and to focus on her return to London and the practicalities of her packing and flight details.

And she didn't have to worry about him contacting her. For starters, he most likely didn't want to have anything more to do with her. As well as having her mobile switched off, he didn't even know where she lived.

She had actually slept on Thursday night. She had lain in bed feeling as though a truck had hit her, sending her sky rocketing helplessly into the air and crash landing back down on the hard pavement, such was the level of her numbness and shock. She had fallen into a dreamless sleep and had been surprised until she remembered that she had had little or no sleep the night before.

She was glad that she was numb, that she couldn't cry, that she was unable to dislodge the concrete lump clogging her throat, much less the steel shutters that had conveniently positioned themselves between her eyes and the rest of the world. She knew the breathtaking waves of pain would come afterwards, but for now she was glad that she had moved through the last thirty-six hours in some kind of mechanical daze.

* * *

Eve almost let her new mobile phone fall into her bath when she heard Alex's gritty voice at the other end.

'Alex!' She sat up in the water and hastily reached out for a towel. Holding her phone with the utmost care, she climbed out of the bath, haphazardly slung a bath sheet around herself and sat down on the edge of the tub.

'I was wondering if you're busy today?' he asked.

She pinched herself to make sure she wasn't dreaming. Forget about her hair appointment and deep conditioning treatment, never mind the seaweed facial. This wasn't the time to play hard to get. Forget, too, about her silly notions of pride. She took a deep breath and told him that she wasn't particularly busy.

'I might take you up on that cup of coffee,' he said.

'Today?'

'Yes, if that suits you?'

'Sure. Em, where would you like to meet?'

'Wherever's most convenient, I suppose,' he said. 'Isn't there a pub in Templeogue? Would that be okay?'

'It would.' She tried to sound composed. 'What time?'

'I suppose around twelve, before it gets busy for lunch?'

It took her twice as long to get dressed. Alex wanted to see her. For coffee. And somewhere quiet, before the Saturday lunchtime hustle and bustle. Was it any wonder that she could hardly do up the buttons of her blouse or apply her mascara?

And this time, she warned herself, she wasn't going to blow it.

Chapter Fifty-six

He was waiting for her, already seated in a corner of the lounge, and he stood up when she arrived. She felt her heart pounding as she walked across to him. As she neared him, she noticed the dark circles beneath his eyes, the tension in his face.

No matter. She would soon wipe that off, wouldn't she? She asked for a white wine, heedless of the early hour, badly needing some fortification.

'Coffee for me, please,' he said to the lounge girl.

'Well, Alex, this is a nice surprise,' she began, shrugging off her jacket. Her silk blouse, pencil-slim skirt and opaque tights had been a good choice. Not blatantly sexy, just slightly suggestive.

'Thanks for coming. I know it was short notice, but I had to see you,' he said, sending her heart into giddy flight.

'You caught me at a good time,' she said, smiling at him.

'So long as I'm not disrupting your Saturday schedule. You'd probably prefer to be shopping or something.'

'No matter,' she shrugged and forced herself to look casual and relaxed. She could hardy admit, after all, that she would have cancelled a trip to the moon for a chance to meet up with him. It was almost like old times, sitting beside Alex like this, with him so near that she could reach out and touch him. And touch him she did, just lightly on the arm as though to make sure that she wasn't imagining things. 'Tell me, have you settled back in Dublin?'

He grinned at her, but his eyes were full of irony. 'No, I haven't.'

'That's too bad,' she said, her blue eyes sending him unmistakable signals. 'I wish there was something I could do to help.'

'As a matter of fact, there probably is,' he began.

She felt a rush of heady exhilaration and was relieved that the lounge girl chose that moment to return with their drinks and distract Alex's attention. It gave her time to absorb his words and try and pull herself together. Never in her wildest dreams had she expected things to move this swiftly. She took a sip of her wine and watched him pour milk into his coffee. He looked strained.

Maybe he was nervous. After all, she had called him all sorts of names before he had left to go to London, and she had said some awful things on Thursday. Maybe he was unsure of his ground with her.

'Alex, I….' She swallowed. How many times had she dreamed of this very moment, wondering if it would ever happen? 'I just wanted to say that I've forgotten all about… well, the words we had before you left for London.' She reached out once more and patted his arm. It felt so right, somehow, to be able to connect with him like this. 'And I shouldn't have spoken the way I did on Thursday, because as far as I'm concerned, it's all water under the bridge.'

'Good,' he said. 'I meant to phone you at the time, to apologise for the misunderstanding. But I was extremely busy, as you can imagine.'

Misunderstanding? Was that what he thought? No matter, it was over and done with.

'No worries,' she smiled. 'This is like old times, isn't it? I'll be more than happy to help you settle back into life in Dublin.'

'The way it is, I won't be able to settle into anything until I find out what's really going on,' he said, giving her a candid look.

'I'm glad you feel like that,' she said, her blue eyes sparkling. 'Why pretend any more? I know you're interested in me and as far as I'm concerned, the past is over and done with. We can easily begin again, make a fresh start….' Her voice faltered. There was something wrong. She watched, almost paralysed with a creeping humiliation, as the expression on his face changed until he was regarding her with total incredulity.

'It seems we have another misunderstanding,' he said, the wintry expression in his narrowed eyes striking ice into her veins.

'What's wrong now? What's wrong with starting over again?' Her voice sounded desperate. She *was* desperate. She was clinging on by her fingernails, but who cared how frantic she sounded? This was Alex Gallagher, for God's sake.

'Eve,' he sighed. She watched with a cold dismay as he looked away and slowly shook his head. Then he looked back at her, his eyes flat and expressionless. 'There was never anything much between us in the first place.'

'Surely we could pick up where we left off?' She had never pleaded like this before, but where he was concerned, her pride was in shreds.

'I'm sorry, but you've got it all wrong. This isn't why I wanted to talk to you or asked you to meet me,' he said. 'I'm trying to make sense of something and I thought you might be able to help.'

How had she been so wrong? How could she have been so stupid as to misinterpret everything? Eve felt a flare of anger. 'Help? Why should I bother helping you out? Once again you've made a right fool of me!' she snapped, reaching for her jacket. 'You're still a sad bastard. I've never been so humiliated in my life.'

'I've put my foot in it again, haven't I?' He gave her a brief, self-deprecating grin that made her heart lurch. 'Look, I'm really sorry, but it wasn't intentional.'

'Yeah, sure.'

'I should have realised… I should never have asked you to meet me like this. You'll have to forgive me, because I'm just not thinking straight right now.'

She stood up to go and she saw his face in the diffused light spilling in from the leaded windowpane. He looked as though something had imploded inside him. Just as he had looked on Thursday evening when he had walked away. And then she knew.

'This has nothing to do with me! It's about Daisy, isn't it? My precious cousin. Oh, God, I don't believe it.'

Alex didn't reply. He sat staring into space as Eve picked up her bag and prepared to stalk off.

'She's welcome to you,' she snapped. 'I hope she makes you happy.' She felt a renewed rush of fury as he absently stirred the dregs of his coffee and completely ignored her. 'The best of luck. You'll need it,' she said bitterly. 'Just wait till you meet mad Marina.'

'Marina?' His voice was terse. 'What's the problem?'

'What's wrong with spending your life in a

bottle of vodka? Not that I blame her,' Eve paused. 'You probably don't know, do you?' Her voice was suddenly amused. 'Not even Daisy knew herself until last week.'

'Knew what?'

'The reason why her mother turned to drink.'

'What are you talking about?'

'Let's see, well, for starters Daisy's father ran off when she was born. He didn't want to know. And best of all,' Eve paused for dramatic effect, 'her twin sister died in a car crash and it was all kept a big secret until recently. So how's that for happy families?' She turned on her heel and was just about to stride off when Alex's hand shot out and grabbed hers. 'Let go of me,' she hissed.

'Sit down,' he hissed back. 'You're not going anywhere until you explain every single one of those outlandish remarks.'

'Talk to Daisy. She'll tell you,' Eve snapped.

'You're not getting away with it that easily,' he clipped. 'You don't drop a nightmare scenario like that onto my lap and walk off.'

'It's true, you know, every single word,' she laughed mirthlessly. 'Your precious Daisy has quite a few skeletons in the closet.'

He released his hold on her. She felt pleased with herself as she began to walk away. She had certainly rattled him. Served him right. It was the least he deserved after the way he had treated her, pretending he wanted to see her on some pretext, when all along it was Daisy he was after. She headed towards the door and on impulse she looked back, trying to think of a suitable parting shot.

She faltered. He was still sitting in the same spot, staring straight ahead and looking so devastated that her heart clenched. In spite of her sickening disappointment, her bubbling anger, her humiliation, she couldn't leave him like this.

Oh yes she could.

She hesitated for what seemed like forever, vaguely aware of the increased bustle as customers began to filter in for lunch, of the aroma of hot food wafting around the lounge, the chink of cutlery, the brisk, cheerful voices coming from the kitchen, the muted light glimmering through the windows. Aware of Alex, looking as though his life had fallen apart. Aware of herself, feeling as though she was suspended in time.

And then she turned on her heel.

Chapter Fifty-seven

Sunday morning, at last. Not much longer now to keep up the façade, to paint a false smile on her face. Daisy was up early and she had finished the last of her packing before Marina came into the kitchen.

'Let's have a big fry-up this morning,' Marina suggested. 'I know it's not your usual breakfast, but it'll set you up until you get back to London.'

Daisy smiled. Marina was certainly pulling out all the stops. Marina rarely, if ever, had a fry for breakfast. She was strictly a coffee and toast person, sometimes not even bothering with the toast.

'You're still coming home for Easter, aren't you?'

'Of course I'll be home,' Daisy assured her mother. Even if it meant staying in the house for the entire weekend so that she wouldn't run the risk of bumping into Eve again, never mind Alex.

She shivered. She could always pretend she had the flu or something and needed to stay in bed. She was good at that, wasn't she? Good at deception. She took a carton of eggs out of the fridge and suggested they have scrambled eggs and toast.

'What time is your flight at?'

'Two-thirty. I've booked the taxi for twelve.'

'Then you've plenty of time.'

Her eyes flicked to the wall clock. Just a couple of hours and thankfully, she would be gone. Back to London. A new address and a new job as soon as possible, she had decided. It would be easy to lose herself, to disappear in the vastness of the city. Just in case. For she didn't want to run the risk of ever seeing him again, standing at the reception desk in Dolan's, with his hands in the pockets of his jeans and that grin on his face.

* * *

When Eve answered the door to Alex shortly after eleven o'clock, her immediate thought was one of sheer relief that she was alone in the house. Her parents had gone out for a Sunday morning walk and Victoria had stayed overnight in Amy's house. Then she realised that she was standing in front of him in her pink dressing gown and furry slippers, her face pale and devoid of make-up, her dark hair tangled and messy, her eyes showing the effects of little or no sleep the night before. No matter, she thought wearily. Alex Gallagher had already witnessed her in action at her worst.

'I was hoping I'd find you at home,' he said curtly, striding into the front room.

'What are you doing here?' Her voice shook and the sight of him standing in the living room made her heart clench. 'You can't just march in like this.'

'I already have,' he smiled grimly.

'What do you want?'

'Don't panic, Eve, I'm not here to kiss and make up.'

He stood in front of the fireplace, his hands clasped behind his back. Kiss and make up? If only. She let that thought spark for a moment before replying, 'I didn't think you were, Alex. I think we've gone beyond that stage, you and I.' She shivered a little in her dressing gown and pushed her messy hair away from her face. He seemed different this morning, she thought, purposeful and determined.

'I'm not leaving here,' he said quietly, 'until I get a full explanation.'

'Explanation of what?'

'Just cut the bullshit. You can scarcely have forgotten what you threw at me yesterday. Most interesting, I might add.' His dark eyes held the glitter of anger.

No, indeed she hadn't, not when everything she had said was still churning around in her mind.

Not when the look on his face as she had marched away had kept her awake half the night. Half the night? More like the whole night. And she couldn't possibly have slept with the hollow ache that weighed down her heart when she finally began to accept, somewhere around four o'clock in the morning, that she had lost him for good. She looked at him for a long, steady moment, remembering the way she had stalked off on him yesterday and the thoughts that had crowded into her head in the small hours of the night. Mingled with those thoughts was a spark of gratitude that he had bothered to turn up on the doorstep and by doing so was giving her a second chance. Not a second chance at getting it together with him, far from it, but a chance to clear the air.

She turned away and looked out the window into the landscaped front garden, and with her back to him she eventually said, 'I didn't go out last night. Quite unusual for me, on a Saturday.'

'What happened? Boyfriend let you down?' His gritty voice dripped scorn.

'Oh no, I had plenty of invitations. No, Alex, I couldn't have gone out last night and tried to pretend I was enjoying myself, not after yesterday.' She wheeled around and her blue eyes searched his, as if to gauge his reaction, but his face was shuttered. 'I was too upset.'

'Upset?' His eyes narrowed in disbelief. 'Funny, I could have sworn you were enjoying yourself.

541

Payback time for Alex. Kick him where it would hurt. Maybe we got our wires crossed, but I don't understand what Daisy has ever done to deserve your outburst.'

'I'm… I'm sorry,' she said, subdued. God, this was every bit as difficult as she had imagined. Alex was looking at her as though she had crawled out from under his shoe.

'You're what?'

'I said I'm sorry, Alex. Look, I've spent the whole night thinking about this.'

'Have you? And what conclusions have you come to? Or are they worth sharing?'

'It's really amazing what can go through your head at four in the morning.'

'Really?'

'I had time to think, you see. Yesterday I went off the deep end. I had always hoped that you and I… that there might be a you and I… I've had feelings for you….' She stopped, unable to continue for a moment, finding it impossible to voice what she felt. She snuck a glance at him and thankfully realised that he seemed to have thawed a little. The expression on his face, although not entirely benign, wasn't half as chilly as when he had first knocked on the door. 'I suppose I realised that I should never have walked off the way I did,' Eve said, praying he might understand and make it easy for her.

'And what brought you to that earth-shattering conclusion?'

542

She shrugged. 'You can laugh at me all you want, but I kind of realised that no matter what happens, I just want to see you happy.'

He lifted a dark eyebrow. 'You could have fooled me. And I'm not laughing at you. Far from it. I'm still a little stunned by what you told me yesterday and I'm finding it difficult to believe.'

'Maybe you should be talking to Daisy. It's not up to me to enlighten you.' She couldn't believe the words coming out of her mouth while Alex remained silent. 'Of course, you walked away from her, didn't you?' Eve said as things suddenly fell into place. 'You had some sort of a row and you walked off. So why did you phone me yesterday? Did you think that silly, stupid Eve would act as a go between?'

He shook his head. 'You're not silly or stupid, Eve. I told you already that I thought your were bubbly and fun loving and there's a lot to be said for that.'

'It's some consolation, I suppose.'

'I haven't seen Daisy since Thursday,' he continued, his eyes sombre. 'And I just wanted to know if she was… maybe in some kind of trouble. That's why I arranged to meet you yesterday. I thought, seeing as you're her cousin, that you might be able to throw some light on things.'

'We're not exactly joined at the hip, Daisy and I. If you ask me, she's always been in trouble.'

'Yeah, I'd guessed,' Alex sighed.

If only she could throw her arms around him,

Eve fretted. If only she could be the one to make him happy. But although he thought she could be bubbly and fun loving, it wasn't enough. She had finally admitted to herself as she tossed and turned that Alex didn't want her. She had finally faced the fact that he didn't love her and that for some reason that was beyond her comprehension, he seemed to be in love with Daisy.

'What can I tell you?' she asked grudgingly. She was mad, wasn't she? No, she wasn't mad, she argued with herself, because the other thing she had finally accepted in the middle of the night was that Alex's happiness meant everything to her. It was far more important than nursing her shattered pride.

'You could start by giving me an idea of what's going on.'

She gulped and looked away. She thought briefly of what might have been and she tried and failed to suppress a sad regret, a regret that she knew would echo forever in her heart. He didn't love her, but he thought she was bubbly and cheerful. That would have to do. It was certainly better than being thought of as some kind of she-devil. Then she began to talk, telling him sketchily and briefly what had happened to Marina and Daisy, and he listened in total silence until she had finished.

'Daisy was running away when she went to London,' Eve tacked on, anxious to fill the silence. 'Of course, you probably know that already.'

'No, I didn't know.'

'Can't say I blame her,' Eve shrugged. 'There was a huge row at her mother's birthday party. Marina was plastered and caused a bad scene with Daisy.'

'I see.'

'I never thought she'd have the guts to stay away as long as she did,' Eve continued in an effort to fill the silence. 'I expected her to come home fairly quickly.'

'Yeah, well, she met me.' Alex suddenly grinned and Eve felt a sharp pang of envy.

'How come you walked off on her the other evening?' she asked in spite of herself.

'That was a misunderstanding,' he said.

'You seem to be making a habit of those,' she attempted to joke. It was better like this, she told herself, far better to be on friendly terms. And it was small consolation to think that she had wiped some of the tension off his face, wasn't it? Already he was looking happier.

He smiled at her, a genuine smile. 'This is one I have to put right as soon as possible.'

'The best of luck. You don't have much time, you know.'

'How's that?'

'She's going back to London, I think maybe this afternoon.'

'What? Are you sure?'

'Yes, I'm almost sure.'

'In that case, Eve, would you do one more thing for me? Would you please tell me where she lives?'

Liz power-walked around the corner of the avenue just in time to see to see a tall, attractive man hurry down the garden path and fling himself into the shiny BMW parked at the kerb. She heard the squeal of tyres as he turned the car and she stalled her fast pace for a moment in order to catch a glimpse of his profile as the car swept past.

'What is it?' Harry asked, pausing alongside her. He had begun to join her on her keep-fit walks. He found the gym rather boring, he admitted, and it was a lot more pleasant to go for a brisk walk with his wife.

'I'm not sure. I think… no, I could be mistaken.' She shook her head.

'Oh, so you finally admit that you do make mistakes?'

She threw her husband an amused glance and linked her arm through his. 'Only very occasionally. No, I've just seen someone coming out of our house… a man.'

'A man? Do you think Eve snuck someone in last night?'

'She didn't go out last night, remember? For once, she stayed at home and went to bed early.'

'Maybe they had a lover's tiff and he just dropped in to make up.'

'We haven't been out all that long, so he scarcely had enough time to make up.'

'How do we know she didn't let him in at three

in the morning and he's disappearing off now while the coast is clear?'

'Harry!' She continued up the avenue in her tracksuit and trainers, thinking that whoever had come out of the house had borne an uncanny resemblance to that lovely man Eve had been seeing last year. Maybe Eve was finally getting it together with him. That would be nice.

Liz still felt troubled by the row they had had at the start of the new year. Eve had pulled the rug from under the careful order of her life with her hurtful remarks. She loved her daughter unconditionally. As far as she was concerned, she had done her best for Eve all her life. She couldn't quite figure out exactly what her daughter had been getting at when she spoke about learning lessons the hard way and things were still a little strained between them.

But who said miracles never happened? You never really knew what was around the corner. Look at Marina now, and Daisy, and the way their lives had turned around. Surely she and Eve could sort things out. If Eve stayed with someone long enough to fall in love, it would help her to grow and mature a little, and she might in turn have some appreciation of how her parents felt about her. Her spirits lifted as she looked at the high, clear February sky. She watched a flock of sparrows scattering and wheeling into the air before lining up in perfect order on the ridge of a neighbour's roof and realised that spring was on the way. She felt instinctively that this year would be a good year.

Inside the house, she went up the carpeted stairs and hesitated outside Eve's bedroom door. She was just about to knock when she heard a funny noise. Unless she was imagining it, there was the sound of muffled sobs coming from Eve's room. She waited, tense as high wire, and listened again. Then she went downstairs to Harry.

He was sitting out in the conservatory with the Sunday newspapers scattered before him. 'Harry? I don't think it's a good idea to say anything to Eve about whoever came out of the house,' she began.

'Whatever you think, Liz.'

'I think our daughter is going to be in need of some extra TLC in the coming weeks.'

Harry lowered the newspaper. 'Doesn't she get enough already?'

'Yes, but right now she seems to be a little upset.'

'What's wrong?'

'I'm not sure, and I'll probably never be told, but at a guess I'd say she's just had her heart broken, poor thing.'

Harry fixed her with a steady look. 'Now Liz, please bear in mind that if Eve has a broken heart, it's not your mission in life to mend it.'

'I know, but I'd just like her to feel she can count on us for support, no matter what.'

'I've no doubt Eve is already aware of that fact.

But you've got to remember that people, including beloved daughters, have to find things out for themselves, the hard way.'

'Do you really think so?'

'Of course. It's the nature of life, isn't it?'

'Were you talking to Eve recently?' Liz looked at him suspiciously.

'No, darling, I just know you too well.' Harry's light blue eyes gleamed. 'And I don't want my precious wife to wear herself out thinking she can wave a magic wand and make everything all right. With the best will in the world, it isn't always possible.'

'Harry Andrews, I want to give you a big hug,' Liz said as she smiled at him and walked across the floor to her husband.

Chapter Fifty-eight

When the doorbell rang, Daisy thought it was the taxi. Her weekend case was ready in the hall, her jacket thrown over it, her bag with her booking confirmation beside it.

'He's a bit early,' she said as Marina followed her into the hall.

'Just as well,' Marina said. 'You'll have time to relax when you get to the airport.'

Daisy opened the door and when she saw Alex standing outside she automatically began to close it again. But he was too quick for her and stuck his foot in the doorway, pushed it back and strode into the hall.

'It seems I'm just in time,' he said, glancing at her case.

She felt stiff and unyielding as he gathered her into his arms, like a cardboard cut-out, as she was held against him, felt his mouth against her forehead, heard his voice whispering over and over how sorry he was. He held her for what seemed like eternity and she drew in the scent of him, the familiar warmth of his arms around her, and after a while she began to relax into him. She didn't notice Marina slip quietly into the front room and didn't realise that the concrete lump constricting her throat had begun to dissolve until the tears began to slip silently down her face.

'I am never, ever letting you out of my sight again,' he murmured. 'I'm so sorry for walking away. Can you forgive me?' He rested his forehead against hers, his mouth so near that her heart missed a beat.

She felt herself begin to shake and he held her tighter, her head cradled into his shoulder, her tears soaking into his jumper, his arms wrapped snugly around her so that her body almost fused with his. He murmured soothing words and after a while her shaking subsided. He drew slightly apart from her and she felt his eyes searching her face. It was almost impossible to look at him.

'Daisy.'

She desperately looked away and her glance darted to her case in the hall. 'My taxi will be here in a minute,' she said in a muffled voice.

'Cancel it.' He took his mobile out of his pocket and passed it over to her.

'I'll miss my flight.'

'You're not getting on that plane.'

'Oh?'

'You're coming with me,' he said crisply. 'I told you I'm not letting you out of my sight again. Now go on, cancel the taxi.'

She took his phone and dialled the number as though on auto pilot and faltered over her words, but somehow the girl at the other end of the line got the message. Silently, she handed him back his phone.

'That's one thing settled,' he grinned as he pulled her back into his arms. And this time she didn't want to move or let go. Something inside her softened and loosened and she needed him to hold her close. She heard him calling to her mother, heard the murmur of their voices and then his arms were falling away from her but only so that he could help her into her jacket and lift her case.

'You do want to come home with me, don't you?' He shot her a glance of concern.

'I guess I won't be needing this.' She smiled through her tears as she plucked her flight confirmation out of her bag and let it flutter to the hall table. She turned to Marina. 'Mum? This is—'

'Alex. I know,' Marina said, looking happy.

'I'll phone you later,' Daisy said, giving her a quick hug.

Alex bent down and kissed Marina's cheek. 'We'll see you soon.'

'I look forward to that,' she said.

Alex's car was parked at the kerb. He stowed Daisy's case in the boot and Marina waved goodbye as he honked the car horn and drove off down the road.

'I think we should go somewhere we can talk,' he said. 'We both know what will happen when I bring you home.'

Daisy's heart leapt as without taking his eyes off the Sunday traffic he lifted her hand briefly and kissed it.

They went to Marlay Park where, taking her hand in the warmth of his, he tucked it into his pocket as they set off on a track that ran through the park.

'How did you know where to find me?' she asked.

'Eve told me,' he explained.

'Eve?' her voice quavered. Up to now, she had refused to think about Eve. She couldn't give space to the thought of her and Alex, together.

'I went out with her a couple of times before I left for London. I found her funny and good for a laugh, maybe a little empty headed. That's all, nothing more. There was never anything between us. Just a couple of dates. Are you okay with that?'

'Yes, yes, I am.' Something nameless eased inside her.

'I called her because I didn't know where you lived, and guessed you wouldn't answer your mobile. I needed to know what was going on. And being your cousin, I figured she might have an idea.'

'We were never what you'd call friends.'

'I'm not surprised,' he smiled. 'She was right when she said that you're not the least bit alike. Thank God.' Daisy smiled. 'She wasn't too happy when she discovered that I only called her to find out about you. I think she had some ridiculous notions about her and me.' Alex shook his head. 'Anyway, to give her her due, she swallowed her pride long enough to tell me a little about what had happened, and she also told me where to find you.'

'She did?'

'Yes. But I want to hear everything from you, every last detail, so there can be no misunderstanding between us. Let's start at the beginning, and I promise to keep my hands off you until you've said everything you want to say.'

She laughed then, and it echoed softly in the clear February air. She found it easy to talk, to let the words flow as they slowly circled the park, where an eggshell blue sky peeped down between branches that glimmered with a pale spring fuzz and the mountains rose before above them, clear and crisp and bluey green, washed in fresh spring sunlight.

She felt lighter and lighter as the words tumbled out.

Long before she came to an end, his arm curled comfortingly around her and he guided her over to a bench. He held her tightly to him as she eventually drew to a faltering close and they sat for a while in silence. He kissed her then, and she kissed him back. He murmured words of comfort, of love. She closed her eyes and buried her face in the crook of his neck as the cool breeze riffled her hair. Dear God, she thought. She was quietly bursting with happiness.

'Just tell me something,' he asked after a while. 'Why couldn't you talk to me all the time we were in London? Couldn't you trust me?'

She thought for a minute. 'I was so appalled at what I had said, I almost couldn't believe it myself. And I was so ashamed at the way I kept it up that it seemed easier to just ignore it,' she whispered. 'As well as that, I thought you'd get fed up with me. I didn't think we'd last.'

'Why not?'

'Because I… well, you know….' She felt colour sting her face as she met his eyes.

'No, I don't know, Daisy O'Neill. I think you'd better elaborate,' he said, and she knew by his face that he was teasing her. 'Tell me, do you think you'll ever try and find your father?'

She looked away. 'I tried already, in London, but I didn't get very far. So I'm not too pushed, because he's never existed for me.'

'Aren't you curious?'

'Not right now. There's been so much to take in over the past few days. There's something else, though,' she continued after a while, 'somewhere I want to go, but I need you to come with me.'

'Daisy, I'll go with you anywhere.'

She told him what she wanted and he immediately agreed.

'And one last question,' he said.

'Yes?'

'Why did you want to see me on Wednesday?'

'I wanted to tell you what had happened so that you could....'

'I could what?'

'I... I needed you to hold me tight,' she said huskily.

He held her tight then and gave her a long, lingering kiss, then asked, 'Why did you suddenly feel that you could talk to me now, when you couldn't tell me before?'

'It was something that happened this week, with my mother. You see, even though she had kept stuff from me, in the end it didn't matter,' Daisy said slowly as she tried to pick out the right words. 'Finding out about my sister and what had happened was a shock, all right, but knowing that I hadn't done anything wrong, and that underneath everything, she's always loved me... well, it was important to know that. And so....' She glanced at him shyly.

'I think that just about answers my question.'

He smiled at her and cupped her face in his hand. 'And I also think that it's about time we got out of here, don't you?'

* * *

He went ahead of her, carrying her case into his bedroom.

'Handy that you were all ready for me when I called,' he teased over his shoulder. 'You can unpack later on... jeez!'

'What's wrong?'

He turned back to her, looking embarrassed. 'I completely forgot. The bedroom. We made a mess, remember? I haven't been back since Thursday morning when we bolted out.'

She followed him in and looked at the tangled sheets and caught her breath as memories exploded.

'I'll get some fresh stuff,' he said, dropping her case and hurrying out to the airing cupboard. They made the bed together, laughing as they smoothed down white sheets and plumped up soft pillows, and Daisy mischievously pulled the duvet across so that it fell more generously on her side of the bed. Alex promptly pulled it back and told her she was being greedy.

Laughter died in her throat as the fresh drift of sheets and pillows were finally in place and she fell into his arms.

Chapter Fifty-nine

The music thundered around her in rolling waves and laser lights angled across tightly packed bodies. Out on the floor, Eve writhed and swayed.

She knew she was looking great. She had just had her hair restyled in a shorter, angular cut and her new make-up was flawlessly applied, eyebrows arching in perfect twin curves, lip gloss shining. Her glittery cropped top moulded her uplifted breasts and her short leather skirt clung to her.

It was almost a week since the Sunday morning that she had mentally said goodbye to Alex and she was getting her life back together. She halted momentarily and frowned. She would have to stop measuring time in terms of Alex. He was completely and utterly out of her life now.

***

Just the other day, her mother had casually raised the subject.

'Eve, there's something I've been meaning to ask you,' she said on Thursday as she prepared vegetables for dinner. Eve had just arrived home from work and had gone into the kitchen to make a cup of coffee. 'It's about something you said on New Year's Eve.'

'God, Mum, I think we'd both had far too much to drink. Let's just forget about it.'

'No, hear me out. You mentioned something about college.'

'College?'

'Or should I say, not going to college. I'd hate to think you felt you missed an opportunity, but at the time, your dad and I didn't think you were the least bit interested, and that's why we didn't push the issue. And we didn't want to put you under any of this hideous points race pressure.'

'Look, it's okay,' Eve shrugged.

'I just wanted to say that if you cared to do anything about it now, at this stage....'

'What?' Eve nearly dropped her cup of coffee. 'Go back to study?'

Liz smiled. 'I think it's obvious how you feel. But have you considered anything else? You hardly want to stay in Foley's forever, and there are alternatives.'

'Like what? One boring job is much the same as another.'

'Not necessarily. What are you interested in, really, I mean? Clothes? Fashion? Hair and beauty?'

'All of those,' Eve grinned.

'There you are. Why don't you consider some of those avenues? There's plenty of scope out there for a bright spark like you. I often wondered why you settled for office work in the first place.'

'It was just the obvious way to go with my basic computer qualification. And I did that course because I felt it was the next best thing compared to going to college, like, well... like Daisy.'

'Oh, Eve,' Liz smiled. 'Talk about mixed messages. You should look to your own gifts. Your Dad and I never expected you to light a fire in the commercial sector of the world. We'd be just as happy if you wanted to be a hairdresser or work in a boutique. Once you're doing what you'd really like to do.'

'I'll think about it,' Eve told her. Maybe it was possible after all that a little light existed at the end of the never-ending tunnel of boring Monday mornings.

'You've heard about Daisy, haven't you?' Liz's voice was so casual that Eve's suspicions were immediately raised. How much did she know? How much could she possibly know?

Eve deliberately looked vague. 'Yeah, I knew already. Victoria saw her in town and she was with one of my exes.'

'So he *is* one of your exes? Alex somebody or other? I thought I recognised the name when Marina told me, but I wasn't sure if they were one and the same.'

Eve shrugged. 'She's welcome to him.'

'It doesn't bother you that he and Daisy….?'

Eve laughed shortly. 'Whatever gave you that idea? I dumped him ages ago.'

'What a coincidence, all the same,' Liz remarked. 'She met him in London and now they're an item. According to Marina, they seemed to have had a bit of a falling out, but he caught up with Daisy last Sunday just before she was about to leave for the airport.'

'Really?' She held her mother's look unflinchingly.

'It's all right for Daisy,' Liz went on. 'I think we all agree that she could do with a bit of romance in her life.'

'She probably could.' Eve willed herself to stay cool.

'But if you ask me, you have the right idea, Eve. It's important to enjoy your life for now, and make the most of your single years. You've got plenty of free and easy years ahead before you need to get tied up in a serious relationship,' Liz said.

'Yeah, I suppose.'

'And I think it will have to be a very special man for you,' Liz continued with a smile. 'So far, I haven't set eyes on anyone who could possibly fit that bill.'

Eve felt a sudden urge to throw herself into her mother's arms. Yes, her parents had indulged her and spoiled her rotten. It was nice, though, to know that her happiness came first with them and to have that unmitigated love as an essential in her life. As for Alex, it was funny to think she had helped to nudge him into Daisy's arms, and just in the nick of time, apparently. But that was love for you, wasn't it?

Absolutely.

She swallowed hard. 'Is Daisy going back to London?'

'She's going back with Alex next weekend, but it's just to collect the rest of her stuff. And I think she wants to say a proper goodbye to her friends,' Liz continued. 'Marina told me that she's already moved into Alex's apartment in Rathfarnham, and he's brought her to meet his family. They certainly didn't waste any time. She was probably living with him in London, I dare say.'

'Yeah, probably.'

'Marina's delighted, of course. She's telling everyone that she's already hearing the patter of tiny feet and hoping for twins....' Liz paused again, but Eve shrugged her shoulders as though it was of no interest to her.

'Personally, Eve,' Liz continued, 'I'm not in any rush for grandchildren, not for years yet, but it's given Marina a new lease of life, thank God.'

Liz began to rinse the vegetables and started to

talk about Victoria's school exams. Eve was relieved that the moment of danger was over and she felt she had somehow passed a test.

She had wondered, in the long stretches of the night, how she was going to cope with seeing Alex and Daisy together, with hearing them being mentioned in the same breath in the course of family conversations, with running into them from time to time, as she surely would. But at least she had got over the first hurdle. And at least she and Alex had parted on friendly terms. She felt a huge sense of relief that she had rescued some of her self-respect at the same time as rescuing Alex.

So she felt she could hold her head up high. And, of course, as far as Liz, Victoria and her friends were concerned, she had dumped Alex. They would never guess that she had carried him in her heart for far too long. She latched onto this thought and held it in front of herself like a shield, and it was a comfort to her as the week finally drew to a close.

She was relatively content as she wriggled and writhed on the dance floor. Saturday night in Dublin and Eve Andrews was on the razz. Whoever she finally hooked up with, he would have to be someone very special. But not for a long time yet. Not while there was still plenty of fun to be had.

And then, as her movements took her to the edge of the dance floor, she saw him through the crush of moving bodies, standing by the bar. He must have been on a spring break, for he looked tanned and healthy. His jeans clung to his narrow hips, his T-shirt was a snug fit.

She had thought about him on and off since New Year's Eve, finally beginning to understand that perhaps she had rocked his world in the same way that Alex had rocked hers. And now, here he was, propping up the bar in D2.

Daniel Richards.

Maybe she should talk to him and try to make amends. Then again, maybe it was better to fade into the crowd and leave him in blissful ignorance.

Any minute now, he would turn around and spot her.

Any minute now....

Epilogue

London, a Sunday morning in early March. A crisp, fresh day with a touch of spring in the air.

They walk along a gravelled path where grass verges are speckled with dew and posies of flowers infuse the air with a sweet scent and splashes of vibrant colour. Some of the headstones are old and difficult to read, some are new and freshly engraved. All of them bear testimonies to love and devotion.

She carries a sheaf of daffodils and his arm is curved around her as they reach the end of the track. She stops and looks down at the simple wooden cross, faded now with time, and she hears the echo of her name shimmering in the air and the sound of childish laughter drifts like a gossamer veil. She drops the daffodils and they fall in shards of yellow dazzle.

565

Peace is so tangible here in this corner of London that she can almost reach out and touch it.

Afterwards he brings her back to her room, where her cases wait inside the door for the early evening flight, and curtains billow in the soft March breeze. He closes the curtains and turns to her and opens his arms.

They make love slowly and sweetly, as outside the sun shimmers incandescently at the zenith of the sky and winks through the curtains. He covers her body with his, covers her love with his, and she laughs with him as he holds her tight and sets her free.

Win
a weekend in
a luxury hotel!

Would you like a chance to stay in the gorgeous Stephen's Green Hotel in the heart of Dublin?

The Stephen's Green Hotel is a stylish boutique hotel that effortlessly combines two beautifully restored historic Georgian houses with a contemporary style. Centrally located, the hotel overlooks Dublin's landmark Stephen's Green Park.

To be in with a chance to win this fabulous prize, all you have to do is answer the following question:

What is the name of the company where Eve works?

INSTRUCTIONS
1. To enter the competition, answer the question.
2. Detach and post this page, along with your name, address and daytime telephone number to:
   Absolutely Love Competition
   Gill & Macmillan
   Hume Avenue
   Park West
   Dublin 12.
3. The entry does not give rise to any contract between Gill & Macmillan Ltd. ('Gill & Macmillan') and the entrant.
4. The competition will be run and determined in accordance with the Rules overleaf.

RULES

1. The instructions overleaf form part of the Rules.

2. Only entries on an original entry form contained at the end of a copy of *Absolutely Love* will be considered.

3. All entries must be received by Gill & Macmillan prior to or not later than 31 December 2005 ('the Closing Date').

4. Gill & Macmillan reserves the right to extend the Closing Date if necessary.

5. Multiple entries will be accepted, but each such entry must be on an original entry form.

6. No cash will be offered in lieu of the prizes available in the competition.

7. Gill & Macmillan will in its absolute discretion decide any matter or question concerning the running of the competition, these Rules, their interpretation or any ancillary matter and any such decision or necessary opinion of Gill & Macmillan will be final and no correspondence will be entered into concerning such a decision.

8. Gill & Macmillan will notify the winner within 30 days of the Closing Date that he/she has been successful.

9. Gill & Macmillan will have no responsibility for, and is not obliged to take into account, any entry lost, damaged or delayed in the post or otherwise.

10. All entries must be sent and received by Gill & Macmillan, by ordinary post. entries received by any means other than ordinary post such as by hand, courier, facsimilie, etc. will not be accepted or considered.

11. The competition is open to residents of the Republic of Ireland, except the author, employees of Gill & Macmillan and their families, and employees and/or administration of O'Callaghan Hotels and this competition.

12. The winner's name may, at Gill & Macmillan's discretion, be used for publicity purposes.

13. The value of this prize does not exceed €1,000. Travel expenses of not more than €100 will be included in the prize. Gill & Macmillan and O'Callaghan Hotels are free from any liability involved in travel to/from and

O'Callaghan
Hotels

For reservations at any of the four Dublin city centre hotels run by the O'Callaghan Group please call Central Reservations at (+ 353) 1 6073900 or log onto www.ocallaghanhotels.com